Opening the car door, Caitlin stepped outside and peered over the hood of the Lexus. "Nancy?" she called.

Both girls stopped and squinted at her.

"Nancy, I'm Lindsay's mom," she explained. "Is she still inside?"

The girl shook her head. "She didn't show up for practice."

"What?"

"I saw her before lunch," the other girl piped up. "But practically, like, right afterward, in my fifth-period English Lit class, she wasn't there . . ."

"Are you sure?" Caitlin asked, walking around to the curb.

The brunette girl nodded. "Her seat's right beside mine, and it was empty. But then a lot of people ditch that class . . ."

Nancy nudged her friend. "Want to get her in trouble?" Then she turned to Caitlin. "I'm sure Lindsay had a good reason for missing the class, Mrs. Stoller."

"And blowing off practice," the other girl said under her breath.

Both girls giggled. Then Nancy waved at her as they moved on down the sidewalk.

Caitlin stood by her car. She felt a horrible pang in her gut.

She glanced over at the double doors and realized that Lindsay wouldn't be coming through them—not now.

Caitlin thought about another high school swimmer—a girl found naked and strangled in some woods about eighty miles away . . .

Books by Kevin O'Brien

ONLY SON

THE NEXT TO DIE

MAKE THEM CRY

WATCH THEM DIE

LEFT FOR DEAD

THE LAST VICTIM

KILLING SPREE

ONE LAST SCREAM

FINAL BREATH

VICIOUS

DISTURBED

TERRIFIED

UNSPEAKABLE

TELL ME YOU'RE SORRY

NO ONE NEEDS TO KNOW

YOU'LL MISS ME WHEN I'M GONE

HIDE YOUR FEAR

Published by Kensington Publishing Corporation

KEVIN O'BRIEN

HIDE YOUR
FEAR

PINNACLE BOOKS
Kensington Publishing Corp.
www.kensingtonbooks.com

PINNACLE BOOKS are published by

Kensington Publishing Corp.
119 West 40th Street
New York, NY 10018

All Kensington titles, imprints, and distributed lines are available at special quantity discounts for bulk purchases for sales promotions, premiums, fund-raising, educational, or institutional use. Special book excerpts or customized printings can also be created to fit specific needs. For details, write or phone the office of the Kensington sales manager: Kensington Publishing Corp., 119 West 40th Street, New York, NY 10018, attn: Sales Department; phone 1-800-221-2647.

ISBN-13: 978-0-7860-3883-1
ISBN-10: 0-7860-3883-7

First printing: August 2017

10 9 8 7 6 5 4 3 2 1

Printed in the United States of America

First electronic edition: August 2017

ISBN-13: 978-0-7860-3884-8
ISBN-10: 0-7860-3884-5

This book is for my friend and neighbor,
John Simmons,
one of the nicest, classiest guys around.

ACKNOWLEDGMENTS

Thanks so much to John Scognamiglio, my brilliant editor and friend, and to everyone at Kensington Books. You're simply the best.

Another great big thank-you goes to my agents, Meg Ruley, Christina Hogrebe, and the terrific team at Jane Rotrosen Agency.

I'm in debt to my Writers Group pals, David Massengill, Garth Stein, Colin McArthur, and John Flick. These guys put in a lot of hours eating pizza and helping me improve on the early draft of this book. Every writer should have a writers group this cool!

Many thanks also to the wonderful people at Kitsap Regional Libraries and King County Libraries. In fact, thanks to librarians everywhere.

Another thank-you goes to Meade Jorgensen for his help with some of the swimming scenes.

Thanks, hugs, and kisses to my fellow Seattle 7 Writers, especially the core members: Garth Stein (again), Jennie Shortridge, Erica Bauermeister, Dave Boling, Carol Cassella, Laurie Frankel, and Suzanne Selfors.

I'd also like to thank the following individuals and groups for their support, encouragement, and friendship: Dan Annear and Chuck Rank, Ben Bauermeister, Pam Binder and the Pacific Northwest Writers Association, A Book for All Seasons, The Book Stall, Marlys

Bourm, Amanda Brooks, Terry and Judine Brooks, Lynn Brunelle, Deb Caletti, George Camper and Shane White, Barbara and John Cegielski, Barbara and Jim Church, Pennie Clark Ianniciello, Anna Cottle and Mary Alice Kier, Tommy Dreiling, Paul Dwoskin, the gang at Elliott Bay Book Company, Bridget Foley and Stephen Susco, Matt Gani, Cate Goethals and Tom Goodwin, Bob and Dana Gold, my friends at Hudson News, Cathy Johnson, Ed and Sue Kelly, Ryan and Eric Kelly, Elizabeth Kinsella, David Korabik, Stafford Lombard, Paul Mariz, Roberta Miner, Dan Monda, Jim Munchel, my friends at The News Group, Meghan O'Neill, Midge Ortiz, the cool people at ReaderLink Distribution Services, Eva Marie Saint and Jeff Hayden, John Saul and Mike Sack, Roseann Stella, Dan Stutesman, Doug and Ann Stutesman, George and Sheila Stydahar, Marc Von Borstel, Michael Wells, Susan Wiggs, and Ruth Young.

Finally, a huge Thank-You to my wonderful family.

CHAPTER ONE

Deception Pass, Washington
Saturday, May 21—1:57 A.M.

"Where are we going?" Sara Goldsmith asked with a tremor in her voice. She glanced in the rearview mirror.

The person—or *thing*—in the backseat of the Goldsmith family SUV didn't utter a word.

The silent passenger's face was hidden behind a clown mask. The mask was a strange pale peach shade, almost translucent—except for the wide scarlet grin, a blue-painted nose, and white stars that framed each eyehole. The stranger wore a black, hooded raincoat and brandished a gun in his—or her—black-gloved hand. Sara couldn't tell if it was a man or a woman. All she could really see was the clown face, leering back at her in the mirror.

A few drops of rain hit the windshield. The SUV's headlights pierced the mist hovering over the two-lane roadway. With the tall evergreens bordering both sides of the thoroughfare, it was almost like driving through an unlit tunnel.

At this time of night, traffic was light on Highway 20. Sara hadn't spotted many cars, not a single police car. But then it wasn't as if she could have flashed her headlights or signaled anyone for help. Her passenger in back seemed to study her every move.

Still, with more cars around, at least she might have hoped for *some* kind of intervention. Right now, she felt so lost and alone—and doomed.

She wondered if she'd ever see her son again.

Sara's window was open a crack. Her shoulder-length, ash-blond hair fluttered in the cool breeze. People were always surprised to hear she was forty-two—or maybe they were just being nice. In the last few months, stress, too much drinking, and not enough sleep had all taken their toll. She looked sallow, tired, and puffy. Her booze of choice was bourbon, specifically Jim Beam, because it was usually on sale at the Safeway in Echo.

With everything that had recently happened to her and her family, she'd come to rely on booze—and sometimes Valium—to put her to sleep every night. She usually didn't start self-medicating until after her thirteen-year-old son, Jarrett, had gone to bed.

Tonight Jarrett was staying over at his friend Jim Munchel's house, leaving her alone at home. Sara realized she'd never actually spent the night by herself in the house before. She blamed so many of her troubles—and even their recent tragedy—on the big, isolated, old Tudor at the edge of town. It had seemed so charming when she and Larry outbid another couple for the place seven months ago. That was before they knew the house had a disturbing history. That was before the creepy, anonymous phone calls, texts, and emails. That was before all the trouble began—the infidelity, the accidents, and the death from which she'd probably never recover. The house on Birch Place was cursed. At least that was what *Bobby* said. Bobby was obviously watching them and sending those cryptic, ominous messages. On the phone, Bobby's raspy, gender-indistinguishable voice reminded her of the demon in *The Exorcist*.

She'd once read that Mercedes McCambridge, the Oscar-winning actress who had dubbed for the demon-possessed Linda Blair, had drunk weird concoctions and choked herself with a scarf to get that gravelly, sinister voice. The demon's superior, all-knowing tone reeked of evil. Bobby sounded the exact same way, croaking at her over the phone.

The first call, which came two weeks after they'd moved in, was disturbing mostly because of that voice. "Are you all settled in?" it whispered. Then the line went dead. Sara tried to dismiss it as a wrong number.

The next call came two weeks later: "You won't have a happy time in that house, Sara."

"Who is this?" she demanded to know. Her phone screen showed UNKNOWN CALLER.

There was a long pause on the other end. "It's Bobby," the raspy-voiced stranger finally purred, "from down the block."

Sara heard a click on the other end. She tried star-six-nine, but a recording told her that the number dialed was unavailable. Sara asked her neighbors if they knew someone named Bobby. She asked a lot of people in Echo the same question. Everyone seemed to know someone named Bobby or Bob or Robert or Roberta. But nobody knew someone with a voice like that.

Bobby's calls became more frequent—and then came the emails, texts, and notes. Bobby never used obscene language or made threats. For Sara, it was almost as if she had a meddling, omniscient neighbor watching her and her family—an unwelcome anonymous friend who relished sharing bad news about things to come.

Bobby didn't have to sign the notes and emails. Sara always knew who they were from, like the piece of notebook paper folded up and stuck under the windshield wiper of the SUV. It was written in a child's scrawl:

Your daughter Michelle is doing things she shouldn't ☹

When Sara asked her daughter if there was any basis in fact to the strange note, Michelle turned livid. "How can you even ask me that? Do you actually believe this stalker freak is telling the truth?"

She and Larry went to the police, who increased patrols on Birch Place. But it didn't do any good. Sara changed her phone number and email server. But Bobby managed to track down her new contact information and got to her nevertheless.

"Jarrett's going to hurt himself on that skateboard someday . . . ☹ " said one email. When Sara tried to

reply, she got the same notice as always: MAILER-DAEMON: UNABLE TO DELIVER.

Within a week, Jarrett wiped out on his skateboard. He got a concussion and a broken arm. He was in the hospital for two days.

It was obvious this person was watching their home. More than that, Bobby seemed to have gotten inside the house at times. He or she seemed to know everything about Sara—her quirks, habits, and vulnerabilities. Bobby knew what was going on with Larry and the kids even before Sara did.

One afternoon, coming home from a brief trip to the Safeway, Sara found a Post-it stuck to her bedroom dresser mirror. She immediately recognized the childlike handwriting:

I don't think Larry is happy with you . . . ☹

Bobby told her about every dose of trouble that was coming her way—the accidents, Larry's philandering, and Michelle's drug problem. Sara couldn't help wondering if this gravelly-voiced phantom was making these things happen—or merely trying to warn her.

After all, how could one person cause all these horrible occurrences? Was it just bad luck? Or was it the house?

"Why don't you just move?" Bobby had asked more than once over the phone. "You should leave this place . . ."

But for months, Larry refused to budge. He didn't think the house was cursed. He didn't believe in curses. Sara had a feeling he didn't even believe Bobby existed.

He seemed to think she was making up this stalker person. She had to show him one of Bobby's emails before he started to believe her. But he still didn't take Bobby seriously. He maintained that they were having a bad patch—that was all. He wasn't about to be forced out of his own home. This *Bobby* person was probably part of some sort of elaborate real estate scam. At least, that was what he told the police when Sara insisted they make their fourth or fifth harassment report.

Ironically, Larry ended up being forced from his house.

Sara had kicked him out eight days ago. Never mind the humiliating circumstances. For the time being, he was staying at the Oak Harbor Best Western. He said he didn't want a divorce. He thought they should see a couples counselor, and if she wanted to unload the house, that was fine with him. In fact, he was all for it.

But Sara refused to have anything to do with Larry. She wouldn't agree to any of his suggestions—except selling the house. They needed to get out of there before something else happened.

With Jarrett spending the night with the Munchels, she'd considered getting a room at the Bayside Bed & Breakfast, the local inn. She didn't want to be alone in that awful house. But it didn't seem worth the peak-season, weekend rate of 190 bucks for just one night. Besides, except for a few minor accidents, nothing bad had actually happened *inside* the house.

So Sara had resolved to brave it alone at home, treat herself to carryout chicken teriyaki from Chop-Chop Delight and *The Sound of Music* on DISH on Demand. She knew it was silly, but she wanted a movie *event*, one that would take up most of the night and help her forget her troubles for a while. She'd always loved *The Sound of Music*. Last year, she'd tried to make a movie night with it for the family. Michelle had been on her mobile device during most of the movie, Jarrett kept saying, "This movie is so gay," and Larry fell asleep about a third of the way through. Sara had ended up shutting off the movie and going to bed early.

Not tonight.

She ate off a TV table and sat in Larry's recliner. No one else in the family ever used it. But Larry had no claim on it tonight—and possibly never again.

The baroness was just breaking up with Captain von Trapp when the house phone rang.

It was 10:07 according to the cable box in the TV console. The UNKNOWN CALLER hung up after three rings. Sara was almost certain it was Bobby. What telemarketer would call at this hour?

Bobby usually called Sara's mobile phone. But then, Bobby probably knew she was alone tonight.

Her heart racing, Sara glanced at the darkened windows of the family room. She couldn't see anything, just her own timid reflection. She had a feeling Bobby was seeing the exact same image—only from outside, somewhere in the dark.

Sara quickly closed the drapes. She double-checked the locks on the doors and first-floor windows. Minutes passed and the phone didn't ring again.

She told herself that the Unknown Caller could have been anybody.

Still, Sara wasn't able to concentrate on the movie after that. Every little sound inside and outside the house became cause for alarm. At least five times, she put the movie on pause to investigate some strange, new noise.

She decided a little Jim Beam would help her relax. But when she opened the kitchen cabinet, she found only one bottle there—about a third full. She could have sworn she'd bought an extra bottle yesterday for backup. Had she gone through it already? Had she gotten that bad about her alcohol consumption? Or was it possible Jarrett had stolen the bottle and taken it to his friend's house? It was just the kind of thing a thirteen-year-old might do. She could see him and his pals all trying to be cool, passing around her bottle of Jim Beam in someone's basement.

It was too late to go out for another bottle. She'd have to stretch out what she had. A carefully measured shot with some ice and a little water helped calm her nerves.

It was after midnight by the time Maria, the captain, and those von Trapp kids had finally fled the Nazis and were hiking over the Alps to a chorus of "Climb Every Mountain."

Sara convinced herself that the call earlier must have been a wrong number. But she was still feeling too edgy to sleep—too edgy and too sober. She poured herself another Jim Beam, straight this time. Then she switched channels to HGTV's *House Hunters*.

She was beginning to nod off when the phone rang, startling her.

She glared at the phone on the TV table and started to get mad. She'd had enough.

Snatching up the cordless, she clicked it on. "What?" she bellowed. "What do you want?"

It was nearly one in the morning. She didn't have to look at the caller ID screen on the cordless to know it read: UNKNOWN CALLER. She knew it was Bobby.

She could hear someone breathing on the other end of the line.

"Goddamn you!" she barked. "What the hell do you want?"

"Jarrett's asking for you, Sara," the caller said in that all-too-familiar crawly voice. "He's very badly hurt. He needs his mommy . . ."

Horrified, Sara listened. She didn't remember a time when Bobby had ever lied to her. For a moment, she couldn't talk or breathe. "What happened?" she finally asked.

"He's going to die if he doesn't get some help."

Hunched forward in the recliner, she clutched the phone tighter. Tears filled her eyes.

"Are you listening to me, Sara?"

"You monster!" she cried. "What have you done to him?"

"Come meet me in front of the teriyaki place where you picked up your dinner earlier. Don't stop to call anyone. Just grab your keys, get in the car, and drive. Do you understand?"

"Where is he?" she asked, getting to her feet. "Is he there with you?"

"If you're not here in ten minutes, I'm going to let Jarrett die."

There was a click on the other end of the line.

With a shaky hand, Sara automatically dialed Jarrett's smartphone. She hoped against hope it was all lie. But after three rings, Jarrett still hadn't picked up. In the middle of the fourth ring, she heard a click.

"Jarrett?" she asked anxiously. "Honey?"

There was no answer. Had it gone to his voice mail? She couldn't tell.

Then she heard a sigh on the other end—and that raspy voice: "Jarrett can't come to the phone, Sara. I already told you that. Now you only have nine minutes to get here. I'm not even sure Jarrett will live that long. He's lost a lot of blood."

Then the line went dead.

Sara dropped the cordless onto the seat of Larry's recliner and ran to grab her purse off the kitchen counter. Frantically searching for her keys, she headed for the side door that faced the detached garage. At last she found the keys. She stepped outside and shut the door behind her. It locked automatically.

The garage's door was just a couple of steps away. In her rattled state, Sara couldn't get the key in the lock. Tears streamed down her face. All she could think about was her son, stabbed or shot by this maniac. Was her boy still alive?

She finally got the key in the lock and opened the door. Stepping into the darkened garage, she blindly reached over and flicked on the light switch.

Nothing happened.

She tried the switch next to it. Still nothing.

But the electricity was working. Their second refrigerator was humming—over by the kids' bicycles. She couldn't see it in the blackness, but she could hear it.

Was someone else in the garage with her?

Sara saw the outline of the SUV. She pressed the

Unlock button on her key fob. The vehicle's emergency lights flashed for a second, and the interior light went on.

Making her way around the front of the SUV, Sara opened the driver's door. She reached inside for the remote on the sun visor and then pressed the button to open the garage door. There was a click. The garage light went on, and the motor overhead started up.

Sara was about to jump inside the car, but she hesitated. She'd meant to check if anyone was hiding inside the SUV.

But she was too late.

A shadowy figure popped up in the backseat.

Sara gasped. A hooded clown face grinned at her. She could see the gun in the stranger's gloved hand. It was pointed at her.

Over the mechanics of the garage door opening, Sara heard that all-too-familiar gravelly voice behind the clown mask: "Get in and drive, Sara, and maybe we'll reach Jarrett in time to save him."

Her heart racing, she climbed behind the wheel and started up the car. She looked into the rearview mirror and tried to stop shaking. "We're not going anywhere until you tell me what's happened to my son."

"My partner got a little carried away and shot him."

Sara let out a feeble cry and covered her mouth with her hand.

"You didn't think I worked alone, did you?" Bobby asked behind the mask. "Jarrett's in a safe place. He seems stable for now—"

"But you just said he might not last even ten minutes," she cut in.

"Ten minutes or ten hours, who knows? As I said, he's lost some blood, and he's asking for you. My partner is texting me updates on Jarrett's condition. The sooner we reach them, the sooner you can get your son to a hospital. Now, let's go before the garage door closes on us. We're wasting time sitting here, Sara . . ."

That had been nearly an hour ago.

So many times when Bobby had telephoned in the last few months, Sara had asked, "Who are you? Why are you doing this?"

She'd never gotten an answer.

During their journey tonight, she asked those same questions—over and over again. But her passenger didn't respond. Sara still wondered if Bobby was behind everything that had happened—or just the gleeful harbinger of horrible news.

As they drove by a sign for Deception Pass, Bobby took a phone out from the pocket of that dark raincoat and checked it. "Jarrett's lost consciousness, but his breathing is steady."

Sara tightened her grip on the steering wheel. They were headed for the bridge. Was Jarrett somewhere on the mainland?

Three months ago, her daughter had died from a heroin overdose in an alley behind a bar on Highway 99 in North Seattle. She wondered if Jarrett was destined to die in Seattle, too. After the bridge, it would be at least another ninety miles to Seattle. "How much farther?" she asked, her voice cracking.

"Not too much. Keep driving, Sara."

She had a feeling that behind the disguise, her passenger had a grin that matched the one on the clown face. Bobby must have felt extremely smug to see her so unhinged and helpless. Sara tried not to cry but couldn't help it. Jarrett seemed so far away.

She saw the Deception Pass Bridge ahead, partially obscured by a cloud of mist. The old, narrow, two-lane viaduct had two spans suspended 180 feet over the choppy waters of Skagit Bay and the Strait of Juan de Fuca. The nearly thousand-foot span connected Whidbey Island with tiny Pass Island; the second section was just over five hundred feet—connecting Pass Island to Fidalgo Island and the mainland. Lights along the pedestrian walk railing helped navigate the way.

But the mist and rain on the windshield obscured Sara's view. She switched on the wipers. The road felt slick beneath the SUV's tires.

Just last week, another person—some poor, miserable woman—had leaped to her death from this bridge. It hadn't been reported on TV, and *The Seattle Times* had buried the story in the paper's back pages. That seemed to be the local media's policy: *Don't report it, don't give people ideas.* She'd once read on the Internet that close to 450 suicides had occurred on Deception Pass Bridge since its construction in 1935.

It was strange that she would remember that right now.

Hers was the only vehicle on the old bridge. With her window open a crack, Sara heard the wind—and the water rushing far below.

"I don't have much gas left," she announced edgily, "less than a quarter of a tank. I don't know where you're taking me, but if we're headed to Seattle—or even Everett—we'll have to stop for gas."

"At the end of the bridge, you'll turn into the parking area for the tourists."

She eyed the clown mask in her rearview mirror. "Is that where you've got Jarrett? Is that where he is?"

"You'll see . . ."

During the day, Deception Pass State Park was crammed with people, most of them taking pictures. Sara imagined that, at night, the place might have been a lovers' lane or a spot for teens to hang out and smoke or drink. But at this hour—on this cold, drizzly night—the park was probably deserted.

Biting her lip, Sara switched on her indicator and turned into the lot for the Deception Pass Park. Beyond the rain-beaded windshield, she didn't see any other cars there. Certainly, Bobby's partner had a car. She'd imagined the two of them speeding away in another vehicle while she tried to save her dying son.

Of course, her scenario was based on the foolish assumption that Bobby and Partner were human—with some traces of compassion.

They hadn't brought her all this way in order to save her son's life. They'd forced her to come here for some other reason. Did they want her to watch Jarrett die?

Sara glanced around the empty lot. There was no sign of anyone. The lights of the bridge peeked through the tall evergreens bordering the lot. It was too dark to see the water, but she could still hear the rushing current.

"What's going on?" she asked. "Where's Jarrett? Is he even here?"

"Park the car."

Sara pulled into the first parking spot she saw. She swiveled around and glared at the figure in the backseat.

"Okay, where is he?" she asked anxiously. "Where have you got my son?"

Bobby nodded toward the front passenger side. "Check the glove compartment, Sara. Go on . . ."

She turned toward the dashboard and pressed the button on the glove compartment. The panel door fell open. She noticed a bottle of Jim Beam in there.

"I thought Jarrett had made off with this," she murmured, taking the bourbon out of the glove compartment. "But it was you . . ."

"Why not have a hit?" croaked Bobby.

Though she was tempted, Sara quickly shook her head. "Where's Jarrett?"

"He's at his friend Jim Munchel's house—asleep, I assume. Jarrett probably doesn't even realize his phone is missing. But then, he really isn't too bright, is he?"

"What are you saying?" Sara whispered, clutching the bottle to her chest. "You mean my son's all right?"

"Snug as a bug in a rug," Bobby replied from behind the mask. "Aren't I the naughty one to tell such a lie? But I needed you here, Sara, and I needed you to cooperate . . ."

Sara let out a long sigh. Jarrett was safe.

"Now, after a scare like that, I'd say you need a drink. Go ahead . . ."

"I'm fine," she lied. The truth was, she desperately wanted a hit of bourbon—just to calm her nerves. But she needed to keep a clear head right now.

"I know you want it," the gravelly-voiced stranger purred. "Don't pretend. I've watched you when you think you're all alone, Sara. You drink yourself into a stupor and stagger up to bed. Go ahead, have a few gulps. You'll feel better. Drink up." Bobby raised the gun a bit. "In fact, I insist."

Sara glanced down at the bottle in her grasp—and then into the eyeholes of the clown mask.

"Go ahead . . ." it said.

She unscrewed the top and realized the seal was broken. It had already been opened. She hesitated. "What are you going to do to me?"

"You don't want to hear the answer to that while you're sober."

Sara didn't move.

"Better you hear it after a few gulps," Bobby whispered. "I crushed up some of your Valium and put it in there to help things along. You just need to relax, Sara. I'm simply trying to make this easy on you. Now, go ahead, take a hit. Swallow it down like a good girl."

Sara thought about her dead daughter and her ruined marriage. What did she have to live for anyway? She didn't care anymore. A big part of her was already dead.

She brought the bottle to her lips and took a gulp. The bourbon burned going down, but then almost immediately it warmed her and made her feel better. She wiped her mouth and stared at the figure in the backseat. "What—what are you trying to *make easy* for me? What are you planning to do?"

"Take another healthy swig, and I'll tell you."

The truth was she desperately wanted another blast of the bourbon. She took two more gulps from the bottle. "All right," she gasped. "What are you trying to *make easy* for me?"

"Dying," Bobby answered.

Sara wasn't sure she heard right. "What?"

The bottle slipped out of her hand, and bourbon spilled down the front of her. She could smell it on herself.

She heard a sinister cackle from behind the mask. "The police will know you were drinking, of course. And they'll assume that at some point, on your way to the bridge, you tripped and hit your head . . ."

On her way to the bridge?

Before she could ask what that meant, Sara saw Bobby raise the gun—near the ceiling of the SUV. In an instant, the butt of the weapon came slamming down on her head.

She heard it smack against her skull. The pain was excruciating.

Everything turned black.

But Sara could still smell the Jim Beam, and she could still hear the rushing current.

The Seattle Times, Monday, May 23:

ANOTHER DECEPTION PASS SUICIDE
*Echo Woman Hangs Herself
From Bridge's Walkway*

Only eight days after a Monroe woman leaped to her death from Deception Pass Bridge, the Western Washington landmark became the site of another apparent suicide. Early Saturday morning, traffic on the bridge

was halted for two hours after motorists reported someone hanging by the neck from a
rope tied to the railing of the pedestrian
walkway.

Friends of the victim, Sara Rogan Goldsmith, 42, of Echo, Washington, said she was
still despondent over the drug-related death of
her daughter, Michelle, 16, in February . . .

The article mentioned that Sara had called the police on several occasions to report that someone was
harassing her, but the authorities were unable to sub-
stantiate her claims.

Apparently, the notes and emails from Bobby that
she shared with the police were neither threatening nor
malicious enough for them to be too concerned. There
was every indication that Sara was depressed and mentally unbalanced.

The piece listed her survivors as her husband, Dr.
Lawrence Goldsmith, 44, and a son, Jarrett, 13. No
mention was made of Sara and Larry's marital problems.

The article was buried in the back pages of the front
section of that Monday-morning edition.

On page two of the same newspaper was a seemingly unrelated article. Unlike the story about Sara,
this one featured a photograph. It was a school portrait
of a pretty teenage girl with a narrow face and straight,
shoulder-length blond hair. She had a dimpled smile.

She was Monica Leary, a junior at Capital High
School in Olympia. Monica had attended a party at a
friend's house that Saturday night. The friend lived

only two blocks away from the Learys' house on Gold-crest Drive. Monica had left the party early, 10:30 P.M., because she was competing in a very important swim meet the following morning.

She never reached home.

CHAPTER TWO

Everett, Washington
Sunday, October 23—2:17 P.M.

Aaron Brenner hurried out of the locker room in his Speedos. Frazzled and out of breath, he threw on his warm-up jacket.

Most of the other swimmers milling around the Olympic-size pool had already shed their warm-up clothes. The bleachers were packed. A big banner across the railing in front of the first row of seats read:

MARINER HIGH SCHOOL
Go Marauders!

Occasionally, a group of spectators shouted out that second line—over the noise and chatter echoing off the tiled walls.

Aaron was a junior and one of the star swimmers on the opposing team, the Mount Vernon Bulldogs. This was an important meet, and he'd missed the team bus here. Carrying his goggles and warm-up pants, Aaron hurried toward his teammates and Coach Gunderson on the other side of the pool.

Someone in the crowd whistled. Then from the same general direction, Aaron heard some girls laughing and squealing. No matter how noisy a place got, the giggling of high school girls somehow always managed to be heard. Aaron realized it was about him. With his black hair, dark eyes, bronze complexion, and sinewy build, he was quite handsome. But Aaron still thought of himself as skinny and awkward. Maybe that was because he always compared himself to his dad, who was part-Hawaiian and a surfer and a major stud as far as the ladies were concerned. "He was too good-looking for his own good!" Aaron's mother often said about his estranged father.

Aaron thought he could never measure up to what his father once was.

So—whenever girls whistled at him, or giggled and whispered to each other in his presence, his best friend, Nestor, had to remind him: "Those girls aren't making fun of you, stupid. They think you're hot. Enjoy it."

But Aaron couldn't really enjoy the attention right now.

The coach was glaring at him, the trademark Gunderson scowl.

Aaron approached him. "I'm really sorry I'm late, Coach. I was—"

"I don't want to hear any excuses," Gunderson muttered. "Late is unacceptable."

Lanky and balding, the coach was in his late forties. Today he had on one of his Izod knockoff sport shirts from JC Penney, a yellow model. He held up his hand—thumb and forefinger almost touching. "I was this close to eliminating you, Brenner. You're up first in the fifty-freestyle, and you have about ninety seconds to limber up for it. Be ready."

"Yes, sir," he said, nodding a few more times than necessary.

Aaron quickly tossed his warm-up pants on the bench, where some of his teammates were waiting. Among them sat Nestor, the only black swimmer on the team. He'd already taken off his warm-up gear, exposing his skinny, splotchy body to the scrutiny of the spectators and home team. Nestor had the pigmentation condition called vitiligo.

"It's the same thing Michael Jackson had," Aaron would explain when people asked what was wrong with his friend. Except for a few pale spots on his left cheek, Nestor's face was unaffected by the condition. But his chest, torso, and neck were like a map of dark brown against an almost chalky beige—with odd, jagged borders between the conflicting colors. Aaron had to admire his friend. Not only was he a good swimmer, he had a lot of guts. Every time Nestor took off his warm-up clothes for a meet, he'd have to ignore the stares and murmurs. And it wasn't because people thought he was hot.

Getting to his feet, Nestor squinted at Aaron and silently mouthed: "*What happened?*"

Aaron just shook his head and rolled his eyes. Then with a feeble wave at his teammates, he started to walk around the pool. It had become a sort of superstitious ritual for him: one lap around the deck before the start

of a meet. Lately, he'd taken that time to search the
bleachers for college coaches he'd been soliciting. It was
a bit early in the year, but Aaron had already emailed ré-
sumés and video links to seven different universities—
mostly in Washington and Oregon.

Without a swimming scholarship, he couldn't afford college. The coaches were supposed to let him
know when they were coming to watch him at a meet.
But that wasn't always the case, and sometimes they
sent—unannounced—an assistant coach in their place.
Aaron had Googled the coaches and their assistants,
and he knew most of their faces. As he made his way
around the pool, he tried to find one of them in the
crowd.

He was also looking for his mother. When they'd
talked on the phone an hour ago, he'd told her not to
bother coming. He was so mad at her. Still, he couldn't
help wondering if she was there in the bleachers somewhere. But, so far, Aaron didn't see her.

He kept his hands in the pockets of his warm-up
jacket as he ambled toward the other side of the pool
and scanned the crowd. He didn't recognize anyone—
except a bizarre-looking, fortysomething man who had
been at Aaron's last three meets. The man was pale
with helmet-shaped, copper-colored hair that looked like
a bad wig. He wore big, thick-lens glasses that made him
resemble a cartoon mosquito. In the humid pool area, he
had to be sweltering in his fuzzy black V-neck sweater.
The weird guy grinned at him—and gave a thumbs-up
signal.

Bewildered, Aaron worked up a smile and nodded,
but he kept moving. He wondered if Mr. Mosquito was

the father of one of his teammates or maybe some college assistant coach.

He finished his walk around the pool deck, shed the warm-up jacket, and grabbed his goggles. Then he started to swing his arms and stretch to limber up.

Nestor approached him. "So what the hell happened?"

"I don't want to talk about it," Aaron muttered.

"Weren't you supposed to get a ride from your mom? Did she flake out at the last minute?"

That was exactly what had happened. Aaron frowned at him. "What part of 'I don't want to talk about it' didn't you understand?"

Nestor sighed and slapped his shoulder. "It's cool. Get in there and kill'm, dude."

Coach Gunderson came up to him and whispered some advice about his main competition on the Marauders: a cocky, good-looking senior named Dante Bellini. Aaron didn't quite hear what he said, but he nodded anyway.

He'd already started to get into his own zone, and the only things he listened for now were the whistle signals from the referee and the starters.

With a few short blasts of his whistle, the ref called the swimmers to their blocks. In the next lane was Bellini. With his multicolored swimming cap and buffed body, he looked like he belonged on the cover of *Men's Fitness*. Bellini grinned and muttered something to him. Aaron had no idea what the guy said, but he nodded once again. Then he put on his goggles.

The long whistle from the starter prompted Aaron to

get in position on the block. "Swimmers, take your marks!" the man announced.

Usually, from here on, Aaron was like a robot. He didn't focus on anything except his lane in the pool in front of him. But for some reason, this time, he looked up. Through his goggles, he saw that strange-looking man in the bleachers smirking at him.

The starting horn beeped.

Aaron pushed off the block and dove into the cool water.

Once under the surface, he always thought of himself as a machine—just speeding forward. The splashing water from his furious kicks had the sound of a powerful engine. The 50-yard freestyle was like an aquatic version of a drag race. At the same time, everything had to be perfect, no mistakes. He usually did both laps without a breath. He knew how many kicks he usually took before reaching the other side of the pool, but something was off this time. The wall seemed to sneak up on him, and he suddenly realized he was about to ram into it. He hesitated—like a total idiot. He lost time pushing off for the second lap.

It threw him, and he started thinking about Bellini in the next lane, about his mother making him miss the team bus here, and about that bizarre-looking man in the bleachers, who may or may not have been a college scout.

Aaron knew he'd lost the race with ten yards to go.

In fact, he came in third—at 22.38 seconds, way off his best, behind Bellini and one of his own teammates.

Bellini later beat him out again in the 400-yard freestyle.

Aaron figured no college coach or scout in their right mind would want him now. He noticed Mr. Mosquito had vacated his spot in the bleachers, and the meet wasn't even over yet. The guy must have left sometime after the 50-yard freestyle defeat.

He tried to be happy for Nestor, who won in the 100-yard backstroke. But Aaron kept brooding about his own defeat. As if he didn't feel lousy enough, he had to endure Coach Gunderson in the locker room afterward, reminding him that he'd let down the entire team. Aaron tried to finish dressing while the coach stood by his locker chewing him out. "You said you wouldn't be taking the team bus—that you'd get to the meet on your own, which means you're responsible for showing up on time. Ten minutes early is on time. On time is late. And late is unacceptable . . ."

And *blah, blah, blah.* That was Coach Gunderson's spin on the Vince Lombardi quote about team punctuality. He gave the speech practically every week— whenever someone was even *almost late* for the team bus. Aaron didn't want to hear any more. But Gunderson went on and on.

How did he expect to win a race when he showed up for the meet at the last minute—with no time to warm up? Where was he? Did he know how disrespectful that was to his teammates?

Aaron just shrugged and said he was sorry.

"Y'know, I was worried about you," the coach grumbled. "That swimmer from East Wenatchee, the one who went missing and then last week was discovered drowned—the police think he might have been

murdered, maybe part of a pattern. It's happened before . . ."

Aaron had heard about that, too. The kid's name was
Chris something, and apparently he'd been the latest high
school swimmer to disappear. The kids were all from
Washington and Oregon. Only a few had gone missing
over the last two years, and some of them could have
run away. No one could say for sure they'd all been abducted or murdered. Aaron didn't know any of them.
He hadn't seen anything on the news or online about it
yet, just a lot of buzz among the guys on the swim
team. He hadn't said anything to his mom about it, because he didn't want her to worry.

Aaron figured the coach was only bringing it up
now to make him feel even more crappy about arriving
late to the meet.

Gunderson glanced around and seemed to realize
they were the only ones left in the locker room. "Well,
hurry up and get dressed," he grumbled. "Let's not
keep the bus waiting."

"I've got a ride," Aaron said, sitting down on a bench
to put on his sneakers. "My aunt lives close by, and she's
picking me up." That was a lie. To get to the meet, Aaron
had ridden his bike to the downtown stop in Mount Vernon and loaded it on the rack at the front of the public
bus. Then after thirty minutes, he got off in Everett and
furiously pedaled to the high school.

His bike was parked by a side entrance to the school.
It would have been easy to load it in the luggage area of
the team bus and go back with the rest of the guys. But
he didn't want to face his teammates after losing the

meet for them. Plus he just needed to be alone for a while.

The coach stood over him. "So—this aunt of yours, is she on her way?"

Aaron nodded a few more times than necessary. "She just texted. She's in the parking lot, waiting for me now." The lies were really mounting up.

"Fine." Gunderson sighed. "See you at practice to-morrow—on time."

He turned away and lumbered out of the locker room.

A minute later, Aaron was zipping up his backpack when the locker room door swung open again. Nestor stopped in the doorway. He wore his hooded red sweatshirt and carried a duffel bag. "You're not taking the bus back?" he asked.

Aaron shook his head. "And put up with Gunderson glaring at me the whole time? No thanks."

"How are you getting home?"

"There's a bus to downtown Mount Vernon that leaves in about forty minutes," Aaron said, hoisting his pack over his shoulder. "I got my bike parked outside."

"So that's how you got here," Nestor murmured. "Listen, next time your mom says she can drive you to a meet, tell her no thanks."

Aaron worked up a halfhearted smile. Though it was the truth, he didn't like hearing that his mother was a screw-up—not even from his best friend. Nestor meant well. "Thanks," he said. He nodded toward the toilets. "Listen, I got to take a leak. The bus is waiting. You better haul ass or Gunderson will be on your case, too."

Nestor glanced down at the floor for a moment and nodded.

"You really blew them away in the hundred back-stroke, dude," Aaron said. "Way to go."

"Hey, about time you said something, man." Nestor's face lit up. "I mean, c'mon, I was like a shark—fast, furious, and deadly."

"Except a shark on its back," Aaron smiled. "Seriously, you were awesome. I'll call you tonight. Okay?" Then he headed toward the bathroom area, and the smile faded from his face.

"Later!" he heard Nestor call.

Aaron didn't really need to pee. He just felt so miserable. Not even a pep talk from his best friend could help.

He stood by the sinks for a few moments, making sure Nestor had left. He caught his reflection in the wide mirror above the sink counter. Once in a while, someone would mention that he looked like Keanu Reeves—especially when Keanu had shorter hair, like in *Speed*. When Aaron was growing up, other kids sometimes asked if he was part-Asian. That was thanks to his Hawaiian father.

Aaron had spent the first eight years of his life in Honolulu. It was where he fell in love with the water and learned to swim. His dad worked nights as a bartender. His mom was an artist, painting mostly in watercolor—beach and landscape scenes. She waited tables during the day. As a kid, Aaron used to watch his dad in action at the beach—when his dad was supposed to be watching him. His father would stick him with friends, admirers who were all too willing to babysit

Jason Hale's little boy, as long as it meant the King of the Beach would come sit with them after conquering some waves. His father actually had groupies. Back before Aaron was born, his dad had posed naked for a photographer. In the shot, he held a big pineapple in front of his crotch. It became a popular postcard—with different greetings written across it, everything from "*Aloha!*" to "*Hand Picked in Hawaii!*" It still sold in a lot of the tacky tourist shops. His dad might have made a fortune if he hadn't signed away the photo rights for cash to buy a new surfboard. In a way, he was kind of an institution. He was pretty dazzling—and friendly toward everyone. Looking back, Aaron figured—between the beach and the bar—his old man must have been getting laid all the time.

That became quite clear to Aaron's mother after a while. She divorced his dad and took Aaron back home to Mount Vernon, where they lived with her ailing mother. Swimming at the Skagit Valley Family YMCA was his only break from a strange new school and the sick, bedridden woman at home. It was up to Aaron to take care of her a lot of the time, because his mom was always taking these spur-of-the-moment trips to Bellingham, LaConner, the San Juan Islands, or Seattle to meet with some art gallery owner or potential buyer. She often missed dinners and sometimes didn't come home until the next day. Aaron's grandmother would grouse about how irresponsible his mother was—usually while eating the Progresso ravioli or soup, or the hot dog or the frozen pizza nine-year-old Aaron had heated up for her.

His grandmother died a week before his tenth birthday. He and his mother continued to live in the house. She got a job as a checker at Haggen Food and Pharmacy but still painted. And she still took off for hours at a time to push her work at galleries. Aaron was fine on his own. After school and during the summers, he rode his bike to the YMCA. He idolized Matt Biondi, Nathan Adrian, and Michael Phelps. He was thrilled to join the freshman swim team when he started at Mount Vernon High School. At last, he could compete with someone besides himself. He often sent emails and texts to his dad about his accomplishments on the team. His father wasn't very responsive. No matter how long Aaron's email, the response was practically always the same:

> Congrats! Way to go!
> Dad
>
> Sent from my iPhone

After a while, Aaron stopped trying to solicit any kind of interest from his father.

Last Christmas, he'd gotten a $15 Target gift card from his dad inside a holiday photo card:

MELE KALIKIMAKA!

from The Hales
JASON, AMBER, CARSON & SHAWNA

It showed his dad on the beach with his current family, all of them in sport clothes: a twentysomething blond wife and two toddler kids—half-siblings Aaron

had never met. His father had gotten paunchy. The
card was signed "Happy Holidays!" probably by the
wife—unless his dad had suddenly taken to putting little circles over his I's.

Aaron remembered a time when he'd adored his father—and when his mother had been there for him.
But he'd come to realize that his pretty, blond mom
and his hunky *King of the Beach* dad were horribly
inept parents.

Still, with his mother, he always wanted to believe
she'd turn herself around and be there for him—for a
change. He wanted to depend on her.

In his grandmother's house, he'd found several
Peanuts cartoon books his mom had owned decades
ago. Aaron had devoured them as a kid. He remembered the cartoon panels with Lucy holding the football for Charlie Brown to punt. Always at the last
minute, she snatched it up, leaving Charlie to kick at
the air and careen back on his ass. Each time Charlie
went to kick that ball, he seemed to think Lucy would
actually hold it for him—for a change. That was how
Aaron felt with his mother when she promised to be
there for him. He kept thinking: *She really means it
this time. It's okay, she'll be there. I won't end up
falling on my ass.*

It had happened again today. She'd said she wanted
to go to his meet but needed him to be the navigator
because she didn't have a GPS in her car or on her
phone. His mom never had any problems finding these
various art galleries out of town. But the prospect of
driving thirty miles to a high school in Everett seemed
to intimidate her. She'd said she had to meet with a

gallery owner in LaConner in the morning but would be back before noon—with plenty of time for them to beat the team bus to Mariner High School.

Aaron figured it was his own damn fault. He knew what time the team bus was supposed to leave. When his mother hadn't called or shown up by twelve thirty, he could have still hopped on his bike and pedaled to school and caught the team bus. But he stuck it out, thinking his mother would be there at any minute. He figured she probably wasn't answering his calls and texts because she was on the phone with someone else while driving. She did that a lot.

She finally called him at five minutes after one, saying she was just leaving LaConner and that someone was very interested in one of her paintings.

Aaron was furious. "The meet is in fifty-five minutes! What the hell? Why didn't you call me? Damn it, Mom . . ."

"I'll be there in twenty minutes at the most, I promise. We can still make the meet in plenty of time—"

"No, we can't!" he shot back. "Forget it. I'll get there on my own."

"I'm on my way!" she said. "If we're a little late, it's not like they're going to start the meet without you. You're their star swimmer."

"What kind of bullshit is that?" he cried. "It doesn't work that way. How goddamn clueless are you? Of course they're going to start the meet without me. Jesus, Mom!" He rubbed his forehead. "Listen, forget it. I need to hang up and figure out how I'm getting to Everett."

"Aaron, I'll be there in—"

"At this point, Mom, I'm so pissed off, you could show up here right now and I wouldn't want you driving me. I don't even want you at the meet. You'll probably bring me bad luck."

Then he'd hung up. That was the last thing he'd said to his mother.

Now, as he left the locker room, Aaron took his phone from the pocket of his hoodie. He checked his messages. There were none. His mother hadn't tried to call back.

Once home, he'd probably spend the rest of the evening apologizing to her.

Or would she even be there when he got home?

He stepped outside. It was getting dark and the streetlights were on. The sudden autumn chill made him shudder. Fallen leaves skittered across the school lot, which was practically empty. He turned a corner and spotted his bike in the distance by the school's side entrance—on the rack where he'd locked it. No one else was around except for a woman with her son. The kid looked about ten years old—at least from behind. They were about thirty feet ahead of him on the sidewalk.

It occurred to Aaron that his mom would have called—if not to apologize, then to make him feel guilty for being so mean to her on the phone. At the very least, she would have left a message asking if he'd made it to Everett okay.

She'd said earlier that someone might be buying one of her paintings—and he hadn't responded to that at all. His mom had helped get him a job bagging groceries at Haggen three nights a week. Aaron often worked there with his mom for part of her shift. He'd seen how she was treated by some customers. He'd seen how tough and degrading the job could get. Selling a painting meant so much to her. And here when she'd told him about a possible sale today, all he could do was chew her out for not being there in time to drive him to a meet.

No wonder she hadn't called.

And then there was the possibility that she could have been in an accident—rushing to see him at his swim meet.

Aaron speed-dialed her number and started counting the ringtones.

"Oh, no!" someone cried out.

Aaron froze. He saw the mother and son—several yards in front of him. The kid fell to the ground with a thud. As if in shock, the mother just stood there, looking down at the helpless boy. "Oh, no!" she repeated in a feeble, shaky voice.

Switching off the phone, Aaron ran toward them. The kid seemed to have fainted or collapsed. The panic-stricken mother still hadn't moved. All she did was twitch and frantically wave her hands in front of her.

Aaron scooped the boy off the ground. He was surprisingly heavy—and up close the kid looked more like a growth-stunted twelve- or thirteen-year-old. He had black hair, a slightly chubby face, and traces of teenage acne. He moaned and started to regain consciousness in Aaron's arms.

"He—he's had these spells before," the mother said—in a breathless, childlike tone that made Aaron think she was drunk or just kind of daffy. "Can you— can you help us to the van? I have a little mattress in back for him . . ."

The boy moaned again as Aaron set him back on his feet. He led the kid toward a silver minivan that was parked not too far away from the bike rack.

"Thank you so much!" he heard the woman say in her silly little-girl voice. He glanced at her for a moment. He noticed the thin, pale, thirtyish brunette had a bruise around one eye.

Pressing a button on her key fob, she unlocked the back of the minivan and then opened the door. Aaron saw a scrawny-looking mattress there—beside a mess of blankets.

The boy groaned once more and slumped in Aaron's grasp. It was hard holding him up.

"If you could get in first," the woman said, "it'll be easier to pull him onto the mattress. Then I'll help you from out here . . ."

Climbing inside, Aaron kept his arms wrapped around the kid and tried to hoist him up onto the mattress.

But something was off. He noticed the kid was smirking. Aaron's hands were momentarily trapped, squeezed between the boy's shoulders and the mattress.

"You were doing really well until the second lap, Aaron," someone said.

He swiveled around and came face-to-face with the strange-looking man, the one with the big glasses and the copper-colored hair. He was grinning at him from the front passenger seat. He had a rag in one hand and wore yellow rubber gloves.

Before Aaron could move, the kid grabbed him by the arms.

The man lurched toward him, covering Aaron's mouth and nose with the moist rag. The cloth had a chemical smell to it.

Struggling, Aaron held his breath and tried to pull away. He managed to break free from the boy. But a sudden dizziness overwhelmed him. He was so weak, he could hardly move.

The kid scurried out from under him and jumped out of the van.

Aaron felt his whole body shutting down. He couldn't put up a fight anymore. The man was pushing him toward the mattress.

"Your timing was off, too, Aaron," grunted the man, hovering over him. "We'll have to work on that . . ."

Just before he lost consciousness, Aaron heard the boy giggling.

CHAPTER THREE

Echo, Washington
Tuesday, October 25—4:22 P.M.

Some slob had left today's *Seattle Times* in disarray at the end of the long reading table in the Echo Public Library's Grand Room.

With a sigh, Caitlin Stoller plopped down on the chair at the table. She started to reassemble the newspaper sections and pages in their proper order. At first, she didn't notice the article on page one about the missing teenage boy from Mount Vernon High School.

Caitlin was thirty-nine, and the recently appointed assistant head librarian. She was thin with shoulder-length, tawny red hair and freckles. She wore khaki slacks and a petite dark blue cardigan. One of her new co-workers, Myra, called her "Ms. J.Crew" because of the preppy way she looked and dressed. A more accurate moniker would have been "Ms. Outlet Mall."

She'd always been frugal, but Caitlin had put herself on an even stricter budget after buying an old four-bedroom Tudor-style house on Birch Place last month—to the tune of $309,000. The same house would have cost about a million in Seattle or Portland. And it was quite a deal in Echo, too. The seller was eager to unload it because he and his wife had separated. The wife ended up killing herself. Caitlin asked the real estate agent if the woman had committed suicide in the house.

"Oh, no, no," the agent had assured her. "It wasn't on the premises. As I mentioned, she and Dr. Goldsmith were separated at the time."

Caitlin had hated taking advantage of someone else's misfortune. She'd tried a few other houses in Echo, but kept coming back to that old Tudor on Birch. The place had charm and character—and a huge, wooded front yard that gave them some privacy.

They still weren't completely moved in. About a dozen unpacked boxes sat in the basement—mostly junk the kids hadn't touched in years but still couldn't part with. Her eleven-year-old son, Gabe, must have owned a dozen different video game systems. And just what the hell was her sixteen-year-old daughter, Lindsay, planning to do with her homemade volcano exhibit from a science fair three years ago? Okay, so she'd won a sec-ond-place ribbon for it, but the papier-mâché mountain took up an entire large-sized moving box. Did Lindsay intend to hold on to the thing for the rest of her life? It didn't even erupt anymore.

"Dad helped me make it," Lindsay had argued—in defense of keeping it.

So her useless old science project was now taking up room in the basement of their new house.

There were also several boxes of Caitlin's books and knickknacks in the guest bedroom upstairs. She hadn't had much time to unpack—what with getting the kids settled in new schools and trying to make a good impression her first few weeks at work.

It was a challenging time for the staff because they were moving into a brand-new library once construction was complete in December.

As Caitlin put today's *Seattle Times* back together, she couldn't help feeling a little sad that they were going to tear down this beautiful old place. The library was a slightly decaying, white-pillared, redbrick mansion in downtown Echo. It was always drafty, and they had problems with the plumbing. The lavatories had handwritten signs by the toilets: *Please hold handle down until flushing is complete. Thank you!* During heavy rains, the lower level flooded—sometimes up to two inches of water. That explained why the gloomy basement always smelled so musty—as did the bound sets of magazines from their periodical archives down there.

But the Grand Room was beautiful with a big fireplace, which was always lit from October through April. It warmed the room and cast faint, flickering shadows on the high ceiling—with its art deco chandelier. All the trim was original wood paneling from the thirties, which someone had meticulously copied for the library's checkout counter. The worn, slightly tattered sofas and easy chairs were practically antiques—as were most of the reading lamps. It was a lovely space. But Caitlin realized her son, Gabe, was probably right when he said it looked like the living room of a haunted house in a black-and-white horror movie. That was especially true around eight o'clock, when the place was empty—and she was working the closing shift alone. That was when she noticed all the little clicks and squeaks from the old mansion settling.

With the lights dimmed, the aisles between the bookshelves on one side of the Grand Room became black pockets where anyone could be hiding. All of the other areas of the library suddenly seemed just as sinister: the periodical section in the basement, which was creepy enough in the daytime; the children's reading room, where anybody could lurk in the shadows amid the oversized stuffed animals; and upstairs in the fiction section—with its balcony that overlooked the Grand Room. How easy it would be for some stalker to sneak up there, then wait and watch as the library emptied out.

Caitlin had worked the closing shift only a few times—and hated it.

But now, at dusk, with the fire blazing and a few customers quietly reading, the room seemed so peaceful and cozy.

She got off work at five thirty tonight, thank God. She had a pound of ground beef thawing in the refrigerator. The kids liked Sloppy Joes. Maybe they'd stop hating her for a night or two if they got Sloppy Joes and Tater Tots for dinner tonight.

The move to Echo had been her idea. For Lindsay and Gabe, it meant saying good-bye to their lifelong friends in Portland and starting anew in this nothing little island town that didn't even have a McDonald's.

Caitlin finally put the newspaper together and noticed a headline at the bottom of page one. The accompanying photo showed a dark-haired, handsome teenager.

MOUNT VERNON TEEN MISSING SINCE SUNDAY

SWIMMER VANISHES AFTER COMPETITION AT MARINER HIGH SCHOOL

Police fear pattern in teen disappearances

Hunched over the library table, Caitlin anxiously read the article. She couldn't help thinking about Lindsay, who was on the varsity swim team at her high school. The missing boy, Aaron Brenner, was a year older than Lindsay. His parents were divorced, too. Caitlin wondered if Lindsay knew him or had heard of him. Her team had had a meet at Mariner High just last week. The school was in Everett, a thirty-minute ferry ride from Echo.

It could have been Lindsay.

The article pointed out that in August, another swimmer, sixteen-year-old Christopher Whalen, went missing from his home in Wenatchee. His divorced mother had left him alone while she went to a play at his sister's grade school. When the mother and sister returned, Chris was gone. His bike and the second car were still in the garage. There was no sign of a struggle.

His naked body had washed up on a Wenatchee River bank in Leavenworth just five days ago. He'd drowned. There were also signs of head trauma. The police were still trying to piece together the circumstances of his death.

Three months before Christopher Whalen's disappearance, another swimmer—seventeen-year-old Monica Leary, from Capital High School in Olympia—vanished after a party at a friend's house. She was still missing.

The article gave a description of her: "blonde, green eyes, five feet tall, 117 pounds, slender, birthmark on her neck."

The article listed four other teenage swimmers who had disappeared within the last two years:

Julie Reynard, 18, from Salem, OR, missing
    since 3/14/15
Cooper Rydel, 16, from Longview, WA, missing
    since 5/2/15
James Lessing, 17, from Bellingham, WA,
    missing since 1/27/16
Paula Sibley-Martz, 17, from Tacoma, WA,
    missing since 3/11/16

Of the four, only Paula was eventually found—three weeks after her disappearance. Hikers discovered her naked body in some woods near Lake Sammamish. She'd been strangled.

The article mentioned that Paula's father, Gordon Martz, of Missoula, Montana, had offered a reward for any information regarding his daughter's whereabouts. The girl's mother, Janice Sibley of Tacoma, had identified the remains.

Obviously, Pamela's parents were divorced—or at least separated. So were Christopher Whalen's parents.

Caitlin wondered about the other missing swimmers. Were their parents divorced or separated as well? If so, that made her daughter a perfect fit for this disturbing pattern.

Lindsay walked a mile and a half home from her

swim practice at the recreation center every day after
school—always alone. She hadn't made many friends
yet.

It would be dark out by the time she finished practice tonight.

Setting the newspaper on top of the stack of recent
editions on the shelf, Caitlin hurried back behind the
counter. She ducked into the employee break room and
pulled her phone from her purse. She moved toward
the break room door so that she could keep an eye on
the checkout counter. She quickly texted her daughter:

> Ill pick up after swim practice. Look for me out-
> - side rec center. Text me back 2 confirm. OK?
> See u soon! XX

She had just finished sending the text when one of
their regulars, Ken Meekley, strutted though the front
door. He was tall, thin, and about forty years old—with
intense dark eyes and a slightly sallow complexion.
His brown hair was parted on the side and ceding to
gray. At first glance, Caitlin had thought he was sort
of handsome. But then after a few encounters, she'd
changed her mind about him. Maybe it was because he
came on a little too strong—to the point that Caitlin
tensed up whenever he walked into the library.

She closed the break room door and made her way
to the counter.

Ken had on his red Windbreaker. Caitlin had never
seen him without it—even back when the weather was
hot. Heading toward the counter, he grinned at her and

brandished a copy of *Truth Like the Sun*, which he'd checked out last week.

"Great recommendation!" he said, giving her the thumbs-up signal. "You were correct-a-mundo when you said I'd like this one. Then again, you know I'm a sucker for anything to do with Seattle history, especially the World's Fair."

The book made a loud bang as he slapped it down on the counter. Several people in the Grand Room looked up from their reading.

Caitlin tried to smile instead of cringe. "Well, I'm glad it was a hit with you, Ken," she said quietly.

Leaning on the counter, he gave her a playful pout. "It's really not fair, Caitlin. I mean, you know me so well, and you won't give me a chance to get better acquainted with you."

"Well, I—I'm just terribly busy . . ."

She could tell he was trying so hard to be smooth, but he just came across as awkward.

He nodded at the phone in her hand and smirked. "What's this? Are you making calls on company time? Should I report this to the library board?"

"I was texting my daughter about something, that's all."

"So—how are Lindsay and Gabe?" he asked. "How's she doing on the swim team?"

"Fine, they're both fine, thanks," Caitlin replied, keeping the pleasant smile plastered on her face. But she could feel a crack in the façade.

About a month ago, in a weak moment, she'd made the mistake of saying something to Ken Meekley about her children, mentioning them by name. Ever since, whenever she had to wait on Ken, he always asked about her kids—by name—as if he knew them or had met them. He was probably just trying to be friendly and polite. But somehow, it unnerved her—especially today.

Ken drummed his fingers on the countertop. "Do you think one of these nights Lindsay and Gabe could get along without their very attractive mother for a few hours so I could take her out to dinner—maybe show her some of Echo's hot spots?"

"Sorry." She shrugged. "I'm flattered, but as I said, I really don't have the time, Ken. Thanks anyway . . ."

He sighed. "Well, maybe I'll just have to steal a library book or break some other rule around here to get your attention."

She let out a skittish laugh. "Oh, I hope not . . ."

"See ya, Caitlin." Ken winked at her, then turned away and started for the door.

"Hot crap on a cracker," someone muttered. "He was just in here yesterday . . ."

Caitlin turned around.

Myra had emerged from the children's reading room, and now she stepped behind the counter to join Caitlin. She was in her early thirties, with close-cropped blond hair and a cute dimpled smile. She wore jeans and a loose-fitting purple top that helped camouflage her weight struggles.

During Caitlin's first week at the library, Myra hadn't once flashed that dimpled smile her way. It was obvious Myra resented having some new person come in and take a position over her. Caitlin had been hired to help with the transition from the old library to the new facility. The head librarian, seventy-nine-year-old Della Zegers, was still quite sharp and spry—and not at all ready to retire. It took Della, Myra, and the part-time staff a few days to warm up to Caitlin, which they did once they realized she wasn't replacing anyone. But Myra could still be a bit icy and caustic toward her at times.

"So—is it all set?" she asked, moving closer to Caitlin. "Are you and Creepy Ken going on a date? You can join the last five women who had dates with Ken. They're now buried in his basement. But at least they got a Taco Time dinner out of it."

"Well, I'm holding out for Applebee's for my last meal." Caitlin sighed. "So—no, I won't be going out with Ken anytime soon. I'll leave the field open for you." She nodded toward the children's reading room. "How are things in toddler paradise?"

"Tolerable," Myra murmured. "A couple of the mothers are actually sticking around and watching their own children for a change, instead of expecting me to babysit the little brats. Mind if I step out for a cigarette?"

"Go for it," Caitlin replied. "Is it okay with you if I leave a little early tonight? I want to pick up my daughter from swim practice . . ."

It was fine with Myra. So Caitlin cut out of work fifteen minutes early.

As she headed toward her Lexus in the parking lot, she buttoned up her peacoat to ward off the breeze from the water.

Echo's harbor was quiet—almost deserted. The ferry was on its fall schedule with only six crossings daily. As the cold weather crept in, this part of town almost seemed to shut down.

Caitlin heard it used to be a lot busier until a few years ago when the community recreation center—with its gym, yoga studio, and pool—was built about a mile inland. Soon Safeway, Starbucks, T-Mobile, and several other stores and restaurants popped up there. Meanwhile, businesses here near the harbor closed one after another—until it was practically a ghost town. But a handful of retail establishments and the library were still hanging in there. It helped that during the summer, Echo attracted a lot of tourists, thanks to whale-watching tours and two nearby wineries. Every summer weekend, they had an arts and crafts street fair near the ferry landing. A lot of people felt the area was starting to revitalize.

But the powers that be were building the new library inland—near the community center, of course.

Caitlin still hadn't heard back from Lindsay—not even her daughter's usual texted "K" to acknowledge she'd gotten the message. She told herself Lindsay had probably been in the pool all this time, practicing with the rest of the team. No point in pushing the panic button yet.

The Lexus was backed into a diagonal space under a streetlight at the edge of the library lot. Just a few feet away from the car, Caitlin stopped dead. She noticed a slip of white paper stuck under the windshield wiper. She walked over and plucked the note out from under the wiper blade and squinted at the childlike handwriting:

Have a nice day, Caitlin! ☺

She immediately thought of Ken Meekley.

Who else would leave her such a well-meaning, yet unsettlingly weird message? And Ken had just been in the library flirting with her fifteen minutes ago. How did he know which car in the lot was hers? Then again, this was the same guy who had instantly memorized her children's names after she'd mentioned them in passing a few weeks ago.

With a sigh, Caitlin folded up the message and quickly shoved it in the pocket of her peacoat.

"Do you think Ken has any idea how creepy he really is?" Myra had asked Caitlin a while back. "Or is he clueless?"

Maybe he's just lonely—like so many of us, Caitlin had wanted to answer. But in her response, she'd merely shrugged and chuckled halfheartedly.

Climbing into the driver's seat, she wondered how much Myra knew about her. Everyone was probably aware that she was divorced, but Caitlin hadn't talked about it with anybody. Still, there was Google. Some of what she'd gone through in the last two years had made *The Oregonian*. Her ex-husband, Russ, had given the newspaper a very candid—brave—interview last year. Caitlin couldn't help wondering if Myra had read all about her.

Or maybe Ken had.

Caitlin shuddered. She started up the car, switched on the headlights, and started toward the lot exit. She turned onto Main Street and then checked the digital clock on the dash: 5:19 P.M.

No doubt, her son Gabe was home and in his room right now. Having snacked on Mountain Dew and

Barbecue Lay's, he was at his desk, drawing mazes—or perhaps something inspired by *Dungeons & Dragons* or M. C. Escher. He was a good artist. Caitlin didn't want to discourage that in him. But she wished he'd go out and make some friends.

The newness of Echo wasn't to blame for the way Gabe seemed to hibernate. He'd started to isolate himself more and more after his older brother, Cliff, was killed two years ago.

For a while, she and Russ had him seeing a therapist, who wanted to prescribe medication. All the while, Gabe had insisted that he just preferred to be by himself so he could draw his pictures. So they decided to leave him alone and let him do what he wanted.

Caitlin figured, hell, he'd found a better way to cope than any of them—and he was becoming a gifted artist in the process.

What Russ had become was someone totally different from the sweet guy she'd married.

He wasn't the clear-eyed, healthy, gregarious guy she'd first met at the Dragonfly Coffee House in Portland. Back then, she hadn't considered him particularly handsome. But he was sort of offbeat cute, and whenever the two of them talked, Russ made her feel like the most important person in the world. He was an electrician, a fitness nut, and he read a new book every two or three days. He used to joke that he fell in love with her because she was a librarian.

Russ was a good father, too. That didn't mean the two of them never argued over whose turn it was to get up in the middle of the night with the screaming babies. But as the kids got older, he was always doing things with them—ice-skating at Lloyd Center, kite-flying in the park, or swimming at the Laurelhurst pool.

Cliff was the middle child, and the firstborn son. With his wavy brown hair and goofy smile, he looked like his father. He loved basketball. His favorite movie ever was *Hoosiers*. He must have seen it at least twenty times. When he got at all excited, he stuttered.

It happened on a Saturday in May, two years ago—just a week after Cliff's eleventh birthday. Russ wanted to return a book to the library and pick up a biography on FDR he'd placed on hold. If he'd just waited a couple of days, Caitlin could have done it for him. But Russ was looking for an excuse to get out on his bike. Cliff wanted to go with him.

They both had their helmets on. When Russ took the kids bike riding, he always made sure they wore their bicycle helmets.

But the way things happened, the helmets didn't really make any difference that day.

Twenty-two-year-old Mackenzie Burke was driving the blue Toyota Camry her parents had given her for college graduation. She was also texting a friend about getting together that night with some other girlfriends for dinner.

Mackenzie hadn't correctly judged the distance of the curve in the road ahead. She'd failed to notice a Yield sign for merging traffic—and the two bicyclists who had pulled in front of her.

She'd been looking at her phone at the time.

The vehicle plowed into Cliff first. He and his mountain bike went careening off the road. Cliff flew over the handlebars and slammed headfirst into a telephone pole, breaking his neck. He died instantly.

Russ was catapulted off his bicycle and thrown against a parked SUV. He claimed that even when it was happening—past the sound of glass shattering, screeching brakes, and the SUV's shrill alarm, he tried to listen for Cliff. He hoped to hear him crying out—or stuttering the way he did when he was upset. Russ said he'd been so concerned about their son, he didn't even realize the extent of his own injuries. He was in pain, lying on the pavement amid broken glass from the SUV's windows—a few feet away from his mangled bicycle. He tried to get up but couldn't even move. At first he thought that he'd landed in a puddle, because he was wet. Then he realized he was covered in his own blood.

That was when he blacked out.

The doctor said he was lucky his spinal cord had remained intact. But Russ had a fractured clavicle, two ruptured discs, and a shattered right femur. The left leg was broken—as was his right wrist—and he'd suffered extensive nerve damage. The doctors had to surgically fuse together vertebrae in his neck. He also had multiple cuts and lacerations. Not counting the surgeries, Russ accrued a total of ninety-three stitches.

Three days after the accident, the doctors told Caitlin that Russ would be able to walk again with extensive physical therapy. Because of the drugs they were giving him to reduce the pain, Russ was too out of it to comprehend most of what the doctors told him. But they advised Caitlin not to expect things to return to normal anytime within the year.

She had a feeling they were wrong. Things would never return to normal.

All the while, Mackenzie Burke's parents' lawyers and insurance representatives were barraging Caitlin with calls, faxes, emails, and forms. It was their way of cooperating. Their insurance company was paying Russ's hospital bills, and they'd offered a big settlement—to make sure Mackenzie didn't have to face any criminal charges. All she got was a slap on the wrist and a suspended license.

Seven weeks after the accident, while Russ was moved from the hospital to an inpatient rehab facility, Caitlin couldn't help thinking Mackenzie was probably driving again—in a brand-new car. Hell, the girl might have even succumbed to texting behind the wheel once again—only a little more carefully this time around.

Russ would be at the rehab facility for three months. Caitlin worried about Lindsay and Gabe as they grieved over their brother. Finances were tight because Russ couldn't work. They were supposed to have settlement money, but Russ had it tied up in stocks and bonds they couldn't touch. He insisted on paying all the bills and handling their accounting while in rehab. He said it gave him a sense of purpose. At the time of the accident, he'd been in the middle of remodeling their kitchen. For those next few months, Caitlin felt like they were living in an abandoned construction zone. She cooked their meals in a toaster oven or microwave, or on their George Foreman grill. She kept telling herself that things would get better once Russ came home.

She couldn't have been more wrong.

Waiting at one of Echo's few stoplights, Caitlin realized she had tears in her eyes. The accident had happened two years ago, and she was still crying about it. She pulled a Kleenex from her purse and wiped her eyes and blew her nose.

The light changed to green, but the blue MINI Cooper in front of her didn't move.

"C'mon," Caitlin muttered, stuffing the used tissue in the cup holder. "The light couldn't get any greener if you watered it, honey."

She was about to tap the horn when the MINI Cooper finally pulled into the intersection.

As she followed the slow vehicle and watched it occasionally veer over the yellow centerline, Caitlin felt herself bristling. She could see the driver was a woman, who seemed to keep looking down at something every few seconds. Caitlin knew what the other driver was doing.

And she thought of Mackenzie Burke.

"Stupid jerk," she hissed, gripping the wheel more tightly. Yet she also felt this strangely satisfying rush—a valid reason to get really angry at someone or just people in general. She was tempted to lay on her horn. But she kept a safe distance behind. She wondered if the driver would look up in time to see the stoplight at the intersection ahead.

The MINI Cooper stopped at the light, but not without a little screech from its brakes.

The recreation center was four blocks up the street, but Caitlin couldn't help herself. She pulled into the right-turn lane—beside the MINI Cooper. With a shaky hand, she lowered her window. She could clearly see into the other car now. Sure enough, the woman at the wheel had a phone in her hand, and she was moving both thumbs over the keypad. This woman needed to be told off.

Caitlin tapped on her horn. "Hey!" she yelled out the window.

The woman didn't look up.

"Hey, you!" Caitlin screamed.

The other driver finally glanced her way, but she didn't put the phone down.

"Stop texting and driving!" Caitlin's heart was racing. She hated confrontations—but she couldn't help it. She was a woman with a mission. People needed to know when they were endangering other people's lives.

The driver shook her head and waved her away as if she couldn't be bothered. Then she turned all her attention to her phone again.

"You're going to kill somebody!" Caitlin shouted, tapping her horn again. "Just how important is that stupid text?"

The front passenger window of the MINI Cooper went down. The woman took one texting hand away from her phone—long enough to flip the bird at Caitlin. "Mind your own business, you crazy fucking bitch!"

The window went up again. The woman went back to her texting.

"What is wrong with you?" Caitlin cried. "My God—"

A car horn blared, startling her. Caitlin realized someone behind her wanted to turn right. She felt like such an idiot. She was in the right-turn-only lane. She checked traffic in the intersection and then turned—onto a street that would take her out of her way.

She couldn't stop shaking. She was so angry and frustrated she wanted to hit somebody. There were way too many Mackenzie Burkes out on the roads. And like someone with an old score to settle, Caitlin was almost always on the lookout for them. So practically every time she got behind the wheel, she'd notice someone texting while driving—and her blood would boil.

At the first intersection, Caitlin turned left so she'd be back on track to Central Avenue and the community recreation center. She took a few deep breaths. Maybe that awful woman was right. Maybe she was a crazy bitch, a woman obsessed. And she'd only drive herself even crazier going after all the Mackenzie Burkes in this world. It wasn't going to make a difference. She wasn't going to save any lives—or bring her son back.

She turned onto Central, which became more and more commercial with every passing block—one little strip mall after another. She saw the Echo Recreation and Fitness Center coming up on her right. It was a big ugly building, cold gray concrete with tiny windows. It looked like some government building in a former Soviet bloc country.

Caitlin turned into the vast lot, pulled up in front of the center's main entrance and parked behind three other cars—all in a row. She wondered if the drivers were all nervous mothers like herself, each one making sure her daughter wouldn't be the next missing swimmer. She wondered if any of them had already lost a child—as she had.

She had to live with the constant fear that it could happen again.

Caitlin switched off her headlights and the ignition. She checked her phone again. Still no answer from Lindsay. She decided to phone her instead of texting. It rang four times and then went to voice mail. "*Hi, this is Lindsay,*" her daughter said on the recorded greeting. "*If you want to leave a message, you know the drill. Bye!*"

Caitlin listened to the beep. "Hey, Lind," she said with a little edge in her tone. She couldn't suppress it. "I guess you haven't gotten my text yet. You're probably still in the pool. Anyway, it's . . ." She glanced at her watch. "It's just past five thirty, and I'm parked here outside the rec center—by the main entrance. I'm waiting for you. I—well, I hope to see you soon. If you've already wrapped up practice and are on your way home, call me. Okay?"

Just as she clicked off, Caitlin noticed three girls stepping out the center's double doors. They had their backpacks over their shoulders and their mobile devices in their hands. Gazes fixed on their phones, they seemed to ignore each other. Caitlin didn't know their names, but she'd been to enough swim meets to recognize Lindsay's teammates.

Several more girls followed. Two of them hopped into the car directly in front of Caitlin. Three girls piled into the first vehicle, an SUV. One girl got into the middle car.

Biting her lip, Caitlin watched the three cars pull away from the curb, one after the other.

She nervously drummed her fingers on the steering

wheel and waited for Lindsay to step outside. "C'mon, Lind," she murmured. "Please, honey . . ."

A few stragglers wandered out. Caitlin had a feeling this was the last of them. She tried to convince herself that maybe Lindsay was staying late. It would be like her to push herself and stay at practice longer than the others.

Caitlin recognized the pretty redhead among the stragglers. Her name was Nancy Abbe. Lindsay said Nancy was the best swimmer on the team—besides herself, all modesty aside. Nancy was talking with one of her teammates—a skinny, tall brunette.

Opening the car door, Caitlin stepped outside and peered over the hood of the Lexus. "Nancy?" she called.

Both girls stopped and squinted at her.

"Nancy, I'm Lindsay's mom," she explained. "Is she still inside?"

The girl shook her head. "She didn't show up for practice."

"What?"

"I saw her before lunch," the other girl piped up. "But practically, like, right afterward, in my fifth-period English Lit class, she wasn't there . . ."

"Are you sure?" Caitlin asked, walking around to the curb.

The brunette girl nodded. "Her seat's right beside mine, and it was empty. But then a lot of people ditch that class . . ."

Nancy nudged her friend. "Want to get her in trouble?" Then she turned to Caitlin. "I'm sure Lindsay had a good reason for missing the class, Mrs. Stoller."

"And blowing off practice," the other girl said under her breath.

Both girls giggled. Then Nancy waved at her as they moved on down the sidewalk.

Caitlin stood by her car. She felt a horrible pang in her gut.

She glanced over at the double doors and realized Lindsay wouldn't be coming through them—not now.

Caitlin thought about another high school swimmer—a girl found naked and strangled in some woods about eighty miles away.

CHAPTER FOUR

He woke up, shivering and scared.

Aaron had no idea where he was. His head throbbed so badly he didn't even want to move. But he was freezing—and he had to pee.

It took a few moments for him to realize he was clad only in his underwear. The cot he was sleeping on didn't have any blankets or sheets. There wasn't even a pillow. He wondered how long he'd been unconscious.

Aaron sat up and a wave of nausea overwhelmed him. Still, he got to his feet. The floor was concrete—and cold. His teeth started chattering, and that made his head ache even more. The dimly lit room seemed to be spinning. He rubbed his eyes and glanced around for a door to the bathroom. He spotted a toilet in the corner, beside a small sink.

Where was he anyway?

"Hello?" he yelled, panicked. His throat was sore—and dry. "Is anyone there? Hey . . ."

He started to cough and staggered to the toilet.

Aaron braced a hand against the wall to keep his balance while he peed. He had a vague memory of standing in this spot before. A man had been behind him, holding him by the arm while he urinated. It was like a bizarre dream. He remembered now: he'd been awoken by the man, who guided him from the cot to the toilet. "C'mon, I'm not going to have you pissing in bed, chum," he'd muttered. After Aaron had finished, the guy had given him a shot, which must have put him back to sleep. How long ago was that?

Now he was dying of thirst. After flushing the toilet, Aaron bent over the sink and slurped from the faucet. The water tasted a little rusty, but it was cold and wet, and he guzzled it.

His last clear memory was struggling with that creepy guy, the one with the big glasses and the toupee. They'd been in the back of a minivan. The guy had slapped a rag over Aaron's mouth. It had been soaked in something, probably chloroform. Whatever the guy had used, the stuff had left a slight chemical burn. Aaron felt it now as he turned off the water and wiped his mouth. He winced. His lips and nose were raw.

He still had no idea where he was. He started to cry. "Hello?" he called out.

There was no answer.

Rubbing his bare arms and shoulders to ward off the cold, he glanced around—at the toilet and sink, a dresser, the cot, and an empty bookcase beside it. The drab gray cinder-block walls were decorated with corny, "inspirational" posters. They were photos of swimmers and divers—no one famous or identifiable. The captions read: "DETERMINATION WINS!" and "ACHIEVE EXCELLENCE," and "EVERY ACCOMPLISHMENT STARTS WITH THE DECISION TO TRY!"

Aaron didn't see a window. But there was a vent in the wall—right by the floor—near the cot. He reached down and waved his hand in front of it. No heat. The one door looked like thick steel, and it had a screened speakeasy-type opening at eye level. But the other side of the screen was boarded up. The door didn't have a knob or a handle.

Above him, in the center of the ceiling, was what looked like a surveillance camera—encased in a plastic dome with perforations on the bottom. A pinpoint green light was by the lens.

He wasn't completely alone. Someone was watching him.

Aaron wiped his tears away. But he was still cold and terrified, and he missed his mom.

He walked over to the door and grabbed the screened opening. But when he tried to pull the door open, it didn't budge. "Hello?" he called in a shaky voice. "Is anyone there?"

No response.

"Can anybody hear me?" he cried.

He smelled something very familiar—the chlorine agent used in some swimming pools. Was there an indoor pool nearby?

Aaron banged on the metal door. "What's going on? Where am I?"

He heard a woman's voice—distant and muffled: "Chris, is that you? Are you back?"

He wasn't alone after all.

"Who's there?" he called. He pounded on the door again. "Hello? Who's there? Is anybody there?"

It sounded like someone shushed him. But it didn't seem to come from the other side of the thick door. He glanced back at the vent near the floor. "Say something!" he called. "Who are you?"

Whoever it was, they weren't responding.

"Is anyone there? I heard you before. Please . . . say something . . ."

There was no answer.

Frustrated, Aaron turned and started banging against the door once more. "Let me out of here!" he yelled. The tears started to stream down his face. "Can you hear me? Can anyone hear me?"

"No one can hear you, Aaron—except me."

He froze and gazed up at the ceiling. The voice had come through a speaker above him. Aaron realized it must be up there with the camera.

"You can scream all you want, and it won't do you any good," the man said. He spoke in a gentle, condescending manner—as if he were reprimanding a slow-witted child. "In fact, it'll just do you *bad*, Aaron. I like my peace and quiet. You don't want to disturb that. If you do, I'll just have to punish you—"

"What do you want?" Aaron asked, staring up at the camera. He wiped away his tears. To keep from trembling, he folded his arms in front of him.

"What I want is your cooperation," replied the voice from above. "Depending on your behavior and what you accomplish, you'll soon see that I can make your time here extremely comfortable or . . . well, let's just say you don't want to upset me, Aaron. You look cold. There's a blanket in the bottom drawer of the dresser."

He looked over toward the dresser—and then up at the camera again.

"Go on, boy, get it," the man said, obviously watching his every move. "I know you're cold. I control the heat to that room . . ."

Aaron went to the dresser and opened the bottom drawer.

"I control *you*, Aaron. Know that, remember that . . ."

He pulled out the coverlet—for a kid's twin-size bed. It had illustrations from the first Chris Pine *Star Trek* movie years ago. Aaron wondered if the bedspread had once belonged to the dwarfish kid who had helped set him up. Or did it belong to some other child, who had died in here?

It didn't matter. Aaron wrapped the blanket around his shoulders and shuddered gratefully at the immediate warmth it provided. "Where am I?" he asked, gazing up at the camera. "How long have I been here? What day is it?"

"It's Tuesday afternoon. You're very far from home. And just how soon you'll get back there is completely up to you. Look at those posters on the wall, Aaron. Learn from them. You're going to practice and practice—like never before. I have a pool. And I'll put you on a training schedule—along with a strict diet. You're all mine now. And in the end, you'll thank me for this. I'm going to help make you into a champion swimmer. No more settling for second or third place . . ."

"The missing swimmers," Aaron murmured—almost to himself. He'd been too cold, scared, and disoriented to realize until now. "My God, that's why I'm here. That's why you picked me . . ."

"You'll be surprised at how much you can accomplish, Aaron—when your life depends on it," the man said. "Not just your life, but—well, if I don't think you're giving me one hundred percent, I may just call on your mother. I'll surprise her some night when she's leaving Haggen Foods. Or maybe I'll pay a little visit to that black friend of yours with the spotty skin. There'll be one less freak in the world. I will have your full cooperation, Aaron. You sit there quietly and think about that for the next few hours."

"Wait!" Aaron cried. "No, please, listen to me—"

But he heard a click, almost like someone hanging up a phone.

He was alone—and even more terrified than before. He was hungry as hell, too. He couldn't believe it was Tuesday already. He'd lost two days.

His mom was probably going out of her mind with worry. He wondered if his father even knew something was wrong.

No one had any idea where he was.

But maybe he wasn't completely alone. That other voice he'd heard, the girl, was she one of the swimmers who had disappeared? Was she locked up in another room like this somewhere nearby?

"Hello?" he yelled. "Can anyone hear me? Is anyone there?"

There was no answer.

Aaron had a feeling she could hear him. Was she afraid to talk? Was the man watching her, too—and listening?

Earlier, she'd thought he was someone named Chris. "*Is that you?*" she'd asked. "*Are you back?*"

Chris was the name of the swimmer from Eastmont High, the one whose corpse had been dragged out of the Wenatchee River last week. *Chris Something*.

Aaron glanced over at the cot that Chris Something must have slept on before him.

He didn't care who was watching. He started to cry.

CHAPTER FIVE

"*The T-Mobile customer you are calling is not available right now,*" announced the woman on the recording. "*Please try your call again later.*"

Then the woman said the same thing in Spanish.

There was no message option—no way for Caitlin to tell Lindsay how worried she was about her. That generic recording meant that sometime after she'd left the last message for her daughter—less than twenty minutes ago—Lindsay's phone had been shut off or damaged.

Her stomach in knots, Caitlin clicked off her phone. She was in Lindsay's bedroom. Gabe stood in the doorway. Looks-wise, he took after her. He was pale and skinny, with unruly red hair and freckles.

She'd telephoned Gabe from the recreation center to make sure Lindsay hadn't come home. She hadn't. Gabe didn't have any idea where Lindsay might be.

Caitlin had already talked to Lindsay's swim coach and a couple of her teammates. None of them had seen

Lindsay since lunch period. *Over five hours ago*, Caitlin had thought, wondering if she'd ever see Lindsay again.

From the rec center, she'd called the police to report her daughter missing. They'd asked for a description. She'd told them: sixteen, pretty, slender, blue eyes, long brown hair—no tattoos, scars or facial piercings. She couldn't recall if Lindsay had been wearing jeans or khaki slacks with her black sweater this morning. What kind of mother was she that she couldn't remember a thing like that?

The police had asked if it was possible that Lindsay might have run away. Considering how unhappy she'd been since moving away from Portland, it was certainly possible. The cop on the phone had told her to go home. They'd send an officer over within the hour to make a report.

Caitlin was still waiting for the police to show up, still hoping against hope that Lindsay would call. Now she knew her daughter's phone wasn't working. She wondered if this was how it started for the parents of each of the missing swimmers.

She'd already lost one child. She couldn't bear it if she lost another.

"What are you looking for?" Gabe asked.

"Lindsay's night-guard," she answered, setting down her phone and opening the top drawer of the dresser. "It's in a pink plastic case . . ." She figured if Lindsay had gone off on her own, she would have taken along her night-guard among other things.

"Yeah, I know what the case looks like," Gabe said, scratching the back of his neck. "She usually leaves it near wherever she slept last—which could be any-where lately."

Every night, Lindsay started out in her own bed, but then after about an hour or two she'd go sleep on the family room sofa in front of the TV or in the spare bunk in Gabe's room. This was a pattern she'd started since they'd moved into the Birch Place house.

Still, her bedroom looked quite lived in—with clothes scattered on the pink shag carpet or draped over the old Pier 1 Imports furniture. Her white fake fur beanbag chair had at least three tops flung over it. One shelf on the white bookcase held Lindsay's swimming trophies and team photos. A *Hunger Games* movie poster had a center spot on the wall—amid snapshots, postcards, and drawings by her Portland friends. Above the unmade and un-slept-in bed was a travel poster. "*Portland Is Happening Now!*" it said, amid cartoons of various hip attractions in the Rose City. Caitlin often wondered if Lindsay had put up that poster just to stick it to her dear old mother—as another reminder that she wished they'd never moved away. As if she didn't vocalize enough how much she missed her friends and her fa-ther.

Maybe she did run away. Caitlin almost hoped for that right now.

"She conked out on the couch again last night," Gabe said. "But I didn't see the night-guard anywhere around when I was watching TV this afternoon. If she ran away, she would've taken it with her. I'll bet she packed her Clearasil, too. She wouldn't go anywhere for the night without her zit cream."

"Sweetie, you're brilliant." Caitlin mussed his hair

as she brushed past him. She hurried into the kids' bathroom and opened the beveled-mirror medicine cabinet above the sink.

She'd just bought a new tube of Vanishing Formula Clearasil for Lindsay last week. But she didn't see it on any of the shelves. No night-guard, no Clearasil. Lindsay had probably stashed a change of clothes in her backpack as she'd left for school this morning.

Heading into Lindsay's bedroom again, she gazed at the poster above her bed. Lindsay stayed in touch with her longtime friend, Roseann Stella, in Portland. Caitlin grabbed her phone from the dresser top. Caitlin still had Roseann's number on her contact list.

She clicked on the number and then reached over and patted Gabe's shoulder. He looked as worried as she was.

"Hello?" Roseann answered on the third ring. "Mrs. Stoller?"

"Hi, Roseann," she said edgily. "Listen, I'm sorry to bother you, but I'm really worried about Lindsay. No one at her new school has seen her since lunch today, and she's not answering her phone. I've already called the police. Do you have any idea where she might be?"

"Ah—no, I'm sorry, Mrs. Stoller . . ."

"Please, Roseann, if you know anything—anything at all . . ." She took a deep breath. "When's the last time you spoke with her? Did she say anything to you about wanting to run away?"

"We—we talked on Sunday night, Mrs. Stoller," the girl said, a bit hesitant in her tone. "God, I hate ratting on her. But well, you know Lindsay really misses her dad. She said she wanted to go see him and stay the night—only she figured you wouldn't let her."

Caitlin couldn't believe it. "So you think she might be in Portland right now—or on her way there to see her father?"

"Not Portland, Seattle," Roseann said. "Mr. Stoller moved to Seattle, like, a couple of weeks ago. Didn't you know?"

Caitlin had no idea. And here she was hearing it from Lindsay's friend. Her ex-husband had moved from Portland to Seattle without telling her a damn thing about it. But obviously, he'd told Lindsay. Caitlin realized what must have happened today. Her daughter had ditched school at lunchtime, walked to the two o'clock ferry to Mukilteo, and then caught a bus to Seattle to see her father.

Caitlin couldn't help wondering if Russ was in on this scheme.

The whole idea behind the divorce and them relocating to Echo had been to put a substantial distance between Russ and her—as well as Russ and the kids. He'd agreed to that—in one of his more lucid, unselfish moments.

With the phone to her ear, Caitlin stared at Gabe. "So—you're pretty certain Lindsay decided to visit her dad in Seattle today. Is that right, Roseann?"

"Yeah, but Mrs. Stoller, Lindsay's just worried about him being alone and all. Please don't let on that I told you. She'd be so ticked . . ."

"It's all right." She sighed. "I won't say anything. I appreciate your help, Roseann, I really do. Thanks. Take care, honey."

Once she clicked off with Lindsay's friend, she frowned at Gabe. "Did you know about your dad moving to Seattle, too?"

Gabe squinted at her. "He's in Seattle? You mean, like, he's living there now?"

She nodded. "So I hear."

Obviously, it was a guarded secret between father and daughter.

Why should she be so surprised? It wasn't the first time Russ had kept her in the dark about something.

"So—that's where Lindsay is?" Gabe asked. "I don't get it . . ."

"Neither do I, but I'm going to straighten it out." She stroked his head and tried to calm down for his sake. "Thanks for helping me, sweetie. It might be a while longer before we get around to dinner. Are you terribly hungry?"

"I'm okay," he said, his eyes still narrowed at her. "But—why didn't Dad tell us that he moved to Seattle?"

"That's what I hope to find out," she replied. "Listen, why don't you go back to your drawing? I'll let you know about dinner—and everything else—in a little while. I just need to make another phone call."

"Are you calling Dad?"

She nodded. "Yes, right after I call the police and tell them to cancel the search party. You can talk with your dad later."

"Don't be too mad at him, okay?" Gabe said.

She kissed the top of his head and gave him a gentle push toward the hall. As Gabe wandered back to his room, she phoned the police and told them she knew where her daughter was after all. She apologized and thanked them. All the while, she felt like an idiot for not checking with Russ before calling them. But then, she'd had no idea he'd moved to Seattle.

She hung up and then turned toward Lindsay's bed and stared at the framed photo on the nightstand. It was of Lindsay when she was five, sitting in her dad's lap. There were several other photos of Russ on the wall, but none of her.

Caitlin couldn't help feeling a little hurt.

What had happened to Russ had been as hard on the kids as it had been for her. But while she had to push him away for their own survival, Lindsay seemed to become more and more devoted to him—blindly so.

Caitlin remembered when Russ finally came home from the rehab facility. He was still on crutches. He'd always been so robust and healthy. But he'd returned to them looking sallow, shaky, and on edge. It was alarming because she'd just seen him two days before, and he hadn't looked bad at all. She probably should have known something was wrong. Every day, she drove him to a physical therapist—in a pretty sketchy part of town. Russ always insisted she drop him off and come back later to pick him up. Eventually, he did get better—and there were times, brief as they were, when Russ was his old self again. He went back to work. But after a few weeks, his boss called her at home to ask where Russ was. Apparently, this wasn't the first time since his return that Russ had failed to appear at the office—or a job site.

When she asked Russ about it, he said that some days he just couldn't make himself go to work. So he'd drive to the park to sit by the river and think. He certainly wasn't going to the gym, which the doctor had recommended to help him heal faster—mentally as well as physically. He used to love working out. But since returning home, he'd lost all interest in exercise. His navy blue gym bag moved farther and farther toward the back of their bedroom closet.

One afternoon she liberated his gym bag from its closet prison. She planned to leave it by his side of the bed—a not-too-subtle inducement to get some exercise. The satchel was stuffed with his old workout clothes. She took them out to throw them in the wash.

That was when Caitlin found the freezer bag containing a thin rubber hose, several syringes, and an old spoon with a scorched underside.

He'd been weaned off painkillers while still in the hospital. But he said he fell back on them at the rehabilitation facility. He blamed an orderly and another patient for getting him hooked on morphine—and then heroin. Russ was handling the family's finances while at the rehab facility, and he'd become quite clever at hiding the losses. He'd gone through nearly all their money from the settlement. He'd never had it in any special accounts.

For a while, Caitlin had unwittingly been driving him every day to his supplier—and then picking him up after he'd had his fix.

She wondered how the hell she couldn't have seen this coming.

Russ begged her to forgive him, and he promised to quit. They told the kids about it together. And he got some help. He even agreed to be interviewed in *The Oregonian,* hoping to help other addicts in recovery.

He was clean for five months.

By the time Caitlin discovered he'd relapsed, he'd gone through all their money. The bank foreclosed on their home. Russ vowed to put in overtime and get them financially solvent again. If he just had his dose twice a day, he could continue working and no one would be the wiser. How different was that from those guys who slug back a couple of martinis every night when they get home from the office? How different was his situation from people who have to take antidepressants or some other kind of medication?

He wasn't promising to quit this time. He was trying to talk her into letting him continue as a functioning addict.

Caitlin refused to listen to his arguments.

At the same time, her mother was dying of pancreatic cancer. Her mom had always adored Russ, but Caitlin couldn't keep any secrets from her. Her mother made it clear that she didn't want to leave her daughter a three-hundred-thousand-dollar inheritance if the money was going to end up paying for the poison her son-in-law injected in his arm—or between his toes.

Caitlin remembered driving her mother to one of the many doctor's appointments near the end. "I can get the lawyers to put the money in a trust for Lindsay and Gabe—for when they turn twenty-one," her mother said, sitting in the passenger seat. Her face was slightly puffy and her complexion had a yellow tinge from all her medications. Her hair still hadn't grown back after the unsuccessful chemotherapy, so she was wearing a beige-colored, close-cropped wig.

"But that's years away," her mother continued. "And I think you need that money now."

Tightening her grip on the steering wheel, Caitlin tried to focus on the road ahead. "Mom, seriously, do whatever you want with the money," she said. "I don't like talking about this inheritance stuff. You're going to get better . . ."

"Well, that's not very realistic, is it?" her mother murmured. "And it's not realistic to think Russ will get better any time soon, either. Listen to me, Catie, I can set up that trust. But I know you and the children really need the money *now*. If you divorce him, I'll make sure you get it all. It'll be a fresh start for you and the children. But I can't leave you the money as long as you're still married to Russ. He'd just end up using it for drugs. It pains me to say this, Catie, because he used to be such a dear man. But the children and you won't see a dime of the inheritance. And you know I'm right about that. Think about it, Catie, and let me know what you want to do. But we don't have a lot of time."

When Caitlin told Russ last May that she was divorcing him and taking the kids, she didn't mention her mother—or the inheritance. Russ was hurt, but he agreed that it was probably the best thing for everyone. However, by the time he moved out of their apartment, he was barely talking to her. When her mother died in July, Russ didn't even come to the funeral.

After she received the inheritance, Caitlin offered to pay for Russ to get help at one of the top rehab/recovery facilities in Oregon—to the tune of eight thousand dollars. He claimed he knew a better place that didn't cost quite as much—if she just gave him the money. Of course, that was a lie.

She took the kids and moved to Echo—and let him know that she'd still pay for a recovery program when he was truly ready. He told her she was right to put some distance between him and the children. But he didn't tell that to Lindsay or Gabe. The kids had no idea how better off they were. So—they felt sorry for their poor abandoned father and did nothing to hide their resentment toward her, especially Lindsay.

Caitlin glanced at her daughter's bedroom wall again: about five or six photos of Russ—like he was a rock star or something.

With a sigh, she found his number on her phone and clicked on it. It rang twice before he picked up. "Hey, babe, I was just going to call you," he said.

"Is Lindsay there with you?" she asked.

"Yeah, listen, I hope you weren't too worried . . ."

"Well, what do you think?" she shot back. "I started calling her two hours ago. She disappeared from school. She wasn't at swim practice. I was going out of my mind. I even called the police. So she's there with you now—in your *Seattle apartment*?"

"Listen, I was going to tell you about the move," Russ said. "I was just waiting for—"

"But Lindsay's there?"

"Yes, I told you, she's here, she's safe . . ."

Caitlin could hear Lindsay talking in the background.

"Lind says she meant to call you back, but her phone battery ran out—"

"There's a ferry to Echo that leaves Mukilteo at eight o'clock," Caitlin said. "And I want you to put her on it. If you still have your car, drive her there, or go to Mukilteo with her on the bus. I don't want her traveling alone. In case you haven't seen the news, there's someone in the area abducting high school swimmers. A boy from Mount Vernon just disappeared on Sunday. Can I count on you to get her to the ferry, Russ?"

"Of course," he said. "Listen, Caitlin, I've been clean for almost three weeks now. I'm past the worst part of the withdrawal. I'm in a really good program—and it's free. That's why I moved here. And I have a job."

"That's wonderful, Russ," she said in a quiet voice. Tears came to her eyes. She knew he was trying, but she still couldn't trust him. He'd lied to her about quitting before.

"I can borrow a car from my sponsor," he said. "I'll drive Lind to the ferry . . ."

Caitlin could hear her daughter protesting in the background.

On the other end, she heard him shush Lindsay. Then he got back on the line. "Listen, if you're really worried, I'll get on the ferry and make the crossing with her. Maybe I can stick around for an hour or two. I'd really like to see the house and visit with Gabe—and you . . ."

"I'm sorry, but that's not a good idea," she said, hoping he didn't hear the quaver in her voice. She cleared her throat. "The last ferry leaves Echo at nine twenty. That wouldn't give you much time for a visit. Besides, I'm not in the best of moods right now. Just—just get

Lindsay to Mukilteo in time for the eight o'clock crossing, okay? Please?"

"Fine," he muttered.

She was about to thank him and say she was really proud of him for his efforts—or something along those lines. But he hung up.

Caitlin clicked off the phone and took a few deep breaths.

The phone rang in her hand.

She immediately clicked it on. "Russ? Russ, I think we might have been cut off, I—"

She fell silent. There was someone on the other end, but they weren't saying anything. Caitlin glanced at the caller ID: UNKNOWN CALLER.

"Hello?" Caitlin said.

Then a gravelly voice came on the line: "She's going to give you a lot of trouble."

"What?"

There was a click, and the line went dead.

CHAPTER SIX

Curled up on the cot with the *Star Trek* blanket over him, Aaron tried to keep warm. He missed home so much that he ached. He missed his mom. No one knew where he was. He felt utterly doomed.

The overhead light in his cell must have been on some sort of automatic timer. It shut off, and in its place was a blue-hued night-light.

His captor had left him some items in the second drawer of the dresser—including a new toothbrush, a tube of Crest, a bar of Irish Spring, and a towel. He figured the guy wouldn't have provided him with that stuff if he was going to kill him right away.

So, how long did this psycho plan on keeping him here?

Aaron also found a cheap, battery-operated alarm clock in the drawer. It was ticking. If the setting was correct, it was now 11:40. Until the night-light had gone on, Aaron hadn't been sure if that was at night or in the morning. From the way the windowless cell kept getting colder and colder, it had felt like night. Now he knew.

The drawer also held a change of underwear. But unlike the unopened toothpaste and toiletries, the T-shirt and white briefs looked secondhand. Had they belonged to the dead kid, Chris Something? Out of desperation for warmth, Aaron donned the T-shirt, but he wasn't about to put on hand-me-down undershorts.

Also in the drawer—and more welcome than anything else—were two PowerBars and a small pack of turkey jerky. Aaron was ravenous. If it was really Tuesday, as his captor had claimed, that meant he hadn't eaten in two days. Aaron wolfed down one of the PowerBars and then tore open the jerky pack with his teeth and ate four sticks. He decided to pace himself with the second PowerBar and the two remaining sticks of jerky. He was still hungry but had no idea how long this meager food supply was supposed to last. Aaron slurped water from the faucet to keep hydrated. Between the food and the water, his awful headache was starting to wane.

He'd searched every inch of the small cell and saw no possibility of escape. The vent down near the floor was about twelve inches across. If he managed to pry off the screen, he still couldn't fit in there. Even if he was standing on the bed, he couldn't reach the ceiling to feel for any loose panels. There was a weird metal panel on the wall near the door. It looked like some kind of drawer, but he couldn't get it open. Having seen *The Shawshank Redemption* about five times, Aaron even checked behind the inspirational posters to see if someone had started digging a tunnel. But he was out of luck.

It had been about five hours since the man had talked to him over the speaker system. He'd been instructed to "sit quietly and think" for a while. But what Aaron kept thinking about was that girl who had briefly called to him from somewhere outside this cell. She'd thought he was that missing swimmer, Chris. Obviously, she didn't know this Chris person was dead. Later, at one point, she'd shushed him. Who was she?

He had to know. Despite his captor's instructions, Aaron couldn't just sit quietly. Several times in the last few hours, he'd leaned against the crack in the steel door and softly called out, asking if anyone was there or if anyone could hear him. "Please, answer me!" he'd begged a couple of times.

There was no response.

He knew he was pushing his luck each time he tried to call out to the girl.

So he'd given up, retreated to the cot, and curled into a ball. He'd hoped to fall asleep—just for a while to make the time go by, just for an escape.

But he lay there awake, wondering what this man wanted from him. He kept thinking back to that bizarre-looking guy with the bad wig and the big glasses, grinning at him and giving him the thumbs-up from the stands at the swim meet. He remembered him from those other meets, too.

Was it really all about becoming a better swimmer? Or did the guy have some sexual demands in mind? Aaron was pretty sure his abductor hadn't done anything to him while he'd slept for nearly forty-eight hours—except peel off his outer clothes. Maybe the creep had fondled him while he'd been out cold. There was no way of knowing for sure. Aaron remembered what he'd been told over the speaker: "*You're all mine now.*" That could mean anything.

Even if he tried to cooperate, how long before he did the wrong thing—or before his captor grew bored with him? How long before he ended up dead and dumped along some riverbank?

"Hey, are you still there?" he heard the girl whisper.

It was barely audible, but Aaron quickly sat up. The voice seemed to come from inside the room. He glanced down at the vent.

He was about to answer but hesitated. The tiny green light was still on by the camera on the ceiling. Even in the dark room, the camera could still be recording him—thanks to the blue night-light. Aaron scooted over toward the foot of the bed—near the vent. He covered his mouth. "Can you—can you hear me?" he whispered nervously.

"Yes, that's perfect," she replied quietly. "I think the microphone is up near the camera and doesn't pick up much in here. Just don't talk any louder. We don't want him to catch us. Are you a swimmer?"

"Yeah, I—I'm in high school," he said behind his hand. "My name's Aaron. I'm from Mount Vernon. Do you know where we are?"

"No," she answered in a faint voice. ". . . swimmer, too . . . Monica Leary . . ."

He eyed the camera and casually slouched down so that he was closer to the vent. "Could you speak up a little?"

"I said my name's Monica Leary, and I'm eighteen. I'm from Olympia. I go to Capital High. He—grabbed me on my way home from a party. I've been here about six months. Have you heard of me?" Her voice cracked a little. "Has there been anything on TV or online about me—anything at all? Or have they given up looking for me?"

"I—I'm sorry, I'm not sure," Aaron murmured. "I haven't been paying much attention to the news. I—"

She shushed him. "Shit, he's coming!" she whispered. "I can't believe he's still awake. Don't make a sound! No matter what you hear, please, don't say a thing . . ."

Aaron listened for footsteps but didn't hear any. He wondered how far away this girl's cell was. Through the vent he heard a faint murmuring but couldn't make out the words. Then the man raised his voice, and it came through clearly. "I don't feel like any games tonight, Monica," he barked. "I'm tired and not in the mood for rough stuff. So don't be a little bitch. C'mon, you know what to do . . ."

She said something back, but the words were indistinguishable.

Aaron leaned even closer to the vent. The man muttered something. It sounded like a command.

After a minute or two, he heard the girl whimpering and crying.

Aaron wanted so much to scream into that vent and tell the scumbag to stop. But he bit his lip. Something horrible was going on. It was happening very close to him, but he couldn't do a damn thing about it. He felt so powerless and miserable and scared.

He moved away from the vent and started nervously

pacing around, his fists clenched. Finally, he curled up on the cot and covered his ears. He couldn't hear any more, but he knew it was still going on. He wanted to cry.

But Aaron stifled his sobs.

She'd told him not to make a sound.

Only a few hours after having woken in this cell, and already Aaron knew he'd have to cooperate if he hoped to survive.

Echo
Tuesday—11:55 P.M.

She'd found the mover's box that held the photo albums. Caitlin was on her second glass of cabernet and couldn't resist paging through the books. She lingered over the old images of when she'd been happy. She sat on the guest room floor amid several unopened boxes from the move. The twin beds and dresser were part of an oak bedroom set she'd inherited from her parents. The walls were still bare, and the windows needed curtains. Caitlin had Bruce Springsteen's *Tunnel of Love* playing at a low volume on the boom box. With the guest room door closed, the kids couldn't hear it down the hall. They'd gone to bed about an hour ago.

She studied a photo of Lindsay, age two, sitting in a high chair and smiling with a face full of chocolate birthday cake.

"She's going to give you a lot of trouble."

Caitlin thought about that strange, gravelly voice on the other end of the phone earlier tonight. She hadn't been able to tell if it was a man or a woman. At first, she'd thought the unknown caller had been referring to Lindsay. After all, she and Russ had just been discussing Lindsay when the phone rang. And she'd been in Lindsay's room. The timing had been almost too much of a coincidence.

But Caitlin told herself it had been just that—a coincidence. It was probably just a wrong number. The caller could have been talking about anyone—or anything. Caitlin knew what the matter was. She was letting this awful news about the missing swimmers unnerve her. She still wanted to kick herself for calling the police this afternoon without first checking in with Russ.

At least he'd gotten their daughter onto the ferry, which had pulled into the terminal at eight thirty. Caitlin—with Gabe in the front passenger seat—had been waiting in the parking lot. Good thing, too, because she was so mad at Lindsay she didn't even want to be sitting next to her. Caitlin was doing her damnedest to keep from losing it.

She had watched Lindsay shuffle along the passenger walkway to the parking lot with that slightly bored, ticked-off look she wore most of the time lately. Her long, straight brown hair ruffled in the breeze, and she hugged her backpack to her chest. She opened the back door and scooted in behind Gabe.

"You are so busted," he muttered.

"Mom, before you bite my head off, I'm sorry, okay?" She shut the car door.

Caitlin didn't say anything. She started the car.

Lindsay let out an exasperated sigh. "I didn't mean to worry you. I was going to call you back after I got your first message, I swear. But I forgot to recharge my phone . . ."

Caitlin reached for *The Seattle Times*, which she'd had Gabe buy at the kiosk by the ferry terminal. She'd folded it in half so Lindsay would see the article on the bottom half of the front page, the one about the high school swimmer who had disappeared in Everett. Barely looking at her daughter, she reached back and handed it to her. "Here, read this," she said. "Then maybe you'll understand why I was freaking out. I called the police, for God's sake."

Turning forward again, she shifted out of Park and headed for the terminal lot exit. She glanced in the rearview mirror for a second. "How could you just take off like that without telling me?"

"I wanted to see Dad," Lindsay replied in a quiet voice that was still slightly defiant. "And I knew you wouldn't let me go."

"So you ditched your afternoon classes and skipped practice. Well, that's great. That's just terrific."

Gabe looked over his shoulder. "How's Dad? What's his place like? Does it have a view of the Space Needle?"

"He says hi," Lindsay answered. "And no, it doesn't have much of a view at all."

Caitlin wondered when Lindsay had found out about Russ's move to Seattle—and how long she'd been keeping it a secret. But she didn't ask. She didn't want to start screaming at her daughter in the car. She was afraid she might have an accident.

"Have you had any dinner?" Caitlin asked curtly. It was a safer question.

"Yeah, Dad bought me a cheeseburger and a shake at the snack place in the Mukilteo ferry terminal."

"We had Sloppy Joes," Gabe piped up.

Caitlin swallowed hard and kept her eyes on the road ahead. "When we get home, I want you to call your swim coach, Ms. Donahue, and apologize for skipping practice. She was worried about you, too. I'll call the principal in the morning and ask if there's any special punishment for students who ditch school."

"Fine," Lindsay said under her breath.

Caitlin glanced in the rearview mirror again. Lindsay glared back at her but then turned her attention to the newspaper article.

No one said a word for the rest of the ride home.

Wordless, they filed through the front doorway of the house. Caitlin double-locked the door and put the chain on. The stony silence was broken by her keys rattling as she plopped them down on the side table in the hallway. She shook her head at Lindsay and then fiercely hugged her. It was either that or slap her—and she didn't do that. "I'm glad you're safe, at least," she muttered.

She didn't wait for Lindsay's response. She hurried upstairs to her bedroom, closed the door, and then took a long shower in the adjoining bathroom. It was one of her deluxe showers—for when she was stressed out. She sat under the shower's spray until the tub filled with water. It was the closest thing she had to a Jacuzzi. It helped calm her down. By the time she toweled off, blow-dried her hair, and changed into flannel pajama bottoms and a long-sleeve tee, it was almost ten. Lindsay was already holed up in her room.

Caitlin had seen the thin crack of light at the threshold under Lindsay's door down the hallway. It had gone out a while ago—around the time Caitlin had returned upstairs with her first glass of wine. She'd been determined to unpack at least three moving boxes tonight, and she was only halfway through this first one.

She closed the photo album and put it back inside the box—on top of the album full of Cliff's baby pictures. If she looked at any more photos tonight, she'd start crying.

She pushed the box aside but then hesitated.

Past Bruce Springsteen's vocals, Caitlin thought she heard footsteps. She quickly reached over and put the boom box on pause.

The floorboards creaked. Someone was in the hall.

She got up, padded to the guest room door, and opened it. Caitlin gasped.

So did Lindsay.

Her daughter stood in the middle of the hallway with her pillow under her arm. She wore gray sweat shorts and a slightly tattered, faded *Powerpuff Girls* T-shirt a friend had given her as a joke ages ago. With tousled hair and her mouth open, Lindsay gaped back at her.

"Sorry I scared you," Caitlin whispered. "Are you okay?"

Lindsay took her night-guard out of her mouth. "I couldn't sleep," she said. "So I thought I'd crash in Gabe's room." She glanced down at the hallway floor for a moment. "I'm really sorry about today. It wasn't like I was running away or anything. I figured I'd go see Dad and surprise him. Then I'd call and let you know where I was. And then maybe as long as I was already there, you'd be okay with me having dinner with Dad or staying over. I didn't mean to worry you."

"Staying over—in Seattle on a school night?" Folding her arms, Caitlin leaned against the doorway frame. "Just how many classes were you intending to skip while you were on this little excursion?"

"There's a ferry at six in the morning," Lindsay said. Her voice started to quaver. "Mom, if you only knew how lonely Dad is. He misses us. And his apartment, it's this dumpy little place. It's so sad. He tries so hard . . ."

"I know, honey. But I thought you understood, he needs to get better before he can be with us again. Until then, you and Gabe can still visit him on the appointed days."

Lindsay wiped her eyes and sniffled. "Why do you have to be such a hard-ass about it?"

"Hey, I get lonely, too, you know," she admitted. "You're not the only one who misses him. Do you think this is the way I want it? This is tough on me, too. Every day it's tough. And then when you disappeared this afternoon, I just about went out of my mind. Did you read that newspaper article?"

Lindsay hugged the pillow to her chest. "Yeah," she nodded. "Like I said, I didn't mean to worry you, Mom."

"Please, just don't ever do that to me again," Caitlin said.

"I won't, I promise."

Caitlin sighed. "I'll see if I can get out of work a little early again tomorrow and pick you up after practice. I don't like the idea of you walking home alone—not when there might be some nutcase out there." She reached over and smoothed Lindsay's hair back away from her face. "And when I call the principal in the morning, I'll ask him to go easy on you for ditching classes . . ."

Lindsay gave her a quick hug, but the pillow was between them; to Caitlin, it felt slightly awkward. "Sorry I called you a hard-ass," Lindsay murmured. Then she ducked into Gabe's room and quietly closed the door.

Caitlin retreated to the guest room. She took a swig of wine. She figured she and Lindsay were good for another twelve or fifteen hours before they were driving each other crazy again.

She spotted a mover's box with *sweaters* written across it in Magic Marker. That would be an easy one to unpack. She opened the box and started to pull it toward the center of the room. A piece of yellow paper from a legal pad had been beneath the box.

Someone had written on it, but the print was tiny—and childlike. Caitlin had to pick up the piece of paper to read what it said:

I'm watching you.

The crying had stopped.

Aaron sat at the foot of his bed—with his ear close to the vent. He hadn't heard a sound for the past several minutes. He figured their shitbag abductor was finished with the girl. She was probably alone in her cell once again.

He looked up at the green light by the monitoring

device on the ceiling. Aaron covered his mouth and softly called into the vent. "Hey, are you all right? Monica? Can you hear me?"

For a few moments, there was no response. Then she murmured something.

"What did you say?" he asked.

"I said, leave me alone."

"What happened? What did he do to you?"

"Shut up!" she hissed. "Goddamn it, just leave me alone."

Then he heard her crying again.

Biting his lip, Aaron curled up on the cot. He tried to go to sleep—though he knew it would be impossible.

Sitting on the guest room floor with the note in her hand, Caitlin heard a noise again. She told herself it was just the old furnace in this old house—this big old house with a creepy basement and so many crannies and closets, so many places for someone to hide.

She stared at the note and wondered how long ago it had been written. The boxes had been sitting here in the guest room for six weeks. The message could have been left there by the movers, maybe some sort of reprimand from their boss. It might not have even been meant for her.

Or maybe the note was left there today—by someone who was still inside the house.

"Shit," she murmured, getting to her feet.

She still wasn't used to this house—or to being alone at night. For seventeen years, she could automatically nudge Russ awake whenever a noise made her nervous or she had a nightmare. The few times she'd made him get up to investigate a strange sound she always accompanied him, hovering behind him most of the way. She'd never been able to sit in bed and wait for him to check the house by himself. After all, what if he didn't come back?

Now she was alone.

She glanced over at the guest room windows—with all the blinds pulled down. No one could see in. No one was watching.

Caitlin padded over to one window and moved the blind slightly so she could peer outside. It was a clear night. The front yard was big and woodsy with a tall hedge bordering it. When she'd bought the place, Caitlin had liked the idea of privacy. But now the house just seemed terribly isolated. Even with the windows open, she doubted anybody would hear her if she screamed. She noticed the neighbor's front porch light on across the way, but all the windows were dark. She glanced down at her front lawn again. With all the trees and bushes—all the shadowy pockets—anyone could be out there now and she wouldn't see them.

She remembered that in one of the boxes there was a tall ornate brass candlestick she never liked and didn't know what to do with. She nervously dug it out of the box.

She kept trying to convince herself that the note wasn't meant for her—that the yellow paper had merely gotten stuck to the box somehow. But after that bizarre phone call hours ago, she couldn't ignore it.

And the smiley face message on her car windshield earlier in the afternoon was undeniably for her. It said:

Have a nice day, Caitlin. She'd assumed it was from Ken Meekley in a lame attempt to flirt with her. But now she wondered if it was connected to this other note and the wrong number. Was it one of those terrible things that come in threes?

Holding the note in her shaky hand, she studied the handwriting. It didn't look like Russ had written the note. Neither Lindsay nor Gabe had penmanship like that. She thought about Ken Meekley again. Did the handwriting match the note she'd discovered on her windshield this afternoon?

She remembered shoving the little piece of paper into the pocket of her peacoat. The coat was hanging in the closet downstairs.

She had to go down there anyway. If she expected to fall asleep tonight, she had to go down there and check every room and closet and behind every curtain. Setting down the candlestick, Caitlin carefully folded the note and slipped it into the pocket of her sweatpants.

She picked up the candlestick again, opened the guest room door, and stepped out to the hallway. A night-light in the kids' bathroom dimly lit the way to the stairs. She quietly checked in on them in Gabe's room. They were both asleep in the bunks.

She probably would have heard if someone had crept upstairs, but she checked her own bedroom—along with the connecting bathroom, even behind the shower curtain. "All clear . . ." she murmured to herself. It was the same in the hallway bath.

Stepping into Lindsay's bedroom, Caitlin got a chill. She wasn't sure why. She didn't see anyone in there or in Lindsay's closet.

She flicked the switch on the wall by the top landing for the light in the downstairs entryway. With trepidation, Caitlin started down the steps. She heard a clicking noise and hesitated.

Now there was a hum.

She realized it was just the refrigerator.

Continuing down to the front hall, Caitlin turned on the ceiling light in the living room—and then the chandelier in the dining room. The front door was still double-locked, the chain fixed in place. She checked the powder room to make sure no one was hiding in there. She opened the front hall closet and saw her peacoat on a hanger. She took the folded message out of her sweatpants pocket to compare both notes. But then she decided to check the rest of the house first. She needed to make sure they were safe.

Down the hall, she switched on the lights to the kitchen and the family room. The curtains and shades were open. Beyond the windows, all she could see was blackness. Maybe her stalker was lurking outside close enough to see her with the candlestick in one hand and the yellow piece of legal paper in the other. Maybe he was smiling as he recognized his own note.

Caitlin stuffed the note back into her pocket. She checked the windows to make sure all of them were locked.

On the circular-top oak breakfast table, she saw another note. Caitlin gasped. She almost knocked over one of the bar stools by the kitchen counter as she rushed over to the table. Swiping the slip of paper off the table, she read what it said:

Need $2 for Whidbey Island Big Brothers
donation today!

It was Gabe's handwriting. She hadn't noticed the note before when she'd been down to get her wine. She set it back down by the lazy Susan with their tacky papier-mâché ghost-and-pumpkin Halloween centerpiece.

Off the family room was a small study with a fireplace centered between two floor-to-ceiling French-style windows. The three big built-in bookshelves were already full of books, many of them first editions signed by the authors when they'd visited her library in Portland. Caitlin poked her head in long enough to make sure nobody was there—and no one's face was pressed up against the glass. Then she retreated to the kitchen and the annex to the basement and outside doors. Both doors were locked.

When she'd first moved in, Caitlin had thought it slightly strange there was a lock on the basement door. But pretty soon she found herself locking it every night.

She hated the thought of going down there right now. But the lock was flimsy, and there were certainly enough tools in one of the boxes downstairs if someone wanted to get past that lock.

Caitlin opened the door, flicked on the light, and started down the basement stairs. She clutched the brass candlestick a little tighter as she made her way into the second family room. It was paneled—with a fake wood floor and a wet bar. The kids didn't use the room much, even though that was where Caitlin had decided to put the bigger-screen TV and a sectional sofa. She'd imagined it would be a great place for Lindsay or Gabe to hang out when their friends came over—just as soon as they made some friends here.

She checked the bathroom, which no one ever used, and then headed into the huge unfinished utility area. Caitlin took a deep breath and switched on the lights. The room housed the furnace, the washer and dryer, and a laundry sink. There was also a long workbench, and on the wall above it a pegboard with strategically placed nails and faded outlines for where each tool was supposed to hang.

This room was where they'd dumped the rest of the unopened moving boxes. Up near the ceiling, exposed pipes ran along the length of the room. It was a gloomy place. Even during the day, the room seemed a bit sinister. Maybe it was because of the outside entrance—a battered old door in a concrete stairwell that led up to ground level. It was on one side of the house off a walkway by some bushes. It seemed like a perfect spot for an intruder to break in.

Caitlin checked the door. *Double-locked.*

At one end of the big room were two storage closets. One of them had the electrical box in it. As Caitlin reached into the first closet to turn on the light, she almost expected someone to grab her hand.

But there was no one in there. The other closet was empty, too.

A third closet, under the stairs, was crammed with wood scrap and old pipes. She figured if some contortionist was able to maneuver their way through all that crap and hide, then kudos to them. They deserved to get whatever the hell they wanted here.

Caitlin retreated back upstairs, turning off each light on the way. She closed the basement door and locked it.

Caitlin told herself to calm down. She'd just checked the entire house. Everything was locked, no intruders, they were fine.

Taking out the note again, she headed toward the front of the house to the hallway closet. She tucked the candlestick under her arm and then reached for her peacoat. From the pocket, she pulled out several pieces of paper—a couple of receipts, an old grocery list, a ferry ticket and the note:

Have a nice day, Caitlin! ☺

The other scraps of paper fell out of her hand as she compared the writing on the two notes.

The handwriting was a match, the same childlike scrawl. Someone had left a note on her windshield seven hours ago—and the same someone had gotten into her home and left another message for her.

I'm watching you, it said.

All that was missing was her name—and that creepy smile.

CHAPTER SEVEN

Wednesday, October 26—8:13 A.M.

Aaron woke up to a strange *whoosh-clank* noise. Startled, he sat up on the cot. He rubbed his eyes and squinted at the cheap clock on the nightstand: a quarter after eight. The last time he'd looked at it, the time had been three hours ago, and his fellow prisoner, Monica—wherever she was—hadn't uttered a sound in hours. He'd given up calling to her through the vent.

It had seemed like the longest night of his life.

The fluorescent overhead light was now on again, and he saw where the *whoosh-clank* noise had come from. The metal panel in the wall had just opened. It was some kind of drawer—like the one in Hannibal Lecter's cell in *Silence of the Lambs*. Aaron remembered that was how they passed things to him through the Plexiglas wall. Wrapping the *Star Trek* blanket around his shoulders, Aaron got up and shuffled over to the drawer.

Inside it were two granola bars, a banana, a container of orange juice, and a container of milk. Aaron gratefully guzzled down the cold sweet juice. He let the blanket drop to the ground as he stood by the drawer and wolfed down the food. He didn't even like granola very much, but he was starving.

Without the blanket, he noticed it was no longer so chilly in the cell. He stepped over to the vent and waved his hand in front of the warm current. He thought of Monica and wondered if she was eating her breakfast now, too. He moved toward the drawer again to finish eating, hovering over it like it was his place at a counter. Every once in a while, he turned and glanced up at the camera on the ceiling. He kept wondering when his abductor would make another announcement.

He wished he had some clothes—and a mirror. No one knew where he was, everything around him was so alien, and he couldn't even see himself. It was almost like he didn't exist—as if he were already dead.

There was no trash bin in the room. So Aaron returned the banana peel and the wrappers to the drawer. He washed out the empty juice and milk containers and returned them to the drawer as well. He figured it was the most sanitary thing to do. Still, he imagined his captor flipping out on him for leaving a mess in the bin—or something just as petty. God only knew what it took for this guy to snap. Aaron wanted to come across as cooperative, a model prisoner. If he gained the guy's trust, it would be easier to lower his guard. Then maybe he'd have a better chance to escape.

Aaron folded the blanket and set it on the cot. Then he went to the sink and brushed his teeth. He was about to wash his face when he heard something from outside. It sounded like splashing.

Maybe the guy wasn't lying. Aaron realized that, indeed, he was somewhere near a pool. It explained the chlorine smell he'd first noticed yesterday. Was this psycho really going to let him out of here—to swim? *I'm going to help make you into a champion swimmer*, he'd said.

Was that all he wanted?

Aaron glanced at the dorky, inspirational swimmer posters on the cinder-block walls.

He heard a shrill whistle and flinched. This was followed by footsteps and someone mumbling. Aaron turned from the sink in time to see the window open in the cell door. The strange-looking man peered in at him. He didn't have the bug-eye glasses on. Nor was he sporting that bad copper-colored wig. His real hair was short and a dull black color that made his complexion look pasty.

"Step back against the wall, Aaron," he said with quiet authority. "And take off your clothes, everything."

Aaron hesitated. He kept thinking that he had to be a model prisoner and gain the guy's trust. But he was also thinking about the sounds he'd heard from Monica's cell last night.

"You heard me," his captor said. "Everything off."

Aaron started to tremble as he backed against the wall with the DETERMINATION WINS poster on it. He pulled the dead kid's undershirt over his head and dropped it on the floor. Then he pulled down his undershorts and stepped out of them. Now naked, he automatically folded his hands in front of his crotch.

There was a clanking sound, and then the door opened. The man stood in the doorway. He wore sneakers, shorts, and a knit sports shirt that hugged his barrel-chested, stocky frame. His arms and legs were chalky white with heavy black hair. A coach's whistle hung from a lanyard around his thick, short neck. He pointed a revolver at Aaron.

"Come with us," he said, stepping back to clear the doorway.

A kid darted in front of him and marched into the cell. He was holding a yardstick. Aaron recognized the short, chubby-faced young teen as the same boy who had faked the seizure the other day. He wore jeans—along with a sports shirt like the man's. Aaron guessed he was the guy's son.

The kid was smirking. He slapped Aaron's bare leg with the yardstick. There was a loud whack, and it stung.

Humiliated, Aaron stepped toward the door. He felt like an animal being led to the slaughterhouse.

"C'mon, move," the kid muttered, tapping him on the butt with the yardstick.

It was all Aaron could do to keep from ripping the damn stick out of the brat's hand and beating the crap out of him with it. But he was obedient. He hurried out to a dimly lit, white-tiled hallway. It looked like part of a locker room. The chlorine smell was stronger now. He could hear more splashing.

With the gun, the man motioned toward an alcove off the corridor. "C'mon, this way," he said. "No one gets into my pool without a thorough scrubbing."

The kid poked the yardstick in his back, and Aaron moved into the alcove. There was a small shower stall—without a curtain or a glass door. A fluorescent overhead light illuminated the tiny space. Aaron turned the shower handle, and water sprayed him. It was cold at first but then warmed up. Both the man and the kid were staring at him.

"That water should be hot," the man barked. "I want to see steam. And use the soap. Get those stinky armpits and that butt crack clean."

Aaron turned the shower handle farther toward the "H." A bar of Irish Spring was in the recessed soap dish. It was still wet and slick. Someone else must have recently washed with it. Aaron soaped himself.

"Scrub between your legs," his captor growled, "around the groin."

His kid snickered.

Aaron was obedient. The hot shower might have actually felt invigorating—if not for this weirdo and his brat gaping at him the whole time.

"Okay, that's enough," the guy said after a while.

Aaron turned the shower knob, and the water shut off with a squeak. The man stepped back and nodded down the little corridor.

Shaking off some of the excess water, Aaron headed in that direction. He put his hands in front of his crotch once again. The kid gave him another light swat on the back of his legs with the stick. It didn't hurt so much as it pissed off Aaron. He turned a corner in the tiled corridor and stopped dead.

Past the open entryway, he saw the huge indoor pool, the same length as his high school pool—twenty-five yards but half the width. On the other side of the pool—against the gray-and-white-tiled wall—were a few green plastic patio chairs. Aaron recognized the boy's mother in one of the seats. She was knitting but glanced up from her work to gape at him.

He could still hear splashing.

A girl bobbed up from the water in the shallow end of the pool. She stood and stared back at him. She was thin with short blond hair. For a second, Aaron thought she was naked, too. But now he saw she was wearing a beige one-piece suit that was almost transparent.

Aaron turned to his captor. "Wait a second. Aren't you going to give me a Speedo or something else to wear?"

"No," the man grunted. "We follow old traditions here. Until the late seventies, in certain high schools and YMCAs, the boys usually swam naked—"

"I've never heard of anything like that," Aaron argued. He nodded toward the girl in the pool. "She's got a suit on. How come I have to—"

"Girls wear suits for modesty's sake," the man said, cutting him off.

Dumbfounded, Aaron just shook his head at him. He figured even if it were true about boys swimming naked before 1970-something, they certainly didn't swim in the raw with clothed girls and women around.

"Well, I'm modest, too," Aaron insisted, still covering his crotch. "I'd like a bathing suit, please."

"That's not how it's done here," the man growled, brandishing the gun. "Now get in the pool—unless you want to do your customary walk-around on the deck first. You see, I've been watching you a while, Aaron."

Aaron just stared at him.

The coach nodded at his son, who gave Aaron a

hard whack across his butt with the yardstick. Against
his bare wet skin, it hurt like hell.

"Just get in the pool!" the girl called to him, her
voice echoing in the pool area.

Flustered, Aaron made a beeline toward the pool,
covering his genitals the whole time. Then he jumped
into the deep end feet first. The water was cool and
bracing. He came to the surface and started treading
water. It was good to be in a pool again, and he felt a
little less humiliated with the water partially obscuring
his nudity. He blinked and saw the girl staring back at
him. She didn't seem very interested—or titillated.
With her head above water, she swam toward him, a
slow freestyle glide. She was kind of pretty and had a
birthmark on her neck. She may as well have been
naked, too. Even below the water's surface, he could
see her nipples through her suit—once she was close
enough.

"Monica?" he whispered, trying not to stare.

She nodded. "Aaron," she murmured. "Listen, don't
make a fuss, and don't worry about being naked. I
couldn't care less—and neither does the Missus . . ."
She nodded toward the woman seated a few feet from
the edge of the pool. The fragile-looking, thirtyish
brunette went back to her knitting. Her black eye from
the other day had faded.

The man stood at poolside near the shallow end. He
jotted something on a clipboard. Meanwhile, the brat
plopped down in one of the plastic chairs and became
mesmerized with his mobile device. All the while, he
absently tapped the yardstick against his foot.

"I trained and competed with two other guys before you—Jim and Chris—and I never once saw either one of them with clothes on," Monica continued. "So I'm kind of used to it."

"Well, I'm not," Aaron muttered. "Listen, this Chris guy you mentioned, was he from Eastmont High in Wenatchee? Was he here for about seven weeks?"

"Why, yes, Chris—Chris Whalen," she said. "Have you heard of him?"

Aaron said nothing and just treaded water for a few moments. He finally nodded. "They found him a few days ago. He's dead."

"God, no," Monica gasped. She shook her head. "I had a feeling . . ."

"I'm sorry," Aaron whispered. "He washed up on a bank of the Wenatchee River. They say he was pretty banged up."

She rubbed her eyes.

Because her face was wet, Aaron couldn't tell if she was crying.

The whistle sounded even louder in the pool area. "Warm-up time!" the man announced. "More warm-up, less talk!"

Their captor strutted past the kid and the woman—past a door and then a window to what looked like a coach's office. A boom box sat on a plastic chair about six feet away from the pool. The plug was connected to a thick outdoor extension cord. He pressed a button on the box, and the theme from *Rocky* resonated through the vast room. Aaron thought of those dippy posters in his cell and wondered if this music was supposed to inspire him, too.

The man consulted his clipboard again and jotted more notes.

"C'mon," Monica whispered, executing a slow back-stroke into one of the lanes—marked at the bottom of the pool. Her voice was shaky. "You need to cooperate with him and do whatever he says. That's where Chris went wrong . . . poor Chris . . ."

Aaron stared at her as he swam sidestroke in the next lane. "Was that what you were doing last night?" he dared to ask. "Cooperating?"

She frowned and then swam away from him.

"Wait . . ." Aaron caught up with her. "I'm sorry. I didn't mean that the way it sounded. Did he—hurt you?"

"No more than usual," she muttered, pausing at the shallow end.

"Does that go on every evening?"

"No, but last night was hardly the first time. I learned early on that he sometimes likes a fight, so usually I just submit and get it over with."

Aaron stared at her. "Am I going to have to . . . ?"

She shook her head. "Unless Jim and Chris were lying, I'm pretty sure he leaves the boys alone."

"Who's Jim?" Aaron asked—with a cautious look toward the man, who had moved into his office for something. He must not have heard what they were saying over the music. The *Rocky* theme finished—and the theme from *Chariots of Fire* started up.

"Jim Lessing," Monica answered, stretching in the water. She changed to a sidestroke. "Have you heard of him? He's a championship swimmer at the University

of Oregon now. He'd been here about four months before the coach abducted me—"

"Coach?" Aaron asked, slowly swimming alongside
her.

"Yeah, *coach*, that's what he wants us to call him.
You might as well know that now. They're all very
careful about how they address each other. They never
use names. He's making it so, later on, we won't be
able to tell the police who they are or where they are.
So he's *coach*, and I call her the Missus and"—she
nodded toward the kid—"the little shit over there is Junior."

"They're all related?"

She nodded. "Yeah, one fucked-up family."

"What were you talking about, 'later on, we won't
be able to tell the police'?"

Monica got water in her mouth and spit it out. "I'm
talking about after he lets us go," she said. "You win
enough races, you make the goals the coach sets for
you, and he gives you your freedom—only you have to
sign something that says you'll never reveal how he
helped you."

Aaron squinted at her. "You really believe he'll just
let us go?"

"You have to earn it. Once I've won sixteen more
races, I'll be going home—like Jim did."

Aaron stared at her. All he could think was: *We're
both going home—like Chris did.* This guy wasn't going
to release either one of them. He was a murderer. Aaron
had heard that several high school swimmers had gone
missing in the last two years, and none of them had
been found alive. And certainly none of them became

college swimming champs. How could she believe that garbage? Maybe after six months under this guy's thumb, it was what she had to believe to keep sane and hopeful.

"I know you think I'm being naive," she said, moving toward the deep end. "But check the bulletin board. It's full of news stories from the Internet about what Jim's doing now. He's set all kinds of records at the University of Oregon. The coach even gave him a medal and a little ceremony before he let him go."

Aaron glanced over at the bulletin board that hung on the wall near the window of the coach's office. But he was too far away to see anything on the board except a photo—and some sheets of paper.

"The only reason Chris was killed was because he was difficult," Monica went on. She clung to the edge of the pool. "I tried to warn him, but from day one, he wouldn't cooperate. He kept trying to escape. And believe me, it's pointless. The coach has a gun, and the Missus has a gun in her knitting bag . . ."

Aaron turned toward the woman and caught her staring. Then she tried to look interested in her knitting again.

"Listen, Monica," he whispered. "Do you really believe this Jim guy wouldn't tell the police anything about this psycho who abducted him and held him prisoner for months—just because he signed some piece of paper?"

"No, he stayed quiet so that I wouldn't end up like Chris," she said. "It was part of the deal. And I'll make the same kind of deal to keep you alive when the coach lets me go."

"You don't know," Aaron said. "It's not just you,

me, and two other guys. A bunch of swimmers have gone missing in the last two years, and none of them have turned up alive—"

A shrill wail from the coach's whistle interrupted Aaron. "Stop the chitchat, and start swimming!" he yelled. "You shouldn't be looking at each other. You should be looking at the bottom of the pool!"

Aaron frowned at Monica, and she gave him an exasperated look. "Just do what he says," she whispered. "I don't want you to end up like Chris."

Then she ducked underwater and pushed off the wall.

It was no surprise to Aaron that the coach was brutal to them, a real sadist.

He kept popping lozenges because he screamed at them so much. And how he loved that stupid whistle. He had a basket of small, hard black rubber balls, and each time he wasn't pleased, he'd hurl one at Aaron or Monica—aiming for their heads, shoulders, or—if they were standing in shallow water—their torsos. It hurt like hell. After a while, both he and Monica were covered with red marks.

One of Junior's jobs seemed to be scooping the rubber balls out of the pool with a net and putting them back in the basket.

"He doesn't pull out the black balls every time," Monica whispered to Aaron during a rare lull while the coach checked his clipboard again. Apparently, this was supposed to be reassuring news.

"Great," he muttered. "What does he use on us the rest of the time, a taser?"

Aaron lost track of how many times he had to hear: "Do ten more laps until you get it right!"

By 11:50, he was exhausted and pissed off and still very scared. He kept hoping they'd stop for lunch hour. Even if he and Monica weren't fed, the son of a bitch and his family would have to eat—and then at least he and Monica could rest for a while. Aaron wanted to ask, *"When do we break for lunch?"* But he remembered *The Shawshank Redemption* again—when one of the new prisoners asked the warden pretty much the same question and got the crap beaten out of him. So Aaron decided to keep his mouth shut and try not to look at the clock.

At 12:15, the coach announced that it was almost lunchtime. But he didn't like Aaron's *"sloppy breathing,"* and they needed to work on that first.

"Oh, no," Monica murmured—with a look of dread.

"I don't want to hear a peep out of you, girlie," the coach said. He had Junior handcuff her to the ladder in the pool.

The coach told Aaron to step out at the shallow end. Aaron obeyed him and got out of the pool. He covered his crotch again, but Junior grabbed his arms and pried his hands away, placing them back by his spine. Then the kid handcuffed him.

"Down on the floor," the coach barked. He kicked off his shoes and peeled off his socks. "Face above the pool."

Trembling, Aaron wasn't sure exactly what he was

supposed to do. Junior guided him and set him in position so that he was lying on the deck—with its slightly scratchy no-slip surface. Aaron's face hovered directly above the steps into the pool. He was gazing into a foot of water.

"Your breathing is too haphazard," the coach said, walking toward him.

Aaron had a view mostly of his feet. They were ugly with dirty, yellow toenails. He didn't know what the guy was talking about. Coach Gunderson never had any complaints about his breathing method.

"You have to get a rhythm down," the coach went on. He stepped into the pool—nearly astride him. Aaron's head was between the coach's chubby, pale, hairy legs. The man dragged him forward. Aaron winced as the rough surface of the floor scratched his chest, thighs, and penis. Still, he didn't cry out. He felt so helpless, but he didn't want the coach to know that.

"You're taking too many breaths, and it's slowing you down," the coach claimed, grabbing the back of Aaron's head. "Let me show you . . ."

The man dunked Aaron's head under the water—nearly slamming his face into the first step inside the pool. The coach held Aaron's head there for what seemed like an eternity. He was saying something, but Aaron couldn't hear him under the surface.

Aaron hadn't taken a good breath beforehand, and now he was swallowing water and choking.

With a tight grip on his hair, the coach jerked his head to one side so he could get a breath. But all Aaron could do was cough out water and gasp.

"See what I mean?" the coach said. "Sloppy, no precision . . ." He shoved Aaron's head back under the surface again.

Aaron squirmed and struggled beneath him. He kept getting water in his nose and mouth. Every time the coach turned his head for him to take a breath, Aaron was wheezing. He thought he was going to drown. He wondered if this was what waterboarding was like. And he wondered when it was going to end.

Several times, the coach had to let go of his hair and then grab it again because he was pulling it out by the roots. As Aaron writhed on the floor, the scratchy deck surface seemed to tear away a layer of skin down the front of him.

The coach was relentless. Whenever Aaron came up for air, he heard him yelling some new instruction. But nothing he said was really useful.

By the time the coach was finished and announced it was time for lunch, Aaron felt as if he'd swallowed half the water in the pool. He was sick. He thought he might throw up.

He hadn't learned a single new thing about breathing.

And he knew, as far as the coach was concerned, it wasn't really a lesson in breathing.

For the coach, it was a lesson about who had all the power.

CHAPTER EIGHT

Echo
Wednesday, October 26—10:55 A.M.

The cop had told her this morning that she should write down a list of potential suspects and relevant information about them. Maybe he'd suggested it to humor her—or keep her preoccupied and out of their hair for a while.

Caitlin had stopped by the precinct station on her way to the library. She told her story to a husky, poker-faced blond policewoman at the front desk. She ended up in the deputy's office, telling it all again to a fortysomething man who looked like Dabney Coleman in *9 to 5*. His office smelled like stale coffee and peppermint Life Savers. He wore a bow tie that was obviously a clip-on, and his desk was a mess. He jotted notes and occasionally scratched his mustache while Caitlin showed him the two cryptic messages.

The deputy didn't think the handwriting was an *exact* match. He said that anyone might have slapped the *I'm Watching You* note on the moving box anywhere between Portland and Echo. He even found a little piece of dried Scotch tape on the back of the yellow paper and proposed that the note might have been taped to the moving box weeks ago. "It may even have accidentally gotten stuck to the box," he said. "You can't ignore that possibility."

Caitlin was forced to acknowledge that, no, the notes weren't really threatening. And neither was the phone call, which, yes, could have been a wrong number. And, no, there hadn't been any signs of forced entry when she'd checked the house. Nothing valuable had been stolen. And finally, yes, she was the same woman who had called yesterday afternoon about her missing daughter, who hadn't really been missing.

She felt like a fool. The deputy told her to hold on to the notes. He gave her his card—with her official case number on it.

At least he'd pretended to take her seriously.

So Caitlin decided to take him seriously and gather some information on her suspects—or rather her one *semi-suspect*.

There was no computer application in the library's system to bring up a list of the library items a customer had checked out—at least, none that Caitlin knew about. But during a lull, while working the checkout desk, she was able to pull up a record of Ken Meekley's late charges and those books and DVDs he'd returned after their due date.

She really didn't know much about him, except that he was a software engineer who worked out of his home. From the way Ken talked, Caitlin was pretty certain he lived alone. She couldn't think of anyone else who might have left her those notes and made that bizarre phone call. She'd asked the kids about the "*I'm watching you*" note. Had either one of them written it? Could one of their Portland friends have stuck the note to the moving boxes as a joke? Neither Lindsay nor Gabe knew anything about it. She called Russ and asked him if he was responsible for either of the messages.

"No, and this is really troubling," he answered. "It sounds like you have a stalker, honey. You said you found this second note in the guest room? Listen, as long as there's a guest room, let me stay over for a few days until this blows over. I don't like the idea of this going on when you and the kids are alone in a new town, in a strange new house . . ."

Caitlin had thanked her ex-husband for his concern but insisted he stay where he was. Maybe Lindsay wasn't totally wrong when she'd accused her of being a hard-ass. But it was bad enough that Russ was in Seattle now. All he had to do was come and stay with them *temporarily*, and pretty soon he'd be there for good. She couldn't help wondering if that might have been Russ's plan. Had he planted those notes—so she'd ask him to move in and protect them? It struck her as a particularly weird and sneaky way to get back into her life. That wasn't like Russ. Then again, because of his drug problem, she didn't really know him anymore—or what he was capable of.

Still, the logistics of Russ coming over to Echo yesterday afternoon to plant a note on her car windshield—when Lindsay was on her way to Seattle to see him—didn't make sense.

Caitlin figured *Ken Meekley, 903 Smugglers Cove,*

Echo, WA was a more viable suspect in this mystery. From his late-charge records, he seemed to be a pretty conscientious library patron. With all the books and DVDs he'd checked out in the last year, he'd been late returning only six items:

Devil in the White City / Larson—Due: 10/26; Returned: 10/30; Charge: $2.00—Paid

Star Trek: Voyages of Imagination / Ayers— Due: 12/11; Returned: 12/18; Charge: $3.50—Paid

The Stranger Beside Me / Rule—Due: 3/7; Returned: 3/9; Charge: $1.00—Paid

This Boy's Life / Wolff—Due: 6/7; Returned: 6/10; Charge: $1.50—Paid

While the City Slept / Sanders—Due: 8/29; Returned: 8/30; Charge: $.50—Paid

Brooklyn / DVD—Due: 9/20; Returned: 9/22; Charge: $1.00—Paid

She found the list a little disconcerting. Of course, Myra's jokes about Ken being a psycho didn't help any. *Devil in the White City* was about a serial killer at the Chicago World's Fair in the 1890s; Ann Rule's *The Stranger Beside Me* was about serial killer Ted Bundy; and *While the City Slept* was about a brutal 2009 double homicide in Seattle.

But did that make Ken Meekley a stalker or a potential murderer? Those three books were extremely popular. And it wasn't like all the books he checked out were about serial killers and true crimes. Hell, they had certain customers who borrowed nothing but grisly thrillers and true crime stories—and most of them were very nice people.

Ken was nice, too. He was just socially awkward—and maybe a little too persistent in his lame attempts to flirt. He was pretty harmless compared to others. She would have taken Ken over the serial texters or cell phone talkers who unfailingly ignored her every time they checked out a book or DVD. Then there were the ones who brought in their dogs, despite the signs that pets weren't allowed. Caitlin loved dogs. She just hated people who didn't think the rules applied to them. And there were customers who were certifiably crazy or just plain rude. There were also ex-customers, people on the *Trespassed* list—the ones who weren't welcome in the library anymore. Della told her they had a forty-year-old man who had groped several women in the library—until Myra caught him molesting a thirteen-year-old girl in the fiction section upstairs. They couldn't find anyone willing to prosecute, so he went free, but he was barred from the library.

One trespassed customer was still giving them trouble. Pierce Anthony was a thin, swarthy man in his late thirties. Apparently he was a heavy drinker, and he was also one of those people who always brought in his dog, a German shepherd. As Della told it, he got nasty to a high school girl who worked there over the summer—all over a two-dollar late charge. He used abusive language.

"He called this sweet girl a *fucking cunt*," Myra clarified. "How's that for classy?"

He, too, was barred from the library. But that didn't stop him. Pierce Anthony sent in his dope of a girlfriend to check out books and DVDs for him on her account—and all the while, he'd wait outside the library for her. With his dog straining on the leash, he'd stand there by the door, glaring through the window at whoever was behind the counter. Often the books or DVDs the girlfriend returned were damaged—pages torn from the books, or discs and cases looking as if they'd been used as the dog's chew toy. But the drippy girlfriend always denied culpability—to the point that Della, Myra, and Caitlin now inspected every book or DVD before they checked it out to her. At least she paid her late charges without an argument.

Before hearing the whole story on Pierce, Caitlin had first noticed him outside the library entrance with the German shepherd. She'd made the mistake of smiling at him and asking the dog's name.

He'd grinned back. "Her name's Queenie. What's yours?"

"I'm Caitlin. I work here."

"I know," he'd replied. Then his smile had faded and he'd muttered something under his breath.

Caitlin remembered almost asking him what he'd said, but seeing that glower on his thin face, she'd decided she was better off just heading into the library. That had been about a month ago. So—he knew her name, and he probably knew her car.

But Caitlin hadn't seen him or the girlfriend in over

a week. It didn't make sense that Pierce Anthony would be stalking her now. She barely knew him. Then again, a lot of women were stalked by guys they barely knew.

"You're daydreaming."

Caitlin blinked and turned to see Ken leaning on the counter—near one end. He had on his red Windbreaker again. He waved the DVD of *Superman Returns* in his hand and started to move toward her. "Is this any good?"

Even though Ken couldn't possibly see the computer, Caitlin quickly paged out of his account. "Ah, I'm not much for comic book action, but my son has seen it about a dozen times," she answered.

"Well, if Gabe likes it, I'll give it a try." He set the disc case on the counter.

Caitlin cringed inside, wishing once again she hadn't told him her kids' names. She opened the case to make sure the DVD was inside.

"I snuck right past you earlier," he said, handing her his library card.

Caitlin scanned it—and entered the DVD code into the computer. She worked up a smile. "Speaking of sneaky," she said ever so casually. "I—I got your note yesterday. That was cute."

"What note?" he asked—with a baffled look.

"The one you left on my windshield," Caitlin said. "You don't have to be coy . . ."

He shrugged. "I have no idea what you're talking about. Somebody left a note on your car windshield and signed my name? What did it say?"

Caitlin quickly shook her head. "It wasn't signed. I

just—well, I thought it might have been from you. Never mind, forget it." She handed him back his card and the DVD.

Ken chuckled. "Well, if they wrote something really profound or beautiful and poetic, I'd love to take credit for it, but I can't."

"It just said, 'Have a nice day,' " Caitlin admitted. "That's all."

"Sounds like a weirdo."

Caitlin said nothing. She was glad Myra wasn't around to hear those words come out of Ken's mouth. The irony would have been too much for her. Caitlin managed a professional smile once again. "The movie's due back next Wednesday, November second. Hope it's a hit with you."

He glanced at the back of the disc case. "Well, anything with Kevin Spacey, Parker Posey, and Eva Marie Saint can't be too bad." He nodded at her. "I'll probably have it back to you tomorrow. Hope you don't get any more strange notes."

"You and me both," she murmured, watching him head out the door.

She figured Ken probably wasn't the one behind those messages. She was a bit disappointed. A part of her sort of wished he'd written them. She had hoped that it was all just harmless, inept flirting—and nothing more.

Now she had to deal with the possibility that it could be something worse, something much, much worse.

*   *   *

Tucking the DVD into the pocket of his red Windbreaker, Ken stepped out of the library. He thought Caitlin seemed to be softening toward him. In a way, it was kind of flattering that she immediately thought of him after someone had left a flirtatious note on her car windshield. Was it wishful thinking on her part? At the same time, he didn't like the idea of someone else out there competing for Caitlin's affections.

He knew Caitlin's car and wondered if he should leave her a nice note on the windshield—and sign it. He heard somewhere that a lot of couples got started that way—with a special private joke between them.

As he headed toward his MINI Cooper, he saw someone in a hooded black raincoat near the edge of the lot. From where he stood, Ken couldn't tell if it was a man or a woman. The stranger's back was to him. He—or she—was approaching Caitlin's Lexus. Almost without breaking stride, the stranger slid a note in between the window and the door on the driver's side.

"Hey!" Ken called. "Hey, you, stop!"

The stranger took off toward an alley in back of the library. Ken chased after the culprit, but stopped by Caitlin's car and swiped the note off the driver's window. He glanced at it. He wasn't sure what it meant:

Were the police any help? ☺

Ken wasn't going to let this person get away. He raced toward the alley—which led to the harbor. "Hey, you, wait! I can see you!" he yelled. No one else was around at this time of morning to help him stop this weirdo. The way the culprit was dressed, all swaddled up like that, he was obviously up to no good.

Ken poured on the speed. He imagined Caitlin thanking him for intervening. He'd be her hero.

He caught up with the stranger by the mouth of the alley. "Hold it right there!" he panted, out of breath. He grabbed the fugitive by the raincoat sleeve.

The stranger swiveled around.

Ken didn't see the person's face right away.

What he saw first was a gun in a gloved hand. It was pointed at him.

Wednesday, October 26—12:55 P.M.

Hello from the desk of Ken Meekley. His living room looks like he raided an Ikea store. There are a couple of large Edward Hopper prints on the walls in cheap frames. His house smells like burnt toast. Right now, I'm killing time & waiting for him to fall asleep.

I didn't plan on this, but I think it might end up working to my advantage. I was pretty lucky the way things turned out. It started with a little run-in with Ken Meekley in the library lot. He's one of Caitlin's regular customers.

Fortunately, that block east of the library was totally deserted. No one saw Ken & me as we walked together to his car. Unfortunately, my note for Caitlin was intercepted. Getting to Ken's MINI Cooper & getting him home suddenly took priority. He was a nervous driver. "Careful with that thing," he kept telling me, eyeing my gun. We were here in ten minutes. More luck, he has an automatic garage door opener & the garage is connected to the house (a slightly tacky 2-bedroom rambler). So no one saw us.

Even more luck, he's a scotch man. Plus I found a whole bunch of prescribed antidepressants in his bathroom medicine cabinet. By the way, Ken also has a message written on the mirror—in some kind of special green crayon he must have bought specifically for these little daily medicine-chest pep talks. It said: Make Somebody Smile Today!

Another little something on display was far more interesting. On his refrigerator, he had a clipping about "Echo's new assistant librarian, Caitlin Stoller"—along with her photo from the Echo Bulletin. I think there's something I can do with this. I noticed his computer printer in the study has a copying function. What will the police think when they find Ken's bedroom practically wallpapered with this clipping and photo of Caitlin?

They'll think they found her stalker, that's what.

With the gun pointed at him, Ken was very cooperative. He cried a little, of course & tried to bargain with me. (Why do they always offer me money? I mean, do I look at all destitute?) But he finally washed down fifteen

antidepressants with about a quart of scotch—
like a good boy. He didn't need as much
persuading as Sara did back in May. I got the
distinct impression that sooner or later, Ken was
planning on doing something along these lines
anyway.

He was cooperative about taking off his clothes,
but wouldn't lose the underpants. So the police
will find him in the bathtub in his boxer shorts. I
don't think that's necessarily suspicious.

He was pretty out of it & again quite obedient
when I told him to sit down in the tub. He didn't
even try to struggle as I tied his hands together
& his feet together. This is a good thing, because
I don't want any rope burn marks on his skin. It
totally compromises the suicide scenario. There
were some muffled protests when I crammed a
washcloth in his mouth. But it didn't last long.

I can still hear him moaning in the bathroom.
He's sounding weaker by the minute. I'll give
him until 1:15. He should be unconscious by
then. I'll go in there & untie him. I don't want
anything getting in the way of his wrists. And I
want him completely out of it when I fill the tub
with water and make the cuts.

Alas, Ken uses disposable razors.

But in a drawer in the kitchen, I've found a box
cutter, and that will do nicely. The blade is very
sharp.

I don't hear him anymore. Either he's dead or he's in a deep sleep. Either way, that's perfect. Less struggle, less mess.

This is actually turning out well for me . . . very, very well indeed. Thank you, Ken.

You're making me smile today. ☺

CHAPTER NINE

With a towel wrapped around him, Aaron headed into his cell and abruptly stopped.

Some furniture had been added to the grim little room: a slightly battered desk with a lamp, some pens and a writing tablet on top of it; a desk chair; a table with a small TV; a bookcase full of books; a pillow, folded sheets, and clothes on the cot; and a mini-refrigerator.

The steel door clanked shut behind him.

Aaron swiveled around in time to see the speakeasy contraption open. The coach peered in at him. "I wasn't too impressed with your efforts today, Aaron," he said. "But you've been provided with some creature comforts on good faith that you'll do better tomorrow. Dinner's at six fifteen and lights-out is at eleven."

The speakeasy door closed.

Aaron turned around again to gaze at his quarters. He'd been training in the pool for the last eight hours—except for a forty-five-minute break for lunch. He'd spent much of that time recovering from nearly having drowned during the coach's "breathing" lesson. His chest and thighs were still red and sore from rubbing against the pool deck's rough surface.

During his break, he'd eaten in here—with the towel wrapped around him. He'd had a peanut butter and jelly sandwich (the jelly bleeding through the white bread), Fritos, and an apple—with a container of milk. The *creature comforts*—as the coach called them—hadn't yet arrived at the time.

Monica had urged him to cooperate. And apparently, these amenities were part of the coach's reward system for Aaron's cooperation.

For the most part, Aaron had done what he was told during this first day of training. He'd grown pretty tired of hearing the coach yell at him, but it beat another breathing lesson. By the afternoon session, he'd almost gotten used to being naked in front of these other people. Then again, he'd spent nearly all of that time in the pool. However, for a while, the coach had become preoccupied with Aaron's dive—and how long he was submerged and propelled forward in the water before breaking to the surface. So the coach had him diving in again and again. After a while, Aaron stopped putting his hands over his genitals between every dive.

But then the coach started videotaping him.

"I don't feel comfortable with you doing that," Aaron announced.

"Well, get your dive right, and maybe then I'll stop," he snapped back. "Meanwhile, I'll keep recording it so you can see how you're screwing up. Now get on your mark, and don't give me any more of your backtalk . . ."

The guy never got in the pool. Instead, he'd make Monica demonstrate in the water certain movements that were meant to improve Aaron's form and technique. Or the creep would stand on the pool deck and pantomime the way Aaron was supposed to swim. He had him and Monica compete in two 400-yard freestyle races. She edged him out in both races. Aaron wasn't exactly surprised. He'd been in a drug-induced sleep for two days and confined in a small cell for the third. He was hardly in the best of shape. At the same time, he wasn't used to having a girl beat him. He was humiliated. Still, he acted like a good sport and congratulated her.

She was ecstatic.

The coach said she was now two points and two days closer to her graduation day—when she'd be released from here. Then he went into this long spiel with Aaron about why he'd come in second—and where he'd made his mistakes. His strokes were sloppy, and he didn't keep his feet up, and blah blah blah. The guy seemed to know a few basic principles of the sport, but he certainly wasn't qualified to coach anyone. He blew his whistle a hell of a lot. And as he went through the motions like he was the voice of authority, Aaron wondered how long he could pretend to take this douche bag seriously.

The answer was obvious. He'd put up with him as long as the guy carried that gun. He had it in a holster on his belt during most of the practice.

Aaron didn't see many opportunities to grab the weapon. Whenever he climbed out of the water, he noticed the coach always kept a distance. Even if the guy was remotely close by, Aaron couldn't imagine lunging at him. Something about being naked made him timid and docile. He hated feeling so powerless.

Still, he was careful to observe the surroundings and everything the coach did. Aaron noticed the Missus and Junior came and went at certain times. But one of them was always there as a backup for the coach. Aaron also noticed they both used the door by the window to the office. Not once did they have to use a key. So that door was unlocked.

He never saw the Missus walk through with their lunches—so there must have been another access to their cells besides that tiled corridor to the pool he'd used earlier.

He noticed white-painted windows up along the top of the wall—near the ceiling. Obviously, this pool was in the basement of a house somewhere.

The coach never had him and Monica out of the water at the same time. One of them always had to be in the pool. Was their captor afraid the two of them might rush him—and wrestle the gun away? Aaron saw that as a possibility, but one of them was bound to get shot—wounded at the very least.

After only a couple of hours with Monica, Aaron realized she wasn't about to attempt an escape. She seemed to be holding on to some weird, misguided plan that she'd eventually get out of there with a good-conduct medal and a pat on the back from the coach. Between their laps and the lessons, she kept saying that Chris would still be alive if only he'd done what the coach had said. She talked about her former fellow prisoner, Jim Lessing, as if he was a great success story.

On his way back to his cell at the end of practice, Aaron got a closer look at the bulletin board with Jim Lessing's photo on it. He was a broad-shouldered, handsome guy with a trace of acne on his face and shoulders. He was extremely pale in the photo, obviously the result of several months of imprisonment. He had a sort of forced smile on his face, and around his neck was a garish blue ribbon that held what looked like an Olympic gold medal. Aaron knew the medal had to be a fake. The background in the photo was the deck to this pool. Monica had said the coach had had a parting ceremony for him. Was that when this picture had been taken? Jim Lessing was cropped at mid-stomach in the photo, and Aaron wondered if he'd been naked while posing for this picture.

He also couldn't help wondering where the kid was buried now or what river his corpse had been dumped in.

All the bulletin board's "news stories" about Jim Lessing's success as a freshman swimmer at the University of Oregon—and his potential as a candidate for the next Olympics—were just Microsoft Word documents. The pages tacked to the board didn't have the look of something copied off the Internet. It was obvious the coach had just made up these stories about Lessing. Aaron didn't notice anything in the "articles" about Lessing having been missing for months. Monica said he'd been a high school senior from Bellingham when he'd been abducted. But there was no mention of that.

Aaron made a mental note to ask Monica—next time he had a chance—how she figured Jim Lessing went right on to college without having to make up for the months he'd missed at the end of his senior year.

He'd glanced over his shoulder at her, obediently waiting and treading water in the deep end of the pool while the Missus and Junior guarded her.

The coach had made Aaron rinse himself off in the shower. Then he'd given him a towel to dry himself before heading back to his cell.

Now alone, Aaron made a beeline to the mini-fridge and opened it. He was slightly disappointed in the food selection inside: three bottles of Gatorade, a bag of carrot sticks, two oranges, a bunch of grapes, and a small pack of individually wrapped American cheese slices. But at least he had some food.

Aaron moved over to the cot to inspect the clothes. They looked secondhand. They'd probably belonged to the dead guys, Jim Lessing and Chris Whalen. But at least the garments were clean—and warm. He threw on a gray sweatshirt and a pair of jeans that were a bit too long. He cuffed them and then put on a pair of white socks that had washed-in dirt marks on the soles. He felt halfway human to be dressed again.

He looked at the small TV. It was the closest thing he had to a mirror. He hadn't actually seen his own reflection since he'd been brought here. He stared at himself for a few moments. Then he realized there might be something on the news about him. How long had he been missing now? Four days? He tried not to think about his mom or home because then he'd start crying. He found the remote and switched on the TV. It seemed to take forever to warm up. One look at the local news, and at least he'd know what city they were in. Were they still in Washington State?

Some Bruce Willis movie came on. Aaron couldn't tell which one it was. It didn't look like one of the *Die Hard* movies. In the bottom corner of the TV screen, it said *Retroplex.* That was one of those all-movies, all-the-time stations. He pressed the channel arrow on the remote. He got a couple of sports stations: college basketball and some snooze of a golf tournament. Then it went back to Bruce Willis. Three stations, that was all. No news stations, no hint of where he was or if anyone was looking for him.

Aaron tried to ignore the pang of homesickness in his gut. Or was it hopelessness?

He left the Bruce Willis movie on—just for background noise so he didn't feel so all alone.

Aaron glanced down at the vent. He wanted to talk to Monica. He wanted to tell her what had happened to his cell. He wanted to convince her that the coach was lying about what had happened to Jim Lessing. He wanted to talk to her and convince her that if they ever expected to get out of here alive, they'd need an escape plan. But Monica had been adamant that they shouldn't communicate through the vent anytime before lights-out—and even then, they had to be very careful about it.

So Aaron took a deep breath and started to put his new secondhand clothes in the dresser. A neat cell would be part of his pretense as a model prisoner. He wondered if that was how they all started out—all the coach's victims. Did they all start out just pretending to cooperate?

Bruce Willis was yelling at somebody. The movie looked like some World War II action drama. All at once, the screen went to gray static.

So much for his creature comforts.

"You were deficient in your dive today, Aaron," the coach announced. He appeared on the TV screen—with the window to his office in the background. Aaron could see the camera on a tripod reflected in a dark part of the glass. "I'm even more concerned about your dive than your breathing. I want you to study these videos for a while—and figure out what you're doing wrong. Compare them to this other video, and you'll see how it should be done. There's a whole lot of room for improvement on your part."

"Oh, shit," he muttered, staring at himself naked on the small TV screen. He looked so scrawny and ridiculous. He felt humiliated. His nude dive into the pool kept repeating—and freezing at times—so he could study his mistakes.

"Your knees aren't bent correctly," the coach said in voice-over—like he knew what the hell he was talking about. "And your arms should be straight out. See how you're leaning too far in?"

"Son of a bitch," Aaron muttered. He tried to change the channel with the remote. But the awful video was broadcast on all the channels. The Off switch didn't even work on the remote. The coach controlled the TV.

The video switched to another angle. It took Aaron a few moments to realize this video wasn't of him. The lighting fooled him. It was another naked teenager, pale and blond-haired—in the exact same spot—diving into the pool. Aaron recognized Jim Lessing.

"Now, watch how Jim pushes off and makes his entry into the water," the coach said. "You can learn from this . . ."

The guy looked so pale and dazed. He was like a zombie. Aaron wondered how long he'd been a prisoner at this point. And how much longer did he have to live?

Aaron stared at the TV screen and shuddered.

For a moment there, he'd thought he was that dead guy.

And he realized there wasn't much difference between them at all.

CHAPTER TEN

Echo
Wednesday, October 26—5:36 P.M.

Heading to her car in the library lot, Caitlin was worried she'd find another note on the windshield. She'd checked earlier during her lunch break—not long after talking with Ken Meekley and found nothing, thank God.

At least Caitlin didn't have to leave work early today.

Lindsay was staying late at practice this afternoon to make up for skipping yesterday. Caitlin had said she'd pick her up at the recreation center at 5:45.

She'd phoned home twice—to make sure Gabe was all right. She didn't have to worry about him walking home. The school bus dropped him off practically at the end of the driveway. But she kept thinking that—despite what the police said—whoever left that second note may have gotten inside the house to do it. She wasn't sure if Gabe was really safe alone at home.

Now as she approached the Lexus, Caitlin buttoned up her peacoat and furtively glanced around. She couldn't help feeling as if someone was watching her.

The library's shady parking lot could have used a few more lights. For all she knew, someone might have been sitting in their car watching her—or hiding in the bushes bordering the lot.

She came up toward the back of the car and noticed what looked like cracks all through the rear window. Caitlin stopped dead. "Oh, no . . ."

But then she realized—it was just the streetlight and some bare branches overhead reflecting in the darkened glass. She felt so silly, standing there with her hand on her heart.

Taking a deep breath, she walked toward the front of the car. Even after that false alarm, she still expected to find another note on her windshield. But there was nothing.

The tires looked fine. There were no scratches on the car. All the windows were intact. Everything looked okay. She climbed inside, started the engine and pulled out of the lot. The car was handling well, no detectable sabotage—yet.

She felt silly again. Talk about paranoid. Obviously, the police thought she was blowing this whole note thing out of proportion. Ever since Cliff's death—and then what happened with Russ—she was always half expecting another horrible shock. *Princess Dark Cloud*, that was her, forever anticipating the worst.

She found Lindsay standing by herself in front of the rec center. Her dark hair was a bit flat and lifeless after being tucked inside a bathing cap for the past couple of hours. She had her backpack slung over her shoulder and her nose in her mobile device.

Pulling up to the curb, Caitlin tapped the horn to get her attention.

"Everybody at school today was talking about the missing swimmers," Lindsay announced, once she climbed inside the car. She shut the door and buckled her seat belt. "Ms. Donahue's freaking out. She wants us to get rides home from practice—or walk home in twos or threes. A couple of girls on the team knew the guy from Mount Vernon who went missing. They said he was really nice. It's so sad. From the photos online, he looked pretty cute . . ."

"You shouldn't talk about him in the past tense like that," Caitlin said, heading out of the lot. "He's not dead yet . . ."

Lindsay checked her iPhone again. "Did you know about this?"

"Know about what?" Caitlin asked with her eyes on the road.

"Before we moved in, the woman who lived in our house killed herself," Lindsay said. "It says in this article that she hung herself from the pedestrian walkway on Deception Pass Bridge. Talk about creepy. And I had to find out from one of the girls on the team. Why didn't you tell me?"

Caitlin sighed. "Well, I didn't see any point in it, honey. You and Gabe were having a tough enough time adjusting to the move. Why upset you more with sad stories about the previous owners? Besides, it's not like she killed herself in the house. She wasn't even living there at the time."

"Who told you that?"

"Sally, the real estate agent," Caitlin replied. She glanced at Lindsay for a moment.

"Well, Sally's full of shit," Lindsay said.

"We bought the house from Dr. Goldsmith, honey. He and Mrs. Goldsmith were separated when she committed suicide."

"Yeah, he moved out when they separated. He was staying in some hotel in Oak Harbor, and she was living in our house when she hung herself. Then the husband moved back into the house for a few months—before unloading the place on us."

Caitlin gripped the wheel a little tighter. "My God," she murmured. "I'm going to kill that real estate agent. She gave me the distinct impression that Mrs. Goldsmith wasn't living in the house at the time. Are you sure about this?"

"Jaime Fleischel told me," Lindsay said. "The Fleischels live just down the street—on Pine. You want to know what else? The Goldsmiths had a daughter who was a year ahead of me, and she killed herself, too. She ran away from home, and they found her three days later, overdosed in an alley behind some sleazy hotel in Seattle."

"Good God," Caitlin whispered.

"I can't believe the real estate agent didn't tell you. That's the chatty woman with the Botox and the bad perm, isn't it?"

Caitlin nodded glumly. "You know, technically, she isn't required to tell us anything unless someone actually dies in the house. Still . . ."

"Ha!" Lindsay said.

"What's that? What do you mean, 'ha'?"

"Jaime said the house is like—cursed. She said a girl was murdered there back in the nineties—"

"No, honey," Caitlin cut in. "Like I say, the real estate agent would be required to tell us something like that."

"And like I say, *ha*," Lindsay replied. "Jaime said somebody broke in and bashed this girl over the head with a hammer. And they never found the killer. It probably happened in my bedroom. No wonder the place gives me the creeps."

"Are you sure this Jaime person isn't just messing with you, Lind? I mean, how does she know so much? Does she work for Wikipedia or something?"

"Her mom grew up here," Lindsay explained. "I tried to look it up on Google but couldn't find anything about the murder. But I got all sorts of stuff on the Goldsmiths—and Jaime was right about them."

Caitlin kept shaking her head over and over as she turned down Birch Place. She'd bought the damn house for a fresh start—something to help change their luck. She'd bought it for its charm and character. All the while, the place was nothing but bad luck for the previous owners—and someone may have even been murdered there. She would try to look it up herself later. If she couldn't find anything online, maybe Della at work knew about it. Della had lived in Echo for over fifty years, and knew everything about the town.

Pulling into their driveway, Caitlin noticed none of the lights were on in the front rooms of the house.

She parked the car in the garage. Then she and Lindsay headed into the house through the side door. As soon as Caitlin unlocked and opened it, she called out to Gabe. "Honey, where are you?"

She noticed the basement door was open. The light was on down there, but she didn't hear the TV. "Gabe?" she called again, starting down the stairs.

Lindsay poked her head in the basement doorway. "Maybe the ghost of Mrs. Goldsmith returned home and took possession of his soul."

Caitlin turned and shot her a look. "You know, I really don't need that right now."

"Sorry," Lindsay called.

At the bottom of the stairs, Caitlin turned into the family room no one ever used. Gabe wasn't there, but the door to the big utility room was open—and she felt a draft. Had someone gotten in through the outside basement door?

"Gabe?" she called—even more panicked this time.

She stepped into the utility room, which managed to look gloomy even with all the lights on. She noticed by the washer, dryer, and laundry sink, a few hangers on the overhead pipes were swaying in the breeze. Then she saw the open door.

"Mom?" Gabe's voice was a bit muffled.

"Gabe, honey, what's going on? Why is this door open?"

He came from around the corner. He was wearing khakis and a blue sweater—and he was filthy. "You should see what I found," he said eagerly. "Come check it out . . ."

"Is everything okay?" Lindsay called from the stairs.

"I'm not sure yet!" Caitlin called back.

She passed the workbench, where Gabe had opened some of their unpacked boxes. The wall above the bench was a cheap wood panel with strategically placed nails and outlines indicating where to hang a hammer and different types of saws.

She followed Gabe around the corner to the little closet under the stairs. He'd cleaned out all the wood scrap, old pipes, and rubbish that had been dumped in there. Caitlin was amazed at the work he'd done—and the size of the cubbyhole. There was actually room to stand and move around on one side of the stairs. She didn't even think the room had a light, but Gabe had unearthed an overhead socket—and a two-plug outlet. He'd mopped the speckled linoleum floor covering. He must have found the wood and brick in there to assemble the small college-style bookcase. She could smell the lemon-scented Pledge—along with a sooty, musty odor. He'd already stocked the shelves with some of his books—along with the lava lamp from his room. It was plugged in, giving the space a homey, retro-bohemian touch. He'd moved in a TV table, a folding chair, and some of his drawing pads.

"I'm going to make this my private clubhouse," Gabe said. "Is that okay, Mom?"

Lindsay came up behind her. "God, it looks like the Unabomber's workspace."

Caitlin shot her another look and turned to Gabe again. "Honey, what you've done here is incredible. But I don't know about the ventilation . . ."

"That's why I left the outside door open, so I could air it out," he explained. "I carried all the crap that was in here up the outside steps and dumped it by the side of the house. I'll take everything out to the curb when they come to collect the garbage on Friday, I promise.

You weren't going to turn this into a broom closet or anything boring like that, were you?"

"No, if—well, if you really want to make it your clubhouse, that's fine with me," she said tentatively.

"Cool! I bet I could even fit an air mattress or a sleeping bag down here—maybe under the lower steps where it's too low to stand . . ."

He seemed so proud of his find—and his work to convert it into his own version of a man-cave. Caitlin didn't want to pooh-pooh it. But she kept thinking that Gabe would be isolating himself even more down here in this little basement hideaway.

"Listen, why don't you go get cleaned up for dinner?" she suggested.

"He's probably covered in asbestos or something like that," Lindsay said.

Caitlin didn't even want to think that her daughter might have a point. She worked up a smile for Gabe. "Throw those clothes in the hamper, and take a shower, okay?"

He nodded and then took a drawing from his sketchpad and put it against the dirty gray wall to see how it looked.

"God, he's such a little freak sometimes," Lindsay muttered, retreating into the other room.

Caitlin heard her heading up the stairs. At least there wasn't a cloud of soot in Gabe's new clubhouse for every step Lindsay took. "C'mon, wrap it up in here, honey," she said. "Dinner will be ready in a half hour."

She went over to the doorway by the laundry sink and stepped outside into the stairwell. She got halfway up the steps when she saw the pile of wood, old blinds, pipes, and other debris by the side of the house. It was such a dark, neglected, creepy spot. She felt a chill and shuddered.

There was an exterior light above the door, but it didn't work. She didn't know whether something was wrong with the switch or the bulb just needed changing. There was still so much she didn't know about this house—from a room her son had just discovered to an old murder her daughter had just told her about.

Caitlin ducked back inside.

She shut the door, locked it, and fixed the chain in place.

Wednesday—11:12 P.M.

"Monica, can you hear me?" he called softly into the vent. "Are you there?"

After a moment, he heard her: "No, I went out for ice cream. What do you think? Not so loud, okay?"

Aaron scowled. She didn't have to be so sarcastic.

He slouched lower on the cot, closer to the vent. He had a book in front of his face—so the camera up on the ceiling couldn't record him talking. The book was about Michael Phelps—and it was still readable under the blue night-light. It was from the library of about two dozen books that had come with the bookcase earlier today. All of them were used and a bit beaten up.

His video "lesson" had gone on for about forty minutes—until he was pretty sick of seeing himself and Jim Lessing naked. Then he had control of the TV again. *The Pink Panther* came on the movie channel. Aaron actually found himself chuckling a little—for the first time in four days. He ate in front of the movie: microwave lasagna—and milk. He didn't like milk with Italian food or pizza. So he stashed it in the mini-fridge and drank a sports drink with dinner instead. He wondered if he might get punished for it.

He found the TV addictive company. Even though he wasn't crazy about the next movie, *The Sting II*, he watched it, occasionally switching to one of the sports channels in hopes that they might have some game he remotely cared about.

The lights had gone out at eleven—along with the TV.

"Is this better?" he whispered behind the Michael Phelps book.

"Yes," she answered. "But listen, you can't make a habit out of this. If he catches us, he'll make our lives totally miserable. You won't believe how long a night can seem without any heat or clothes."

"He put all this stuff in my cell today—including a TV and a little fridge," Aaron said.

"If you want to hold on to it, you better give your best during practice tomorrow. That's how he operates. If you keep losing the races or he doesn't think you're trying hard enough, you get punished. It is supposed to motivate us, create a genuine competition between us. And you know something? It does. That's another reason I shouldn't be talking to you. We're not supposed to be friends, you know."

"Weren't you friends with Jim Lessing?" Aaron asked. He gave a cautious glance over the book—at the green light in the little dome on the ceiling.

"I respect Jim," she answered in a solemn tone. "He's a nice, decent guy, and a good competitor. He's . . ."

Aaron leaned closer to the vent. He wondered why she'd stopped talking.

"Are you okay?" he whispered after a moment.

"Yes, Jim and I are friends," she said finally. "I miss him. I was sad to see him go, but I was happy for him, too."

It dawned on Aaron that she was probably in love with the guy. He wasn't bad-looking, and he was the only guy in Monica's life her first couple of months here—besides the coach and Junior. She saw him every day—naked. And they probably whispered to each other through this same vent practically every night, too. He could imagine how they felt. He barely knew Monica, and already he had feelings for her.

No wonder she didn't want to think that Jim Lessing might be dead.

For her sake, Aaron tried to pretend for a minute or two that the guy might be alive. "What kind of story did he give the police for why he went missing all those months he was here?"

"He said he'd run away and gone hitchhiking across the country," Monica answered.

"And people believed him?"

"Why shouldn't they?"

"If that's the case, I think they would have sent him to a shrink or something."

"I don't know, maybe they did. So what?"

"Well, how come he got into college right away?" Aaron asked, figuring the question he'd saved up since this afternoon would stump her. "Wouldn't he have to make up for all the months of high school he missed?"

"Maybe he made up for it in just a couple of weeks. Jim was very smart."

Aaron sighed and raised the book to cover most of his face. "Listen, Monica," he whispered. "You need to—to consider the possibility that the coach is lying to you about Jim. Those stories on the bulletin board, he could have written them. It could be total bullshit, y'know? I mean, if I end up here for another month and I get out the way your pal Jim supposedly did, I don't care what kind of deal I make with the coach, I'd tell the cops about him and this whole setup. I'd do everything I could to track down this guy and get you out of here."

"Well, maybe Jim *has* told the police about it and they're keeping the investigation a secret. They could be on their way here right now. We don't know for sure."

"Or maybe Jim's dead and his body is hidden somewhere—along with all the others before him," Aaron said. "We can't wait around hoping the cops will find us, Monica. You and me, we need to come up with an escape plan. It's our only chance—"

"Are you crazy?" she hissed. "You sound just like Chris. He wouldn't cooperate. He constantly mouthed off to the coach. He was always telling me how we needed to escape—"

"He was right," Aaron cut in.

"Yeah, well, he tried to escape. And he got out of here, all right. He ended up dead. Maybe that's what happened to the others. It's going to happen to you, too—if you don't change your attitude."

"Listen, I think there's a way for us to get out of here alive. But we have to work together—"

"I don't want to hear it."

"The little shit, Junior, he's always getting up and moving around. All I have to do is grab him and use him as a shield. I can threaten to break his neck. A friend of mine showed me how it's done—just like in the movies. We can get the coach and the Missus to surrender their guns. But you have to work with me on this. You have to distract the coach long enough so I can grab the kid."

"It's too risky. He'll shoot you . . ."

"We can do it. You wait until I'm out of the water. I'll cough a little, and that'll be your signal to fake a cramp or something. Just distract the coach for a few seconds, that's all."

"It's not going to work." She sighed. "Please, let's just drop it."

"No, it'll work—if you'll go along with me. The door by his office is unlocked. We can get out that way—"

"And just how far are you going to get stark naked?"

"We'll lock them in one of the cells. I can get some clothes then."

"It's a stupid plan, Aaron. And he'll be expecting you to try something on your first days here. There are so many things that could go wrong. I have only a few more races until I'm out of here. Don't screw it up for me."

"All you have to do is fake a cramp when I cough, and then I'll take over from there—"

"I don't want to talk about this anymore."

"Monica, do you really believe he'll let you go?"

She shushed him. "He's coming! Don't say anything else, okay? I'll see you tomorrow."

Aaron leaned over the bed—with his ear practically to the vent. He didn't hear anything—no voices, no crying. Was the coach really there? Or was she lying? Maybe she just didn't want to talk anymore about escaping.

Maybe Monica thought if she refused to discuss it with him, he wouldn't try anything tomorrow. Well, after so many months in this place, her thinking was screwed up.

He didn't intend to spend another day here.

CHAPTER ELEVEN

Echo
Wednesday, October 26—11:16 P.M.

Sometimes Facebook was the only way she could keep in touch with her friends in Portland. Lindsay had 211 Facebook friends, and only eleven were from Echo. She was surprised and disappointed at how much fun her Portland friends were having without her. And each new post of hers got fewer and fewer "likes" from the old gang. That kind of irked her, because she "liked" and commented on practically all their posts—including the latest (*God, not again*) photo of Amy Emerson's stupid cat, Amber Merrick's eighty-seventh selfie, and the slice of pizza Dori Lasky ate yesterday. Meanwhile, her post from hours ago had a whopping three likes and absolutely no comments so far.

She thought the post was pretty damn interesting, too. She had posted a photo of their new house alongside a Google image of a woman screaming from some 1950s horror movie. She'd written:

*I just found out today that a girl was murdered in
the house we moved into last month. This is no
joke! It happened back in the 1990s. How's that
for creepy? For all I know it could have
happened in my bedroom. Wish me luck falling
asleep tonight!!!*

No comments, not even a "wow" face; she couldn't
believe it.

Lindsay was sitting on the beanbag chair in her bedroom with her iPhone in front of her and Panic! at the
Disco playing through her earbuds. She'd already finished her homework and was way too nervous to sleep.

She saw a friend request at the top of the Facebook
page. She clicked on it.

Friend request sent from Jeremy Dawson, it read.

Lindsay had never heard of him. She clicked on the
name, and the screen went to his Facebook page. She
blew up the profile picture. He was really cute—with
blue eyes, messy dark brown hair, and a sexy, unshaven
scruffy look. In the cover photo, it looked like he was on
a hike. He wore sunglasses, cargo shorts, and no
shirt—which revealed a swimmer's build and a tan. He
had his arms spread out as if to show off the lake and
the mountains behind him.

Lindsay was pretty sure she'd never seen him before in her life. Was he for real?

He had sixty-two friends. He lived in Echo and attended North Seattle Community College. From his
birthday, she figured out he was nineteen years old.
His favorite movie: *The Departed*; his favorite book:

Catcher in the Rye; favorite band: The Killers; favorite team: Seahawks. Most of his photos were nature shots that he must have taken on his hikes. But there was a selfie of him—shirtless again and sporting a backward baseball cap as he flexed in front of a bathroom mirror.

Really? Was he serious with that?

Still, Lindsay accepted his friend request and told herself that the bathroom selfie was probably just a joke. She also wondered how he knew her.

A number "1" came up on her message icon.

Lindsay clicked on it. "*You are now friends with Jeremy Dawson! Leave Jeremy a message!*"

Lindsay clicked on his name and her thumbs worked rapidly over the letters on her phone screen pad: "*Do we know each other? Have we met?*"

Because of the music pumping through her earbuds, Lindsay didn't hear the knocking on her bedroom door. So she flinched when the door opened.

Her mother poked her head in.

Lindsay pulled one earbud out and turned her phone screen down in her lap. "God, you scared me . . ."

Her mother stepped into the room and folded her arms. She wore a long-sleeve tee and sweatpants. She looked ticked off about something.

"What?" Lindsay asked.

"Were you in my room earlier tonight?"

Lindsay shook her head. "No. Why? What's going on?"

"My Hummel figure—the little boy with the trumpet that was on my dresser—someone broke it. And they didn't even do a good job covering it up. They just kicked the smashed pieces under my dresser."

"Well, don't look at me."

Her mother just kept staring.

"Listen, I know, after yesterday, you probably trust me about as far as you could throw me," Lindsay said, borrowing a phrase from her dad. "But really, Mom, if I broke something of yours, I'd tell you—or at the very least, I'd cover it up better. Try Gabe. I think he's still awake."

"I just talked to him," her mother said. "He swears up and down he hasn't even been in my bedroom for the last few days."

"Well, then—maybe it's the ghost of the girl who was murdered in this house, because it sure wasn't me."

Her mother sighed and shook her head. "I'm so disappointed. I thought I'd raised you kids so that you were both reasonably honest and responsible individuals. I can't believe neither one of you will own up to this."

"It wasn't me!" Lindsay insisted, rolling her eyes. "God, do you want me to open a vein and write down an oath in blood? Did you give Gabe this much shit? Because obviously, he's the one who broke the stupid thing, not me. Every time something goes wrong around here, you blame me. God!"

Her mother narrowed her eyes at her. Then she turned and hurried out of the room, shutting the door behind her.

Lindsay was livid. She didn't know who she was madder at—her mom or her lying little weasel of a brother.

She listened to her mother speaking quietly to Gabe down the hall. She couldn't make out what her mom

was saying, but she heard Gabe's response: "I didn't
do it!"

Why didn't the little brat just admit that he broke the
tacky figurine? It wasn't like their mom ever hit either one
of them. And if she grounded him, why would he care? He
shut himself off in his bedroom all the time anyway.

Lindsay's phone binged.

She glanced down at the Facebook screen. A message had popped up from Jeremy Dawson:

> Hi. Thanks for friending me back. No, we haven't
> actually met. So I guess this is going to sound
> kind of stalker-ish (hope not!), but I swim at the
> rec center & saw you there with the swim team
> on Monday. You were coming in when I was
> leaving. I thought wow & then later, I asked
> around & found out your name. I heard you were
> new in town & figured I'd take a chance & say hi.
> I'm really not a stalker. Honest!

Lindsay cracked a tiny smile, and her thumbs started
working on the phone pad.

> I'm pretty sure that's the first thing a stalker tells
> someone they're stalking: "I'm not a stalker!"

She thought about it and then added a smiley icon.
He messaged back:

> I like a girl with a sense of humor.

> I'm pretty sure that's the second thing a stalker
> tells someone they're stalking.

She giggled at her own remark. This hiker hottie probably thought she was so clever.

He wrote:

You're not going to give me a break, are you?

Not until I know you better. Do you still live at home with your parents?

Guilty. In fact, I'm sitting here in my bedroom in the basement. My grades weren't that hot. So instead of going away to a university, I decided to take a year of community college. Big mistake. All my friends are gone & I'm here with the fossils & my kid sister & I'm bored shitless.

Lindsay smiled. *Fossils*, meaning parents. She'd never heard that before. She continued:

I know what you mean. I moved here from Portland 7 weeks ago. So all my friends aren't around, either. Plus my mother is driving me crazy right now.

Tell me about it. Every weekend I go hiking or camping just to get out of the house . . .

I saw some of the pictures.

Now the weather's getting too cold & crappy for camping. But I lucked out. The fossils and my kid sister are going to Spokane this weekend. I have the house all to myself. Wish I could throw a Halloween party or something, but like I say, none of my friends are around. Do I know you

well enough to ask you on a date for this weekend? What are you doing Friday night?

Lindsay felt a little pang of excitement, but then she
remembered.

Sounds cool, but I have a swim meet in Seattle
on Saturday morning, so Friday night's out.

What about Saturday night?

Lindsay smiled as she typed her reply.

Maybe . . .

With a warm old cardigan over her shoulders,
Caitlin plodded down the stairs to the front hall. She
was upset and decided a glass of cabernet would help
her mellow out a little.

She couldn't believe that neither one of her children
would own up to breaking that Hummel figurine. Russ
had given her the little boy with a trumpet shortly after
Cliff was born. He'd found the thing in an antique store.
Apparently it was a collector's item, but that really didn't
matter to her. The little Hummel figurine was one of the
few things she had left from when they were really happy.

It wasn't at all like either one of her kids to lie to her
about something like this. Obviously it had been an accident. She would have been very forgiving—if the
guilty party had just confessed.

"God, I hate this," she muttered, heading into the
kitchen.

Caitlin opened the cupboard where she kept the wine and started to reach for the bottle she'd opened last night. But it wasn't there.

It didn't make sense. She'd drunk two glasses last night. She'd polished off a bottle of Columbia Crest and opened up some Robert Mondavi for the second glass. The Mondavi bottle was about three quarters full when she put the cork back in. The only wine left on the shelf now was an unopened ridiculously expensive merlot. She'd had a slight buzz last night, but she wasn't so drunk that she would forget knocking off a whole bottle of wine.

Caitlin checked the recycling bin under the sink. There was the empty Columbia Crest bottle, just where she'd put it, but no second bottle. She tried the garbage, cringing as she pushed aside food scraps, coffee grounds, and damp paper towels. She found the empty Robert Mondavi bottle.

"What the hell?" she murmured. It was like someone had hidden it there.

Then she remembered a remark Lindsay had made a few minutes ago about the broken figurine that was swept under the dresser: ". . . *I'd have covered it up better*."

It wasn't like Lindsay to drink alcohol—on the sly or otherwise. She was very conscientious about keeping in training for the swim team. Then again, it wouldn't have been like her daughter to ditch school, skip practice, or run away from home—and she'd pretty much done all those things yesterday.

Caitlin still blamed herself for missing all the signs that Russ was in trouble with drugs. Was she doing that all over again with Lindsay?

Washing her hands, she headed upstairs. She switched off the hallway light. In the darkness, she looked for the telltale strip of light under Lindsay's door. But it wasn't there. Lindsay had already gone to bed.

Caitlin imagined her daughter denying any culpability once again. "*Every time something goes wrong around here, you blame me. God!*"

With a sigh, Caitlin retreated back down to the kitchen and opened the ridiculously expensive merlot. She felt like she was losing her mind. First the Hummel figure *nobody* broke and now the wine in a near full bottle magically evaporating.

"*Well, then—maybe it's the ghost of the girl who was murdered in this house . . .*" Lindsay had said.

With her glass of merlot in hand, Caitlin sat on a stool at the kitchen counter. She opened up her laptop and clicked on Google. She typed in the keywords: Young Woman Murdered, Echo, WA.

The first three pages of search results had to do with Echo Gerard, a University of Washington student who had murdered her roommate over some boy in 2012. It was a notorious case. With all the *Echo Gerard* results, Caitlin understood why Lindsay had given up her Google search for the murder in Echo.

Caitlin tried new keywords: Girl Murdered Bludgeoned Birch Place Echo.

The first six search results were about the infamous Echo Gerard again. But the seventh result caught Caitlin's eye:

TEENAGE GIRL BLUDGEONED TO DEATH IN ECHO HOME
www.theseattletimes.com/news/1992/07/06/echo-wa-killing.html

July 6, 1992—The **girl** was **murdered** around 10 P.M. on
Saturday night July 4th . . . family home on **Birch Place**
in **Echo** . . . **bludgeoned** with a hammer that was found
near the body . . .

Caitlin clicked on the story link. The first thing she
noticed after the headline was the photograph, obviously
a yearbook portrait. The smiling teenager had dark,
shoulder-length corkscrew hair, dimples and braces.
She wore a nineties-style blouse with shoulder pads.

The caption beneath the photo read: "*Murder victim,
Denise Healy, 17, was an accomplished equestrian
and swimmer.*"

"Another swimmer," Caitlin whispered to herself.

The article didn't give the exact address, but said
that the Healy house was on Birch Place in Echo. The
girl's father owned a recreation center in Echo called
Equestream—with a pool and horse stables. The police
believed that Denise Healy was probably killed by an
intruder intent on robbing the house. The murder
weapon was a hammer that Mr. Healy usually kept in
his basement work area. Denise's parents and her
younger brother discovered her body when they returned home from a July 4th fireworks show—held on
the Equestream grounds. Denise hadn't attended because she'd had a bad cold.

Caitlin sipped her merlot and tried new keywords for
the Google search: Denise Healy, Murder, Echo, WA.

She wanted to find out if the police had ever caught
the girl's killer. She also needed to know if Denise
Healy had been murdered in this house. She thought of
the workbench in the basement utility room and the
tool outlines drawn on the pegboard wall. She thought

of the faded outline, and wondered if that was where Mr. Healy's hammer had hung.

There were only six houses on Birch Place, which connected two slightly busier residential streets. Like her house, the others all had large wooded lots. The odds were one in six that this was the house where Denise Healy had been murdered.

Caitlin found a follow-up article from *The Seattle Times* dated July 13, 1992. The headline read: SEARCH CONTINUES FOR KILLER OF ECHO GIRL. The article featured a police composite sketch of a "*shaggy-haired man*" a neighbor had spotted on Birch Place that Saturday night. The rendering made him look like an ugly, sinister version of a young Jackson Browne.

Just a week later, other theories were emerging besides the robbery-gone-wrong scenario:

> Police investigators are trying to determine if the murder is linked to another unsolved crime: the murder of Lilly-Anne Wilde and the disappearance of her friend Jill Ostrander of Bremerton on December 6. Both girls were 16 years old. They were returning from the Kitsap Mall in Silverdale, where they'd met with friends to see the Martin Scorsese film *Cape Fear*. The film finished at 9:45 that Friday night, and the girls said good-bye to their friends. It was the last time anyone saw either one alive.
>
> Lilly-Anne Wilde's car was found on a wooded trail four miles from her home. Wilde had been beaten over the head with a tire iron.

Police determined she'd been dead at least 12 hours when her body was discovered on Saturday afternoon. Jill Ostrander is still missing . . .

Caitlin couldn't help wondering if either one of those girls was a swimmer. The article didn't say.

Nor did it give the Healys' address on Birch Place.

Caitlin couldn't find any more follow-up articles. So—the murder must have remained unsolved. And as far as she was concerned, it would remain unsolved tonight. If she expected to get any rest, she needed to go to bed. As if she could fall asleep. She'd probably be wondering all night where in the house the murder had taken place.

Caitlin was about to switch off the computer when she heard a click from the email box. She opened her email page and saw the new email. She didn't recognize the sender. The subject line read:

Good Evening, Caitlin.

She opened the email. There was just one line:

It happened in Lindsay's bedroom ☺

Thursday, October 27—2:30 A.M.

The light in Caitlin Stoller's bedroom went out at 1:50 a.m. I doubt she'll get much sleep tonight.

She knows about the murder now. I'm guessing she found out the same way Sarah Goldsmith did. Her daughter probably heard about it at school and told her. Those little bitches at the high school are a bloodthirsty group.

I had a busy day yesterday, what with the unexpected visit to Ken Meekley's house. I should be exhausted, but I feel quite energized. Yesterday saw an important milestone. It finally happened. I knew it would eventually. Leave it to young Gabriel Stoller to discover that room under the stairs. I saw him piling all the rubble against the side of the house late yesterday afternoon. It was still there when I left the house a half hour ago.

Does that stupid little boy or his stupid mother realize how close they are now to the heartbeat of that evil house?

They haven't a clue.

No one should be happy in that house. No one should be living there.

They don't know what's in store for them. I've left them alone for quite some time. In fact, I was thinking about it yesterday. This is the longest any of my occupants have had in the house before I made them aware of my presence. I have to admit, Caitlin has fascinated me. Such a contradiction: good looks, good breeding, brains, class & yet so utterly pathetic.

Most of the families who have moved in start out
so happy there. But she's been rather pitiful—
from the very start. Maybe that's why I've left
her & the two brats alone for so long.

Well, we've reached that turning point now.
Caitlin knows I'm watching. She just doesn't
know who to look for. As she left the library late
yesterday afternoon, she was like an amateur spy
in some old movie, constantly looking over her
shoulder. I know she was expecting another note
on the windshield of her car. Well, if not for her
gallant Ken, she would have had one.

When I was in the house earlier today, I
checked. She obviously found the note under the
box in that upstairs bedroom. About time. It's
been there six days.

While I was there, I went through her bedroom
again—and couldn't resist leaving another
calling card.

I removed the bugs I planted in the bedrooms and
kitchen. I've listened in on enough conversations
that I know them pretty well now. I don't want to
risk having them discover any of my bugging
devices. Plus I don't want to lose them. They're
expensive.

I got into the refrigerator, too, while I was there.
We'll see in tomorrow's garbage if the carton of
chocolate milk is in there. That'll mean Gabriel
thought it tasted funny & then I'll just have to be

more careful about how much of that stuff to put in there.

Speaking of drinks, I wonder if she noticed the wine bottle thing tonight.

We'll see.

This is the fun part—when they know something's wrong, but they can't put their finger on it. When they start blaming each other for things that are spoiled, broken, or missing. When they start blaming & doubting themselves.

It's fun to know what they're thinking & wondering—when I have all the answers.

Caitlin's probably just starting to get a vague inkling that they might be in danger.

And me, I already know the exact date when the first one of them will die. ☺

CHAPTER TWELVE

Echo
Thursday, October 27—7:19 A.M.

With the phone to her ear, Caitlin poured Gabe's chocolate milk into his favorite *Simpsons* tumbler. She was warming up a blueberry muffin for him. He sat at the counter with his nose in his history book. "Thanks, Mom," he mumbled, reaching for the glass.

Lindsay was still in the upstairs bathroom. She'd fallen asleep last night on the family room sofa in front of Turner Classic Movies. The Pottery Barn throw was still bunched up in one corner, by the armrest. It was always a crapshoot whether or not Lindsay would have breakfast, and if she did, it was usually a bowl of cereal. So Caitlin decided to let her fend for herself.

She'd already had her own breakfast and was on her third cup of coffee. For the last fifteen minutes, Caitlin had been listening to the "hold" music from AOL customer service. Right now it was "Can't Take My Eyes Off of You." Lindsay claimed she was one of the few people under seventy still using AOL.

Last night, Caitlin had tried responding to that unsettling email, and asked just one question: *Who are you?*

Within a minute, she'd received an automatic response: MAILER DAEMON: UNABLE TO DELIVER, ADDRESS INVALID.

Caitlin immediately closed out of AOL, shut down her computer, and phoned AOL Technical Support. She was on hold for only ten minutes before a representative came on the line—obviously from India. Caitlin gave the woman her AOL user name, her mother's maiden name (Walker), and the name of her first pet (Amos, a turtle). Then she asked if there was a way to ascertain if her account was in use at the moment.

"Yes, we show it is being used right now," the woman replied with her crisp accent.

"Well, it's not me using it," Caitlin said. She hated knowing someone out there was on her account. But at least that explained how this person was able to determine what she'd been Googling—and even what she'd been thinking.

First the note on the car, then the one under the mover's box in the guest room, the strange phone call—and now this. Had the same someone gotten into the house yesterday as well? Had they drank her wine and broken that Hummel figurine? It made no sense.

The customer service rep recommended that Caitlin change her AOL password—and check her credit cards if she did any bill paying online. By the time Caitlin had finished doing all that, it was nearly two in the morning. She'd gone to bed and tried to read—her one escape. But she couldn't concentrate, and after that, she'd barely slept. Having to do without credit cards for the next week or so seemed like the least of her worries.

Changing her password was at best a temporary fix. What good did that do while the culprit was still on her account? They probably knew the new password.

So she'd called AOL again this morning—while drinking her second cup of coffee. Another cup and twenty minutes later, and she was still on hold, waiting for a representative to pick up in Delhi or wherever. She set the warm muffin in front of Gabe, who had drunk nearly all of his chocolate milk. While Caitlin refilled his tumbler, Lindsay wandered into the kitchen and fixed herself a bowl of Honey Nut Cheerios.

"We need to have a talk before you head off to school, kids," Caitlin announced, the phone to her ear. The hold music had switched to "Norwegian Wood."

"Oh, goodie," Lindsay muttered, sitting down at the counter with her brother.

The AOL operator finally picked up. She was perky with a southern accent. Caitlin went through the drill with her again: user name, mother's maiden name, first pet, and her query about the account.

It wasn't in use at the moment.

"Thank you!" Caitlin said. She quickly hung up and then switched on her laptop at the end of the counter. Typing furiously, she followed the instructions for changing her password to CHEERIOS829. August 29 was Lindsay's birthday.

"Are you going to give me the third degree about the bugle boy china figure again?" Lindsay asked. "I told you last night—"

"You did it," Gabe cut in, scowling at his sister. He had a chocolate milk mustache.

"You lying little weasel," Lindsay hissed. "Why don't you just 'fess up? It's not like—"

Caitlin shushed them. She confirmed her new password and then closed out of AOL. She would call the customer service number during her break at work and see if someone was still getting into her account. She switched off her laptop, then leaned on the counter and looked at her two children. "So—neither one of you broke the figurine on my dresser," she said.

Lindsay nodded at her brother. "Obviously he did, because it wasn't me."

"Liar!" Gabe argued.

"Please," Caitlin said. "We have about four minutes before you guys have to catch the bus. The point I'm making is—if neither one of you broke the figurine, it means someone else broke it, possibly an intruder. Maybe it was someone looking for jewelry, but nothing is missing. I keep thinking this has something to do with those notes I told you about . . ."

She took a swallow of coffee. "Now something else kind of weird happened. Practically a whole bottle of wine got drunk—or poured down the drain—yesterday. Do either one of you know what I'm talking about?"

Gabe shook his head.

"Don't look at me," Lindsay said. "I hate the taste of alcohol . . ."

"Is there a chance one of you might think I'm—I'm drinking too much and poured it down the drain?" Caitlin asked, wincing a little. After all, they had a drug addict for a father. Perhaps one of them was worried she'd become an alcoholic.

Gabe shook his head again.

Caitlin grabbed a napkin, reached over, and gently wiped off his chocolate milk mustache.

"Mom, what's going on?" Lindsay asked, squinting at her.

"I wish I knew." She sighed. "Someone got into my computer account. That's what I was doing just now, changing my password. Anyway, with all this going on, I think we need to take some precautions. You'll need to keep your eyes peeled and your phones charged."

She turned to her son. "Gabe, I don't like the idea of you being here in an otherwise empty house for two hours every afternoon. Until we figure this out, starting today, instead of coming home, I'd like you to get off the school bus when it stops near the ferry terminal. From there it's only a couple of blocks to the library. You can do your homework or draw there . . ."

He grimaced. "But, Mom, I want to work on my clubhouse . . ."

"It's just for a few days." She turned to Lindsay. "Gabe and I will pick you up after practice. Meanwhile, don't go wandering off by yourself at any time"—she turned to Gabe—"either of you. We just have to be careful for a while. Okay, promise me?"

A horn sounded outside.

Gabe jumped off the stool. "My bus!"

Grabbing his books and jacket, he ran to the front door.

Caitlin followed him to the doorway. "Don't forget to come to the library after school, honey!"

"I won't forget!" he yelled back as he hurried down the driveway.

Crossing her arms to keep warm, she watched him board the school bus. "You better get ready, Lind," she called into the house. "Your bus should be here any minute now . . ."

"I'm ready," she said, stepping into the front hallway. She threw on her sweater and grabbed her backpack from the banister newel post. "Mom, you know what we should do? We should have Dad come and stay with us for a while."

Caitlin started to shake her head. "Honey, I don't think that's such a good idea. I—"

"Fine," Lindsay said, cutting her off. She brushed past her in the doorway. She stepped down from the front stoop and then swiveled around. She had tears in her eyes. "Y'know, every night I email Dad, and every night he emails back, and he always asks how you're doing. He misses all of us. Why don't you give him another chance? If he were here staying with us, we probably wouldn't have any of these problems . . ."

The brakes on the bus hissed as it pulled to a stop at the end of the driveway. Lindsay glanced at it for a second and then turned back to scowl at her. "I happen to think it's a *great* idea!" she insisted. With that, she turned and ran toward the waiting bus.

Caitlin waited in the doorway until the bus pulled away.

With a sigh, she headed back inside and cleared off the counter. Sure, it would have been easier on everyone to have Russ staying with them—and easier for him to slide back into his old habits. She wanted to think they'd indeed get back together sometime, but not now. It was too soon—and too easy.

At the kitchen sink, she turned on the water and started to wash the dishes. Between changing her online password and warning the kids, she hoped she'd done enough to protect all of them. She debated about calling the police deputy. She could hear herself trying to explain about the broken china figurine and the missing wine: *well, no, nothing valuable was stolen and no, there was no sign of a break-in.* She could have told him about someone hacking into her AOL account. But even the AOL customer service representative had indicated that it wasn't exactly a freak occurrence. The cop would want to know if her credit cards had any erroneous charges. She'd have to tell him: *no, but someone was obviously following my activity online.*

As if that cop didn't already think she was a crackpot.

Caitlin told herself she was doing everything she could for now. She'd have to wait and see what happened next.

She prayed—whatever it was—it didn't happen to either of the kids.

She set Gabe's chocolate milk tumbler on the drying rack and turned off the water.

CHAPTER THIRTEEN

Thursday, October 27—10:08 A.M.

"I'm telling you, it's too risky," Monica whispered. "The coach is on his guard today. You're up against two people with guns. And I know you think you can grab Junior and hold on to him, but he's older and stronger than he looks . . ."

She and Aaron were treading water in the deep end of the pool. It was their "warm-up" time. They weren't supposed to be conversing, but the coach was busy consulting his clipboard—and he couldn't hear them over the boom box, which was playing the theme from *Hawaii Five-0*. Aaron recognized it because he and another bagger at Haggen Foods often played a Name That Tune guessing game to the music that was pumped through the store. The coworker was a fiftyish, balding guy named Milt. He knew the themes to old movies and TV shows really well—and Aaron was beginning to learn them, too. Milt was slightly simpleminded and always had a smile for everybody—even customers who treated him like crap. Aaron missed him right now. He never thought he'd miss working at the store, but he did.

He was so homesick and scared, his stomach ached. He couldn't imagine staying in this place for as long as Monica had. He couldn't imagine staying here another day.

He figured the coach must be statistic-happy because he loved consulting that clipboard, which had several pages attached to it. But he studied the clipboard only when both Aaron and Monica were in the pool. If either of them was on the deck, he rarely took his eyes off them. That was why Aaron needed Monica to distract the coach for a few moments—so he could ambush Junior while the dad wasn't looking.

The little shit was fidgety and restless today. He was dressed in shorts, a sweatshirt, and sneakers. He tapped his yardstick against everything within reach and kept getting up from his chair and walking around the pool. If Junior continued like this, Aaron would have a perfect opportunity to grab him and get him in a choke hold. And if he kept him at the right angle, neither the coach nor the Missus could fire their guns without endangering the kid.

"C'mon, I'm not asking you to do anything except fake a cramp and get their attention for a few seconds," Aaron whispered. "I'll do all the rest. It's no risk for you. The only other thing you'll have to do is pick up the guns after they throw them on the floor. Just keep your distance from the coach—"

"I don't want to do it," she said under her breath. "Chris tried something like this. He tried to surprise the coach and went for his gun. The coach beat him senseless. You should have seen the blood on the floor. It's a miracle none of it got in the pool. Two days later, Chris was gone. Please, for your own sake—"

"Let me worry about that," Aaron whispered. "Just listen for my coughing, and that's your cue to fake a cramp . . ."

With an exasperated sigh, she swam away.

Aaron glanced at Junior, standing at poolside by the shallow end, stirring one end of the yardstick in the water. The Missus was in the same plastic chair from yesterday, intent on her knitting. One side of her face looked slightly bruised once again. Aaron figured either she was accident prone—or the coach beat her. If she did have a gun in her knitting bag like Monica said, would she really use it on either of them? Maybe in a crunch, she'd use it on the coach instead. After all, if the son of a bitch knocked her around, why would she put up with it? She didn't seem to get a particular charge out of any of this, not the way the coach and Junior did.

The coach blew his shrill whistle and then turned down the music on the boom box, propped once again on one of the plastic chairs. "Okay, listen, you two," he announced.

Both Aaron and Monica stopped to look up at him. Aaron was still near the deep end. He grabbed hold of the drain ledge.

Strutting alongside the pool, the coach tapped the clipboard against his chubby thigh. "I hope you're both sufficiently warmed up because we're having a one-hundred breaststroke scrimmage in just a couple of minutes. You're racing for high stakes, chums—five days off your graduation date. Monica, you know what that means for you? You have fourteen days left. If you win this race, you'll be graduating from here in just seven days. Keep winning, and you'll be going home even sooner than that. Considering your competition, I'd say your chances of victory are quite good. We'll see just how *tired* Aaron is today." The coach stopped and frowned at him. "Wasn't that your excuse for losing yesterday?"

Aaron defiantly stared up at him and said nothing.

"All right, get out of the water and on your marks," the coach barked.

Aaron looked at Junior, wandering toward the far side of the pool—near the diving area. He had a stopwatch in his hand.

Aaron stole a glance at Monica. She peered back at him while climbing up the pool ladder. He wasn't sure if she'd actually help him with this escape attempt. They had a good chance—if they just worked together.

Once out of the water, she tugged at the beige one-piece suit that clung to her lithe body.

It was distracting. Aaron couldn't afford to gawk at her. If he got a hard-on, it wouldn't be easy to hide. He hoisted himself out of the water and then kept his hands over his crotch as he headed toward the diving area at the deep end. Junior was just around the corner from there with the stopwatch, but still too far away for Aaron to get to him.

"So—what'll be your excuse for losing today, Aaron?"

the coach asked, chiding him. "Do you enjoy losing to a girl? You even have an advantage because you're not weighed down with a suit."

"If a suit's a handicap, I'll take it," he shot back. He still wasn't completely used to being naked in front of these clothed people.

"You're going to need every advantage today, chum," the coach retorted. "If you lose this race, you might just lose your TV or fridge—or both. It all depends on how well you do and how much effort I see on your part . . ."

Before taking his mark, Aaron stole another glance at Junior, still too far away.

"You might be back down to your skivvies in a cold, empty cell," the coach growled, "if I don't see some improvement."

Aaron told himself that he was never going back into that cell. Still, he wanted to show this son of a bitch what he could do. He wanted to win. He'd do this one last thing before he got the hell out of there and ended this guy's "coaching" career.

Monica was already on her mark. Aaron stepped up on the block, got into position, and focused on the lane in front of him. He tried to tune out everything else—the kid and the Missus watching, the fact that he was naked, that he didn't even have any goggles, and that very soon he'd be risking his life to break out of this place.

He took several deep breaths, and all he saw was the bottom of the pool. He might as well have been at the one at his high school. It was the same size, the same shade of blue.

The high-pitched whistle sounded.

Pushing off, Aaron plunged into the water and propelled forward. He was a machine again—moving and kicking at high speed, breathing methodically, efficiently. His strokes were fast and precise. He never would have admitted it to anyone, but there was something about swimming naked that was so basic and liberating. How could it make him feel so vulnerable out of the water—and so powerful right now?

As he reached the other side of the pool and pushed off for the second lap, he sensed that Monica was trailing behind him by a couple of seconds. He pressed on, drove with his shoulders, and felt himself gaining speed. He was going to win this race. He might even come close to some of his best times.

He was pushing off for his third lap before Monica even reached the wall. He realized how much winning would mean to her—five days off her sentence in this perverted prison. But if he could just grab the kid and use him as a shield, everything would fall into place. They'd get the guns, and they'd throw the coach, the Missus, and Junior into one of the cells. Then they'd call the police. It didn't matter who won this race because they were both "graduating" today.

He was thinking about all this—when Monica inched past him in the next lane. She pushed off for the final lap before him.

Aaron realized he'd lost focus—and a few seconds. He felt so stupid. To make up for lost time, he pressed himself harder and harder. He started to catch up with her. They only had a few strokes left until the finish. He tried to muster up one last burst of speed. He had to reach that wall first.

His fingers scraped against the ledge, and he popped up with a splash. Right beside him, Monica was doing the same thing. Was it a tie? Catching his breath, Aaron stared up at the coach.

"It's Monica—by a tenth of a second," the coach declared. "I think you have a new record for yourself, girl." He glanced over at Junior with the stopwatch.

"Fifty-nine point twenty-eight seconds!" the kid announced.

The coach consulted his clipboard. "That's a personal best, Monica. And you just shaved five days off your graduation."

She let out a grateful cry and turned to Aaron. "I—I couldn't have done it if you—hadn't pushed me. You were so good." Still gasping for air, she put up her hand to high-five him.

Aaron worked up a smile and smacked her hand with his. "I'm going for it," he murmured.

"Wait," she whispered. She grabbed hold of the pool ledge.

"I think I—I know where I might have had a problem," Aaron called out, still breathing hard as he treaded water. His heart pounded furiously. "You were right yesterday about my entry and my breakout. I realize what I'm doing wrong . . ."

Junior shoved the stopwatch back into his pocket and picked up his yardstick. He started to tap it against the diving block.

Aaron pulled himself out of the water and onto the deck.

The coach backed up a few steps.

Aaron noticed Junior wander around the diving block. Now there was nothing but a couple of feet between them. One quick lunge and he'd have the kid in a choke hold.

"Let me show you what I think I did," Aaron said. He cleared his throat and moved toward the block.

The kid backed up a little.

Aaron coughed again. He furtively glanced down at Monica.

She was shaking her head. "Aaron, please, no . . ."

He coughed louder and took another step toward Junior.

"Aaron, don't—"

The coach blew his whistle.

The ear-piercing sound stopped Aaron in his tracks. He glanced over at the coach, who had his gun drawn. He looked at the Missus, who was standing up. She clutched a gun in her shaky hand as well. Aaron didn't understand. He hadn't even made a sudden move for their son yet.

They knew what he was going to do. Had Monica told them?

The kid swung the yardstick at him.

It happened so fast, Aaron didn't even have time to react. He didn't have time to cover his crotch.

The yardstick smacked against his penis and testicles. The pain was excruciating. Aaron fell to his knees and rolled over on the cold tile floor. He wanted to die.

"Good job, son," he heard the coach say.

He heard the kid grunt—like he was throwing a hardball.

Then Aaron felt the yardstick crack and break against the back of his head.

The last thing he heard before he passed out was Monica.

"Aaron, I'm sorry!" she cried. "I'm so sorry . . ."

CHAPTER FOURTEEN

Echo
Thursday, October 27—11:32 A.M.

She felt like a woman obsessed. This was the second time this morning—during a lull—that she had run out to the library's parking lot to make sure a note hadn't been left on her car windshield again. It was starting to drizzle, and was so dark that it looked closer to dusk than noon. From the lot, past the trees, she could see the harbor and the docked boats swaying in the choppy gray waters. It was like a postcard with all the trees and their autumn leaves—so beautiful and windswept.

There was no note on her windshield—and the car looked untouched.

"That's fine—for now," Caitlin murmured to herself.

Heading back toward the library, she pulled her phone from the pocket of her sweater. She found her real estate agent's number and automatically dialed it.

After one ring, it went to voice mail. "Hi, this is Sally Rutledge, and I'm sorry I missed you!" said her professionally perky recorded greeting. "But your call is important to me, so leave a message with the best number to reach you. Have a great day!"

Caitlin stopped at the library entrance, where Della had placed a couple of pumpkins and a slightly lop-sided stuffed burlap witch with a broom. Caitlin waited for the beep. "Hi, Sally, it's Caitlin Stoller. Could you call me as soon as possible? I'm still at 503-555-4159. I think there are some things you forgot to tell me about the house. Or maybe Dr. Goldsmith should have told you, and he didn't. Anyway, please give me a call so we can straighten this out. Thanks a lot."

Caitlin clicked off and shoved the phone back in her sweater pocket. Then she hurried back into the library. She joined Della behind the counter.

The head librarian was a stout, energetic woman with close-cropped silver hair and purple-rimmed cat-eye glasses that she managed to pull off with aplomb. Standing at the computer, she glanced at Caitlin. "Any fan mail?"

"No, thank God," Caitlin whispered. "Sorry to be so preoccupied with this."

"Please," Della said with a dismissive wave. "I don't blame you. I'd be concerned, too."

Caitlin started organizing a short stack of returns by category. "Right now, I just want it to go away."

"When they emailed you, what did they say exactly?"

"It had to do with the house. Apparently, a girl was murdered there back in 1992. Did you know?"

Della nodded. "I would have told you ahead of time if I'd known you were buying the house on Birch

Place. But once I realized you'd put your money down, there didn't seem to be any point in mentioning it."

"So—that Denise person was really killed in the house?" Caitlin asked.

Della sighed. "I'm afraid so."

"Did they ever find the killer?"

"No, and the family just fell apart after that." Della wiped a smudge from her glasses with the bottom front corner of her cardigan. "The Healys were a pretty prominent family in town. Ned Healy was on several civic committees, and he owned one of Echo's big attractions . . ."

"*Equestream*—or something like that, right?"

Della nodded again. She put her glasses back on. "*E-quest-stream*," she said, correcting Caitlin's pronunciation. "It was sort of like a country club—with horse stables, two tennis courts, a pool, and a good restaurant—best burgers in town, though they didn't serve alcohol. That drove a lot of people in town crazy. But Ned was inflexible. He pretty much had a monopoly here. There was no other place around like Equestream. Another thing, they were closed on Sundays," she raised a hand as if taking an oath, "because of the Sabbath, you know. There were some pretty hot summer Sundays when people wanting to go for a swim were—pardon my French—shit-out-of-luck. But Ned refused to budge with his rules . . ."

She leaned in close to Caitlin. She was already whispering but lowered her voice even more. "That man was such a pious pain in the neck. He yanked his children out of public school and homeschooled them so they'd get a *religious* education. Nothing wrong with that, but those poor kids ended up so isolated and friendless. Another thing, people got banned from Equestream—just for swearing on the premises. They wouldn't be allowed back for an entire year. He used to have one of his staff members hide outside the tennis courts—just waiting for someone to break his *no swearing* rule."

Della put a hand over her heart. "And don't get me started on how many books he wanted to ban from here."

"He sounds like a million laughs," Caitlin said.

Della glanced over her shoulder as someone walked into the library. Then she turned to Caitlin again. "I felt so sorry for his daughter. She used to come in here a lot—until Ned decided he didn't want her exposed to some of the books we have . . ."

"You mean smut like *To Kill a Mockingbird* and *The Catcher in the Rye*?"

Della nodded. "Exactly. Anyway, I remember her being so awkward and uncomfortable with people. I mean, how awful to have your father owning one of the most popular places in town—and practically everyone hating him. So when poor Denise was bludgeoned to death, the list of suspects in town was staggering. People didn't know if she'd surprised somebody trying to rob the house or if someone was getting even with Ned Healy by killing his daughter.

"I kind of think it was the latter, because Ned simply fell apart after that." Della slowly shook her head. "It ruined him. He didn't care about anything—and left Equestream in the hands of some terrible managers. He used to run that place like a battleship. I hear he had a very plush office and sleeping quarters there. People used to wonder, with all his money, why he didn't live in a palace. No reflection on that perfectly lovely house you're living in, but it's obvious Ned chose to live rather modestly with his family and go first class all the way with his quarters at Equestream. He spent most of his time there—minding the place down to the last detail. But these new managers let it slide. They spent and lost a small fortune on some sick horses. The stables got awfully seedy—with some shady characters working there. The restaurant went downhill. Even the pool stopped attracting crowds. Less than a year after the girl was killed, Ned ended up blowing his brains out—in his office. Not long after that, his widow drank herself to death. Denise's younger brother got shipped off to relatives in Montana."

"That's horrible," Caitlin murmured. And it didn't happen only to the Healys. She thought of the house's last occupants, the Goldsmiths—and what Lindsay's friend said about the house being cursed.

"You can read about it in the *Echo Announcements*," Della said. "They covered the murder and the follow-up investigations. They did a pretty good job, too—for a little local weekly. I miss the *Announcements*. Now all we have is the *Echo Bulletin,* which is pretty worthless."

Caitlin knew they had old issues of the *Echo Announcements* in the bound-periodicals section down in the basement—from 1972 through 2005, when the newspaper folded. "What happened to Equestream?" she asked.

"They tore down the place in the late nineties, leveled it. That's where they built the recreation center.

It's also the site for our new library." Della looked toward the door as another customer walked in. "Oh, jolly," she muttered.

It was Pierce Anthony's drippy girlfriend, heading over to the DVD section. She wore a trench coat that was rain-wet around the shoulders.

Caitlin immediately glanced at the tall windows on either side of the door. There on the front stoop, standing under an umbrella and holding his German shepherd by a leash, Pierce Anthony glared back at her through the glass.

The high school cafeteria had an entrance from outside—through a small corridor. Not too many people used it. But Lindsay discovered that the corridor was sort of a haven for displaced people to have their lunch—mostly grunge and Goth types, but also people like her who were new to school. A lot of them were eating alone—with their iPhones out as the perfect I'm-not-really-pathetic prop.

She ate Tater Tots with a Diet Coke while surfing Facebook to see what her old friends from Portland were up to. Every once in a while she glanced through the cafeteria doorway at the different girls from the swim team. Her teammates weren't particularly cliquish with each other. A lot of them were in separate packs—making it tough for Lindsay to merge into any one group at a table without an invitation. She still didn't have a good friend yet. And of course, as far as guys were concerned, she was totally invisible—at least, until last night.

A text notice came up on the phone. She saw it was from her mother and frowned a bit.

Just a reminder that I'll be by the rec center around 5:30. How are you doing?

Lindsay sighed and then responded:

K. See you at 5:30.

Another text notice came up. Lindsay rolled her eyes. She wished her mother would give her a break and leave her alone.

But then she saw the text was from Jeremy Dawson:

Hey, really sorry I'll miss u swimming this afternoon. I'd hoped to see u at the rec center, but something came up. Thought of u a lot today. Can u get away tonight? Maybe we can meet somewhere . . .

Lindsay typed her reply:

Sorry, my mother has me on lockdown.
Can I call you? Maybe we can Skype.

She smiled and typed back:

Sure, I'll be around. Sounds like fun.

He texted back:

☺

                          *   *   *

Caitlin scanned the barcode on the library card Pierce
Anthony's girlfriend gave her. The woman was about
thirty-five and thin—with shoulder-length blond hair
that looked like a dye job. The name that came up on
the computer was Kimberly Glotzer.

Kimberly was on her phone, ignoring her. She tossed
the DVD of *The Wolf of Wall Street* on the counter.

Caitlin was reading a note on the computer:

Notify her that *Inglourious Basterds* came back
badly scratched on 10/22. The disc was
inspected and in good condition when she
checked it out on 10/17. If this happens again,
she will have to pay for the disc. No excuses.

Caitlin imagined Myra typing this message and
cursing the whole time. And for some reason, Caitlin
thought of Ned Healy—and how outraged he'd be that
they carried R-rated movies at the library. The backs of
the cases for all the R-movies had an age-limit restric-
tion: *Available Only to Patrons 18 Years of Age and
Older. ID Required for Age Verification.*

Caitlin stared at Kimberly, still on the phone and
still ignoring her. Then she glanced over at the window
by the door and saw Pierce talking on his phone and
smirking back at her. *God, what a creep*, she thought.

Was he the one behind the notes and that email?

She turned to Kimberly, who had her hand out—
waiting for her card and the DVD. "Excuse me," Caitlin
said.

The woman shook her head and held up her index

finger as if to indicate that she couldn't talk for a minute.

Caitlin waited.

With the phone to her ear, Kimberly finally looked at her. "What?"

"There's a note on your account that when you returned *Inglourious Basterds* on Saturday, the disc was badly scratched," Caitlin explained.

"It was that way when we got it," Kimberly argued. "In fact, we couldn't watch it."

"Actually, the disc was inspected when you checked it out on Monday, and it was in fine condition. This has happened before. I need to advise you that if it happens again, you'll be charged for a replacement disc."

"Whatever," Kimberly muttered. Then she spoke into her phone. "Just a minute, okay?"

Caitlin showed her the disc she was checking out. "I'd like you to take a look at this for a minute, please. As you can see, it's in good condition, no scratches or cracks. Before we loan it out to you, I'd like to ask you to—"

"Just forget it," Kimberly interrupted. "I don't need it *that* bad." She snatched her library card off the counter, then turned and flounced out of the library.

"*Badly*," Caitlin said under her breath. She caught a glimpse of Kimberly stashing her phone in her trench coat pocket as she stepped outside. Pierce started talking to her. Then the door shut, and Caitlin couldn't see them anymore.

From the reference section nearby, Della wandered over to the counter.

Caitlin gave her a pinched smile. "I hate people."

"I saw the whole exchange," she said. "I couldn't have handled it better myself. Maybe she'll come to the brilliant conclusion that he's not worth all the trouble. Maybe that's the last we'll see of them both."

"I wouldn't count on it." Caitlin sighed.

"Listen, why don't you go to lunch a little early?" Della suggested. "You could use a break. I'll watch the front desk."

"Well, thanks," Caitlin nodded. "I'll take you up on that."

Lunch was a Special K bar from her purse and another trip out to the parking lot to check on her car. There was nothing on her windshield, and the Lexus looked unharmed. But as she turned around and headed back to the library, Caitlin noticed the burlap witch and one of the pumpkins had been knocked over. There was also a bag of dog crap beside the fallen witch.

"Asshole," Caitlin muttered. She threw the dog poop away in a garbage can at the edge of the lot. Then she went back and set up the pumpkin and witch—looking pretty dilapidated now.

Heading back inside the library, Caitlin shook off the rain and decided Pierce Anthony wasn't her stalker. He was just too obvious and belligerent. Her culprit was subtle and smart—and menacing. She would still consider Pierce Anthony a possibility, but once she had some other candidates, he'd be near the bottom of the list along with Ken Meekley.

She ducked into the bathroom and washed her hands. Then she went down to the basement.

Despite several overhead lights, the bound-periodicals room was dark and gloomy—with a concrete floor and plaster peeling off the walls. The place had a damp musty smell. Three rows of metal shelves held the dusty volumes. The emergency exit had an alarm attached to it—and a sign saying the door remained locked at all times. The doors to the furnace room, electrical room, and a storage room were also locked—with yellowing, faded STAFF ONLY signs on them.

Caitlin found the bound *Echo Announcements* on a shelf near the emergency exit. She knew they had two kick stools down here. Seeing one, she dragged it over to the spot. Its wheels squeaked the whole time. Dusting off the stool, she sat down, pulled her phone out of her purse, and found the number for AOL Customer Support. She dialed it, listened to the menu options, and pressed all the right buttons. They put her on hold.

While she listened to James Taylor's "Fire and Rain," Caitlin hoisted the thick volume for the *Echo Announcements*, July through December 1992, off the shelf. She found an issue dated July 9, 1992. On the cover was a black-and-white photo of what looked like a country club entrance—with a stone post and a sign attached to it. *Equestream Food & Recreation* the sign said in fancy script. A black wreath hung on the post—along with a printed sign: CLOSED DUE TO DEATH IN OUR FAMILY. In the background was a stone-façade building that must have been the restaurant—and a flagpole with the U.S. flag at half-mast.

The headline on the front cover said:

MURDER IN ECHO
POLICE MANHUNT FOR BRUTAL KILLER
Remembering Denise Healy

Caitlin wondered how long Equestream had been closed after the girl's death. How long were the townspeople forced to observe a mourning period for Denise Healy during that hot July before they could play tennis or go swimming and horseback riding again?

The story was on page two—and the *Echo Announcements* didn't spare the photographs. There was a head-and-shoulders snapshot of a smiling Denise with her hair wet. She was obviously in a swimsuit. She proudly held up a medal attached to a ribbon around her neck. Caitlin read the caption: "*Denise Healy won First Place (Teen Girls Division) in the annual swimming competition at Equestream last summer. Former classmates described her as 'shy and smart,' and 'always smiling.'*"

Caitlin stared at the photo of her house, looking a bit spiffier in 1992—with the trees not so full and all the hedges trimmed. An arrow on the photo pointed to what was now Lindsay's bedroom window—on the second floor, at the front, far left. "*Denise Healy died in her bedroom after multiple blows to the head with a hammer,*" the caption said. "*Her parents and brother had been at Equestream's July 4th fireworks show at the time of her death.*"

Caitlin examined the third photograph. "*Happier times for the Healy Family,*" the caption said. Dressed in their Sunday best, the men in suits and ties, and the women in dresses, the two children stood beside their parents, who were seated in front of a fireplace. "*Posing for their Christmas card: Ned and Phyllis Healy with Denise, 16, and Stuart, 11.*"

Caitlin frowned. Another coincidence—the Healy children were the same ages as Lindsay and Gabe.

"This is AOL Technical Support," a woman announced, breaking into the hold music. "Thank you for waiting. This is Erica. May I start with your name, please?"

"Oh, hi . . ." Caitlin gave the woman her name and her story about someone using her account.

It took a moment for Erica to check into it before giving her the good news that the account wasn't currently being used. The new password seemed to be working.

Caitlin thanked her and hung up. Slipping the phone back into her purse, she returned to the story on page two. The article pointed out that the police didn't see any sign of a break-in. Caitlin wondered if maybe back in 1992 the people of Echo didn't worry about locking their doors. But a sixteen-year-old girl alone in the house late at night—wouldn't she be a little cautious? Maybe she'd let in her attacker. Maybe it was someone she knew.

Caitlin couldn't believe her real estate agent hadn't known anything about this. She decided to call her again and reached into her purse.

But then she heard a tinny squeaking sound. She froze.

It lasted only a second—and came from another part of the basement. She realized it must have been the other kick stool. Someone had moved it—or bumped into it.

Caitlin glanced around. She didn't see anybody. She slowly got to her feet and set the heavy volume on top of the footstool. "Is anyone there?" she called nervously.

No answer.

In the rows of volumes on the metal shelves, there were sometimes a few gaps. Through the openings, Caitlin tried to peek into the next aisle—and the aisle after that. She didn't see anyone. Her heart was racing. She thought of that second note: *I'm watching you.*

She told herself that people upstairs would hear her if she screamed. Then it occurred to her: *If there are people upstairs, and I'm scared shitless, why the hell am I still down here?*

Caitlin started toward the stairs, and a shadow swept past her.

She stopped dead.

She heard a sudden clamor. Someone raced up the stairs.

Paralyzed, Caitlin didn't even get a glimpse of who it was. But the footsteps were heavy and hard. It didn't sound like a woman or a child.

She gathered her wits and hurried up the steps after whoever it was. Reaching the top of the stairs, she was out of breath. She glanced around and then went to check the aisles between bookcases. She didn't see anyone.

Della wasn't behind the front desk. Caitlin spotted her in the Grand Room, with the book pushcart. She was shelving some returns. A couple of regulars sat in the easy chairs, their noses in books. A young woman was hunched over her laptop at the long desk. Caitlin didn't spot any suspicious-looking characters. There was no sign of Ken. Had Pierce snuck in and then snuck out again?

She glanced up at the second-floor fiction section

and didn't notice anyone by the railing that overlooked the Grand Room.

She approached Della. "Did you see anybody come in or leave just now?"

Della shook her head. "No, but I haven't been at the desk in the last few minutes. We just got a bunch of new returns."

Caitlin kept glancing around. She was starting to get her breath back.

"Would you look at all these?" Della asked, nodding at the pushcart. "I just did a sweep check. I've said it once, and I'll say it again. These people who pull a book off the shelf and then leave it out someplace on a chair or wherever—they drive me crazy."

"Beats them putting it back on the shelf in the wrong place where no one can find it," Caitlin said. It was her standard comeback to Della's standard lament. She wondered if someone was hiding in one of the lavatories—or in the children's reading room.

"Are you back from lunch already?" Della asked.

"Almost," Caitlin said distractedly. "In about five minutes, okay?"

"Take your time," Della said, returning to her task. "It's not like we're swamped right now."

Caitlin checked the children's reading room. She saw a mother browsing with a toddler boy and a baby in a stroller. There was another woman on her iPhone, sitting by one of the big stuffed animals. Their part-timer, a pretty college-age girl named Chelsea, was seated at one of the small desks with two kids. She was reading to them but paused to glance at Caitlin and smile.

Caitlin nodded and smiled back. Everything looked so normal that she decided not to ask Chelsea if she'd seen anyone suspicious come through there. Instead she checked the bathrooms, knocking on the men's room door before poking her head in and softly calling out: "Anyone in here?" She even checked the stall. Empty.

She made a trip up to the second-floor fiction section and found a middle-aged woman who came in about twice a week. Caitlin still couldn't remember her name. She was glancing at a book and didn't seem to notice Caitlin. No one else was up there.

Heading back down to the desk, she remembered what Della had just said about people leaving books out on chairs. Caitlin realized she'd left the 1992 volume of the *Echo Announcements* on top of the kick stool in the basement.

With some trepidation, she paused at the top of the basement stairs. She took a deep breath and started down the steps. She didn't see anyone. Still, she called out in a shaky voice: "Hello?"

No response.

She hurried toward the emergency exit door, but then she saw the kick stool.

The thick volume wasn't on top of it. She was almost positive she'd left it there.

Caitlin inspected the shelf with the bound *Echo Announcements*. There were no gaps among the books. The volume marked JULY–DECEMBER 1992 was in its place among the others.

She figured she must have put it away after all.

But then she noticed a small slip of paper sticking out among the pages near the front of the volume. She took the big book off the shelf and opened it up. The paper was marking the page she'd been reading—about the murder of Denise Healy. There was writing on the little piece of paper.

All it said was:

Isn't this sad? ☹

Echo
Thursday—2:43 P.M.

The person inside Caitlin's house figured that Caitlin must have had her checkbook with her in her purse. It wasn't with the refill checks in the top drawer of her desk in the study. The first stack of refills started with check number 091. Check number 099 would be perfect. Caitlin wouldn't notice for a while that it was missing.

In the same drawer was an old address book—filled with names, addresses, and numbers—all in Caitlin's very neat handwriting. She would have missed those pages if they were torn out.

So the intruder photographed the pages—enough samples to learn Caitlin's penmanship and forge a letter.

For the signature, there was a copy of the Comcast contract she'd signed when she'd set up cable service to the house. Caitlin wouldn't miss it.

But the real jackpot was finding a box of stationery and envelopes—with her name along the top in a simple, yet stylish print. One thing about Caitlin, at least the woman had good taste. Three sheets of the stationery and two envelopes would be fine. It was just one letter that needed to be sent with the check. The extra stationery was in case of mistakes.

The kitchen was the next spot—just to see if the chocolate milk was still there on the refrigerator shelf. It was. Young Gabriel must have been thirsty this morning. The carton was almost empty. Caitlin had bought another carton still unopened. That was a small challenge, nothing a hypodermic needle couldn't fix. Once the syringe was filled with the solution, all it took was a jab in the top of the carton. After a little shake, the poison was mixed in there pretty well—and there was no evidence of a needle hole in the carton, not even a drip.

If the kid finished that carton of milk in a day, it would finish him. At one or two glasses every twenty-four hours, it would probably take a few more days until he was really sick—and maybe a week before he was dead.

Gabriel Stoller would join the ranks of several children who met their demise while living in this house. He'd be one of the Birch Place Angels.

Poor Caitlin, she was so worried about her problem-child daughter, she wouldn't see it coming.

Poor, stupid Caitlin.

CHAPTER FIFTEEN

A aron woke up feeling sick. His head ached, and he couldn't move.

He couldn't breathe right, either. Someone had slapped a piece of duct tape over his mouth. The tape seemed to be getting loose on one side because he was sweating.

It took him a moment to realize his hands were tied behind him, and his feet were bound together. There must have been a taut piece of rope between his ankles and wrists, because every time he tried to move his legs, he felt it tug at the restrictions around his wrists.

He was naked under a scratchy blanket. He'd been moved from his cell, he knew that much. He was in a car or a van—probably that silver minivan they'd used when they'd abducted him. He figured they'd set him on the same thin mattress in the back, too.

He could hear the coach humming to himself, but couldn't Name That Tune. The sound blended in with the whir of the tires on a highway. Aaron didn't hear any other cars around. The van hadn't stopped or slowed down—at least not in the last few minutes. An occasional pebble ricocheted against the bottom of the vehicle. He imagined them driving down a long, lonely highway. Was it night? The blanket covered his head, and he couldn't shake it off. He didn't see any cracks of light where the coverlet was askew.

Aaron wondered where they were. He wished the coach would stop his stupid humming and turn on the car radio. Then maybe a DJ would come in during a break and announce the city they were broadcasting from. Maybe he'd announce the time, too. Aaron didn't know how long he'd been unconscious.

The last thing he remembered was Junior swatting him in the groin with that damn yardstick. The pain had been so awful that Aaron had almost wanted to die. His lower torso still didn't feel right. He wondered if the kid had done some permanent damage. The little shit smacked him over the head with the yardstick, too. That explained the horrible headache.

The next thing Aaron knew, someone was bent over him, covering his nose and mouth with a damp cloth. They must have used the chloroform on him again. He imagined Junior dutifully helping his dad as they carried him upstairs—and then into a connecting garage where they could dump him in the back of this van without anyone seeing them. Or maybe the guy's house was somewhere out in the country where he didn't have to worry about neighbors seeing or hearing anything.

So his escape plan had been a bit half-baked, but he might have pulled it off—if only Monica had helped him out a little. He wondered if the coach had knocked more days off of her term until "graduation" for what she'd done. She'd ratted on a fellow prisoner. That had to be worth something.

Was that how it had happened with Chris Whalen? Had Monica informed on Chris, too?

And now the same thing was happening to him.

The exact same thing.

Aaron didn't know where he was—or what time it was. But he was almost certain of one thing: he wasn't going back to that cell—or the swimming pool.

The man behind the wheel was taking him somewhere to kill him.

It was his graduation day.

Echo
Thursday—8:13 P.M.

Lindsay put Taylor Swift on pause and pulled out one of her earbuds. "Come in!" she called. She was sitting on her beanbag chair, reading a paperback of *Crime and Punishment*, which may have been a classic, but as far as she was concerned, it was a major snooze-fest.

Her mother opened the bedroom door and poked her head in. "I thought you and Gabe were going to carve pumpkins together. He's almost finished with his. Aren't you coming down?"

Lindsay raised her book from her lap. "Homework," she said.

She was still kind of peeved with her mother and giving her the semi-silent treatment. All through the car ride home, at the supermarket, and during dinner, she could tell her mom was trying to draw her out and engage. She was asking her this and that, acting like nothing was wrong—like this morning had never happened.

If they really had a stalker, the sensible thing to do would be to have her dad come stay with them for a while. What idiot couldn't see the logic in that? Everyone deserved a second chance. Why wouldn't her mother give one to her dad?

She was still hanging in the doorway. "On the way to the store, when I asked if you wanted to carve pumpkins with your brother tonight, you said yes."

Lindsay twirled the earbud cord around her finger. "I was being nice." She sighed. "If you want to know the truth, I can't think of doing anything more dorky."

Her mother frowned. "And now you're *not* being nice."

"I'm sorry," Lindsay said with a roll of her eyes. "What? Am I supposed to forget all about my homework so I can carve a jack-o'-lantern? It'll only get smashed to pieces in a couple of nights . . ."

"Fine," her mother muttered. "I just wish you'd have told me how you really felt before I spent ten dollars on a pumpkin for you."

"All right, I'll carve the stupid thing," she said, exasperated. "I just can't do it now, okay? I really have to read this . . ."

The truth was—Jeremy was supposed to call tonight, and she didn't want her mother anywhere around when that happened.

But she was still lingering in the doorway. She glanced around the room—as if taking it in for the first time. She crossed her arms in front of her. "Actually, I need to talk to you about something . . ."

Lindsay plucked out the other earbud, set the book on her lap, and gazed at her mother. "What?"

"I didn't want to say anything in front of Gabe, but I got another weird note today—at work. Someone was obviously watching me there. I know you think the answer to this is having Dad move in with us for a while. Believe me, I'd like that, too, but it's not a viable option. I'm thinking of you guys, and I'm thinking of your dad—and where he is in his recovery right now—"

"What did the note say?"

Her mother didn't answer. She glanced around the room again—and then at her. "That doesn't matter. But until this blows over—for a while anyway—I think you'll be better off staying in the guest room. In fact, maybe you could make it your bedroom."

Lindsay's eyes narrowed at her. "What?"

"This bedroom is so isolated. You're way down the hall from your brother and me—"

"That's exactly why I like it here."

"You can't like it that much," her mother argued. "You always end up sleeping somewhere else. Listen, you can do whatever you want to make that other room your own, put your personal stamp on it. And I'd feel a lot better if—well, if we're all closer together . . ."

Lindsay could tell that wasn't the real reason for this bedroom switch. It was something else. "Why are you doing this?" she asked. "I'm not going to have any privacy at all. If you really want us all close together to keep us safe, why does Gabe get to have his own little clubhouse way down in that basement closet? You want me in the room right next to you. Is this how you plan to keep an eye on me? Is this because I went to visit Dad the other day? Am I being punished?"

Her mother shook her head. "No, honey. I just don't want you in this room. It's only for a while . . ."

"If it's only for a while, why are you telling me that I can redecorate the guest room and make it mine?"

"Because I want you kids close to me!" she shot back, tears in her eyes. "I'm worried. Don't you get that? I'm really scared, Lindsay. This—this creep has me totally unnerved. Can you just cut me a break and bunk in the guest room for the next few days?"

Lindsay stared at her for a moment, and then she shrugged. "Fine," she said. "God, if you're trying to freak me out, it's working. When do you want me to make this switch?"

"I'll put some clean sheets on the guest room beds for you," her mother said, a little calmer. "Why don't you try sleeping in there tonight? Over the weekend, maybe we can start moving some of your things there."

Lindsay opened her mouth to say something but hesitated. Her mother wasn't making any sense. What did she suddenly have against this bedroom? One minute she was saying this switch was only temporary, and the next she was talking about moving her things into the guest room and putting her personal stamp on the place.

She nodded warily. "Sure, whatever you say."

"Thanks," her mother replied. She glanced around the room—as if reassessing the place one more time.

Then she stepped out to the hallway and closed the door behind her.

Lindsay listened to her retreat down the stairs. She thought for a moment, and then decided to call her father instead of texting him. She really wanted to hear his voice right now.

On her phone, she clicked on his name. It rang three times and went to his voice mail. She sighed and then waited for the beep. "Hi, Dad, it's me," she said in a quiet voice. "I think Mom has officially lost her mind. Actually, it's kind of serious. She has some stalker—probably some local who haunts the library. Anyway, she's a nervous wreck, and she's driving me crazy. I think if you were here, staying with us, it would really help. She doesn't want to ask you. But you should convince her. There's plenty of room—and Gabe and I would love it. Please, talk to her, Dad. Okay? I miss you."

She clicked off.

Russ Stoller felt his phone vibrate.

They had a rule at the Capitol Hill chapter of the Substance Abuse Recovery Alliance. All cell phones needed to be shut off during their meetings in the basement of St. Joseph's Church. About thirty people were at this particular session. And so far, five SARA members had gotten up to address the group. Russ had cringed when Brent had strutted up to the podium to speak. The guy was about forty-five, short, fairly good-looking, a bit overweight, and rich. Yes, anyone who heard him talk just once knew that he had gobs of money. The former cokehead's talks had practically nothing to do with abstaining from drugs and everything to do with the woes of the disgustingly wealthy.

Last week, they'd all heard about the problems Brent had encountered with the people installing his forty-thousand-dollar granite countertops. Two weeks before that, everyone heard how his Cayman Island vacation was ruined by bad service at the four-star hotel. Today's topic was how the auto repair shop detailing his Porsche was screwing him over. Russ asked his sponsor, Paul, if they really had to sit still for this drivel. He was told that everyone's problems were significant and it was all a matter of perspective. But in private he and Paul referred to Brent as Mr. Grey Poupon. He'd been up there at the podium for about ten minutes now.

Shifting restlessly in the folding chair, Russ furtively slipped his phone out of his coat pocket and stole a glance at it. Lindsay had just called. His daughter phoned, texted, or emailed him once a day. Russ was pretty sure she knew how important that made him feel. He'd check her message and call her back during the break.

As he slipped the phone back in his pocket, Russ glanced around to make sure no one was looking. A few seats away, an attractive redhead glared at him. *Busted*, he thought.

But then she broke into a grin and rolled her eyes in Grey Poupon's direction.

Russ smiled back and gave a little nod.

Grey Poupon finally wrapped up, and their group leader announced it was time for a break. Half the group started toward the back of the room, where they had coffee and cookies. The other half headed out the side exit to smoke. That was where Russ went to return Lindsay's call.

It was starting to drizzle again—and chilly enough for him to see his breath. He stepped away from the veil of smoke wafting from his fellow SARA members and reached for his phone.

"Well, that was inspiring, wasn't it?"

He turned and saw the redhead smiling at him. Russ chuckled. "Yes, those earthquake victims in Central America have it easy compared to Brent."

She laughed and put her hand on his arm. "Oh, God, can I please sit next to you during the next half of the meeting? This is my second time here. Everyone is so serious. Not that this isn't serious business for everybody. But that doesn't mean you have to check your sense of humor at the church door, does it?"

"Stick around," Russ advised. "It's a pretty good group. It can get fun."

"I didn't see you talk last week," she said. "Are you getting up there tonight?"

He shrugged. "I don't think I'm quite ready yet."

"Neither am I," she said. "I'm a former coke-user, clean eight weeks now. I'm hoping to stay straight and sober so I can get my husband back—along with my seven-year-old daughter."

"Heroin," Russ said, tapping a finger against his own chest.

"Wow," she murmured.

"Yes, well, I feel if you're going to screw up your life, why go about it half-assed?"

She laughed—and touched his arm again.

"I've been clean eighteen days," he admitted. "And I'm hoping to make myself worthy again for my ex-wife and two kids."

She offered her hand to shake. "Well, put 'r there, pal."

He pumped her hand. "In answer to your question earlier, I'd love it if you sat next to me. My name's Russ."

She nodded. "I'm Bobby."

Echo
Thursday—9:55 P.M.

When her phone chimed out a text notice, Lindsay thought it was her dad finally getting back to her. But then she looked at the screen and saw the text was from Jeremy.

Do u still want to Skype?

Sure.

Lets do it on r laptops. I want to see u on a bigger screen.

She laughed.

K. Give me a few minutes. My laptop's downstairs . . .

Lindsay typed her email address and then clicked off. It was a lie about her laptop. She'd had it on her desk for the past hour, ready for this Skype session.

She'd even tidied up her room a little. But she needed to check her hair and lipstick. After all, this was like a first date. She couldn't help being nervous. The black long-sleeve T-shirt she wore was hardly sexy, but it was fine. He'd already seen her in a swimsuit. And if she were too made-up or too dressy, she'd come across as desperate.

By the time they had their Skype session set up, Lindsay had brushed her hair, applied some mascara, and used some CoverGirl foundation to camouflage a zit on her forehead. She was sitting at her desk.

Jeremy looked like he was at his desk, too. Lindsay was relieved to see he was real—and not part of a fake Facebook account set up by some middle-aged pervert. He looked as cute as his photos, too. He wore a baseball cap backward (an affectation that drove her mother crazy), jeans, and a blue shirt that was unbuttoned down past his chest. Behind him, the bed wasn't made and clothes were scattered around. She imagined telling her Portland friends: "Oh, my new boyfriend is such a slob!"

She was pretty sure that thing on his nightstand in the background was a bong. Should she ask him about it? Did his parents know—and just not care? Marijuana was legal in Washington State, but still.

"Hey," he said, leaning back in his chair and clasping his hands behind his head. "You're looking good. I usually see you wet. Now I know, wet or dry, you look really nice."

"Well, thanks," she said. It felt so awkward. She'd never had a date with a guy before in which—first thing—she was in his bedroom with him. She glanced over her shoulder for a second at the closed door, and then she looked at him. "Can you hear me okay?" she asked. "I need to keep my voice down. I don't want my mother to hear us."

He nodded. "The old lady's on the warpath, huh?"

Lindsay shrugged. "She drives me crazy most of the time, but actually she's not so bad."

"Well, you're lucky. My mother's a total bitch. Don't even get me started. I think it seems even worse with all my friends away at college. I don't have a—a—"

"Distraction . . . an outlet?" she offered.

"Both, yeah, exactly." He smiled. "That's why it felt so great texting with you last night—that and the fact that you're so nice."

"You don't know me that well yet," she replied, blushing. "But thanks."

"No, I can tell—you're smart and nice, and you're not a phony. Did you have a boyfriend in Portland?"

She liked that he remembered where she was from. "Not really, nobody steady."

"Hey, want to go to bed with me?"

She gaped at him and laughed. "What?"

He took off his hat and threw it over his shoulder. "I have to meet with this teacher at the community college at seven fifteen tomorrow, which means I need to catch, like, the first ferry out of here in the morning. So I need to hit the sheets early. Anyway, mind if I get ready for bed while we talk?" He adjusted the camera on his laptop and then stood up.

"Ah, no, I don't mind," she said.

He unbuttoned his shirt and draped it over the desk chair. "I'm mostly a night owl," he said, his voice a little muffled as he stepped farther away from the laptop mic. "I really hate having to go to bed early. Talk about a drag. Do you have to go to bed super early when you have one of your swim meets?"

Lindsay had been to enough boys' swim meets that she should have been used to seeing guys with their shirts off. But this guy was shirtless in his bedroom, and it was different. She was nervous but kind of excited, too.

She squirmed in her desk chair and nodded. "Yeah, most of the time it's lights-out by eleven if there's a morning competition like this Saturday. But it's really . . ." She trailed off and stopped talking as he unzipped his jeans. He stepped out of them and nonchalantly kicked them across the floor. He was wearing gray briefs.

"Sorry this place is such a mess. I should have cleaned up earlier . . ." He picked up a towel and a T-shirt from the unmade bed and tossed them on the floor. Then he approached the camera again, completely blocking it for a few moments as he moved it. He must have placed the laptop on a chair—because the screen was level with his mattress now. "That's better," he said. Reclining across the width of the bed, he rested on one elbow.

"Well, I'm probably keeping you up," she said. "I should go."

"No, don't go," he said, casually scratching his bare chest. "I'm not sure I can wait until Saturday night . . ."

"God, about Saturday," Lindsay said. "I'm not sure if we can get together. My little brother and I are supposed to spend the night in Seattle at my dad's."

"What about Sunday afternoon? My folks aren't

getting back until late. We'll still have the house all to ourselves."

"Well, I think we'll be back by four. I can make up some story for my mom why I have to go out," she said nervously.

"Great. But Sunday's so far away. Can't I see you tomorrow? Just ditch practice . . ."

She laughed. "The day before a meet? Are you kidding me?"

"What about after practice?"

"My mother's picking me up," Lindsay said.

"Boy, when you said that she had you on lockdown, you weren't kidding."

"She's just worried," Lindsay explained. "It's because all those high school swimmers are missing. Have you heard about that?"

"Yeah, it's pretty creepy."

"After swim practice, the girls who don't have rides are supposed to go home in twos or in groups." She worked up a smile. "Hey, so how do I know when we finally meet up, you won't kidnap me or something?"

"Hey, I'm unarmed." He chuckled. He gave the elastic top of his briefs a tug and let them snap back in place. "Ha, only one concealed weapon here. So can you get away during lunch tomorrow?"

"Maybe," she said. She didn't think anyone in the hallway outside the cafeteria would miss her.

"Let's meet someplace near the high school. I'll text you in the morning, okay?"

She nodded. "Cool. Well, I should let you go to sleep . . ."

"Wait," he said. Then he rolled onto his stomach

and pulled down his briefs. For a second, Lindsay saw his penis before he was flat on his stomach again. He was coy about it—but he was still naked. He threw the briefs in the direction of the screen.

Lindsay laughed. She was so taken aback. She kept wondering what her mother would think if she walked in right now. At the same time, it was so daring and fun.

"All right," he said with a cute, wicked grin. "Before you go, you've got to give me something back."

"What are you talking about?" she asked, a bit breathless.

"It's your turn. You have to take off something. I'm lying here totally bare assed."

"Hey, I didn't ask you to get naked," she whispered. She peeked over her shoulder at the door again.

"C'mon, please?" he asked. He shifted his butt from side to side. "Take off your top—just for a second. Give me a thrill—something to last me through the night until I see you tomorrow."

"Forget it." She laughed. But the thought of reciprocating with a little peep show intrigued her. She didn't have her bra on under the black tee. She could flash him.

"Please?" he said. Then he started to whine and whimper—like a puppy dog begging for a treat.

Lindsay pushed back her chair a little, and then she quickly lifted up her tee to show him her breasts.

"Wow, nice!" he said.

Just as quickly, she pulled down the front of the T-shirt. "That's all you get." She knew her face was red, and she felt a little silly. But it was exciting, too.

"Whew, I'm never going to get to sleep now," he said with a chuckle.

"Well, you're just going to have to, because . . ." Lindsay fell silent at the sound of someone coming up the stairs. "Shit, I think I hear my mother," she whispered. "Text me tomorrow, okay?"

Lindsay didn't wait for an answer. She reached over and clicked out of the Skype session. The image on her screen—of a naked young man lying facedown on an unmade bed—was replaced by the Google Chrome home page and a news photo of Vladimir Putin looking angry.

There was a knock on her door.

"Yeah?" she called, her heart racing.

Her mother opened the door and peeked inside at her. "Who were you talking to in here?"

"Roseann," she lied. "We were Skyping."

"It sounded like a boy," her mother said—with a puzzled half smile.

"She has a cold."

Her mother seemed to buy it. "Well, I put clean sheets on both twin beds in the guest room earlier."

Lindsay nodded. "Okay, thanks."

Her mother ducked back into the hallway and closed the door.

Lindsay turned and looked at the laptop screen. Then she touched the front of her T-shirt. Her heart was still pounding. She realized she hardly knew that guy. She wasn't even sure she liked him.

"What the hell did I just do?" she murmured to herself.

* * *

Caitlin headed downstairs.

She figured she'd wait until Lindsay got more comfortable in the guest room, and then she'd tell her where Denise Healy was killed. If she told her now, her daughter would probably freak out—and justifiably so. Caitlin couldn't look inside that room now without wondering where the poor girl's body had been lying. Was there blood on the walls? Caitlin imagined people from all over the island in the summer of 1992, driving down Birch Place for a glimpse at that bedroom window.

It was odd that Lindsay seemed to have forgotten there had been a murder in this house—especially odd since she was the one who had found out about it. Caitlin didn't have a Facebook account, but occasionally she used Lindsay's password to browse around. She'd noticed earlier today that Lindsay had posted something about the murder. It only got a few "likes." Had her daughter stopped thinking about the murder because it didn't seem important to any of her friends on Facebook?

On the plus side, at least Lindsay didn't give her another argument about switching rooms when she'd mentioned changing the guest room bedsheets for her.

Caitlin passed Gabe's jack-o'-lantern at the end of the kitchen counter. It had a crooked smile and a tea light inside it. Lindsay's untouched pumpkin sat beside it. She saw the open basement door, and the lights were on. She called down: "Gabe! Bedtime in ten minutes!"

No response.

Sighing, Caitlin started down the basement stairs. If he was going to make this remote little closet his new

hibernating haven, she'd have to invest in a bullhorn—
or maybe they could work out a signal where she tapped
on one of the steps or something. She passed through
the recreation room and into the large utility room.
"Gabe? Honey, can you hear me?"

He had the radio on.

She checked the basement door to make sure it was
locked and the chain was in place. Passing the workbench, she couldn't help looking at that outline of the
hammer on the tool wall. She shuddered and rubbed
her arms to fight the gooseflesh.

Gabe had closed the door to his little clubhouse—to
isolate himself even more. Caitlin knocked and then
opened it. He was sitting at his desk, drawing. The
walls were covered with his artwork. He'd put a three-
way plug in one of the outlets—for a desk light, the
radio, and his lava lamp. A swirly patterned bathroom
rug she wasn't using covered part of the linoleum
cutout on the floor. The place actually looked cozy.
The little plastic canister of Renuzit they'd bought at
the store earlier tonight managed to camouflage the
dank smell.

"Well, I like what you've done with the place," she
said, folding her arms. "That's a neat maze you're
drawing, too."

Gabe turned down his radio and smiled up at her.
"Thanks, Mom."

On the corner of his desk he had a napkin covered
with Chips Ahoy! crumbs and his *Simpsons* tumbler
with half a sip of chocolate milk left. Caitlin carefully
collected them. "I'm not sure about eating down here,
honey. The crumbs might attract mice."

"I'll do the Dustbuster in here every day," he promised.

She mussed his hair a little. "We'll see. Anyway, wrap it up, Rembrandt. Bedtime is in ten minutes."

Caitlin made it a point not to look again at the tool pegboard with the outline for the hammer as she walked back to the recreation room. Heading up the stairs, she stopped on a middle step and tapped out "Shave and a Haircut," with her foot. She waited.

Gabe knocked back—twice for "Two Bits."

With a smile, Caitlin continued on up to the kitchen. She threw away the napkin and washed out his Simpsons tumbler for the morning.

"Oh, my goodness, I had no idea," Sally Rutledge claimed.

Caitlin's real estate agent hadn't bothered to call back. Caitlin figured the woman was avoiding her. A follow-up call at 10:15 at night was borderline rude, but Caitlin was getting more and more angry that Sally had sold her this house without telling her a damn thing about its grim history. Wasn't she legally—or at least ethically—obligated to inform a client if someone had been murdered in a house?

Gabe had just gone up to bed, and Lindsay was reading *Crime and Punishment* in her room. Caitlin figured neither one of them would hear her in the kitchen, giving their real estate agent a piece of her mind.

"Caitlin, I swear if I'd known something like that happened in the house, I would have told you," she went on. "And not to sound crass, but I'd have at least gotten Dr. Goldsmith to lower the price for you some more."

"That's another thing," Caitlin said. "When you told me that Mrs. Goldsmith killed herself, you made it sound like she wasn't living in the house at the time, but she was."

"Well, I'm sorry you got that impression, Caitlin," she said coolly. "I'm not sure what difference it makes—or what you expect me to do about it now."

"The difference it makes is that I had to find out from my daughter—through someone at her school— that the last occupant of this house killed herself. And twenty years ago, a girl was brutally murdered—bludgeoned to death—in the upstairs bedroom where my daughter now sleeps . . ." *Or rather doesn't sleep*, she thought. Maybe that was why poor Lindsay always ended up nodding off somewhere else every night. The room was probably haunted.

"I can't believe the Goldsmiths lived here for as long as they did and had no idea about Denise Healy's murder," Caitlin pointed out.

"I'm sorry, Caitlin," Sally replied. "But we closed the deal seven weeks ago. At the risk of repeating myself, once again, I don't know what you expect me to do about it."

"Well, that's just it. What can you do about it? What are my options here? Because I feel—swindled. Considering the history of this house, I really don't know if I want to stay on here with my family. I mean, do you think I'm being unreasonable, Sally? If you think so, perhaps you'd like to come over and spend the night here alone, maybe sleep in my daughter's room—just one night, that's all."

"I—I understand completely," Sally said. "As I said, I had no idea about this murder in 1992. Maybe Dr. Goldsmith knew, maybe he didn't. I do know that you got a very good price for the house . . ."

"Well, do you have a contact number for Dr. Goldsmith?" Caitlin asked. "I'd like to talk to him."

She heard a sigh on the other end of the line. "All right, just a sec . . ."

Caitlin waited. She realized it wasn't entirely the real estate agent's fault that she ended up with this *cursed* house. Wasn't that what Lindsay's classmate called it? *Cursed*? Caitlin knew she was just venting right now. The real culprit was this Dr. Goldsmith, who should have been more open about the house's history. After only a few weeks in the house, she'd found out about Denise Healy's murder. Goldsmith must have known about it when he unloaded this place on her. So—what was she going to do—call him up and scream at him? He'd had a rough time while in this house—a child dying, a marriage crumbling. She knew what that was like. And then his wife committed suicide. No wonder the poor guy was anxious to move out of the place.

If she were looking for a settlement or compensation or something, yelling at Goldsmith wouldn't do any good. She'd have to contact a lawyer. Caitlin imagined the attorney looking over all the contracts and telling her there was nothing they could do. A lawyer would probably recommend she sell the place— and not tell any potential buyers about the 1992 murder.

"Caitlin, are you still there?" Sally asked on the other end. She gave her Dr. Goldsmith's phone number and email address.

Caitlin jotted them down.

"Listen, I really sympathize," Sally said. "It might sound a little hokey, but I know some people in your situation, and what they do is they have a house blessing or they'll burn some sage or . . ."

"Or nail a horseshoe above the front door?" Caitlin interjected. "I'll take that under advisement. Thanks, Sally."

She clicked off.

She decided she needed a glass of wine—if her last bottle hadn't magically disappeared.

Caitlin was heading for the cupboard when the phone rang again. She automatically assumed it was Sally calling back—with another suggestion about "smudging" the house or sprinkling it with holy water or something. Then again, maybe she just didn't like being hung up on.

But when Caitlin went to grab the phone, she saw it was Russ.

"No," she said resolutely. She set the phone back down on the counter. She was better off with a glass of wine. She let it go to voice mail.

He hung up without leaving a message.

She went back to the cupboard and poured herself a glass of merlot. She took one sip, and just then, she spotted someone—or something—darting past her big kitchen window, the one over the sink.

Caitlin gasped and dropped her wineglass. It crashed onto the laminated wood floor, spreading wine and shards of glass halfway across the room.

She'd barely gotten a glimpse of whoever—or what-ever—it was. It was a tall, dark figure, close to the win-dow. But she couldn't see it now. All she saw was her scared reflection and Gabe's glowing jack-o'-lantern in the darkened glass.

Hurrying over to the kitchen door, she switched on the outside light. The backyard was just a small patch of lawn before trees, shrubs, and woods took over. She didn't see anyone out there amid the shadows. There were a few trees gently swaying and some leaves drift-ing across the grass, but nothing else.

Caitlin wondered if she'd merely caught a glimpse of her own reflection. Was she really that on edge? *You're scared of your own shadow.*

Her heart was still fluttering as she reached up and lowered the mini-blinds. On each side of the large win-dow, there was a tiny, square accent window with a lit-tle stained-glass crest in the center of it. But those windows didn't have any shades.

Gabe had left the door open down to the basement. Caitlin closed and locked it. She grimaced at the mess on the floor and then started toward the broom closet.

The phone rang again.

She sighed. "Come on, Russ, please . . ." Still, she snatched her phone off the counter and clicked it on. "All right, what is it?" she asked.

There was a pause. Suddenly, she realized it might not be Russ.

"I can still see you, Caitlin," someone whispered in a gravelly voice.

Then there was a click on the other end.

* * *

"If you think of anything else, call this number," the policewoman said, handing Caitlin a business card. She looked like Jennifer Lawrence. She wore a bulky police jacket and had her dark blond hair in a ponytail.

For a while, both Lindsay and Gabe were spellbound to have a couple of cops in the house, answering a 9-1-1 call. The kids had gone from window to window while the J. Law look-alike and a second officer—a stocky, fiftyish man—had searched the front, side, and back yards with their flashlights. They'd watched the beams swirling around in the darkness. But Lindsay had seemed to grow bored and had gone back up to the guest room about fifteen minutes ago—around the same time the second cop left in his patrol car. Gabe, however, was still fascinated by the whole episode—and by the pretty officer. He sat in the middle of the stairs, in sweatpants and a T-shirt, watching Caitlin and the policewoman in the front hallway.

"Your new case number is on that card," said the cop.

"What if this person comes back?" Caitlin asked.

"Don't hesitate to call nine-one-one," the woman answered. "But I'm pretty sure we've scared him away, whoever it was. We'll put an extra patrol on the block tonight. I don't think he'll come back. In the past, this guy never did any window-peeping two nights in a row . . ."

"Pardon me?" Caitlin stared at her. "You mean, you have a regular Peeping Tom in the neighborhood?"

The pretty cop looked stumped for a moment. "Ah, no, I'm talking about this house," she said. "There were incidents like this with the previous owner. They changed the locks on the doors and windows, and added a couple of lights outside at the end of the driveway. That seemed to take care of it for a while. But I'd recommend more lights—and maybe a surveillance camera."

"Let me get this straight," Caitlin said. "You mean this same thing happened here before—to the Goldsmiths?"

"Well, yes, we were called here on a few occasions," the cop explained. "But we never found any sign of a break-in or even an attempted break-in. As I said, some more lights and security cameras might be your best bet for thwarting any prowlers. Deputy Dana is handling your case. He'll get a full report on this—and the other recent incidents. You'll be hearing from him if he gets any leads . . ."

Caitlin just kept staring at her.

All she could think about was Dr. Goldsmith—and how relieved he must have been to unload this house on some unsuspecting poor fool.

She'd gotten more than she'd bargained for when purchasing this house seven weeks ago. The place had come with its own dark history—and its own stalker.

Friday, October 28—1:35 A.M.

Another milestone! Caitlin's first 9-1-1 call & police visit to the house. (If you want to get technical, her trip to the police station the other morning was the actual first contact with the authorities, but the cops actually coming to the house with lights-a-flashing—that's really something!)

I had a feeling Caitlin spotted me outside from her kitchen window. But what could she tell the police? Someone in dark clothes and a black ski mask was in her backyard. I can hear her trying to convince them it was the same trespasser who drank her wine & broke her little trumpet boy figurine. Forget the Echo Police! This is something for the FBI! They must have had a hard time trying not to laugh in her face.

Another busy, busy day. Winding down, I once again watched the Skype session with lovely Lindsay flashing her pert titties. It was perfect.

Stupid girl.

It's strange, but I've been in that bedroom several times since they moved in, but I've always been so focused on finding what I need & mindful of the time I have to poke around. There's never a minute to reflect while I'm actually there. It took watching the Skype session a second time tonight for me to feel transported in time. Seeing those swimming trophies and certificates on her bookshelf made it seem like July 4th, 1992, all over again—my first time in that bedroom. I could almost smell Denise Healy's cheap lavender perfume.

I remember Denise looking down at me with the light behind her. Her rather plain face was swallowed up in the shadows. She kept dabbing her nose because she had a cold. We were whispering, which wasn't really necessary since no one was home. The others had gone to watch the fireworks at Equestream. She was telling me about her swimming trophies and medals. They weren't just from Equestream. She claimed to have won a whole bunch of awards from school competitions before she and Stuart got yanked out of public school for Ned's homeschooling.

"I'd really love to see them," I whispered to Denise, smiling up at her. "Won't you let me come up to your bedroom and take a look? I promise I won't stay long . . ."

It took a little persuading. I had to keep telling her that no one would ever know I'd been up in her bedroom. We had plenty of time. Her family wasn't coming back for at least another hour or two. It would be our secret.

"If I let you come up, you have to swear you won't try anything funny," Denise said.

I crossed my heart for her.

She finally gave in.

Another stupid girl.

I didn't have any shoes on & my feet were filthy. I told her I didn't want to track any dirt around the house, so she gave me some clean socks from the dryer.

I remember thinking she might spot her father's hammer in my hand as we passed through the kitchen. So I tucked it between the back waistband of my jeans & my spine. I'd requested a house tour & Denise was all too pleased to show me the place. She kept bragging about how much their "state of the art" entertainment system cost & how old this or that antique was. Maybe she thought I'd like her more if I knew how rich her family was. I noticed she'd pulled down all the shades & closed all the curtains in the front of the house. She explained that she didn't want people seeing me in the house.

She made everything so easy for me.

Denise walked up the front stairs ahead of me. I noticed what seemed like a deliberate wiggle in her navy blue short-shorts. She had a nice little body. The shorts, along with her red & white striped tee, must have been her July 4th outfit. She was wearing flip-flops, too, and I remember listening to them slap against her heels as we headed down the hallway to her room.

"My parents and Stuart's rooms are back there," she said, with a dismissive wave at the rooms behind us. I supposed I'd pumped her up into thinking her bedroom was some wonderful attraction, the crown jewel of her Healy House Tour.

There were pictures of horses on the walls, a canopy bed, & lots of pink. She had a mix tape playing on her boom box, a Michael Jackson song I'd never heard before, "Black or White."

"It came out about five months ago," she told me. "You don't know this song at all? Don't you listen to the radio?"

"I told you, I get horrible reception," I said. "That transistor only picks up one station—from Everett, and all they play are oldies." I heard "Louie, Louie" about five times a day. I remember Denise giving me that radio, and being quite touched. She really did have a good heart. She was just weak & stupid.

Denise showed me her bookshelves full of swimming and equestrian awards. I acted impressed. There was a marksman certificate up there on the shelf, too. She kept a gun in her nightstand drawer. She'd told me about it in one of our furtive, whispered conversations. She said every member of the family had a gun.

She started talking about the Olympics in Barcelona in a couple of weeks. She was a fan of all these women swimmers I'd never heard of. While she went on and on, I felt the hammer pressed against my spine.

I remember Madonna's "Rescue Me" was next on her mix tape. Looking back now, it was pretty ironic.

"I had a poster of Madonna up in here, but my dad made me take it down," she told me. "He thinks she's 'morally corrupt.'"

"He's a fucking hypocrite," I muttered.

Then she got all pissy and started to defend him, the fool. I told her that she was a prisoner in this house. (Again, the irony!) She didn't even know how miserable & sad she was. I knew—from all our talks.

"Listen, let's run away tonight," I told her, grabbing her arm. "You don't have to stay here. We can steal some of the stuff you showed me. Your mother probably has a ton of jewelry. There's a regular surplus of valuable crap here. We can hock it and have enough to live on for months. We can go anywhere, Denise."

She uttered a skittish laugh and shook her head. "Are you kidding me? My dad will track us down . . ."

"He can't, not if we stick together," I said. "Listen, I'm walking out of here, and I want you to come with me . . ."

I pleaded & begged, but she wasn't even listening. She took a wad of Kleenex out of her pocket and blew her nose. I kept telling her that I didn't want to leave without her.

"Oh, God, I never should have let you come up here," she whimpered.

I remember seeing fear in her eyes. I knew right then—if she wasn't coming with me, she'd have to die.

She seemed to know it, too. She turned & started for her nightstand. She was going after the gun.

She was still a couple of feet away from the nightstand when I hit her on the back of the head with the hammer. I heard something crack.

The groan that came out of her sounded like the cry of a feeble old woman—a strange warbled wail. She staggered & swiveled around and gazed at me, wide eyed. She looked so astonished. What did she expect?

I hit her again—just above her forehead. Blood splattered me.

She collapsed on the floor in front of me. I stared down at her. She wasn't moving at all. The blood matted down her hair and made a dark puddle on the pink shag carpet. One of her flip-flops had fallen off.

I knew I had time before the family returned.

I went to the bathroom down the hall and took a long, warm shower. It was heavenly.

I got some clothes, some of Phyllis's jewels, two of the guns, & some antiques from downstairs— all stuff that was easy to carry & pawn.

I remember as I left the house by the back door, I thought it was probably for the best that it happened the way it did. I probably would have had to kill her while we were on the road. She would have slowed me down.

And all it took was just two hammer blows.
She'd died a lot easier than Lilly-Anne . . .

Aaron kept wriggling his hands until the rope burned his wrists. But it didn't seem to do any good. The restraints didn't feel any looser.

He'd finally managed to shrug off part of the coverlet. Still, for all his efforts, he couldn't see much. It was dark in the back of the van. Out the rear window, there wasn't any view—just blackness, occasionally interrupted by the sweeping headlight beams of a passing car.

Then for the last half hour or so, Aaron didn't notice any headlights at all. He saw the tops of evergreens against the night sky. He felt the car slow down several times to take various curves in the road. At one point, he felt his ears pop. He realized they were up in the mountains somewhere—in the woods.

This was where he was going to die.

The coach was still humming to himself.

Aaron was so thirsty, it hurt to swallow. Still, he kept poking his tongue past his dry lips and moving his jaw until the duct tape across his mouth started to loosen. His sweat and tears had helped slacken the adhesive even more. The tape dangled off one cheek now. He could have screamed out if he wanted. But it wouldn't have done any good. Who would hear him? It would only alert the coach that he was conscious and struggling to get free.

His hands had been tied in back of him for so long that his shoulders ached. Aaron desperately glanced around for something sharp in the back of the van, something to cut the ropes around his wrists and ankles—something he could use to stab the coach. But he didn't see anything.

Frustrated, Aaron tried to roll over, and he crushed his arms. He gasped at the pain.

The coach stopped humming.

Aaron tried not to cry or make a sound.

"We're almost home," the coach said. "Stop fidgeting."

Aaron couldn't see him, but he imagined the crazy bastard at the wheel of the van—and the dark, winding wooded road ahead.

"Whose home—yours?" Aaron finally asked in a shaky voice.

"No, yours, chum," the man replied. "It sounds like somebody got the duct tape off his big mouth. Well, fine with me. Gives me someone to talk to."

"Where are you taking me?"

"It didn't work out with you—and that's the way it goes sometimes. So I'm taking you home."

"You mean, Mount Vernon?"

"No, this will be your new home. You'll be here quite a while, too." He chuckled and then muttered, "Eternity, in fact."

It took Aaron a moment to figure out what he'd just said. He started to cry. He frantically tugged at the ropes and kicked. It didn't matter how much it hurt.

"Sometimes it just doesn't work out with certain swimmers," the coach went on. "Didn't work out with the last guy, either. And he was a better swimmer than you. Such a waste, all that potential . . ."

"I'll try harder," Aaron heard himself say.

"No, you're too much trouble. You were about to escape—or at least, you were about to try. You were going to grab my kid—"

"I'm sorry, I really am," Aaron said. Tears streamed down his face. His throat was closing up on him. "But—isn't it the duty of every prisoner to try to escape? Wouldn't you have tried the same thing if you were me? Put yourself in my place for a second. I'm scared! I miss my home. I miss my mom—and my friends . . ." He gasped. "Please, I don't want to die . . ."

"Should have thought about that earlier," the coach said.

Aaron could feel the car slowing down. They turned onto a bumpy road. He heard loose gravel crunching under the weight of the tires. They were on a trail in the woods somewhere. All he could see out the rear window were trees, so dense they blocked out the night sky.

"Listen, you don't have to do this," he said. "I've learned my lesson, I have. I—I'll be your best swimmer ever. I'll make you so proud of me. Just give me another chance, okay?"

There was no response. The coach was humming softly again.

"I've never worked with a better coach than you," Aaron lied. Maybe he could appeal to the guy's vanity. "I'm just not used to the setup, y'know? I think—I think your teaching methods are better than any coach I've had in competitive swimming. I mean, in just one day, you got me to—to realize how—how I'm screwing up my dive, my entry. I know with your help, I'm going to do better . . ."

The van slowed down to a crawl and took another turn. They seemed to be on a dirt trail. Aaron heard branches brushing against the side of the van and twigs snapping.

The coach was still humming. The son of a bitch wasn't even listening to him.

The van came to a stop.

"No, please," Aaron cried. "Turn back, please. Can't we go back? I won't give you any more trouble, I promise. Please, I don't want to die . . ."

The coach parked and turned off the engine. He opened the front door.

Aaron felt the chilly night air, and he heard the sound of water rushing against rocks. Chris Whalen was found naked on a riverbank. Was that where the coach was taking him now?

"No, wait . . ." Aaron pleaded. He couldn't stop shaking. Snot dripped from his nose onto the dangling piece of tape. "Please, don't. I understand now. I fucked up. I won't do it again, I promise. Please . . ."

The coach climbed out of the front seat and shut the door. Aaron heard him walk around to the back. There was a clink from the lock, and the back door opened up.

Aaron squinted at him and shook his head.

"C'mon, let's go," the coach said, tugging at the mattress. He grabbed Aaron's arm.

Aaron tried to recoil. "No . . ."

"Don't give me any more trouble," he growled. "You're just making it harder for yourself, chum." He pulled him out of the back of the van.

The mattress slid out at the same time—cushioning Aaron as he fell and landed on his side. Still, it knocked the wind out of him. The coach moved behind him and ripped the piece of tape from his cheek. Then he put his hand on his throat. Helpless, Aaron started to squirm.

"Hold still, damn it," the coach grunted. He wrapped some sort of thick strap around Aaron's neck—and then he tightened it.

Aaron thrashed around, certain the coach was going to strangle him. He cried out.

"Scream all you want," the man hissed. "I know this area. No one's around for miles . . ."

Aaron heard a rattling sound. He rolled back and saw the coach standing over him with a chained leash in one hand and his gun in the other.

He gave the leash a little yank. "Get up."

Aaron felt it tug at his neck. He obeyed him.

He was naked, shivering cold, and wearing a dog collar. He realized this was how he was going to die.

"Down that trail there," the coach said, nodding to a narrow dirt path through the trees and shrubs. "Get going."

Aaron started down the trail, his bare feet stomping over twigs and rocks on the cold, hard ground. He could see his breath. But he couldn't see anything else unless it was directly in front of him. After that, it was just darkness.

He heard the rushing stream. They were getting closer to it. Branches scraped against his naked torso and legs. He started to slow down. He had no idea how he might get out of this.

The coach jerked the leash and cracked the slack against Aaron's spine. "C'mon, quit stalling . . ."

Aaron winced. He stumbled on a tree root and almost fell. It was hard to get his balance back with his hands tied behind him. "Goddamn it, I can't see!" he bellowed.

"Move!" the coach barked.

He continued on. But he couldn't stop shaking, and he couldn't hold back anymore. "What the hell is wrong with you?" he screamed. "Why are you doing this? You sick, twisted fuck! What kind of pervert are you? Making me swim naked—while your stupid wife and kid watch. What the hell is that about? What kind of father are you? What kind of person are you? I heard you raping Monica the other night, you lowlife scum piece of shit . . ."

The coach said nothing. His pull on the leash got tighter and tighter—until Aaron couldn't speak anymore. It finally slackened as Aaron stumbled into a clearing next to a rocky stream.

"Keep going—into the water," the coach said.

It didn't look deep enough to drown in. But then, all the coach had to do was knock him out and hold his head under the water. He'd already demonstrated that he was quite good at that.

Aaron thought about rushing him. But what could he do with his hands tied behind his back? Plus the bastard had a gun.

The ground was rock-strewn and wet. Every step closer to the stream was torture on his feet. The water was like ice.

"I'm a good person!" Aaron announced past his chattering teeth. "And you're not. I'm so much better than you. There's nothing you can do to me that will ever change that . . ."

The coach yanked the leash again—making him spin around. Before Aaron knew what was happening, he felt the man punch him in the stomach. It was sudden and fierce. He fell to his knees onto the stones and pebbles in the riverbed. He tried to get a breath, but couldn't.

He would have fallen facedown into the stream, but the coach still held him up by the leash.

"You still don't seem to understand," the man whispered. "What you say doesn't matter, because I own you. You're mine . . ."

He kept tugging at the leash and pulled Aaron back up to his feet.

"You won't die here tonight, Aaron," he said. "But if you ever disappoint me again, you'll wish you had."

CHAPTER SIXTEEN

Echo
Friday, October 28—10:34 A.M.

She didn't care about the fall of the Roman Empire. Lindsay's main concern at the moment was Jeremy, who had just texted her. But her World History teacher, Ms. Freeman, was a total Nazi when it came to iPhones, insisting they be turned off at the start of class. Like everyone else, Lindsay had merely set her phone in silent mode. She had several good excuses for bending the rules today—in case Freeman caught her checking her phone: she was waiting to hear back from her dad; someone was stalking her mother; and most of all, she was supposed to meet Jeremy during lunch hour today but didn't know where. Not that she would actually use Jeremy as an excuse to Freeman, but the other two defenses were legitimate.

Her dad had texted back late last night, saying he'd been in one of his SARA meetings when she'd called and he would try to get in touch with her mom. She'd texted him again this morning to let him know the police had been by to check out some prowler in their backyard last night. Lindsay had figured this would really motivate her dad to come stay with them. But ultimately it was up to her mother, who was still being pretty stubborn and stupid about the whole thing.

The way her mom had talked at breakfast this morning, this stalker might have come with the house—like roaches or squeaky pipes. At least that was how she made it sound. Lindsay wondered if all this had anything to do with what Jaime Fleischel had said the other day about a murder that occurred in the house back in the 1990s. Was it really true? Lindsay hadn't been able to confirm it online. Still, if a girl had really been killed there twenty-some years ago, maybe the slayer was still hanging around the scene of the crime. Or perhaps some morbid murder-fan freak had become obsessed with the house—and whoever was living in it. Then again, maybe Jaime was just messing with her.

Lindsay hated to admit it even to herself, but her mother had been right about switching bedrooms last night. Sleeping in the room right next to her mother had had its advantages after such a scary, weird evening. Lindsay had felt a little more secure, knowing her mom was awake and hearing all the same noises she heard. She'd actually slept through the night without changing beds.

Her biggest concern right now was Jeremy Dawson. She couldn't believe she'd shown her boobs to him last night. Talk about dumb. He probably thought she was a total slut—or at least a lot more sexually sophisticated than she was. Would he still be interested in her if he knew she was a virgin? He certainly wasn't inexperienced—what with his bong there on the nightstand and getting naked right in front of her like it was a regular thing he did. He was college age, and here she was still waiting to get her learner's permit.

She had no idea what they'd be doing for their date on Sunday afternoon. But he'd said his parents and kid sister would be gone until late. Maybe he expected her to come over to his house and have sex with him.

Ms. Freeman was talking about Caligula, which should have been fascinating because Lindsay knew some famous porn movie had been named after him; however, the way Freeman talked about him, he wasn't very interesting at all.

The bell finally rang, and Lindsay whipped out her phone—as did about half her classmates. Over the din, Ms. Freeman yelled out their reading assignment for the weekend. Lindsay looked at Jeremy's text:

Let's meet by the basketball court on Hillshire Rd, 3 blks from the school at 12:15. Don't tell anyone. OK?

Lindsay glanced at the rain slashing against the classroom window. She knew where the basketball court was—right on the edge of some woods. There was a tall chain-link fence around the court—and next to it, a small playground and a squat little brick building that had restrooms. It was one of those spots that seemed perfectly nice during the day when people were around. But at night, it could be downright creepy.

Lindsay told herself that it would be fine during the day. She looked at his message again. *Don't tell anyone.* Who would she tell?

She texted back: K.

* * *

He woke up and squinted at the clock on the nightstand. It was just past eleven. The coach had let him sleep.

Aaron couldn't believe he was almost grateful to find himself surrounded once again by these four dull gray windowless walls. He was lying on the cot with the *Star Trek* comforter over him. He had on a T-shirt and undershorts—and he didn't care who they used to belong to.

The coach had given him a shot of something after they'd walked back to the van last night. The next thing Aaron knew, he was blindfolded and being led naked into a house and down some steps. Then he got a waft of that chlorine smell and knew he was back in the coach's basement. He was still shivering from the cold.

The coach took the blindfold off him, cut the rope around his hands, and pushed him into the shower stall. The warm water was a shock at first, but then it seemed to melt away the chill in his bones. Aaron saw the scratches covering his body from all the branches in the woods. His feet looked beat up—like he'd been marching for miles barefoot. He noticed the burn marks on his wrists and ankles from the ropes.

He just wanted to sit down in the shower stall and curl up into a ball.

But the coach was standing there, glaring at him. He made Aaron turn off the water, and then he threw him a towel.

Aaron dried off. He was so tired and depleted it didn't even occur to him that he might try to escape at this point. The coach wasn't really on his guard. His gun was in the holster. But all that didn't matter. Aaron was like an obedient zombie.

He wasn't surprised to find his cell stripped of all the amenities—no more TV or fridge or books. But he could see by the blue night-light that he still had a blanket and pillow on the bed—along with the underwear. There was also a big steaming bowl of chicken noodle soup on the desk. He actually thanked the coach for it. He was pretty sure it was just Campbell's, but he hadn't tasted anything so good in a long, long time.

Between the hot shower and the soup, Aaron wondered why the coach was being so nice to him. He'd thought the son of a bitch would have thrown him—cold, shivering, and naked—into the empty cell only to sleep on the floor without so much as a tea towel to cover himself. Why was the coach being so nice?

Then as Aaron sat slurping chicken soup at his desk—in someone else's underwear, it occurred to him. The coach was simply taking care of his investment. How could he expect to get a peak swimming performance out of some kid who had the flu or pneumonia? Aaron realized it would be a waste of time and cell space if he ended up sick and bedridden for the next week. The coach was just being practical.

After finishing his soup, Aaron flopped down on the cot and checked the clock on the nightstand. It was close to three in the morning.

He heard Monica's voice whispering through the vent: "Aaron, are you there?"

He didn't utter a word or make a sound.

"Aaron, please, I'm sorry!" she called softly. "I heard voices a while ago. Please, answer me. Tell me it's you. I understand if you're mad. But talk to me, okay? Aaron? Is someone there? Is it somebody new? Hello?"

Aaron remembered taking the coverlet and pulling it over his head so he could block out the sound of her voice.

Now, hours later, he could hear her in the pool. He heard the coach's whistle, the theme from *Rocky*, and water splashing. Apparently, the coach had decided to let him rest this morning. The bastard really was looking out for his health, wasn't he?

Last night's precautions seemed to have paid off—at least so far. Aaron didn't feel sick or headachy, no sign of a scratchy throat. Outside of feeling a bit beat-up and sore, he was fine. Still, he didn't get up from the cot.

He lay there and thought about Monica and how she'd betrayed him.

He would rest up, and then he'd beat the crap out of her for their next race—and the next one, and the race after that.

She thought she was getting out of here soon. But no, from now on, he'd be the one stacking up wins. He'd be the one to go home first.

Then he realized something, and Aaron suddenly felt sick.

He was thinking just how the coach wanted him to think.

Echo
Friday—11:37 A.M.

"Marie?" the stocky, brassy-haired nurse asked. Holding a clipboard to her chest, she'd just stepped into the waiting room.

Caitlin was still filling out the new patient form for

Camper & Goldsmith Skin Specialists. There was another woman sitting across from her in the small anteroom, reading a *People* magazine. It took Caitlin a moment to realize the other woman wasn't Marie. *She* was Marie—Marie Milliken, her middle and maiden names. It was the alias she'd given to the receptionist in Dr. Goldsmith's office when she'd called from the library an hour ago.

She turned to the nurse and smiled. "Yes?"

The nurse nodded at the form in Caitlin's lap. "You can finish filling that out in the examining room."

Getting to her feet, Caitlin followed her down a hallway. She was ushered into the small room—with a cushioned examination table on hydraulics and beside it, a standing examination lamp that looked like something out of *Star Trek.* The place smelled like Noxzema. The mini-blinds were tilted, so she could see out the rain-beaded window, but people probably couldn't see in. She had a view of the water.

"And what is it we're seeing Dr. Goldsmith about today?" the nurse asked, closing the door behind her.

Caitlin hung up her coat and umbrella on one of the hooks on the wall near the door. "Ah, I have this mole on my arm. I don't like the look of it." She rolled up her sleeve to show her a birthmark that hadn't changed at all.

"Well, Marie, in that case, I don't think you need to change into a gown. Why don't you sit down and make yourself comfortable? The doctor will be with you shortly."

"Thank you," Caitlin said. "And thank you for squeezing me in on such short notice."

"No problem," the nurse said. Then she ducked out to the hallway and closed the door.

Caitlin went back to the form, which wasn't any good because it didn't have her real name or address on it. How she was going to pay for this appointment was up for grabs, too—since the name on her checks wasn't the one she'd written down here on the form. Plus she'd chopped up all her credit cards night before last. Maybe Dr. Goldsmith wouldn't charge her for the session. It would be a small compensation for the fact that he'd sold her a house that seemed to have come with a stalker.

Shortly after the police left last night, she'd emailed and texted him the same message:

Hello, Dr. Goldsmith,

I've encountered a troubling issue with the house, and I'm hoping you can shed some light on the situation. The real estate agent can't help me. I'd like to nip this in the bud immediately. Please get in touch with me as soon as possible. This is an urgent matter. Thanks very much.

Sincerely,
Caitlin Stoller

She included her phone number in both messages. Of course, she was overanxious for a response. By 10:45 this morning, she figured he wasn't going to get in touch with her at all. Why should he? He'd unloaded a *cursed* house on her, the site of a notorious local murder that now had its own stalker. This was lawsuit-worthy stuff. But before getting lawyers involved, she wanted to get some sort of explanation from Goldsmith.

So Caitlin had decided to go to him. She discovered his office was only three blocks from the library. She couldn't use her real name, or he'd never have agreed to see her. So she'd called his office on the library line with this fake name and a fake story about a suspected melanoma.

She finished filling out the form—but left it unsigned. Then she pulled out her phone to reread a text Russ had sent her this morning:

Lind says u had the police over because of this stalker last night. I wish u'd let me come stay there with u. I'll sleep on the sofa. I promise not to get too comfortable. I'll only stay there until this creep backs off or the police catch him. I'm worried!!! Call me. XXX

Caitlin didn't care what he said. Less than six months ago, he was trying to convince her that she should allow him to be a "functioning" heroin addict: *"So I take a little something to get me through the day . . ."*

She hadn't replied yet.

There was a knock on the examining room door.

She slipped the phone back in her purse. "Yes, come in!" she called.

Dr. Goldsmith stepped into the room and closed the door behind him. "Hello, Marie?" he asked, extending a hand.

Caitlin shook it. "Hi."

"I'm Dr. Goldsmith," he said. He was about fifty,

lean, and bald with glasses and a salt-and-pepper goa-tee. He was a perfect advertisement for his business, because his light olive complexion was nearly flaw-less. He pulled a stool on wheels in front of her chair and sat down. "So you have a mole on your arm that is giving you some concerns."

"Yes," she answered, rolling up her sleeve. She showed him her arm.

He took hold of her wrist and bent forward to study the birthmark. "So did you just move to town?"

Caitlin looked at the top of his bald head. "Yes, about six weeks ago . . ." It was a perfect segue for ad-mitting the real reason for this visit. But she was sur-prised to see him pull a magnifying glass from his white lab jacket. He was frowning at her mole. "What—does it look bad?" she asked.

"Even borders, color is fine," he murmured. "I don't see anything to be concerned about here. Is this a new mole—or have you had it a while?"

"Since birth," she said. "I just wasn't sure if it changed color on me . . ."

He pushed away—and rolled himself on the stool toward the counter, where he opened a drawer. He pulled out a brochure, rolled back to her, and handed her the little leaflet. *All About Melanomas*, it said on the cover—along with three photos of nasty looking moles.

"Here's some bedtime reading for you," he said. "I think you're fine. But you were right to come here. It's always better to have these things checked out . . ."

"Thank you," Caitlin said.

"Was that the only area of concern?" he asked.

"Not exactly," she replied, and then she took a deep breath. "Dr. Goldsmith, I—I have another reason for coming here." She held up the new patient form. "I couldn't sign this, because Marie Milliken isn't my real name. I'm Caitlin Stoller. I was afraid if I used my real name, you wouldn't want to see me."

Behind the glasses, his eyes narrowed at her.

"Did you get my text or my email?" she asked.

He nodded glumly. "The text you sent me at one o'clock this morning—the one that woke me up? Yes, I got it—and the email." He sighed and stood up. The wheeled stool moved on its own for a few inches. "Listen, I think—"

"I'm sorry to have bothered you so late," Caitlin cut in. "But I sent you that note right after the police left last night. You see, I had a prowler—someone lurking around the house. Does that sound familiar, Dr. Goldsmith? Because the whole situation was pretty familiar to the police who responded to my nine-one-one call. They told me they had several such calls from your wife."

He shook his head. "I really don't think this is the time or place—"

"I'm asking for your help," Caitlin said. She got to her feet. "I'm asking you to be an honest and decent guy here. When I first put an offer on that house, you should have told me that it came with a stalker. This guy didn't go away when you moved, Dr. Goldsmith. He's still there—watching us, sending me notes, phoning me. He's even gotten into my email account. Was he doing the same thing to you—or your wife? I need to know."

He stood there with his hand on the doorknob. He wouldn't look her in the eye.

"I have a daughter—the same age as your daughter when she died," Caitlin continued, her voice shaking. "And I have a son, eleven years old. I'm scared something's going to happen to one of them. I know you had some tragedies and setbacks in that house. I sympathize. I had a son who died two years ago, and I'm recently divorced. But I need to ask you. Do you think it's possible this stalker I inherited had anything to do with the—the tragedies you suffered while you were living in that house? I need to know if my children are in danger . . ."

He cleared his throat and glanced down at the floor. "My wife developed some psychological problems after the death of our daughter," he said—almost tonelessly, as if reading the words off a page. "Near the end, she telephoned the police several times, but you can ask them and they'll tell you. They never found any evidence that someone was lurking around the house or trying to break in."

He finally looked at her and sighed. "I called the police on a couple of occasions shortly after my wife's suicide because, for a while, my son and I—we had people coming up to the house to peek in the windows. Some of those morbidly curious types aren't very tactful or sensitive. But that stopped after a week or so." He frowned at her. "Is there anything else you'd like to ask me?"

"I don't think your wife was imagining things," Caitlin said steadily. "And at the very least, you should have told me or the real estate agent about the murder in the house back in 1992."

He quickly shook his head. "I don't know anything about that." Then he opened the door.

Caitlin thought his reaction was pretty strange. He didn't seem surprised, just perturbed.

"The person who sold you the house didn't tell you that a girl was killed in one of the bedrooms upstairs?" she pressed.

He shook his head. "We bought the house from an estate. The woman who used to run the Bayside B and B purchased the place, but she died in an auto accident about a year or so before we bought the place. Now, if you don't have any other questions . . ."

"Actually, I have one," she said. "How could you have lived in a house and not be the least bit curious when someone tells you a murder occurred there twenty-some years ago?" Her eyes wrestled with his.

"Because I had enough bad things happen to my family while we lived in that place," he replied. "I'm not interested in anything else that went on there. Now you're welcome to come back here as a patient, Ms. Stoller. But if you have any other questions about the house, I suggest you ask the real estate agent."

He stepped out to the corridor. Caitlin gathered her coat and umbrella and followed him.

"I won't charge you for this visit," he said. Then he nodded toward the door at the end of the hallway.

"Thank you," she said evenly. She was shaking inside. "I'll take you up on that offer to become one of your patients, Dr. Goldsmith. I'd like you to see me and

my children for regular checkups. I really want you to
know my family—in case something terrible happens to
one of us in that house, something you could have
helped prevent."

He said nothing.

Caitlin turned and walked down the hallway—and
out the door.

"Can you get me a list of the people who have
owned the house through the years?" Caitlin asked.
Huddled under an umbrella, she hurried down the sidewalk across from the waterfront. Wet leaves were strewn
along the pavement, and Caitlin kept a lookout for pud-
dles. She had the real estate woman, Sally Rutledge,
on the phone. "I need contact information for them,
too," she added, "everyone who lived there from the
Healys in nineteen eighty-or-ninety-something—up
until the Goldsmiths."

She heard Sally sigh on the other end of the line.
"Well, I suppose I could get a history of the house sales
from the Recorder of Deeds or the Assessor's Office . . ."

"I'd appreciate it, thanks," Caitlin replied. *You owe
me at least that much*, she thought.

"I'll get back to you tonight or tomorrow," Sally
said. "But I'm not sure how I can find you all the current contact information. I mean, some of these people
might be dead."

"That's what I'm afraid of," Caitlin said. "And it's
what I need to find out."

After she clicked off, she called Lindsay. It was

Lindsay's lunch hour and she could have picked up, but it went to voice mail.

Caitlin waited for the beep: "Hi, honey, I need to ask you for a big favor. I think there's a Goldsmith at your high school. My guess is that he's a freshman. I know it sounds weird, but could you find this Goldsmith boy and introduce yourself to him? It shouldn't be too hard, right? I mean, you just ask around and when you meet him, tell him that you now live in his old house. I need you to find out if they had a prowler when they lived there. Ask if someone was stalking his mother or his sister. Remember, they're both dead now—so try to be tactful and delicate. Okay, honey? Can you do that? Does this make any sense to you? Probably not. So— well, call me just as soon as you get this, okay? Thanks."

Caitlin clicked off and then glanced at her wristwatch: 12:25. She hoped her daughter called her back by one.

"Please, don't leave me hanging again, Lindsay," she murmured.

Lindsay debated whether or not to pick up when she saw the call was from her mother. To keep out of the rain, she stood under the overlapping roof of the little brick building—by the water fountain and between the restroom entrances. The basketball court and the kiddy park were deserted. She'd been waiting there nearly fifteen minutes, and still no sign of Jeremy.

She figured if she talked to her mother now, her mom would catch on that she was doing something she shouldn't. Her mother had a sixth sense like that. And the truth was, right now Lindsay didn't feel very good about any of this. Was Jeremy standing her up? A part of her almost hoped he would.

On her phone, she went to her image gallery and studied the two photos of him that she'd downloaded from Facebook—his shirtless, nature-lover pictures. He was awfully cute. But she didn't really know him— and he didn't really know her. He'd seen her boobs. But he didn't know her. God, if her mother ever found out, she'd kill her. Hell, her mom would have a cow that she was merely getting together with some guy she'd met online.

It wasn't exactly an ideal place for a rendezvous with someone who was practically a stranger—in a vacant park beside these dark woods. She'd noticed a paved path that led into the little forest. The trees and their branches swayed slightly in the rain. Everything was so brown and wet.

Jeremy really could have picked a better place, especially in this rain. She watched it steadily drip off the bars of the jungle gym. A couple of swings on the swing set were moving on their own and squeaking.

Where the hell was he?

She checked her mom's message. Talk about bizarre. Her mom wanted her to hunt down this Goldsmith kid and pump him about his dead mother and sister—and someone who might have been stalking them.

Lindsay suddenly remembered something else her mother wanted her to do. At breakfast yesterday, she'd made her promise not to go off anywhere by herself for the next few days.

Lindsay felt this pang of dread in her gut. What was she doing here anyway? This Jeremy guy had already made her do something incredibly stupid. She was just setting herself up to do something asinine again.

Out of the corner of her eye, she noticed something over by the trees.

Somebody tall and thin—their face obscured in the shadows of a hoodie—emerged from the woods. The lone figure hurried along the path, which led past the basketball court to the park. Was it Jeremy? She wondered if Jeremy could be the stalker her mother had tried to warn her about. Lindsay still couldn't make out the person's face.

She wanted to run but was afraid if she did, this guy would chase her down and tackle her. No one else was around to hear her screams. Lindsay tightened her grip on her small collapsed umbrella, thinking she might have to fight off this stranger with it.

He was coming closer. She could see him now. Pale and fortyish, he had a sort of sinister look on his thin face and kept walking at a fast clip. He passed the basketball court and zeroed in on her. He stared back at her and then broke into a leering grin.

Lindsay backed into the brick wall.

"How about this liquid sunshine?" he called. And then he hurried past her.

"Yeah!" Lindsay called back. She let out a weak little laugh.

She glanced at the time on her phone. Jeremy was twenty-five minutes late.

She opened her umbrella and started back toward the school. She decided to text the jerk and tell him their rendezvous was officially kaput—as was their Sunday-afternoon date. Her hand was still a little shaky as she pulled up his number.

After one ring, there was a strange beep, and a recording came on: *"The number you have dialed is no longer in service. Please hang up and try again . . ."*

She tried him again, and the same error message answered.

There was another beep, this time from an incoming text. Caitlin thought it might be Jeremy, explaining why he was late. But the text was from one of the girls on the swim team, Susan Lodge. All it said was: *Is this you?*

There was a video attachment. Lindsay clicked on it. "Oh, shit, no," she whispered.

Out of desperation for something to eat, Caitlin bought a bag of yogurt-covered pretzels and a Diet Coke from the vending machines in the ferry terminal on her way back to the library. Some lunch. She ate it in the cramped break room of the library while typing a rather long text to Russ:

> Thanks for the offer to come stay with us, but I need to handle this on my own. You have to focus on getting better. I'll try to explain to Lindsay. She and Gabe are looking forward to seeing u and roughing it in sleeping bags Sat night. Meanwhile, please don't contact me for a while. Let's talk right before Thanksgiving. Maybe we can all be together for the holiday.

Until then, take care and keep getting better.
Thanks. XXXX

Sitting at the little café table with her stale snack, Caitlin tried not to start crying. Then she sent the text before she could change her mind.

She glanced at her watch: 12:45. She'd taken an early lunch to go see Goldsmith, and she should have been back to work by now. She'd also phoned Lindsay twenty minutes ago—without a callback or text yet. She would wait until one o'clock before she went into panic mode.

Caitlin was cleaning up the remnants of her meager lunch when her cell phone beeped. She prayed the text was from Lindsay. But the phone display read: SENDER UNKNOWN. She winced and warily clicked on the text. She didn't quite understand the message:

Mommy's little girl. I told you she'd be trouble.

There was a video attachment. Biting her lip, Caitlin clicked on the icon.

It was a video of Lindsay at her desk in her bedroom. Caitlin was pretty certain it had been taken last night—close to when she'd checked in on Lindsay the second time. The soundtrack was slightly garbled, but it sounded like a guy laughing and then whimpering like a dog. Lindsay had this strange smirk on her face—like someone had just told her a dirty joke. She was blushing. She leaned back in the chair, lifted her black T-shirt, and showed off her bare breasts. "*Oh, wow, nice!*" someone said offscreen. Then Lindsay lowered the front of her shirt to cover herself again. She was still smiling but rolled her eyes a little.

Caitlin slowly shook her head. "Dear God, Lindsay, no . . ." she whispered.

The clip lasted only a few seconds, but it was on a loop—so it started all over again.

Cringing, Caitlin clicked it off. How could her daughter have done something so reckless and stupid? It was the kind of thing that could end up on the Internet. Caitlin remembered last night hearing Lindsay talking to someone who sounded like a boy. Lindsay had said it was Roseann—with a cold. And she'd believed her. It was obvious—Lindsay had flashed some boy while talking to him on the phone or via Skype. And how many of his friends had now seen this clip?

She speed-dialed Lindsay and listened to the first ringtone. "C'mon, c'mon, pick up. Don't do this to me . . ." There was a click on the other end of the line. "Lindsay?" she asked.

"Mom, I can't really talk right now—"

"Yes, you can," she said. "I just saw a video of you."

"Oh, God, he sent it to you, too?" her daughter cried. "Oh, shit, no. He sent it to *everybody* at school. I've had—like—twenty different people call me in the last few minutes. And I don't even know some of them!" She let out a sob, and when she spoke again, her voice cracked. "Mom, I'm so sorry. This is so humiliating. I'm supposed to go to English Lit class in about five minutes. I'd rather slit my own throat. I'm standing in the rain—across the street from the school. I can't show my face in there . . ."

"You know the person who sent this video to everyone?" Caitlin asked.

She could hear Lindsay crying on the other end of the line. "Some boy . . ."

The door to the break room opened, and Myra peered in at her. "Do you think you'll be coming back from your lunch break sometime this month?" she asked. "I'm getting kind of hungry here—like I'm about to eat my own arm."

"I'm sorry, there's sort of a crisis with my daughter at school," Caitlin said. "I'll be done in a couple of minutes."

With a sigh, Myra ducked back into the library and closed the door.

Caitlin got back on the phone. "Honey, what boy? How did this happen?"

"It's this guy I met through Facebook," she explained. "He was cute and seemed nice. He said he lives in Echo and goes to community college in North Seattle. We were flirting on Skype last night, and it just got silly. I'm so—so stupid. Obviously, it was a setup. Someone decided to punk the new kid in school and totally humiliate me."

"Wait a minute, I'm confused," Caitlin said. "Who is this boy? Is he at the high school or in a community college or what?"

"I think he must be a friend or a brother of someone in my class—or maybe even some upperclassman I don't know. The whole thing was a setup. He friended me on Facebook and messaged me, and he seemed real. But now—well, now his phone number isn't working and his Facebook page is gone. Oh, Mom, what am I going to do? I've got, like, three minutes before I have to go to class."

Caitlin took a deep breath. "Well, I don't want you to be alone," she said calmly. "What I said yesterday morning still goes. I don't like the idea of you standing outside of school all by yourself. One option is—well, go to the nurse's office. Tell them you're sick and I'm on my way to pick you up. I'll get there as soon as I can. You can skip practice today and the swim meet tomorrow. Then maybe by Monday when you go back to school, all this will be old news."

"Yeah, like that's really going to happen," Lindsay muttered, sniffling. "God, I never want to set foot inside that school again. Listen, Mom, maybe I can go stay with Dad for a while . . ."

"No, that's not an option," she replied. "You need to leave him alone so he can get well. There's another choice for you, honey. Just go to your class. If anyone says anything—well, remember in seventh grade when you got that award at the school assembly and you tripped going up to the stage?"

"Thanks for reminding me. And your point is?"

"My point is that everybody laughed, and it could have been awful. But when you got onto the stage, you curtsied and made a funny face and you got through it."

"Mom, I was utterly humiliated."

"They gave out a bunch of awards at that thing, and you ended up getting more applause than anybody. You tripped, and you acted like '*So what? I tripped.*' You didn't burst into tears or run away or hide. You laughed at yourself and then dismissed it. Well, it's the same thing here. You tripped. Everybody does a dumb thing once in a while. Forgive yourself and move on."

"Do you forgive me?" Lindsay asked in a quiet voice.

Caitlin sighed. "Oh, honey, of course not."

Her daughter actually laughed.

"Seriously, it's going to take a while for me to get over this," she said. "But we'll worry about that later. Just go to your class—"

"Oh, crap, that's the bell," Lindsay said. "Okay. I tripped. *Aren't I dumb?* It's not the end of the world. Don't hang my head in shame, I got it. Thanks, Mom."

"Call me after your class!" Caitlin said.

But Lindsay had already hung up.

Caitlin hurried out of the break room and took over for a slightly put-out Myra at the front desk. She had several customers in a row but could barely keep her mind on her work. She kept thinking about how Lindsay had been set up for this schoolwide humiliation. Caitlin now realized she'd been so busy trying to talk Lindsay off the ledge that she'd forgotten who had sent her the video in the first place—along with another cryptic note.

How had her stalker gotten a copy of the video? Was it through some connection at the high school? Or had this anonymous creep orchestrated the whole thing?

Lindsay said an older boy had friended her on Facebook. Caitlin wondered if this boy was the same person who had written those notes, made those phone calls, and hacked into her online account. Was he the one with the crawly, raspy voice? Then again, maybe her stalker had hired a handsome young man to seduce Lindsay over the Internet.

During the first lull, Caitlin sent her daughter an-other text:

> Hope ur doing okay. Just shrug it off if people
> are being too jerky. Also be careful. If this boy
> shows up at school or tries to contact u again,
> call me immediately. He could be dangerous. He
> could be connected to this stalker person. Watch
> out for strangers at the school, too. Whoever set
> you up might want to see how it's affecting you
> there. Once again, don't wander off any place
> alone. Call me before swim practice. OK? Love
> you.

Just a minute later, Caitlin got a response:

> K. Taking a lot of heat but surviving so far.
> Thanks.

"Hey, Lindsay!" the husky, loudmouth jock called to her from across the crowded hallway. Lindsay had just gotten out of her last class. She did her best to pre-tend she didn't hear him over the slamming lockers and all the chatter—which was probably about her. She kept on walking to her locker.

"Hey, Lindsay!" he yelled again, persistent. She didn't even know the guy, but she figured he must have been on the football team because he was wearing a varsity jacket. "Lindsay, show us your tits!"

Several people in the corridor laughed.

"Show us your tits, Lindsay!" he repeated. It sounded like he was trying to start a chant with everyone.

Pausing at her locker, Lindsay turned and gave him her best blasé look. "Again? You've already seen them, haven't you? God, ask somebody else and give me a break!"

He seemed stumped for a moment, and it shut him up. A few people laughed.

The last three hours had been so bizarre. She'd slipped away during lunch hour, as usual—the invisible girl. An hour later she'd returned to school, and it was like she was a Kardashian or something.

And she wasn't a fan of the Kardashians.

But she took her mother's advice—for a change. She tried to act like what she'd done was dumb but no big deal.

Was that you in that video? It was the standard question hurled at her in hallways and whispered to her during her last three classes. Her reply got more creative as the afternoon wore on:

Yes, that was me, pretty stupid, huh?

Yeah, I got punked.

Yes, I did it for charity.

No, that's my twin sister who's in an asylum—she shows her breasts to everybody.

People pointed at her, stared and whispered to each other. Some kids sneered or shook their heads in disapproval like she was some big mega-whore. Guys leered at her.

Before her Biology teacher, Ms. Feicht, walked in for the last class of the day, Lindsay's crush, Nick Hurley—who until that moment didn't seem to know she was alive—stood up in front of a nearly full class and announced: "Hey, maybe Lindsay will give us a show!"

She forced a laugh. "Oh, please, you can see a lot more of me with the suits they give us on the girls' swim team. You want a show? We'll give you a show. Come to Seattle and watch us beat Roosevelt tomorrow . . ."

Thank God a few of her teammates were in the class, and they applauded. One of their boyfriends whistled. And from the front of the classroom, Nick smiled and winked at her.

Lindsay felt herself blushing. She tried to act as cool as possible, but she was completely embarrassed. The only reason Nick paid attention to her now was because he probably thought she was easy. She wanted to scream out: "Is there anyone in this school who *hasn't* seen my boobs?"

She kept up a good front but couldn't get past how stupid and pathetic she looked in the video. To her, it wasn't the least bit sexy.

All afternoon at school while people were staring at her, Lindsay kept an eye out for Jeremy—if that was even his real name. She didn't see him anywhere. She didn't notice any suspicious-looking men lurking around the school hallways or grounds, either. She still half expected some classmate or upperclassman to spring the news on her that she'd been punked and so-and-so's older brother was the one who did the striptease for her on Skype. But that didn't happen.

"Hey, aren't you Lindsay Stoller, the one in the video?"

Lindsay took her jacket, backpack, and umbrella out of her locker and then slammed the door shut. She turned around and gazed down at a short, skinny, gawky-looking kid—obviously an undersized freshman. She resisted the urge to tell him, "*Leave me alone, pipsqueak.*" The kid looked kind of sweet, and he had an ugly scar on his forehead. Plus it looked like he had a couple of his geeky colleagues behind him, watching his every move. One was terribly overweight. The other kid was even shorter than his scar-faced friend and had a pubic mustache.

"You were in that video, weren't you?" the kid pressed.

Lindsay rolled her eyes at him. "Yes, that was me. And no, you can't touch them."

"Y'know, you live in my old house," the boy said.

"You're one of the Goldbergs?" Lindsay asked, grabbing his arm. She remembered her mother's voice mail about him.

"Goldsmith," the kid said, looking a bit flummoxed. "Jarrett Goldsmith . . ."

"I really want to talk with you, Jarrett," she said. "Do you have a minute? Could you walk with me for a while? The girls' swim team bus leaves for the rec center in, like, five minutes. Would you mind?"

Visibly awestruck, he shook his head. "No problem," he murmured. He turned to glance at his friends.

The chubby one gave him the thumbs-up signal—like he'd officially scored big-time with the school's current "it" girl.

"So—how come you did it?" Jarrett Goldsmith asked,

tagging alongside her down the noisy hallway. "I mean, why did you show your—your breasts like that? Who were you showing them to?"

Lindsay waved the question away. "I was set up. Some guy I met online pretended to like me, and he got me into this whole *'show me yours, and I'll show you mine'* thing on Skype. I didn't know he was recording it and planning to send it to the entire school. Anyway, I need to ask you—"

She noticed the kid had stopped dead. He stared at her and blinked.

Lindsay stopped, too. "What? What is it?"

He looked like he'd just swallowed something awful. But then he quickly shook his head. "Um— nothing," he said, moving again. "You were gonna ask me a question . . ."

Her mother wanted to know about a prowler, but Lindsay was curious about something else. "Is it true that some girl got murdered in that house back in the early nineties?" she asked.

He nodded. "Yeah, someone bashed her brains out with a hammer. It happened in the bedroom that's down the hall . . ."

"That's my bedroom," Lindsay murmured.

"My sister had that room, too," he said. "But she moved closer to my parents and me after we found out."

Lindsay was dumbstruck. Did her mother know? That might explain why her mom wanted her to move into the guest room.

"My mom had some woman come over and burn incest in there."

"Incense," Lindsay said.

"Yeah, sage or something like that. Then they turned it into a guest room. But it didn't matter. Nobody really liked going in there after that."

"How did you find out about the murder?" Lindsay asked.

"It was pretty creepy," Jarrett said. "About two months after we moved in, my mom and dad woke up one morning and found someone had shoved a copy of a newspaper article about the murder under the door."

"They slipped something under your front door?"

He shook his head. "Not the front door, under their bedroom door. Someone must have broken into the house in the middle of the night while we were all asleep. They didn't steal anything. They just left a copy of the newspaper article."

Lindsay stared at him and slowly shook her head. "Did your parents call the police?"

"Yeah, but there wasn't much they could do. We ended up getting the locks changed."

"Hey, Lindsay!" some guy called. "Shake your tits for me, Lindsay! Let's see you shake them!"

She tried to ignore the jerk and kept walking toward the side door. "So do you think someone was, like, watching your house?"

Jarrett looked over his shoulder at her heckler.

Lindsay nudged him. "Did anything like that weird break-in ever happen again?"

"Oh, yeah." He nodded. "My mom said someone was following her around, leaving her these bizarre notes, and calling her. She was pretty sure they even tried to kill me." He pointed to the scar on his forehead. "This is from when I wiped out on my skateboard. And this person said it was gonna happen—like just days before it did. Seriously, I almost got killed. And it wasn't my fault. The wheel fell off. My mom said this person must have tinkered with my skateboard. I told her if she'd let me keep it in my bedroom instead of the garage, the accident never would have happened. I was a really good skateboarder before the accident. You should have seen me. Now I have a balance problem . . ."

Lindsay opened the door, and they headed outside. The rain had dwindled to a dull, light drizzle. It didn't warrant opening her umbrella. She noticed the girls' swim team bus waiting by the curb. "Listen, I know about your sister and your mom," she said. "I'm really sorry. I had a brother who died two years ago. It sucks. Do you think what happened to them might have been because of this person who was hanging around your mother?"

He stopped by the bike racks and gave a sad shrug. "Sometimes I think so, but my dad says definitely not."

"Why do you think so?" Lindsay asked.

"Because we were in that house for only, like, eight months, and all sorts of weird things happened. My sister and I were pretty close, and Michelle never had any drug problems until we moved into that place. My parents were happy when we moved in there. And by the time my dad and I moved out—well . . ." He shrugged again.

Lindsay put her hand on his shoulder. "Are you and

your dad okay now? I mean, do you think this stalker guy is still hanging around?"

"We haven't seen anybody since we moved out," Jarrett said. "But then—my dad and me never did. It was just my mom. And she wasn't crazy or anything—like some people say."

"Well, I don't think she was crazy, either, because somebody's still hanging around that house. My mother's pretty sure of it." Lindsay worked up a smile for him. "Listen, I need to catch my bus. But thanks for talking to me—and for not saying anything smart-alecky about my boobs."

She gave his shoulder a pat and then started for the bus.

"Hey, Lindsay?" he called.

She stopped and turned to him again.

Jarrett Goldsmith shuffled up to her. He looked a bit hesitant. "You know what you told me earlier—about how some guy set you up?"

She adjusted the backpack on her shoulders. "Yes?"

"Well, I probably shouldn't be telling you this," he said. "But the same thing happened to my dad. A few months after my sister died, and things weren't going so well with my folks, my dad met this woman online. They—well, they sexted and exchanged pictures of themselves, y'know, like sex pictures?"

Speechless, Lindsay nodded.

"It turned out to be a setup," Jarrett explained, wincing a little. "My dad's pictures and sexting stuff got sent to practically everybody who came to my sister's funeral. After it happened, the lady disappeared. My dad never really met her—except online. So he couldn't track her down."

"How did you find out about this?" Lindsay asked.

"Practically everybody knew. My parents split up. My dad lost a lot of his patients because of it. That was practically all anybody talked about for a couple of weeks—until my mom killed herself."

He had tears in his eyes. "Nobody says anything about it anymore. The only reason I bring it up is because it's kind of weird—you living in our old house and the same thing happening to you."

Lindsay gently touched his cheek. "Well, thank you for telling me."

Now she knew why Jarrett had looked so perplexed when she'd explained about the Skyping session with Jeremy. But she was still surprised that he would tell her something so intimate and humiliating about his father.

The bus driver honked the horn.

"Take care, Jarrett," she said. Then she turned and ran to catch her bus.

"There she is!" one of her teammates announced, once Lindsay had climbed aboard the bus.

"You going to bother wearing a suit for practice?" another girl asked.

"Yeah, yeah," Lindsay said. She rolled her eyes and gave a little curtsey. Then she took a seat. She looked out the window at Jarrett Goldsmith.

He waved at her.

She studied the puny boy—and the scar on his forehead. It was a souvenir from his time in that house—a place that seemed to have claimed the lives of his mother and sister. And the poor kid had barely survived himself.

Lindsay realized when he told her that story about his father, it was a warning.

She raised her hand to wave at him. Then the bus pulled away.

CHAPTER SEVENTEEN

Friday—7:50 P.M.—Day 160

Aaron isn't talking to me. I told him I'M SORRY about 20 times while we were practicing today. He doesn't seem to understand it was for his own good that I told C about his escape plans ("for his own good," ugh, I sound like Dad). If Aaron had actually grabbed Jr., C would have shot him. He'd be dead right now. It was a stupid escape idea. Aaron had no chance of getting out of here. I saved his life. I sound like a broken record ("a broken record," I'm quoting Dad again), because I wrote this all down in here last night, too— after C took Aaron away.

I was doing Aaron a favor. I saved his life. So why do I feel so guilty?

Monica didn't write anything about her whispered conversations with Aaron through the vent. She'd told the coach that Aaron had mentioned his escape plan the day before—in the pool. She couldn't risk sharing certain things with her journal—like how she really felt about *C, the Missus*, and *Jr.*, and the fact that she'd been communicating through the vent with her co-captives late at night.

It was a no-brainer that the coach had access to her journals. She'd filled out two and a half of the bound blank journals since that day in May when she'd woken up to find herself locked in this cell. All three journals were on her bookshelf. There didn't seem any point in hiding them—what with the camera watching her 24/7. Plus the Missus and Junior often came into her cell while she was in the pool. One day in mid-June she'd tried an experiment. She'd put her journal on the shelf upside down. Then when she returned from practice, the diary was right-side up. She figured the Missus or Junior must have taken the journal and photocopied her recent entries—so the coach could read what she had to say. She'd been self-censoring most of what went into her journal anyway, figuring the coach might confiscate them someday. But occasionally she wrote from the heart. She'd even revealed a lot about her crush on Jim Lessing.

She wrote about the coach raping her and all the other seedy stuff he forced her to do. Monica figured he ought to know how repulsed she was. She hoped to shame the slimy pig for forcing himself on her. But she also wondered if reading about it only turned him on even more.

Still, she treasured her journals. Jim had said he wasn't given a journal to write in. She wasn't sure why. Maybe the coach thought journal writing was a girl thing. Whatever, she just knew that without her journal writing and the swim sessions, she would have gone crazy in this horrible place.

Her journals and her co-captives had kept her from totally losing it. That was one reason it hurt to know how much Aaron hated her right now.

I swam by myself most of the morning today and was off my game. Then shortly after lunch break, C brought Aaron out to join me. His body was covered with scratches and his feet were all banged up. Like I say, he refused to talk to me and tell me what happened to him last night. I've never seen such a change in anyone. Just yesterday, he was so sweet. But today, when I tried to talk to him, he just muttered "fuck you" under his breath and ignored me the rest of the session. He wouldn't even look at me. I've never been on the receiving end of so much hostility and bitterness. It was horrible.

We had two freestyle scrimmages and Aaron won them both. I'd like to say I let him win, but I didn't. He beat me fair and square. He didn't even seem glad about winning. I tried to be a good sport and congratulated him. But he turned his back to me. C seemed pretty amused by the whole thing. He's got it so we're real competitors now.

I was glad to see I wasn't punished because of my losses this afternoon. None of my "creature comforts" (as C calls them) have been taken away. I've gotten pretty used to my TV, fridge, and other things. C knocked some more days off my graduation date for letting him know about Aaron's plans. Maybe that's why I feel so guilty. I'm like Judas and the 40 pieces of silver—or was it gold? Still, I know in my heart of hearts I did the right thing for Aaron.

Anyway, I'm down to only six more days. If C decides to add bonus days to a race, it could be even sooner than that. But now I'm wondering if I'll ever beat Aaron again. With his hatred of me, he's become a super-fierce competitor. What if he keeps on winning and winning? Will I ever get out of here?

Monica heard a clank at the door. Even though her journal was no secret, she still quickly closed it and slipped it under a book on her desk. The little peephole slat in the door opened.

"It's been a while since I've taken some pictures," the coach announced.

She suddenly felt sick. The last photo session had been about three weeks ago. In each session, she was naked, of course—or pretty close to it. After having her strip down to nothing, he would toss her a pair of hand-cuffs and have her put one cuff around her ankle and the other around a pipe that ran from the floor to the ceiling in one corner of the room. He sometimes made her wear certain outfits—like this awful lingerie from some sex shop. Sometimes she had to don different hats or masks. Once it was kneesocks and saddle shoes. Sometimes he gave her props to pose with—gross adult stuff like vibrators or childlike things such as teddy bears and dolls. Once she had to cover herself with baby oil.

He made her do all sorts of degrading things for his camera. She'd once asked Jim if the coach ever made him pose for porn photographs. He'd said no way.

Here the guys thought having to swim naked was this big humiliation. They had no idea how debasing it got for her.

"C'mon, you know the drill, Monica," the coach said quietly. "Now, get in position over by the pipe. Take off those clothes . . ."

Swallowing hard, she got to her feet and shuffled over toward the corner of her cell. Monica told herself this might be the last time.

She heard the door unlock—and the handcuffs rattling.

Echo
Friday, October 29—8:19 p.m.

"God, this is so gross," Lindsay complained. She stood near the sink, scooping the guts and seeds out of her pumpkin. "How can something as good as pumpkin pie start out this disgusting? It's enough to gag a maggot." With a spoon, she plopped some slimy orange-colored pulp onto a sheet of newspaper.

"Said the girl who has never helped her mother prepare a turkey for Thanksgiving," Caitlin replied under her breath.

She sat at the counter with the computer in front of her. The real estate agent had emailed her a list of the house's previous owners, and Caitlin was reviewing it now.

Gabe had retreated to his man cave under the stairs. Caitlin was worried about him. They'd ordered pizza tonight, and he'd had only one slice. Lindsay maintained that Poppy's Pizza of Echo was garbage compared to Ken's Artisan Pizza in Portland. Usually that never stopped Gabe. But tonight, he'd said he wasn't feeling well.

Caitlin had been so concerned about Lindsay all afternoon that she hadn't given much thought to her son. A few of his classmates had heard from their older siblings that Gabe's sister had shown her boobs on the Internet. The downloaded video got picked up pretty quickly by several sixth, seventh, and eighth graders at the school. Gabe had been the target of a lot of teasing—but unlike Lindsay, the poor kid hadn't had any time at all to prepare himself for it.

He'd shuffled into the library at 3:40 and burst into tears. By the time Caitlin calmed him down, explained, and apologized—and apologized for Lindsay—he seemed listless and sullen.

Lindsay had apologized to him, too. But he was still pretty withdrawn—and obviously disappointed in his older sister. Caitlin figured they should give him some alone time. She'd go down to the basement and check in on him later.

Oddly enough, according to Lindsay, her dad had

actually taken the news in his stride. Caitlin had made her phone him. The kids were staying with him the next day, and he'd be at Lindsay's swim meet in the morning. It was better he hear the news from his daughter than overhear someone talking about it at the meet. Besides, Caitlin had figured that someone had gone out of their way to send her the video, so they'd probably sent it to Russ, too. But he hadn't known a thing about it.

"I thought once I told him he'd have a heart attack or something," Lindsay had reported. "But he was, like, '*You kids and your stupid phones*,' and, '*I hope you're not seeing that boy again.*' Yeah, like that's going to happen."

Caitlin had expected a more severe reaction, too. It wasn't exactly the type of thing a father took well. It was a bit disconcerting. Caitlin wondered if he was completely *there* when Lindsay had called him this afternoon. Was he using again? Or maybe SARA was teaching him how to meditate, lower his stress levels, and mellow out—*really* mellow out.

She wondered why she couldn't just be happy that he'd handled it okay. Why did she have to question everything he did?

Caitlin scrolled down the computer screen and studied the list of the house's previous owners—or maybe *previous victims* was a more appropriate term to describe these people:

Dr. & Mrs. Lawrence Goldsmith—November
    2015–August 2016
276 Anchor Way

Echo, WA 98236 (current address; wife, Sara
　　now deceased)

Bank of America—October 2013–November
　　2015
692 Main Street
Echo, WA 98236 (bank took over the place when
　　Carrie died in 10/13)

Carrie Augusta Sewell (deceased)—February
　　2013–October 2013
c/o Bayside Bed & Breakfast
78 Bayside Road
Echo, WA 98236

Chandler (deceased) & Elaine Hecht—August
　　2011–February 2013
P. O. Box 8971
Port Angeles, WA 98363 (can't verify if this is
　　current)

Island Bank—May 1994–August 2011
442 Bayshore Drive
Oak Harbor, WA 98277
(Note: The house was vacant during this period;
　　it caught fire in 8/94, and again in 6/06)

Mr. & Mrs. Randall "Ned" Healy (both
　　deceased)—March 1983–May 1994

Caitlin was alarmed by the number of former owners who were dead. What were the odds? She wondered if Denise Healy was the only person to actually
die in the house. Did any of the other previous occu-

pants besides the Healys and the Goldsmiths have children who died while they were living here?

Another thing that bothered her: since the Healys' tenure, the only people to stay in the house for more than a year were the Hechts. Then again, it must have taken a while to fix up the place after it had remained vacant for seventeen years. Their actual occupancy in the house was probably like the others—a year or less.

Lindsay's friend was right. The place seemed *cursed.* Or maybe all this *bad luck* had been perpetrated by the stalker she'd inherited from the Goldsmiths.

She kept coming back to the name at the top of the list. Thanks to Lindsay—and Jarrett Goldsmith—Caitlin now knew that Dr. Goldsmith had lied to her. The Goldsmiths did have a stalker, and the good doctor also knew about Denise Healy's murder in 1992. The fact that someone had slipped a news clipping about it under their bedroom door late one night was very unsettling. It meant their stalker had indeed gotten inside the house at times. This person may have been responsible for Sara Goldsmith's suicide, Michelle's drug overdose, or Jarrett's skateboarding accident. There was every indication this same stalker orchestrated the sexting scandal that ruined the Goldsmiths' marriage.

Small wonder Larry Goldsmith didn't want to talk about any of it with her. Still, that didn't justify his blatantly lying to her earlier in his office today.

She looked over the top of the computer at Lindsay, still scooping the insides out of her pumpkin. "Honey, did Jarrett specify that the person his father was caught sexting with was a woman?" she asked.

Lindsay nodded. "Yeah, he said it was a *lady*. What—do you think his dad is gay or something?"

Caitlin sighed. "I'm just grasping at straws here. I thought maybe the same guy who set you up might have set him up, too. I really wish we knew a little bit more about this boyfriend of yours. Too bad his Facebook page is gone. Even if all the information were a lie, at least I'd see what he looks like. Maybe I'd recognize him from the library."

Lindsay rinsed off her hands and dried them. "I downloaded his picture," she said, reaching for her phone. "I still have it."

"You're kidding," Caitlin said, straightening up in the chair. "Let's see . . ."

"I'll show it to you if you promise never to call him my *boyfriend* again," she said, searching for the file. "Here he is . . . here's the snake . . ."

Lindsay held out her phone, and Caitlin squinted at the photo on the small screen. He was standing in front of some scenic overlook, shirtless. He was lean and swarthy. "I can't really see his face," she said. "Could you email it to me?"

Lindsay retracted the phone, and her thumbs worked rapidly over the small keypad. "It's sent," she announced.

Caitlin's computer chimed the signal for a new email. She opened the file and gazed at the enlarged photo. The first thing she noticed was that he was no kid. "Honey, I'm sorry, but look at him. He's high school age like the stars of *Grease* were high school age."

"He didn't say he was in high school," Lindsay pointed out. "He said he was in community college. He's nineteen."

"I think he's closer to twenty-five or thirty," Caitlin observed. He was attractive in a sexy-dangerous way. But he also looked a bit sleazy. "I don't think he's the type I'd find hanging around the library. He doesn't seem familiar at all. And you know, I'm sorry, but he looks a little strung out—like he's partied a bit too much."

"I thought he might be the older brother of some classmate," Lindsay said. "But now I'm not so sure . . ."

Even in the healthy outside setting, the guy calling himself Jeremy looked like someone who took a lot of drugs. Caitlin was getting to know the signs now—a certain look in the eyes, bad teeth, and sometimes the complexion. She couldn't help thinking this young man might be a hustler. That would make sense—hiring a male prostitute to take off his clothes and dupe a teenage girl into doing the same on Skype.

The basement door squeaked.

Caitlin glanced up from her computer to see Gabe in the doorway. His face was like chalk and his eyes didn't seem to focus. He held on to the doorknob like it was the only thing that kept him from collapsing.

"Honey?" she said, getting to her feet.

"I threw up," he said. "I'm sorry . . ."

"Oh, God, gross," Lindsay said, backing into the sink. "Don't do it in here!"

Caitlin could smell the vomit as she rushed up to him. Some of it had splattered onto his Trail Blazers sweatshirt. She felt his forehead. He was burning up. "C'mon, honey," she said. "Let's get you cleaned up and in bed. Think you can make it upstairs?"

He nodded. "I'm pretty sure I'm okay now," he said weakly. "I'm sorry, I made a real mess down there."

"Is it like Barf-o-Rama in *Stand by Me*?" Lindsay asked.

Gabe cracked a weak smile and chuckled a little. "Seriously . . ."

"Give me your sweatshirt, dopey," Lindsay said, holding out her hand. "I'll put it in the wash."

Caitlin helped him pull the sweatshirt over his head and then handed the soiled, smelly thing to Lindsay. She led Gabe up the stairs to the bathroom, where she had him swish some Scope in his mouth.

Getting ready for bed, Gabe moved like an arthritic old man. Caitlin pulled the "barf bowl" from the back of the linen closet. She took his temperature: 99.4. Gabe said he was feeling much better. He was worried that if he was officially sick, he wouldn't get to spend the night at his dad's place in Seattle tomorrow.

After twenty minutes, she left him with his TV on the Syfy channel—along with a glass of water and the barf bowl at his bedside.

In the basement, Lindsay already had the washing machine churning. She said she was cleaning Gabe's soiled sweatshirt and the bathroom rug from Gabe's clubhouse. Lindsay was also mopping up the linoleum sheet that covered the floor in the little room. The smell was atrocious. She had a T-shirt tied around the bottom half of her face—obviously to mute the odor. Lindsay glanced over her shoulder for a second. "God, I thought cleaning out that pumpkin was gross. How's Gabe? Did he hurl again?"

"No, I—I think he's going to be okay," Caitlin said, fanning the air in front of her face. "Honey, thank you for doing this . . ."

"It's okay, I'm almost finished." She sighed and then went back to work. "Besides, you helped me clean up some of my mess today. I owed you."

Caitlin smiled. Her daughter never ceased to surprise her.

Gabe was asleep. He hadn't thrown up again. No encore, thank God.

Lindsay was upstairs, moving her things into the guest room. Jarrett had told her where in the house Denise Healy had been murdered. So she didn't need any further persuading to switch rooms. She'd already packed for the overnight at her dad's place in Seattle, and she had her swim meet there in the morning. She'd be going to bed soon.

Caitlin was listening for her—should she come down to say good night. Caitlin didn't want her daughter catching her at the computer in the study—looking at *Rent-a-Stud Escort Service*.

She'd already been on two other sites: *Hot Guys for Rent* and *Discreet Male Escorts*. Each site had dozens of guys for rent in the Everett, Seattle, and Tacoma area. She must have viewed a couple hundred photos of men—all ages, sizes, and colors, in all stages of dress and undress. She was agog at some of the explicit selfies—and also at how many of these guys seemed to think backward baseball caps were the coolest thing ever.

Rent-a-Stud had three ads listed on every page. Each ad had several tiny indistinguishable photos that had to be clicked on and enlarged so she could see the guy's face. Caitlin was on page twenty-three of twenty-nine.

Their information was in coded icons, which took her a while to figure out. A dollar bill sign meant the guy in the post was a prostitute; a cartoon hand meant he gave massages; a camera meant he'd pose for photos—or did it mean he'd done porn? She really wasn't sure. Most of the guys showed all three icons. And most of them had the international male symbol in one corner of their post, which Caitlin assumed meant they were trying to attract male clients. Only one guy in about twenty had the female symbol on their ad. About thirty percent had both symbols. Caitlin figured "Jeremy" could have any combination of symbols and coded icons in his post—if he was even in here among these rent boys.

She was beginning to think her theory about him being a prostitute was way off. Plus it seemed too easy: uncover the guy in one of these posts, make a date with him, and then find out who hired him to seduce Lindsay online. She'd get his cooperation somehow. After all, her daughter was a minor. She could have him arrested. He'd gotten naked in front of her and solicited her during a Skype session. That had to be a chargeable offense.

Then she saw someone who looked like him—right between *Young Asian Hottie* and *Well-Hung Silver Fox*. The tiny photos had more than a passing resemblance to the shirtless, nature-loving creep who had set up her daughter. *Smooth & Sexy Jock* had all the symbols by his moniker—along with a brief description:

> Handsome, muscular, masculine jock with zero attitude. Couples, gay, bi, straights are welcome. No judgment, just pleasure and fantasy fulfillment. All fotos are recent! Fall Special: $200 for 90 min. Convenient downtown Seattle location. Click here to read the reviews for Dack!

Caitlin ignored the reviews and clicked on the first photo—a selfie of him at a beach, flexing his arm. He was shirtless and had on the requisite backward baseball cap. It was the same cap he wore in the picture Lindsay had of him.

There was an email and a phone contact for him.

Caitlin had decided to ride the ferry with the kids to Mukilteo in the morning—just to make sure they were okay and Russ was there to pick them up. She would call from a phone booth in the Mukilteo ferry terminal and try to book an appointment for that day.

She'd planned on swinging by the bank on the way to the ferry anyway.

She would just have to remember to pick up an extra two hundred dollars—for the fall special.

"You don't even know how I ended up here, do you?" he heard her whispering through the vent. Monica had been rambling on and on for the last half hour, trying to get a response from him.

Aaron was lying on his cot in the darkened cell—

with his head close to the vent. Since his first night here, he'd slept with his feet near the vent. But he'd switched positions tonight so he could hear her voice. Of course, Monica couldn't know for sure if he was listening, because he hadn't uttered a word to her. He was still furious at her. All her apologies and rationalizations didn't change the fact that she'd screwed him over. It was strange how being so angry at someone made the time fly by in this prison. To have some kind of emotion besides fear was a welcome distraction. It wasn't like he could be angry at the coach, because the son of a bitch wasn't even human. But Monica was supposed to be his friend. So he could be full of righteous indignation over what she'd done. As angry as he was, he still liked hearing her voice, and he liked hearing her say she was sorry. He just wasn't ready to let her off the hook yet.

"I was at this party at my friend Katie Martinsen's house," Monica went on. "Katie usually gives the best parties, but this one was kind of a drag. All the wrong people showed up. Anyway, I used a swim meet in the morning as an excuse for leaving early. By early, I mean around ten thirty. I do that a lot—use a swim meet or swim practice as an excuse to get out of bad parties or bad dates. Don't you?"

Aaron said nothing. She was just trying to get a response from him for about the fiftieth time tonight. With his hands behind his head, he stared up at the ceiling.

"Okay, so anyway, I was walking home. Katie lives only, like, two blocks from me. I was only—God, like, a minute away from my house when this van pulled up.

I figured, okay, be careful. But then I see this woman at the wheel and a boy in the front passenger seat. So I wasn't worried. Well, it was the Missus and Junior. And suddenly this guy popped out from behind the hedge in the Bensingers' front yard. Before I knew it, he knocked me down and covered my mouth and nose with this rag. And then, well, you know the rest . . ."

You woke up here, Aaron thought. But he refused to say it out loud.

"That was back in May," she went on. "I missed a whole summer vacation—a whole bunch of parties, swimming at the lake, our family July Fourth picnic, going back to school. This was supposed to be my senior year, the best year of my life, right? I should have spent the summer picking out colleges, going after scholarships, getting tan. God, I miss the sun. Don't you?"

Aaron wasn't falling for it.

"And cue the silence," she said.

Despite his resolve, he cracked a smile.

"I didn't ask if you have any brothers or sisters," she continued. "I'm the youngest of three. I have an older sister who was going to spend her last year of college in Brussels. I figure she must have stayed home after I disappeared. Or maybe my father talked her into going anyway. It's not like she could do anything to help. My mom ran off with this guy about ten years ago. She lives in Atlanta with him and his family. I haven't seen her in, like, five years, but she still calls about once a month. It's just my dad and me at home. God, I worry about him all alone now. I worry about him worrying about me. Isn't that weird? Are your parents still together?"

He wanted to tell her *no*. He wanted to tell her everything about his folks, his childhood in Hawaii, his grandmother, and everything. But he bit his lip and kept staring at the ceiling.

"My brother and his wife live close by—in Lacey," she continued. "Their daughter, Jessica, is eighteen months old. Wait, no she's not. Jessie's two now. I missed her birthday. I'm her godmother and I missed her birthday. She was just starting to talk a little and stand on her own when I was taken. I'll bet she's walking now. God, I missed all that, too . . ."

Suddenly, Aaron couldn't hear anything. He scooted closer to the vent and realized she was crying. He felt awful. He wanted to say something, but what? *Everything's going to be okay?* That would be a lie.

When she started talking again, her voice was a little raspy and she sounded desperately cheerful. "I—I wonder if Jessie will recognize me when she sees me again. Of course, if you keep swimming the way you did this afternoon, I'll never win another race—and I'll never get out of here."

He glanced around his stark, shadowy cell, bathed in blue from the night-light. His two wins today didn't translate into any rewards. The TV and mini-fridge were still locked up somewhere—probably until he really dazzled the coach in the next race or two. Maybe then he'd get them back.

She still talked about winning races as if that was her ticket to freedom. She was probably looking forward to getting a medal—like her friend, Jim, got. Aaron wondered if all the other swimmers got medals, too.

"Are you ever going to talk to me again, Aaron?" she asked quietly.

He sighed. "I'm sorry I told you to fuck off today."

"You didn't tell me to fuck off, you told me, 'fuck you.'"

"Same difference," he said. "Either way, it was pretty creepy of me. Sorry."

"Are we friends again?" she asked.

"Sure," he said.

It reminded him of the fights he had with his mom. No matter how much she drove him crazy and how many times she'd screwed up, he always forgave her—or he wound up apologizing to her. He missed her so much right now. He was almost certain he'd never see her again.

"Listen, we better stop talking," he said, his voice a bit shaky. "We're pushing our luck here."

Now that he was ready to talk to her, he couldn't—because he was crying and he didn't want her to know.

"Sure, I understand," she whispered. "G'night, Aaron."

"Night," he said, and then he covered his mouth.

He was crying because he missed his mother. And he was crying for Monica, who thought she'd be going home in a few days.

Maybe when it happened, the coach would take mercy on her and kill her quickly—before she realized how wrong she was.

CHAPTER EIGHTEEN

Darrington, Washington
Saturday, October 29—7:44 A.M.

A dele prayed he wouldn't notice it.

Her husband, Tim, was at the wheel of their Jeep Cherokee. They drove on an old, narrow, barely-two-lane road that snaked through the woods of the Boulder River Wilderness area. Tim had found out before leaving their campsite that Route 530 was down to one lane in several spots, and they should expect delays. So he was taking the back roads to Interstate 5. Tim was an avid camper. Adele tolerated it. At least this campsite had offered cabins—and theirs had included a fireplace. It sure beat the old days when they used to pitch a tent and roughed it with sleeping bags.

They were both retired now—empty nesters, which was why they could take off and go camping on Thursday for a couple of nights. That was just about enough for Adele. Her favorite part of these rustic excursions was this drive back in the morning. They always stopped for a big breakfast at Bradley's Diner in Darrington on their way home to Lynnwood. Traditionally, that was when they let their diets go to hell. Neither one of them had eaten in anticipation of the big meal. They were approximately twenty minutes away from hotcakes, scrambled eggs, bacon, fresh fruit, and coffee. But there was a bump in the road. Actually, it wasn't a bump—and it was more to the side of the road.

It was a dead raccoon.

Adele hoped Tim wouldn't spot the carcass up ahead. There was a good chance he'd mistake it for one of the big rocks along the road's shoulder. Plus it was a dark, drizzly morning. Adele listened to the squeaky windshield wipers and said nothing. But all the while, she was thinking: *Please keep going, keep going.*

"Oh, no, would you look at that?" Tim announced. The Cherokee slowed to a stop. "Poor little critter."

"Honey, it's raining, and I'm hungry," Adele said. "Can't we dispense with the funeral service this one time and just say a little prayer for it on our way to Bradley's?"

"It'll only take twenty minutes to give the guy a decent burial, and all God's creatures are entitled to—"

"Why can't you just let nature take its course?" she cut in. "I mean, by burying him, you're depriving some other forest animal of their dinner. Besides, we can't park here. We'll block traffic."

"What traffic?" he said, backing up the Jeep. "And there's a trail right behind us here. We'll go up and find a nice little clearing for his final resting place. Twenty minutes . . ."

It never failed. Whenever he saw a dead animal by the side of the road, softhearted, animal-loving Tim had to bury it. He kept a shovel, large trash bags, gloves, and a rope in the back of the Jeep specifically for these impromptu burials. So far, they'd buried two deer, several possums and raccoons, even some stray dogs and cats and countless squirrels. It drove Adele crazy, but it was one reason why she loved him, too.

She figured it was easier not to argue with him and get the ceremony over with.

Tim was right. The trail led to a small clearing in the woods—a perfect little burial ground. He gave her the shovel to get started on the grave, and then he headed back down to the road with his gloves, a plastic bag, and some rope so he could collect the raccoon carcass from the roadside.

In her rain slicker and gardening gloves (she came prepared, too), Adele found a spot where the ground looked soft. It appeared as if some forest animals had been scratching at the soil. It gave her a head start. "I love how he leaves me alone here to break ground," she muttered to herself as she began to dig. "I could get attacked by a bear and meanwhile he's saying a benediction over some stupid dead raccoon . . ."

Adele continued to dig and found herself humming the Beatles song "Rocky Raccoon." The tune would probably stick in her head the rest of the day.

She'd dug down nearly two feet in only ten minutes. She wasn't sure if it was the rain or what, but the ground was loose and workable. Tim would be impressed by her progress.

She wondered what was taking him so long. Maybe he was the one getting attacked by a bear. There were cougars in these mountains, too. Adele glanced at her wristwatch. She'd dig for two more minutes, and if she didn't see him coming up the trail with Rocky, she'd go down to the roadside and see what was taking so long. After all, he was in his heart attack years.

The grave was now about two feet wide and over two feet deep. Bent over it, Adele was mindful of her lower back. She also became aware of an awful smell. She wondered if an animal had recently buried some not-so-fresh bones here. Maybe that was why the ground was sort of soft.

She carefully scooped up another few mounds of earth—then she hit something. With the tip of the shovel, she pushed the dirt around and saw something gold. It looked like a big gold coin. Had she actually uncovered honest-to-God buried treasure?

As she bent closer to the ground to retrieve the discovery, the stench was unbearable. Adele held her breath and reached down for the coin. It was stuck to something. She brushed the dirt away and saw it was a medallion—attached to a faded, tattered blue ribbon. She gave it a tug, but something was holding the ribbon down.

Adele had to come up for air. She glanced over her shoulder and saw Tim lumbering up the trail, dragging the loaded trash bag behind him. "I know you hate doing this, honey," he called. "But all of God's creatures deserve a decent burial . . ."

She waved at him, then turned and took a deep breath. With the shovel, she gently scraped away at the layers of dirt beside the medallion. It looked like an Olympic medal. She kept scraping.

Then she saw a face staring back at her from the dirt. It was mostly gray-brown skin stretched over a skull. The hair was short and caked with dry mud.

Adele gaped down at it, unable to move or scream.

She realized why the gold medallion was stuck.

The ribbon with the medal was around the corpse's neck.

Mukilteo, Washington
Saturday—9:20 A.M.

Caitlin managed to veer out of the lane of cars disembarking from the ferry. Then she pulled into the terminal parking lot.

Russ was waiting there, leaning against a double-parked Toyota Corolla with Virginia plates. It had to be a rental. She wondered how much he'd spent to lease it for the weekend.

He smiled and waved. He looked good—healthy. He wore his navy blue fisherman's sweater, which looked perfect on him in the harbor setting. It had been over a month since she'd seen him. She was overwhelmed with about a hundred different conflicting emotions—mostly yearning. She'd taken a few extra minutes this morning with her hair and makeup. She'd put on a pink blouse that he'd always liked—and twice, she'd nearly changed out of it. She didn't want him back, not yet. So why was she trying to make herself attractive for him?

Lindsay and Gabe scurried out of the car. They grabbed their overnight bags and then ran to Russ and

threw their arms around him. Caitlin remained behind
the wheel with the engine idling. She rolled down her
window.

She'd already broken her own resolve for a morato-
rium on all contact with Russ and texted him early this
morning. She'd had a good excuse. She wanted him to
know that Gabe had thrown up last night and he had to
take it easy today—not too much excitement, not too
much food. His temperature had been normal this
morning. Still, she'd restricted him to tea and toast for
breakfast. Gabe claimed he felt fine and blamed the
school's cafeteria food for last night's upset stomach.

The kids loaded their bags into Russ's rental. Caitlin
could hear them arguing about who would ride shotgun,
and then Lindsay finally conceded to Gabe. Meanwhile,
Russ ambled toward her with sort of a melancholy
smile on his face. He leaned close to her car window
and put a hand on the roof. "Well, so far we're doing a
bang-up job of 'cooling it' for a while until Thanksgiving," he said. "But I'm really glad to see you again,
honey."

"You look good," she admitted.

"I'm being good," he said. "Clean for twenty
days."

"That's wonderful, Russ," she said, working up a
smile. She'd been down this road before with him.
Caitlin took a deep breath and rested her elbow on the
window edge. "Listen, like I said in my text, no junk
food for Gabe, and keep an eye on him. This swim
meet is really important to Lindsay. And be prepared,
because of her—*Internet exposure*—she might have

some loud, off-color remarks from the bleachers today. So try not to lose it . . ."

"I know, I figured as much." He gave her one of those *I'll handle it* nods. Then he touched her arm. "I've missed you."

Her blouse and jacket sleeves were between her arm and his hand, but somehow it still felt so intimate. "Me too," she muttered. Then she pulled her arm away to look at her wristwatch. "You've got less than an hour to get Lindsay to the high school."

"We're fine." He sighed. "I've got it on my GPS."

Caitlin planted both hands on the steering wheel. "Russ, you know I meant it when I said we should 'cool it' for the next few weeks."

"What about this stalker?" he asked.

"I'm taking care of it," she replied. She looked over toward his rental. "You're double-parked, and the kids are waiting. Have a good time today."

He frowned a tiny bit. "Okay, but call me if you need anything. I'll leave it up to you to get in touch. I promise I won't call or text or show up at your door."

"Thanks," she said.

He started to turn away but hesitated and glanced back at her. "I always liked that blouse on you," he whispered. Then he hurried toward his car.

She waited until he climbed into the Corolla and pulled out of the lot. Then she started to drive around in search of a parking spot. She tried to hold back the tears, but it was impossible. She managed to find a space while sobbing. But by the time she slipped her folded-up dollar bills into the pay box's numbered slot, Caitlin had dried her eyes and pulled herself together.

Inside the small ferry terminal, she noticed an elderly man talking on the pay phone. She'd paid for two hours of parking and figured she'd be on the phone for only a few minutes. Would she even be able to get ahold of Jeremy—or Dack or whatever he called himself?

People were still milling around the station, waiting to board the ferry back to Echo. Caitlin took out some quarters and the scrap of paper with Dack's phone number on it. On the wall beside the pay phone was a rack of brochures. She noticed one for the Bayside Bed & Breakfast. The B and B was a short walk from the ferry landing in Echo, not far from the library. Caitlin had walked past it several times—a beautiful old Cape Cod style mansion. She remembered the list that Sally, the real estate woman, had given her: *Carrie Augusta Sewell (deceased)*.

Sewell, the former owner of the Bayside B&B, had bought the Birch Place house about three years ago. Larry Goldsmith had said she'd died in a car accident. He'd bought the property from the bank, which took it over after Carrie's death.

Caitlin wondered who was running the bed-and-breakfast now. Did they have any details about the car accident? Considering the history of the Birch Place house, maybe it wasn't really an accident.

The old man finally hung up the pay phone and shuffled toward the ferry passenger walkway.

Making a beeline to the phone, Caitlin grabbed the receiver and dialed the number for Dack. An automated operator's voice told her the call required one dollar and twenty-five cents. Caitlin slipped her quarters into the slot and listened to the clicking sound on the other end. It was almost like change jingling. Then the ringtones started: one, two, three. Biting her lip, she waited for the voice mail greeting to come on.

"Yeah, hello?" someone said, clearing his throat. He sounded as if he'd just woken up.

"Hi, is Dack there?" she asked.

"Speaking."

"My name is—ah—" she glanced out the window, "Pier, and I was hoping you have an opening today for a massage. I pulled out my shoulder—"

"Hold on a sec," he interrupted.

Caitlin wondered why the hell she was telling him a lie about her shoulder. That wasn't the kind of massage he offered. Was he checking her phone number? Could he see that she was calling from a pay phone in Mukilteo?

"Yeah," he said, getting back on the line. "How does twelve o'clock sound? You can be my 'nooner.' Ha!"

She managed a weak laugh. "That would be fine. What's the address?"

He gave her an address on Western Avenue in Belltown, just north of downtown Seattle. The apartment number was 949. Caitlin scribbled it down on the front of the Bayside B&B brochure.

"For first-time customers, it's cash only," he pointed out.

"That's fine," Caitlin said. "Two hundred dollars, right?"

"Right, the fall special. See you at noon, Pier. Ciao!" The way he said it, he sounded like he was calling someone to dinner.

Then he hung up before she could say good-bye.

Caitlin glanced at his address on the front of the brochure. She had over two hours until she had to be there. As she hung up the phone, she noticed the sign flashing above the entrance to the ferry passenger walkway: *Echo—Now Boarding*.

Hurrying toward the walkway, she pulled out her Orca Pass card and swiped it at the turnstile. Once on the ferry, she sat down and took her cell phone from her purse. She dialed the number on the brochure. She half expected to get a voice mail.

A woman picked up: "Good morning, Bayside Bed and Breakfast, this is Sandra. How can I help you?"

"Hi," Caitlin said, suddenly a little stumped. She should have thought of what to say before calling the place. "Ah, I have some friends who'll be visiting, and I wanted to see if I could get a tour before I make reservations."

"When are they coming in and how many rooms will you need?" the woman asked.

Caitlin noticed the ferry had started moving. "Well, I'm not sure how many or how soon exactly," she said. "Probably two rooms, sometime within the month. I was hoping I could take a tour today, maybe talk to someone there about the B and B's history—you know, interesting tidbits, information about the owners, that sort of thing. I figured my friends might like to know a little bit about the place where they'll be staying."

"Well, I'm Sandra, I'm the owner," the woman said. "I'm probably the best person to talk to."

"Oh?" Caitlin tried to sound mildly surprised. "I thought the owner was someone named Carrie."

"No, I'm sorry to say that Carrie passed away about three years ago. She left the B and B to me. Pardon me, but I didn't get your name."

She hesitated, but then figured there was no reason to lie. "Caitlin Stoller."

"Well, Caitlin, you said you wanted to come in today, but we're going to be busy this afternoon. We have a big group arriving."

"What about now?" Caitlin asked.

"Most of the rooms are being cleaned right now, but I can show you the common areas. Would that be all right?"

"That would be great, thank you," she said.

"How soon can I expect you, Caitlin?"

"I'm on my way," she replied, looking out at the open water. "I'll be there in about twenty-five minutes."

"I have a confession," said the B and B's owner. "Your name rang a bell earlier, and then I realized you're the new librarian. The story was in the *Echo Bulletin* last month—along with your picture, which didn't do you justice."

The tall, thin, fortyish woman had introduced herself at the front door. Her name was Sandra Watts, and despite her slightly hard-edged features, she was pretty—with soft-looking, shoulder-length, pale blond hair. She smelled of patchouli, and wore a floral-patterned blouse and black skirt.

She'd already shown Caitlin the dining room—with a built-in breakfront and a dining table that sat twelve.

The centerpiece was a cornucopia of baby pumpkins surrounded by orange and black votives for Halloween. Sandra had explained that the breakfast buffet was from six until ten every morning.

Caitlin had wondered how she could steer the conversation to Carrie Sewell, the Birch Place house she'd owned, and her death. Caitlin figured since Sandra had inherited the B and B, she and Carrie must have been close.

The living room's big picture window had a sweeping view of the beach and the water. There was a stone fireplace and tasteful, elegant furniture. Still, the B and B seemed just on the brink of decay. Caitlin had noticed a small water stain in one corner of the ceiling. And the Oriental rug was so worn, it almost looked tattered.

Sandra had just explained that guests could use the living room until midnight every night. Then as a *by the way*, she mentioned that she knew who Caitlin was.

Caitlin figured it was a good thing she hadn't given a fake name over the phone. "Well, I don't think I've seen you at the library," was all she could think of to say.

"I've only been by a couple of times in the last month," Sandra said, "probably on your days off. Anyway, I'm sorry I can't show you any of our bedrooms right now, but there are a couple of photos in our brochure, which I see you have." She nodded toward Caitlin's purse—with the brochure sticking out. "And there are even more pictures online. Would you like to see the patio? It's lovely this time of year, and we have some Halloween decorations out . . ."

"Actually, Sandra, I have a confession, too," Caitlin said. "It's true I'm looking for a place where my friends can stay while they're here in town. But I was also very curious about Carrie Sewell. I'm assuming she was a friend of yours . . ."

Sandra's eyes narrowed. "Yes, I suppose you could say Carrie and I were friends. I managed this B and B for her for a year before she died."

"Well, I moved into a house on Birch Place that Carrie used to own," Caitlin said.

Sandra's jaw dropped. "My God, so you bought that place?"

"You look slightly horrified . . ."

She quickly shook her head. "No, I only—well, it's just that your new house has an interesting history attached to it, that's all."

"You mean, like the murder there in 1992?" Caitlin asked.

"So you know about that . . ."

"I didn't know about it when I bought the place," Caitlin admitted. "Did Carrie know?"

"Yes, but she wasn't planning to live there. She wanted to turn it into a second B and B. She figured what the guests didn't know about the murder wouldn't hurt them. And after all, it is a beautiful home. I've been inside it several times."

"Really?"

"Oh, yes. Carrie had big plans for that house . . ."

Sandra stopped talking just as a maid wandered in with a feather duster. The stocky, thirtysomething brunette wore a full apron and thin plastic gloves. She was chewing gum. She started dusting the furniture.

"Anita, did you finish the front two bedrooms already?" Sandra asked.

"Everything but the towels," the maid replied in slightly broken English. "I'm still waiting for them."

Sandra rubbed her forehead. "Oh, God, yes, all right." She sighed and then smiled at Caitlin. "I'm handling the laundry today. How would you like a *real* tour of the place? You can come down to the basement with me and help me fold towels."

Caitlin laughed. "Sure."

She followed Sandra through a spacious modern kitchen and then down a metal staircase to a large, slightly dismal, unfinished utility room. Along one wall were several chain-link cages that looked like storage units. Someone had already pulled out the Thanksgiving decorations for outside: plastic pilgrims and a large turkey. The two big washers and dryers made a loud mechanical hum. The metal shelf beside them was full of Costco-size containers of detergent, bleach, and dryer sheets, among other things.

Pushing up her sleeves, Sandra donned a pair of thin rubber gloves—from another big box on the shelf. Then she unloaded some white towels from the dryer and dumped them in a plastic laundry basket. "So where was I?" she asked, her back to Caitlin.

"Ah, you were in my house," Caitlin said.

"That's right, I had to go over there sometimes to talk to Carrie or run errands for her." She hauled the basket over to a table beside an ironing board. She shook out a towel and started folding it.

"May I help?" Caitlin asked, setting her purse on one end of the ironing board.

"Oh, no, I was kidding earlier. I have this. Anyway, Carrie first got it in her head to buy the house in 2012. The couple who lived there had run into some bad luck, and they were looking to sell the place."

"What kind of bad luck?"

"Well, for one, their marriage went down the toilet," she said, folding another towel and starting a stack on the ironing board. "And I'm pretty sure they had a child who died, too."

"You mean, while they were living in the house?" Caitlin asked. If that was the case, it was a regular pattern with the Birch Place property: a broken marriage and a dead child.

"I can't say for sure. It happened before I came to Echo. When I was hired on here as assistant manager, Carrie was already quite interested in the house. The couple—I forget their names . . ."

"Hecht," Caitlin remembered out loud.

"That's it. The Hechts, they had two kids in addition to the one who had died. Besides that, the Hechts had some financial woes, too. See what I mean, bad luck? I guess the house was a real money pit for them. It had been uninhabited for years and years when they bought it. I guess they started to fix it up, and they weren't quite done when everything went sour. They put it up for sale. Carrie played it smart and waited several months before buying the place. By then I think the Hechts were divorced, and they'd knocked about eighty thousand off the original asking price. Carrie thought she was getting a real bargain, the poor thing."

"What do you mean?" Caitlin asked.

"Well, her luck with the house wasn't much better."

Sandra went back to the machines, emptied one of the washers, and put the wet towels in the dryer. "First she had to borrow from the bank to buy the place. Then she hired this carpenter, Lance Spangler, to do the remodel. He'd worked on the house for the Hechts. Carrie had all sorts of ideas, some of them undoing things he'd done for the Hechts—like tearing out a linen closet upstairs to make it a bathroom so each bedroom had its own bath. Down in the basement, she wanted two bedrooms, plus a Jack and Jill bath. Carrie and Lance spent a lot of time going over the plans together—in the house. FYI, Lance was in his mid-forties and not too hard on the eyes. He was married, but he never let that stop him. And Carrie—well, she was a reasonably attractive widow, fifty-five, no kids . . ."

Sandra turned on the dryer and talked louder to be heard over the noise. "Pretty soon, it was all over town about how Lance and Carrie were 'christening' every room in the house—if you get my drift." She raised her eyebrows at Caitlin, then returned to the ironing board and loaded the folded towels into the basket. "Anyway, they didn't get much work done on the house, that's for sure. I went over there one afternoon when Carrie was sick, and Lance wasn't doing a damn thing except talking on his cell phone. And while I was there, he came on to me—big-time. We're talking about a hot August afternoon, and he was all sweaty in his T-shirt, jeans, and tool belt. I mean, I'm not kidding. It was something out of a housewife's steamy fantasy. If Carrie hadn't been my boss and my friend, I might have been tempted."

She folded her arms and leaned against the table.

"You know, I wish I'd told Carrie what a he-slut hound dog the guy was. Maybe it would have made a difference—or maybe not. When they weren't at the house, they'd drive off in his truck together—always out of town to this antique dealer for doorknobs and hinges or to that lumber mill for a certain piece of wood. Everyone said they were going off to some No-Tell Motel for a little 'afternoon delight.' They were driving back from one of these trips on a rainy October afternoon when the brakes on Lance's truck failed. And that was that."

Sandra let out a long sigh. "It was a mountain road. They were both killed. Carrie left everything to me. I was kind of shocked. I had no idea. We'd only known each other for a little over a year. Anyway, I got this B and B, and the bank got the house."

Caitlin said nothing. She was thinking about the Hechts' child and Lance Spangler—two more deaths associated with that house, two more victims who weren't mentioned on the real estate agent's list of previous owners.

Sandra grabbed the basket of folded towels. "Well, I'll be glad to show you two of our bedrooms now—if you're still interested."

"Thank you," Caitlin said. "But I've taken up too much of your time already."

"It's no bother. I need to restock the bathrooms anyway."

Caitlin glanced at her watch. "Actually, I need to catch the next ferry out. I have a noon appointment in Seattle. I should get going."

Sandra gave her an odd sidelong glance—like she was disappointed.

Caitlin wondered if she should have gone on pretending to be interested in the B and B. She thought she'd pretty much come clean about her motives for this visit when she'd told Sandra she was living in the house Carrie had owned.

"Okay," Sandra said with an awkward smile. "Then I'll walk you to the door."

Caitlin followed her to the stairs. "I want to thank you for telling me about Carrie—and the house."

"No problem," she answered, carrying the basket up the steps. "I figure you own the place now, you should know what went on there."

"Did Carrie ever say anything to you about a stalker?"

"Well, she was convinced someone was watching her and Lance in the house," Sandra replied. "She said she used to find these strange notes everywhere. And we kept getting hang-ups at the B and B. If you ask me, I think it was Scary Teri."

Caitlin stopped at the top of the stairs. This all sounded way too familiar. "Who's Scary Teri?"

"Teri Spangler, Lance's long-suffering and insufferable wife," Sandra explained. They continued on through the kitchen. "We called her Scary Teri. I mean, no wonder Lance strayed. She was pretty crazy. For example, she hurled a rock through the window at the house on Birch—while her husband and Carrie were there. They didn't have any doubt about who had done it. They saw her car speed away. The next night somebody did more rock throwing—here at the B and B. She broke two windows. Scary Teri, she was a real piece of work . . ."

"*Was?* What happened to her?"

"I didn't mean to make it sound like she's dead. I'm pretty sure she's still around. Last I heard, she lives in Oak Harbor. You know, between you and me, I wouldn't be the least bit surprised if Scary Teri had something to do with those brakes going out on Lance's car. I'm just saying . . ."

They passed through the dining room. Then Sandra set the basket on a bench in the front hallway. "So—that's an awfully big house for just one person," she said. "I can't remember if the *Bulletin* article said you were married or not."

"Divorced," Caitlin said.

Sandra opened the door for her. "Any kids?"

She nodded. "Three—I mean, two." It had been a while since she'd made that mistake. "Ah, my oldest died a couple of years ago—bicycle accident."

"I'm so sorry," Sandra murmured. "Listen, come back and get the rest of the tour some other time, okay?"

Caitlin paused in the doorway, which was decorated with fake cobwebs—and real pumpkins on either side. She nodded. "Thank you, Sandra." Then she started down the front steps.

"Caitlin, one more thing," Sandra said. "I can give you and your kids a discount here—if ever you need a place to stay."

Caitlin stared at her in the doorway, the wind ruffling her blond hair. She looked so somber. "That house has been bad luck for everyone who's ever lived there," Sandra said. "And you seem like a very nice person. Just know you have another place to stay here in town."

"Well, thank you," Caitlin murmured, a bit dazed.

Sandra nodded. Then she ducked back inside and closed the door.

She was forty minutes early for her appointment with Dack—or Jeremy or whatever the hell his real name was. She'd found parking within two blocks of his building, a modern high-rise with balconies overlooking Olympic Sculpture Park and Elliott Bay. It looked like a pricey, pretty, well-kept place. Caitlin wondered how a young male prostitute could afford it. Maybe he was pretty well kept, too. Then again, at two hundred dollars for each ninety-minute session, he only had to service five customers to make a thousand a day. Plus he probably got paid extra for special assignments—like the scam he pulled on Lindsay.

Who had hired him? On the ferry from Echo to Mukilteo, she'd thought about how she would get him to talk. Money, of course. But then she didn't have much more than the extra two hundred on her. If that didn't work, she'd threaten to go to the police.

She still wasn't sure why someone had decided to target Lindsay. Larry Goldsmith had been publicly humiliated with the exposure of his Internet sex activities. And his wife ended up committing suicide. Was this whole *Jeremy* ruse designed to humiliate Lindsay to the point that she might take her own life? Was this an attempt to cause another child's death at the Birch Place house?

The talk with Sandra Watts had been informative. Caitlin wondered if Teri Spangler was the force behind the house's *bad luck.* Her husband had worked for two of its owners. Sandra had said that Teri was crazy. Maybe *Scary Teri* had some sort of resentment for everyone who lived in this house her husband had worked on. If she and Lance had grown up in Echo, they would have been teenagers when Denise Healy was bludgeoned to death in the house. Maybe one of them had a connection to Denise's unsolved murder.

On the ferry, Caitlin had Googled *Teri Spangler, Echo,* and couldn't find anything. She varied the spelling to *Terry* and *Terri,* and still couldn't come up with a viable link. She tried *Lance and Teri Spangler* on Google Images, and after three pages of pictures, she finally uncovered a blurry photo posted on the Facebook page of an Everett woman, Loretta Bigelow. It was a snapshot from a party in May 2012. Loretta's caption read: "*I'm not drunk in this picture, I swear! So nice to meet Lance & Teri Spangler. Nice couple!*"

Caitlin guessed Loretta was the laughing redhead who had a cocktail in her hand. She posed with a couple. With his longish sandy hair and mustache, the handsome husband looked like a country music star. Hanging on his shoulder, the wife was a cute, buxom brunette with an off-the-shoulder curly perm that was out of style even back in 2012. She wore an ugly ruffled green dress that looked like a bad bridesmaid's gown. Was this *Scary Teri*? Caitlin didn't remember ever seeing the woman in the library.

She wished she knew more about this woman. She probably wouldn't have much luck tracking down Loretta Bigelow and asking her about Teri. After all, Loretta had just met Teri and Lance at that party. She probably never saw them again after that night. Caitlin decided she was better off trying to track down Elaine Hecht. Lance had worked for the Hechts, too.

With time to kill before her appointment, she hiked up the collar of her jacket and wandered into Sculpture Park. The outdoor museum was nine acres of modern art pieces and designs amid paved walkways. The manicured lawn was still a lush green. The downtown park overlooked the waterfront Myrtle Edwards Park.

Caitlin didn't want to stray far from Dack's building. She sat down on a bench, which was uphill from a twenty-foot-tall steel and fiberglass typewriter eraser—with the rubber wheel seemingly stuck in the grass and the bristles blowing in the wind.

This would be a neat place to take the kids, she thought. But she was too nervous and distracted to enjoy it now. Pulling out her phone, she looked at the photo of Teri Spangler again. She would show it to Dack and ask if this was the woman who had hired him to seduce Lindsay online.

She realized she must have looked like one of those idiots who go to a museum and spend the entire time gaping at their phones. She checked her watch. Throughout the day, off and on, she'd been shopping online for home security companies. If she called some places now, maybe one of them could come over on Monday and make an assessment. She wanted all new locks on the doors—including the one in the basement, especially the one in the basement; motion detector spotlights around the outside of the house; and an alarm system. All the companies were on the mainland, the closest one in Everett.

With the wind sweeping up from the bay, Caitlin sat shivering on the park bench as she called several home security businesses. It was frustrating. The soonest anyone could ferry over to the island was next Thursday.

"Would it bump me up to a sooner appointment if I told you that I recently moved into a house where someone was murdered twenty-five years ago?" Caitlin asked the last salesman. "I have two kids, and someone's been stalking me."

"What about Wednesday morning at eleven?" he asked.

She rolled her eyes. "That would be great. Thank you. If something opens up before that, would you let me know?"

He recommended that in the meantime she buy some spotlights and heavy-duty extension cords at a hardware store and strategically place the lights around the house. It wasn't a bad idea. Caitlin thanked him. She would feel better staying alone in that house tonight if the grounds were lit up.

She glanced at her watch again. It was about a minute before noon. *I'll be late for my male prostitute*, she thought with a skittish laugh.

Getting to her feet, Caitlin hurried up the walkway toward Western Avenue. The building was just across the street. She stopped at a lighted pedestrian crossing as traffic zipped by.

Just as Caitlin looked up at the walk signal, she heard a loud thud and shattering glass.

Someone screamed. Tires screeched.

Caitlin looked around for the traffic accident—or what had sounded like one. Then she saw the white Prius parked across the street—at the corner of Dack's building. A large, black blob had smashed into the car's roof and blown apart the windshield.

It took Caitlin a moment to realize the blob was a person. She saw the blood streaming down the side of the mangled white car.

Traffic had stopped.

Glancing up at Dack's building, she saw a curtain fluttering in an open sliding-glass door to a balcony.

Breathless, she counted the stories. It was the ninth floor.

She hurried across the street, where a crowd was gathering. She gazed at the crumpled, bloody thing on top of the Prius. Already, a crimson pool was forming on the pavement—at the side of the car.

She couldn't see his face. He was wearing a black T-shirt and black jeans.

"Has anyone called nine-one-one?" a woman asked in a shrill voice that rose over the murmuring from the crowd.

People were gasping in shock and revulsion. One woman was crying. Several onlookers were asking what had happened.

"Oh, shit, look at that!" one young man declared, chuckling.

"I think it's that guy from nine," Caitlin heard a man

say. "With all his drugs and partying, I knew something like this was going to happen . . ."

"The police are on their way!" someone else announced.

Instinctively, Caitlin turned and pushed her way through the crowd. She just had to get out of there. She thought she was going to be sick.

She heard a police siren in the distance.

She started toward her car but stopped to glance over her shoulder. She wondered if someone was watching her.

Traffic was at a standstill on Western Avenue. But she noticed one thing moving.

The wind had caught someone's lost baseball hat. Seemingly on its own, it floated and skipped across the pavement.

CHAPTER NINETEEN

Something was wrong.

According to his nightstand clock, it was 12:10. A banana, a granola bar and a container of cold orange juice had been passed through the drawer to him around breakfast time. And just minutes ago, a cold ham and cheese sandwich, Goldfish, and a container of milk had been doled out to him for lunch. In between the food deliveries, time had dragged and dragged. Aaron didn't realize how their grueling practice sessions in the pool had made the hours here move so much faster. Anxious and bored, he was going crazy. He kept busy by exercising—mostly push-ups, kicks, and stretches.

He finally took a chance and quietly called to Monica through the vent. "Hey? What's going on? Do you know? Why aren't we practicing?"

She shushed him. "It's Saturday. There are swim meets. He's probably out scouting swimmers."

Aaron said nothing. He slowly sat down on the edge of the cot.

The coach was already shopping for a replacement for one of them.

Seattle
Saturday, October 29—12:55 P.M.

Her team lost the meet. But Lindsay came in first in the 100-yard breaststroke and took second place in the 200-yard freestyle. So—it wasn't a total disaster.

Lindsay had braced herself for some hecklers. Except for someone shouting out "Hey, Lindsay, show us your stuff!" right before the 200-yard freestyle, there had been nothing. She hadn't noticed who had yelled it out. And the comment hadn't even necessarily been lewd. It wasn't exactly inappropriate to yell that during a sports competition.

Her dad was in a desperately upbeat mood during the drive to his apartment in Capitol Hill. It must have been really important to him that she and Gabe have a good time this weekend. Or maybe he thought she needed cheering up because her team had lost. A bunch of her teammates had asked her to join them at Pacific Place for a shop and calorie fest. Lindsay was flattered they'd asked. She took it as a sign that she'd made some friends on the team. But she'd told them no thanks. She felt obliged to stay with her dad today.

He was making a big deal out of the fact that he'd be taking them to Dick's Drive-In for lunch after they dropped off their bags at his place. As she sat in the front passenger seat of his rental car, Lindsay decided not to say anything. But she imagined Gabe downing those greasy burgers and fries, and then puking his guts out again.

In the lobby of her father's crummy apartment building, he asked which one of them wanted to get his mail out of the mailbox—like they were little kids who still got a kick out of crap like that. *Okay, now, you can push the button in the elevator.* Why the hell would she want to get his mail? Again, Lindsay decided to keep her mouth shut. Gabe volunteered. He pulled out a Macy's flier and a letter. "You got a letter from Mom!" he announced.

The surprised smile on her dad's face was heartbreaking. He eagerly grabbed the letter out of Gabe's hand and thanked him.

As soon as they got up to his dumpy apartment on the third floor, he excused himself, ducked into his bedroom, and closed the door.

Setting down her backpack, Lindsay saw the rolled-up sleeping bags in one corner of the living room. They didn't exactly look new. He must have bought them used. She hoped he'd washed them. She hated to even think it, but what if they carried lice or bedbugs?

On his sad little dining table, he had some mini-carnations in a water glass. Lindsay knew he must have bought the flowers to pretty up the place for their visit.

Moving closer to the bedroom, she thought she heard him talking to someone on the phone: "No, I'm not kidding . . ." he whispered. "Listen, do you know somebody?"

Suddenly the bedroom door opened, and Lindsay stepped back. Startled, she gaped at her father.

He had the phone to his ear. "I'm talking with one of my SARA friends," he said. "Sit tight, and we'll head out for lunch in just a few minutes."

Then he shut the door again.

He was true to his word. Quite soon, they were back in the car, on their way to Dick's Drive-In. "We're almost there," he announced, pulling in front of a seedy-looking little storefront on Union Avenue. "I just have to make a quick stop in here. Stay put, kids."

Lindsay gazed at the sign in the store window:

E-Z CASH EXPRESS
Checks Cashed—Payday Loans
MONEY ORDERS—BAIL BONDS
Quick, Easy & Confidential!

He climbed out of the car and hurried into the place. Lindsay noticed her mother's letter in his hand.

Russ signed the back of the check and got out his driver's license. He was so excited, he shook a little.

He stepped behind a young man who was already at the cashier's window. The Plexiglas looked bullet-proof. There were two security cameras up near the ceiling. Russ wasn't sure if it was the other customer or the place, but something smelled like bad BO—alcohol and sweat. While he waited, he took out Caitlin's letter and read it again:

Dear Russ,

   *I know things are tuff for you right now, so
here's some money to make things easier for a
while. Don't think about paying me back for
now. Please don't say anything to the kids about
this. And please, don't contact me. If you send
the money back, I'll be hurt. Same thing goes if
you try to contact me. I don't even want you to
thank me. Let's never talk about it. Okay? I hope
you understand.*

                         Caitlin

The tone of the note didn't sound like her. In all the
time he'd known her, she'd never signed a note or letter to him, *Caitlin*. It was always *Love, Me*. Even the
notes she'd written to him after their separation had
been signed *Love, Me*. She also wouldn't have spelled
tough that way, not his librarian wife.

But it was her stationery, and the handwriting
looked like hers. Plus the message—about not contacting her—sure was familiar.

Finally, the check she'd sent was for four thousand
dollars.

So Russ didn't question it. He was too busy thinking
about what he wanted to buy with the money—just as
soon as he got the kids on the ferry tomorrow.

Echo
Saturday—3:18 P.M.

   Caitlin shoved the spiked holder into the ground,
adjusted the base, and then screwed in the floodlight

bulb. She wore a dark blue sweatshirt and had her hair in a ponytail. She was filthy from kneeling on the grass and trudging around in the dirt. She figured her face was particularly grimy because she kept crying and then wiping the tears away with her soiled hands.

This was the sixth and last outdoor light she'd installed around the house: two in front, two in back, one on each side. She'd wrapped duct tape around the plug connections to the heavy extension cords, which ran along the foundation of the house to the outdoor socket. She prayed the six floodlights wouldn't blow a fuse.

She'd done a lot of praying in the last three hours—along with all her sobbing.

As soon as she'd pulled out of her parking spot two blocks from Dack's building, Caitlin realized she was leaving the scene of a crime. Suicide or murder, it was still a crime. And she didn't think it was suicide. She should have remained there and talked to the police. And tell them what? That she had an appointment with this prostitute? That he'd solicited her teenage daughter online and sent semi-nude images of her to everyone in her school? She would have been making Lindsay's silly little mistake into an even bigger public humiliation. And by talking to the police, she might as well offer herself as a suspect—if it was indeed murder. After all, she was there when it happened, and she had a good reason for wanting him dead.

It was obvious she'd been set up. Someone must have known about her noon appointment with Dack. Maybe he'd told this certain someone about "Pier" calling to book a massage—from a pay phone at the Mukilteo ferry terminal. Dack plunged from that balcony at noon, the exact time of their appointment. That was no coincidence. It happened when it did so she would see it—and possibly be framed for it.

She wondered if Dack had an appointment book. His phone records probably showed the calls to Lindsay. And the Skype session was probably still on his computer.

Driving on Interstate 5, Caitlin kept thinking that at any minute her phone would ring, and it would be the police wanting to know about her involvement with Dack. Or maybe they wanted to talk to her daughter about this dead male prostitute.

Caitlin's stomach was in knots. She was so distracted that she started to drift into another lane—and narrowly missed sideswiping a VW bug.

When she saw the sign for Aurora Village Mall, she pulled off the interstate. She had a teary breakdown in a stall in the women's restroom of Home Depot. She managed to pull herself together and then texted Lindsay. She had to make sure the police hadn't contacted her daughter yet.

Just checking in. How did u do at the meet?

Caitlin wasn't even out of the bathroom when Lindsay responded:

We lost, but I won the 100 yd breaststroke. CU tomorrow XX

At least for now, her daughter was okay. She texted back:

Way to go! I'm so proud of u. CU XXX

At Home Depot, Caitlin bought the floodlights, the spiked stands, and the extension cords. She paid for everything with a check. She really missed having credit cards.

As she merged back onto I-5 heading to Mukilteo, Caitlin realized she'd have to tell Lindsay about *Jeremy*'s death. More and more, she kept thinking she should call the police. Of course, she could probably kiss off her job at the library when it came out that she'd had an appointment with a male prostitute who had died under mysterious circumstances.

A part of her still clung to the impossible hope that someone else—and not Dack—had fallen from that ninth-floor balcony. On the ferry, she tried to find some information online. She'd checked the latest Seattle news, but there was nothing about a hustler's death in Belltown. She had checked again when she'd returned home, but there hadn't been anything.

She collected the duct tape, leftover wrappers, and bulb boxes, then plodded back into the house and tried the front hall switch that powered the outdoor socket. The lights worked, and she hadn't blown a fuse. The place would be lit up like Buckingham Palace tonight. So at least it would be easy for the cops to find the house when they came to arrest her for leaving the scene of a crime and withholding information in a murder investigation.

There was still time to call them and offer a full report.

Instead, Caitlin decided to make sure no one had gotten inside the house during her long absence today. She'd be alone here all night and wanted to double-check everything now.

No one was hiding in any of the closets upstairs. She checked the windows on the first floor to make sure they were all locked. The kitchen door was still double-locked and dead-bolted.

Then she braved the basement. As she stepped into the utility room, the smell of stale vomit hit her. Lindsay must have missed some spots in Gabe's clubhouse. Either that or she hadn't thoroughly rinsed off the mop.

Caitlin quickly unlocked and opened the basement door. Then she warily sniffed the mop, which Lindsay had left by the laundry sink. It didn't smell too awful. But Caitlin gave it a good rinse anyway. Then she checked Gabe's clubhouse—and grimaced.

The horrid smell was definitely coming from here. While the floor looked clean at first glance, she could see some of the vomit had gone past the edge of the old linoleum and down onto the plank floor below. Even Gabe's Renuzit canister couldn't camouflage the smell.

"Oh, shit," Caitlin muttered nervously. She hated being down in this scary basement when she was alone in the house—even during the daytime. Yet she couldn't just allow that smell to fester. She started to empty out Gabe's clubhouse—the chair, the desk, the makeshift bookshelf and everything on it. All the while, Caitlin tried to hold her breath.

She also kept glancing at her watch. She didn't want to miss the local news at five in case there was something on Dack's death.

The little room didn't have any molding to hold down the linoleum piece. It was cut to fit the closet but felt slightly loose underfoot. Caitlin hoped it wasn't glued to the floor. She slipped her fingers under the linoleum's slightly brittle edges at the doorway and started to lift it. She felt some resistance as the piece bent and scraped against the wall. The vomit smell was definitely stronger. As she struggled to move the linoleum sheet out of the room, she held her breath and kept her head turned to one side. Moving the sheet toward the open door, she saw worn strips of old double-stick tape on the underside. She leaned the old linoleum piece against the door.

With a sigh, Caitlin grabbed the mop and headed back toward Gabe's clubhouse. At the doorway, she stopped dead.

She hadn't seen it when she'd moved the linoleum cutout. She'd had her head turned away because of the smell. But she saw it now. On the plank floor, just about where Gabe's desk had been, there was a trapdoor. From an outline on the wood, it appeared to have had a lock on it at one time.

"What the hell?" Caitlin murmured. She couldn't figure out what it was. Maybe it was access to the plumbing or some kind of drainage thing.

Caitlin thought she heard a noise upstairs. She stepped back and glanced at the open basement door. Had someone snuck in while she was clearing out the clubhouse and wrestling with the linoleum sheet? She stood still for a moment and listened. Nothing.

She hated it down here. And now she hated it even

more because there was another unknown thing in this already creepy part of the house.

As she reached down to pull at the wooden trap-door, Caitlin imagined rodents or insects suddenly scurrying out. One side of the panel was on hinges that squeaked when she lifted it. The light from over her shoulder illuminated what looked like a dirt floor about nine feet down. Was it another room? There weren't any stairs and no ladder.

She pulled her iPhone out of her sweatshirt pocket, bent closer to the opening, and turned on the flashlight app. The space had a stale, musty smell that was almost as bad as the vomit smell in Gabe's clubhouse. The hidden underground space was about the size of one of the bedrooms—and full of cobwebs. The walls were unfinished, concrete posts and exposed wood. She noticed another laundry sink down there.

Bending down a little farther until her head was just past the opening, Caitlin saw a pull-string light socket on the ceiling. There was no bulb. Did the socket even work? From where she was, she'd have to be a contortionist to reach over and screw in a bulb. The blood started to rush to her head.

Caitlin straightened up and retreated to the utility room, where she breathed in some fresh air by the open basement door. What was that room supposed to be? If it was a wine or fruit cellar, there should have been some racks or shelves.

She could see her breath as she stood by the open door for a moment. Then she got a new lightbulb out of one of the boxes on the workbench. Her eyes avoided the outline of the hammer on the empty pegboard wall.

She told herself that maybe Chandler and Elaine Hecht had put up the tool board when they renovated the house years ago. Maybe that wasn't where Ned Healy kept the hammer that someone used to murder his daughter.

Another thing that came with the house—besides the tool board and workbench—was an old ten-foot-tall ladder. It was lying on its side on the floor along the wall opposite the bench.

She moved a couple of boxes of Christmas decorations and grabbed the ladder. It was more awkward than heavy. It was also dusty, with a few spiderwebs between the rungs. Hauling it into Gabe's clubhouse, she banged the ladder against the underside of the stairs a couple of times before she was able to lower it into the hidden room below. The ladder almost seemed tailor-made for the cellar's height—and perhaps it was.

Caitlin retrieved the lightbulb from the workbench, then hurried back to the clubhouse. She hesitated. What if the ladder broke or she fell? She was here all alone. She could end up trapped down in that damp, dusty pit.

She touched her phone in the front pocket of her sweatshirt. If she got stranded, she could always call somebody. She could tell them the basement door was open. *Just follow the barf smell once you get in*, she imagined telling them. She let out a weak laugh.

She shoved the lightbulb in her sweatshirt pocket and then climbed down two rungs of the ladder. It felt steady, but she was shaking. Caitlin skittishly stepped down a few more rungs until she was looking up at the opening above her—and the light in Gabe's clubhouse.

She was surrounded by darkness. She kept imagining the worst. What if the light up there suddenly went off? What if the door to Gabe's clubhouse slammed shut and locked her in here?

With a trembling hand, she managed to screw the bulb into the socket. She held her breath for a second and then pulled the string.

The light went on, almost blinding her for a moment.

"My God," she murmured, looking around as she clung to the ladder. She stepped down to the floor. It wasn't dirt. It was concrete covered with a layer of dust. The laundry sink had no plumbing fixtures. It was just a shell. Beside it, Caitlin noticed a stopped-up hole on the floor—and just above that on the wall, some old pipes that had been capped off. Had a toilet been there at one time?

A metal four-socket outlet box was near the floor in one corner of the room—with visible wires running up the wall. There were no windows or doors. The only way out of the room was back up that ladder and through the trapdoor.

The light above wasn't very strong. Caitlin took out her phone again and used the flashlight to take a better look at the unfinished walls. Some of the concrete posts had old pieces of tape on them—rolled up and smashed. Remnants of yellowing paper were still stuck to some of the tape pieces. Obviously, at one time, someone had displayed some pictures, signs, or posters down here.

She didn't see any loose papers, debris, or trash on the floor. It was like the place had been cleaned out and stripped down. But over in another corner, on the floor, something shiny caught Caitlin's eye, something someone must have missed. She fixed the light on it and took a step closer.

It was a girl's tortoiseshell hair clip.

Caitlin glanced around again and shuddered.

As far as she could tell, this room hadn't been used as a wine cellar, a fruit cellar or a storage area.

But there was every indication it had been used as a prison cell.

CHAPTER TWENTY

Silverdale, Washington
Friday, December 6, 1991—10:02 P.M.

Jill Ostrander sat in the front seat of her friend's Honda Accord and said nothing. She watched the snow outside and fidgeted with the tortoiseshell barrette that kept her new hairstyle in place. It was more than a new hairstyle. It had been a major project. Jill had ditched her last two classes this afternoon to hurry home and transform herself from plain old brown to Clairol Dark Caramel Blonde. She parted her hair on one side and clipped it back for a more sophisticated look. She could have had her mother, who was a professional hairdresser, do it. But Jill wasn't about to let that bitch touch her hair. They barely tolerated each other lately. Jill thought her mother was tacky—and she had atrocious taste in men, too. Each new boyfriend was worse than the next, and several of them had tried to hit on Jill at one time or another.

Jill figured if she had her own boyfriend, things wouldn't be so bad at home. For one, she'd have a good excuse to spend even less time there.

That was why tonight was so important to her. She and her best friend, Lilly-Anne Wilde, were supposed to meet some of their friends at Kitsap Mall for dinner and the 7:40 showing of *Cape Fear* tonight. Mitch Towner, one of the coolest guys in their sophomore class, was among them. Jill had a crush on him. The new look she'd spent all afternoon creating had been mostly for him.

But Lilly-Anne had sabotaged the entire evening.

She sat at the wheel, singing along with Mariah Carey, whose "Emotions" was on the radio. The snow came down pretty heavily, and the highway had turned slick. Lilly-Anne didn't seem fazed. She had the wipers on but didn't slow down much. And it wasn't just her driving; it was her whole attitude. She was acting like nothing was wrong at all—at least, for a while.

Then she suddenly reached over and turned down the radio. "Okay, what?" she said. "You've been a major drag tonight. So what's with the silent treatment?"

"What's with *you*—hanging on Mitch all night?" Jill asked. "You know I like him. Yet you were practically *molesting* him during the scary parts of the movie! It was disgusting—"

"Oh, please, I was not," Lilly-Anne said, hands on the wheel.

Mitch had sat between the two of them. When Robert De Niro had bitten that woman's cheek off, Jill had grabbed Mitch's thigh. But he'd barely noticed, because Lilly-Anne had practically crawled into his lap.

"And earlier, at Red Robin, you were playing footsy with him under the table," Jill continued. "I saw!"

"Well, he started it. I didn't."

"Then you had to announce to everybody, 'Hey, how do you like Jill's new dye job?' God, I wanted to kill you. Could you possibly *be* any bitchier?"

"I thought you wanted people to notice it," Lilly-Anne said.

The car suddenly skidded into the other lane.

Lilly-Anne just laughed and quickly veered back into her own lane. Jill braced her hand against the dashboard and felt her stomach lurch. "God, watch it!"

"Get over yourself!" Lilly-Anne moaned. "I know what I'm doing. I'm a good driver. I'm serious, you're such a drag lately."

"Well, could you slow down at least? You're really making me nervous."

"Drag, drag, drag," Lilly-Anne said.

Jill felt the car speeding up. The snow accumulated on the windshield between wipe intervals—so that for a moment or two, they were driving practically blind. "You're not funny!" Jill protested. "I'm serious! Slow down!"

"You said you wanted to take the turnoff here?" her friend asked, grinning. She jerked the wheel and they swerved onto an off-ramp.

Panic-stricken, Jill thought they were about to spin out of control. The tires squealed as the car weaved and skidded uphill to a rural road. It wasn't even their exit. Jill didn't know this road at all. It ran along some dark woods. She didn't see any other cars around. A layer of snow blanketed the pavement, making the driving even more treacherous. There weren't any street-lights, but the snow seemed to illuminate everything.

It was actually kind of pretty, but at this point Jill just wanted to go home—as much as she loathed it there. She'd already had a shitty night. She didn't need a car accident to make it even shittier.

She was still holding on to the dashboard. "God, what's wrong with you? Are you high? You're high, aren't you?"

Lilly-Anne just giggled.

Jill remembered, after the movie, Lilly-Anne and Tiffany had gone into the restroom and stayed there a while. Everybody knew Tiffany was a big cokehead.

Jill took a deep breath. "Listen, let's just get back on the highway and head home—while the roads are still drivable. I don't want to be stranded here . . ."

"I've got to show you something," Lilly-Anne said, eyeing the forest on their right. "I did this with Jeff during the first snow last year. It's only going to take ten minutes, and then we'll turn around and get back on the highway."

"Oh, shit, I hate this. Where are you taking me?"

"There's a trail into these woods." Lilly-Anne finally slowed down. "I promise, it'll be such a rush . . ."

"Oh, my God, you *are* high. Would you please turn this car—"

"There it is!" Lilly-Anne hit the brakes and turned the wheel. The car skidded and almost overshot the trail. Lilly-Anne jerked the steering wheel and the car half spun again before it seemed to correct itself.

All the while, Jill clutched her heart.

They started into the woods. Except for a few spots, snow covered up the trail. But a series of reflectors posted along the way guided them. Jill could hear gravel under the tires. As scared as she was, she had to agree with Lilly-Anne that it was beautiful—driving through these snowy woods at night. Her friend had slowed down a bit, too. The snow seemed to be in slow motion. For a couple of minutes, it was so quiet and serene—almost magical.

But then The Crystals came on the radio, singing "Santa Claus Is Coming to Town," and Lilly-Anne cranked it up. She loudly sang along. The car started speeding up again.

Jill figured, what the hell, and she joined in.

That was when they hit something.

It might have been just a pothole or a rock in the road, but the sudden jolt silenced them.

"Shit, what was that?" Jill asked, rattled. She glanced back and didn't see anything in the rear window. But she could feel the car hobbling and listing to the passenger side. "Great, just great," she moaned. "I think we have a flat! Of all places . . ."

"Fuck," Lilly-Anne muttered. Then she repeated it about ten times. She stopped and turned off the engine. Dead silence. The snow continued to come down.

"Well, I watched my brother change a tire once," Lilly-Anne finally announced. "And he's a moron, so it can't be that difficult."

Repeating "fuck" a few more times, she scooted out of the car.

In stony silence, Jill climbed out the passenger side. But she slammed her door shut.

"Don't say anything, okay?" Lilly-Anne warned. She opened the trunk.

Jill wondered how many miles they were from

home—or from *anything*. It didn't help that they'd just been to a scary movie. She could see her breath and rubbed her arms to warm herself. She'd worn a light jacket, figuring she wouldn't need to bundle up for the quick walk from the parking lot to the mall entrance.

She was so mad at her friend right now, but she didn't say a word.

"Okay, so here's the spare," Lilly-Anne said, bent over the trunk. "And the jack—and the tire iron thingee . . ." She dropped both black tools onto the thin layer of snow.

Jill glanced down the road and saw a pinpoint of light in the darkness. As she stared at it, the tiny beacon seemed to be getting closer and bigger. It morphed into two lights.

"Someone's coming," she whispered.

Lilly-Anne turned around. "Thank God, we're going to get some help . . ."

But Jill wasn't so sure.

A dark minivan came into view and started to slow down.

"Hey!" Lilly-Anne waved. "Why is he stopping back there? Maybe he doesn't see us . . ." She ran back to the driver's door and opened it.

Jill saw the hazard lights go on. Her friend emerged from the Accord and waved again. But Jill didn't move. She had an eerie feeling about this minivan.

It hadn't moved, either. It was just close enough that Jill had to squint in the blinding headlights. So no doubt, the driver saw them. But no one had gotten out of the vehicle yet.

"What's his problem?" Lilly-Anne asked. She stopped waving. "Can't he see we're in trouble here?"

Jill kept rubbing her arms to fight off the chill—and the feeling that something awful was about to happen. She wished she had a gun or some mace in her purse. She glanced down at the tire iron in the snow. She reached down and grabbed it.

"This guy's starting to give me the creeps," Lilly-Anne whispered.

They both watched as the minivan lurched forward a couple of feet. But then it started to back up. The forest was so quiet Jill could hear the engine humming—even as the vehicle moved farther and farther away.

"Wait a second!" Lilly-Anne yelled, waving her arms again. "What are you doing? Help! Come back here and help us!"

The minivan's driver must have switched off the headlights or turned around. The van seemed to disappear. Jill couldn't hear the engine anymore. Though the snow illuminated the woods, there was no sign of the vehicle.

"Asshole!" Lilly-Anne screamed. Her voice seemed to echo.

Jill shook her head at her. "You're the asshole—for getting us stuck here."

The man in the minivan hadn't driven away. He'd merely backed up far enough so that the two stranded girls could no longer see his van.

He was pretty sure they hadn't noticed him when he'd followed them from the mall. Once they'd gotten off the highway and onto the rural road, he'd shut off his headlights and stayed on their tail. Though the snow was coming down steadily, everything was so bright he'd had no trouble navigating the road and keeping up with them—even through the woods.

Now he got a pair of binoculars out of the back and watched them as the girls struggled with the spare tire. It was such a quiet night he could even hear them sometimes—especially when they raised their voices.

He clearly heard the screams.

He saw it happen.

And he just stood there, watching through the binoculars. Watching and smiling.

He didn't make a move to intercede. When it was over, he returned the binoculars to the minivan. He'd left the back door open, so the interior light was on. He found his little kit—the one with the bottle of chloroform and the washcloth.

In the distance, he heard one of them crying.

Turning, he saw the girl with the dark blond hair. She was staggering up the trail—toward him. As she came closer, he could see blood on the front of her coat. It was on her sleeves and hands. "Help!" she screamed. "Oh, God, help me! Somebody killed my friend!"

He stood by the minivan, staring at her.

She stopped just a few feet in front of him. She had tears in her eyes and snot dripping from her nose. "Help me . . ." she gasped, her breath visible in the cold night air. "Someone killed my friend . . ."

He nodded and smiled. "I know. I saw everything, girlie."

She gazed at him.

The man hauled back and punched her in the face. She collapsed onto the snow-covered ground. The thud seemed to echo in the still woods.

He could see he'd knocked her out. He didn't want her coming to anytime soon. So he turned back toward the vehicle and reached for his kit.

He knew this girl needed saving.

CHAPTER TWENTY-ONE

Echo
Saturday, October 29—4:41 P.M.

Caitlin heard the beep on the other end of the line.

"Hello, Teri," she said into her phone. "My name is Caitlin Stoller, and I live at Sixty-Seven Birch Place in Echo. I'm sorry to bother you. It—ah, seems like a strange request, but I'm hoping you might know something about my house and its history. I heard your late husband worked on this place for two different owners. It seems like a long shot, but I thought you might still have some of his work papers or blueprints. It would be a tremendous help to me. Even if you don't, could you call me back? I'll try to explain myself more clearly . . ."

Caitlin left her phone number and thanked Teri before clicking off.

"No, that didn't sound awkward at all," she muttered to herself, frowning. "I'm sure she's just dying to talk to me now."

She sat in the family room with the TV on Mute,

waiting for the news to come on. Her hair was still wet from a quick shower.

After installing the floodlights near the house and then poking around in that gloomy subterranean cell, she'd been filthy. While she showered, Caitlin kept remembering what Della had said about Denise Healy being so awkward, how she'd been pulled out of school and forbidden by her father to go to the library. Maybe it was Denise's tortoiseshell barrette on the floor of that hidden cell below the basement. Caitlin had heard stories of people locking up their children. Perhaps Denise Healy had been a prisoner in her own home.

Caitlin wished she knew a little bit more about the Healys—and this house. She figured two people might be able to tell her something about the house, at least. One was the widow of the contractor who helped redesign and reconstruct the place for two different buyers. The other was Elaine Hecht, who with her late husband had lived here after the Healys.

To Caitlin's amazement, both Teri Spangler of Oak Harbor and Elaine Hecht of Port Angeles had phone numbers listed with Directory Assistance. She'd even gotten the operator to track down a Stuart Healy in one of the five Washington State area codes: 360.

She tried the number, and a man answered: "Hello?"

"Hello, is Stuart Healy there, please?"

"You got him," the man said. "Who's this? I don't recognize your name on the thingamajig here . . ." He sounded elderly.

"My name's Caitlin, and I'm looking for a Stuart

Healy who used to live on Birch Place in Echo. He should be about thirty-five by now . . ."

"Well, this is the first time in a long, long while someone has mistaken me for being thirty-five. I'm eighty-nine, honey . . ."

She should have known it wouldn't be that easy getting ahold of the right Stuart Healy. Caitlin thanked the man for his time and hung up.

Then, pacing back and forth in front of the TV, she tried the number for Elaine Hecht.

"Yeah, hello?" It sounded like a boy around Gabe's age.

"Is Mrs. Hecht there, please?"

"MOM!" he yelled—almost in the telephone. "Phone for you!"

There was a muffled response somewhere within the Hecht home.

"Who's calling?" he asked, getting back on the line.

"My name's Caitlin. Your mother doesn't know me, I'm—"

"YOU DON'T KNOW HER!" the boy screamed.

She could hear more muffled talk, and then finally, "Yes, hello?"

"Hi, Elaine," she said. "Your son is right. You don't know me. My name's Caitlin Stoller. Are you the Elaine Hecht who used to live at Sixty-Seven Birch Place in Echo?"

There was a silence.

Caitlin stopped pacing for a moment. "Hello?"

"Yes, I lived there for a while. What's this about?"

"Well, I'm living there now," Caitlin explained.

"Oh?"

"I'm talking to you from your old family room. I'm looking over at the kitchen right now—at the two little stained-glass windows on either side of the big window over the sink." She figured this would convince Elaine she was on the level.

But there was more silence on the other end.

"I've been looking into the house's history," Caitlin went on, "and I understand you moved in a few years after the Healy family moved out."

"Yes, quite a few years," she said guardedly. "I'm sorry, but I'm still not sure I understand the reason for this call . . ."

"No, I'm sorry," Caitlin said, "for calling you out of the blue like this. If you could just hear me out for a minute, maybe I can explain. I'm divorced, and I moved into the house about seven weeks ago with my two children, and now I'm discovering some things about the place that are kind of strange. For example, you know that broom closet under the stairs in the basement?"

More silence. "Oh, yes—yes, for a minute I didn't remember," Elaine Hecht finally answered. "But yes, we never used that room. The people before us—"

"The Healys," Caitlin chimed in.

"Yes, they had it crammed with all sorts of junk—old pieces of wood, rusty pipes, you name it. I'm afraid we never got around to cleaning it out."

Caitlin started pacing again. "Well, my son—he's eleven—he decided to clear it out and make the room his clubhouse. Anyway, just today I discovered a trapdoor in the floor. There's a whole other room below that little closet. It almost looks like a cell."

"How bizarre," Elaine Hecht said. "Well, I—I don't know a thing about it."

"Did you know the Healys at all?" Caitlin asked.

"No, not at all," she replied, "never met them."

"Did you hear about the daughter? Did anyone tell you?"

There was a pause. "You know, now isn't a very good time to talk. My son is here with a friend, and we're heading out the door. I'm just about to put on my chauffeur hat. Could we talk tomorrow?"

"Of course," Caitlin said, sitting down on the sofa arm.

"Are you free in the morning? I'm seeing my sister in Coupeville tomorrow. I can swing by on the way— if you don't mind me coming over."

"Wow, no, that would be great," Caitlin said. "Do you need directions?"

"I think I can remember."

Caitlin laughed. "Of course. Ah, is ten thirty okay?"

"That's perfect," she replied. "It'll give me some time to work up the courage I need to step inside that place again."

Caitlin was dumbfounded for a moment. "Was your time in this house really that bad?"

"I'll explain when I see you," Elaine Hecht said. "I'm glad you called, Caitlin. This gives me an excuse to go back there. It's something I've always felt I must do. See you tomorrow."

"See you, and thanks."

Caitlin clicked off.

She didn't have time to let their conversation sink

in, because the news was starting. She put down the phone and grabbed the remote.

"Breaking News," said the announcer over the image of people in hazmat suits digging in some woods. A tent was pitched amid ambulances and cop cars. Yellow police tape stretched across trees and bushes. Though Caitlin couldn't see rain, the place looked muddy and wet. Police, reporters, and camera crews mobbed what must have once been a remote little spot.

"A grisly discovery outside Darrington: two bodies have been uncovered near the Boulder River Wilderness Area, and police believe there may be even more. Stay tuned for the full story. King-Five coverage begins now!"

Caitlin had been expecting the top story to be about the man who fell from the ninth floor of a downtown Seattle high-rise.

"Good evening," said the pretty brunette anchor. *"I'm Emily Cantrell, and we have breaking news out of Darrington . . ."*

Caitlin switched channels to another local newscast, hoping to find something about Jeremy or Dack or whatever his real name was. Instead, she saw more footage of the grim excavation in a forest. Someone was explaining in voice-over: *"A retired couple from Lynnwood, heading back from a camping trip near Boulder River, discovered a shallow grave—"*

She switched channels again to a third local news show, only to find another view of the woods—and a handsome, mustached reporter in a dark rain slicker. He was interviewing a thirtysomething Asian man who must have been a plainclothes cop. His name had flashed off the screen just after Caitlin had changed channels.

"I understand they've just found a third body," the reporter said into his handheld mic. *"Can you confirm that?"*

The cop nodded. *"Yes, a third victim has been uncovered—not far from the other two graves. So far we can tell you that two of the victims are young males. The third is a young female."*

"And the crew here is still digging, looking for more bodies," the reporter interjected. *"Has a cause of death been determined yet? Any clue as to how or when they were killed?"*

"No, I don't have that information right now. We're waiting for the medical examiner on that."

"Is it true that each of the victims was wearing a ribbon with a medal on it around their necks—something similar to an Olympic medal?"

The detective hesitated. *"I can't confirm that right now."*

Wide eyed, Caitlin stared at the screen.

"Do the police believe this discovery is in any way linked to the disappearance of several teenage swimmers in Washington and Oregon in the past two years?" the reporter pressed.

"It's too soon to say," the plainclothesman replied, starting to move away from the mic. *"Right now, we're still trying to identify the victims. Then we'll be notifying the next of kin. You'll have a statement as soon as we have more information."* He turned away from the camera.

The screen showed a yearbook-type portrait of a

cute, smiling redhead. Meanwhile the reporter explained in voice-over that Julie Reynard of Salem, Oregon, was the first teen swimmer reported missing—back on March 14 of last year. Then, in quick succession, came photos of three other missing swimmers—with their names under their photos.

"Two more swimmers who were also missing were later found dead," the reporter said—over pictures of Paula Sibley-Martz and Chris Whelan. Caitlin remembered that the girl was strangled and the boy had drowned.

"Seventeen-year-old Aaron Brenner of Mount Vernon High School was the last swimmer to disappear, six days ago after a swim meet in Everett," the reporter continued—over footage of the good-looking young man in a Speedo and warm-up jacket walking around the corner of an indoor pool. He seemed to catch the camera recording him and gave a shy smile and a subtle wave.

Her eyes watering, Caitlin winced. It broke her heart to think this sweet-looking kid could be one of the corpses they were digging up right now. She thought of the poor parents of all these young athletes whose lives had been cut short.

The broadcast switched back to the news anchor— on this station, it was an older blonde in a pink blazer. *"In Belltown today,"* she announced, *"traffic on Western Avenue came to a standstill for three hours after a twenty-nine-year-old man plunged to his death from his ninth-floor apartment in a Belltown high-rise."* The photo displayed over the anchor's shoulder was unmistakably Lindsay's seducer, Jeremy—aka Dack. It looked like his driver's license picture. *"The victim has been identified as Neal Thomas Huggins, a model who worked in the adult entertainment industry. Police found narcotics in his apartment—along with an apparent suicide note, taped to his bathroom mirror."*

The blonde worked up a smile. *"Employees at Boeing got some good news today—"*

Caitlin switched channels. She got a pretty Asian reporter in a red raincoat in front of Dack's building. *". . . police say the note read: 'Too much partying, no more thrills, nothing left to live for.' Huggins was twenty-nine years old. This is Lisa Nguyen reporting from Belltown . . ."*

Caitlin pressed the Mute button on the remote.

She couldn't understand it. Why had Jeremy-Dack-Neal decided to dive off his balcony just when she was supposed to have met with him? She still wondered about his phone records and his laptop. Maybe he had his phone on him when he went off that balcony.

One possibility was that someone had killed him, made it look like suicide, and then taken his phone and computer. Whoever had hired this hustler to scam Lindsay probably needed to erase all evidence of their correspondence. They had to cover their tracks. Getting a suicide note would have been easy. With a gun to his head, Neal Thomas Huggins would have written anything. The whole thing could have been staged to look like an open-shut case of suicide to minimize the police investigation. And the timing of it ensured that she was there to see him die.

Caitlin imagined someone watching her while she

was at Sculpture Park. Maybe Jeremy-Dack-Neal had thought the killer was her when he'd buzzed the person in.

It made sense. The computer and phone weren't in the apartment—or they'd been erased somehow. Otherwise, the police would have called her or Lindsay by now.

Her phone rang. Caitlin practically jumped off the sofa arm.

She grabbed the phone off the cushion and switched it on. "Hello?" she asked nervously.

There was silence.

Biting her lip, she gazed at the phone screen: UNKNOWN CALLER.

"Who is this?" she demanded.

"I'm Teri Spangler," the woman said. She sounded peeved. "I know who you are. I got your message. I have nothing to say to you. I don't want anything to do with that house. Do you understand?"

"Well, no, I don't understand," Caitlin said. "I didn't mean to be rude or disrespectful—"

"Don't ever fucking call me again. Do you got that?"

There was a click on the other end.

Dazed, Caitlin pressed the End button, and then she double-checked the last-call records. Directory Assistance had a listed number for Teri Spangler. But obviously she also had another phone.

Caitlin had a feeling this wasn't the first time Scary Teri had phoned her and come up as UNKNOWN CALLER.

CHAPTER TWENTY-TWO

Saturday, October 29—5:50 P.M.

> *Dear Mom,*
> *I'm going to ask the person who is holding me here to please send this letter to you. I'm hoping they'll honor my request . . .*

Aaron was kind of proud of that very adult, rather formal sentence. He figured throwing the word *honor* in there might persuade the coach to mail the letter—maybe some mailbox out of town, where he'd be at a swim meet on his next *scouting* mission.

Without the usual practice session, Aaron's day had moved by so slowly, *"like molasses in January,"* as his grandmother used to say. Though he'd only had the TV for one day, he really missed it. After so much reading and calisthenics to keep from getting bored, he'd decided to write to his mother, and maybe Nestor, too. Even if they never got the letters, it was at least something to do. Thank God he had a pen and a lined writing tablet.

The more he thought about it, he'd probably be better off asking the Missus to send his letter. After all,
she was a mother, wasn't she? It was a pretty good bet
that the coach beat her. The son of a bitch certainly
didn't pay much attention to her all day long. Aaron
decided if he was nice to her and smiled at her occasionally during practice, maybe she'd actually start to
care about him. Maybe she wouldn't just sit still and
let him die.

> *First off, I want you to know I'm OK. I admit
> I'm pretty scared, but I'm doing all right and
> getting a lot of excersize (Sp? Wish I had spell-
> check here). The worst part about this is not
> knowing if or when I'm coming home.*
>
> *The other bad part is knowing how worried
> you must be. Please remember to take care of
> yourself. You never do when you're stressed
> about something. Try not to drink too much, and
> be sure to eat. Sorry to nag.*
>
> *I'm also really sorry for acting like such a
> jerk to you last Sunday. I didn't mean anything I
> said. I think I was just freaking out about the
> meet and things, but that's no excuse. I don't say
> it very much, but you're a good mom. I miss you
> a lot.*
>
> *I hope you sold that painting they were look-
> ing at . . .*

Aaron stopped writing at the *whoosh-clank* of the
meal drawer opening.

Jumping up from the desk chair, he rushed over to the receptacle, where a microwaved Stouffer's macaroni and cheese dinner and a microwaved Green Giant peas and carrots side dish were side by side—with a napkin, plastic fork, and a milk container.

"Thank you!" Aaron called. "And—thank you for the soup the other night! It was really good, comforting . . ."

He kept thinking that he needed for her to like him if he hoped to survive. At the same time, weird as it seemed, he sort of felt sorry for her. And it didn't hurt to be nice.

He listened but didn't hear anything for a few moments.

"You're welcome!" she finally called back in her little-girl voice.

Echo
Saturday—7:04 P.M.

Hers was the only car in the library parking lot. A light drizzle dotted the windshield. The library had closed over an hour ago, and the big, empty mansion looked dark and foreboding. Except for a few cars that passed by on the way to the 7:40 ferry, this part of town seemed practically deserted.

Caitlin sat in the front seat with her phone in her hand. Since seeing the news, she must have taken the phone out at least five times to call Lindsay—or the Seattle Police. Then she always put it away again. Caitlin figured she would have heard something by now if the police had contacted Lindsay. And Lindsay would have called if she'd seen the news report of the "suicide."

Caitlin didn't want to go to the authorities without talking to Lindsay first. She needed to tell her in person about Jeremy-Dack-Neal, and then brace her for any repercussions once they called the Seattle Police.

She put the phone back in her purse, took a deep breath, and climbed out of the car. Heading toward the library entrance, she held on to her keys—and a piece of paper. On it were the library's alarm code and some notes she'd jotted down at home earlier.

Since she hadn't had much luck on her Google hunt for information on Teri Spangler, Caitlin had turned her attention once again to Stuart Healy. She tried finding him through his father with the keywords: *Randall Ned Healy, Echo, Suicide.*

A June 13, 1993, *Seattle Times* obituary said Healy died of "*a self-inflicted gun wound to the head.*" There was no mention of financial problems with Equestream. But the article gave a possible explanation for the suicide: "*Business associates indicated that Healy had been battling depression since the murder of his daughter, Denise, 16, on July 4, 1992. The murder remains unsolved.*" The article listed all of Ned's civic interests in addition to Equestream. His wife, Phyllis Arnett Healy, and son, Stuart, were noted as the only survivors.

Caitlin remembered Della saying that after Phyllis drank herself to death, Stuart was shipped off to relatives in Montana.

There was nothing on Google about Phyllis Healy's death.

But Caitlin had the list the real estate agent had given her, and it showed the bank took over ownership of the house in May 1994. So Phyllis must have died around that time. Though *The Seattle Times* didn't carry an obituary on her, the old *Echo Announcements* must have had something. Maybe they even had the name of the relatives who had taken young Stuart Healy under their wing.

Caitlin kept thinking the trouble with the house had started with the Healys.

Even though she loathed the idea of coming back home after dark, conducting another room-to-room check, and trying to get settled all over again, Caitlin had decided to step out.

She'd grabbed her coat and purse, the piece of paper with all her notes, and a small steak knife from the kitchen. She'd wrapped the blade in a paper towel to make sure she didn't cut herself reaching into her coat pocket. Then she'd headed out the door and double-locked it.

Now she stood in front of the library entrance. She took another deep breath and unlocked the library door.

There wasn't much time to get used to the dim surroundings inside, because the warning alarm started beeping the moment she opened the door. Caitlin had two minutes to deactivate it before a call went through to the security company. She closed and locked the door behind her and then charged into the Grand Room.

Darting around the checkout desk, she headed into the break room to the alarm box. The incessant beeping seemed to get louder and louder by the second. But she got the code numbers punched in.

The silence was lovely—for a while, anyway.

Then it was too quiet. She could hear every little squeak and click of the old mansion. Gabe's comparison of the library's Grand Room to the living room of a haunted house in an old horror film was spot-on. Even when Caitlin switched on a couple of the overhead art deco lights, the room still had an aged, seedy grandeur. It needed some people, more light, and a fire in the fireplace to become sort of homey.

Of course, this part of the library seemed downright cozy compared to where she was headed.

Caitlin switched on the basement lights and started down the creaky metal staircase to the periodical archives. She caught a whiff of that stale, dank odor. It was particularly bad tonight because of the rain. Walking toward the back corner, she eyed the metal shelves full of volumes. As with her last visit, she paid particular attention to the gaps where she could see into the next aisle. She told herself that she was alone down here. There wasn't another soul in the entire building. And the doors were locked. She was fine.

From all the rain lately, there was a small puddle on the concrete floor—beside the fire door. Caitlin found the kick stool where she'd left it the other day. Taking off her peacoat, she pulled the knife from the pocket and then draped her coat over a fire extinguisher on a wall bracket. She sat on the stool, put down her purse, and carefully set the knife in her lap. Then she pulled the *Echo Announcements (January–June, 1994)* from the shelf. Blowing off the dust, she opened it and started looking for Phyllis Healy's obituary—sometime in April or May.

All the while, she tried to ignore the sounds of the old building, sounds she wouldn't have even heard during the day when other people were around.

She found the obituary in an issue dated April 23. "*Phyllis Arnett Healy, 49, passed away after a long illness,*" it said. The paper had recycled the Healy family Christmas card photo they'd published two years before, when Denise had been murdered. But there was another picture of the brunette Phyllis, a candid close-up of her smiling and squinting in the sun. She looked a bit frumpy and older than her age. There wasn't much written about Phyllis's activities—besides raising two children, burying one of them, and then burying her husband. Her parents were Warren and Yvonne Arnett of Great Falls, Montana, both deceased. Warren had been president of Arnett-Montana, Inc. Oil Refineries from 1966 until his death in 1984.

Obviously, Phyllis had come from money.

The article showed she was survived by her son, Stuart, 13, and a sister and brother-in-law, Meredith (Arnett) and Charles Rigby of Kalispell, Montana.

Caitlin took a pen out of her purse and scribbled down the names.

The lights flickered.

Caitlin froze for a moment. "It's just a brown-out," she murmured. But she quickly closed the volume and returned it to the shelf.

Grabbing her purse and coat, she hurried back upstairs. All the while, she held the steak knife in her hand. At this point, she just wanted to get out of there.

As she reached the top of the stairs, she heard a sudden rumble in another part of the library. Panic stricken, she stood still and waited. The sound had come from over by the front door.

It took a moment for her to figure out it was just someone using the night drop. "Oh, Jesus," she whispered, a hand on her heart. She watched the shadows from the headlights sweeping across the front windows. "Okay, okay, relax. You just need to get out of here . . ."

Two minutes later, the alarm was set and she was outside, locking the library door. With the knife now in her coat pocket, she pressed the unlock button on her key fob and watched the lights flash on her Lexus. She ran to the car and climbed into the driver's seat.

At least there was no message on the windshield tonight. But then she realized she hadn't thought to check the backseat. Caitlin swiveled around to look back there.

Nothing—just some gum wrappers that must have fallen out of one of the kids' pockets.

Catching her breath, she flicked the switch that locked the car doors. She took her phone out of her purse and clicked onto Google Search. She typed in the keywords: Charles, Meredith Rigby, Kalispell, MT.

"Oh, shit, no," she murmured, looking at the first result to come up:

KALISPELL COUPLE MURDERED VACATIONING IN MEXICO

www.dailyinterlake.com/news/1990/02/26/2000

February 26, 2000—Charles and Meredith Rigby of Kalispell were robbed and murdered on Tuesday while vacationing in Mexico City, Mexico . . .

Stuart Healy was probably in college when his aunt and uncle were killed.

Caitlin clicked on the article. The Rigbys were shot during a holdup after leaving a restaurant. According to the news story, Mexico City police didn't have any suspects in the double homicide. The article concluded: *Meredith Rigby is survived by a nephew, Stuart.*

Caitlin stared at her phone and slowly shook her head.

Practically everyone associated with that damn house seemed cursed.

"It really makes for a long, long day, doesn't it?" he heard Monica whisper through the vent. "This happened the weekend before he brought Chris in—and again a week before you came here. He's scouting for my replacement. I'll bet he's out of town right now. So I wouldn't expect practice tomorrow."

"Swell," Aaron muttered.

From the foot of his cot, he looked around the little cell, bathed in the blue night-light. No practice meant he'd be cooped up in here without a break from the monotony for at least another twenty-four hours. If someone had told him the day before yesterday that he'd actually miss those awful practice sessions, he would have said they were crazy.

"It's good news for me," Monica said. "It means he's probably releasing me sometime this week."

"It's not good news, Monica. It means he's going to kill you sometime this week. You still don't get it, do you?"

"All I know is that I'm getting out of here," she replied. "And if it's anything like how he released Jim, I'll have to agree to a ton of conditions. He wouldn't put me through all that if he planned on killing me."

"He's putting you through that so you won't raise a fuss when he takes you out to kill you," Aaron whispered. "Listen to me. Once he gets you outside, if you see a chance for escaping—any chance—for God's sake, grab it. He's not taking you home. He's going to take you into some woods, then kill you and bury you. I know, because he almost did it to me."

Monica didn't answer.

Aaron figured once the coach got her drugged and into the van, her chances for survival were terrible. But at least there was a chance. Maybe she was better off than he was, trying to warm up to the Missus, hoping she'd eventually help him. After finishing his microwave dinner tonight, he'd set the used containers back in the metal drawer—along with a note:

Thank you very much. I think you're a very kind person.

Aaron

The drawer had *whoosh-clanked* around seven o'clock, and he'd hoped it was her, and not Junior, collecting the leftover containers. He figured even if the coach was home tonight, it wouldn't be him. Aaron couldn't imagine the guy ever cleaning up after someone's dinner—not even his own.

"You still there?" Aaron whispered, covering his mouth so the camera didn't record him talking.

"Yes," Monica replied.

"All your talk about getting out this week," Aaron said. "I wouldn't count on it, because I'm not letting you win any races."

"I wouldn't be so sure about that."

"I mean it," he said. "It's not going to happen. And I'll be saving your life . . ."

"Aaron, please," she whispered. "I really need to get out of here. I've been feeling so—so dead already. I can't keep living in this place. I—I can't take another week . . ."

It sounded like she was crying.

Aaron heard something else, too. He shushed her. "I think someone's coming!" he whispered.

He listened to the footsteps outside his cell. Maybe Monica was wrong about the coach being out of town. Aaron expected to see the speakeasy-cover slide open on his cell door. Instead, the pass-through drawer opened.

Whoosh-clank.

It had never opened this time of night. Aaron climbed off the cot and went to check the drawer.

Inside was an apple.

CHAPTER TWENTY-THREE

Echo
Sunday, October 30—10:42 A.M.

Caitlin opened the front door and immediately told herself not to stare.

The right side of Elaine Hecht's face was badly scarred. Elaine was in her early forties, and the rest of her face was pretty—with a near-flawless creamy complexion. She had a full figure and wore tan slacks with a black sweater. Her auburn hair was cut in a pageboy with bangs that swept over and partially covered the burn marks. Caitlin remembered when she was a child, a neighbor friend's brother held her Barbie doll over the stove—singeing off some hair and melting the plastic on one side of Barbie's face until it bubbled. Elaine Hecht's face reminded her of that doll.

"Elaine?" she said, shaking her hand. She'd worn a lavender sweater with jeans for her visitor. "Hi, I'm Caitlin. Please, come on in."

Elaine hesitated. "Did you see my car sitting in your driveway for the last ten minutes? I was trying to talk myself into coming up and ringing the bell. I have some pretty awful memories of this place." She laughed nervously. "I guess that's a terrible thing to say to the new owner."

"No, that's exactly why I wanted to talk with you," Caitlin admitted. She opened the door wider and backed into the foyer. "I really want to know what it was like for you and your family living here. A friend of my daughter's said this house is cursed. Crazy as it sounds, I'm wondering if this girl might be right about this place."

"It's not so crazy," Elaine murmured.

Caitlin waited for her to step inside.

With an awkward shrug, her guest finally stepped over the threshold and glanced around. "Oh, my, it really isn't very different at all."

"Can I get you some coffee, a glass of water, or a Coke?" Caitlin offered.

"No, thanks," she said. "I really can't stay long. I'm sure when you called me yesterday you didn't intend to give me a tour today."

"No, please, come in and have a look," Caitlin said. "In fact, I used your visit as an excuse to straighten up this morning . . ."

That was true.

She'd fallen asleep on the family room sofa last night. She'd had a pillow from her bed and a blanket. She'd also had the small steak knife—within easy reaching distance just under the sofa. Caitlin had decided not to even attempt falling asleep upstairs. She somehow felt safer downstairs—with Gregory Peck keeping her company on Turner Classic Movies. She realized why Lindsay preferred the couch and the TV to her own bed.

In addition to some classic movies, Caitlin had also caught the eleven o'clock news. There had been no change in their coverage of the Belltown high-rise "suicide." In fact, it was the exact same segment. But they'd reported more activity in those woods outside Darrington. The police had found three more bodies—for a total of six so far. Three of the victims were unidentified females. Police had confirmation on the other three. They were among the swimmers who had vanished: Julie Reynard, Cooper Rydel, and Jim Lessing. That left two missing swimmers still unaccounted for: Monica Leary and Aaron Brenner.

As of last night, the police were still digging and searching for more bodies in the mass grave.

Though the sofa was comfortable, Caitlin barely slept. Of course, it didn't help that she had floodlights shining on the house. Even with the drapes and blinds shut, the light beamed through the cracks.

She'd drifted in and out of sleep, and finally gotten up around eight o'clock to clean for Elaine Hecht's visit.

The house's former owner was still standing in the foyer, still visibly apprehensive.

"You know, this was like a ghost house when we bought it," she said. "We got it cheap because it was so neglected. We felt like Jimmy Stewart and Donna Reed moving into that deserted, ramshackle house in *It's a Wonderful Life*."

"I understand you hired Lance Spangler to help whip it into shape," Caitlin said.

Looking at her, Elaine cocked her head to one side. "Well, you've certainly done your research, haven't you?"

"The woman who runs the B and B told me," Caitlin explained, leaning against the newel post. "Her old boss bought the place from the bank after you moved out. Lance worked for her, too. I hear he was quite the ladies' man."

Elaine gave a little shrug. "My older brother came over during the reconstruction and met him. My brother's gay. He said Lance looked like a 1980s porn star. So that's what we all called him after that, the Porn Star. I got a flirtatious vibe from him, but he wasn't my type. Besides, I was still very much in love with my husband when we bought this place. I thought we were very, very happy." She rubbed the back of her neck and winced a little as if she had a pain.

Caitlin didn't say anything for a moment. "Did you ever meet Lance's wife, Teri?" she finally asked.

Elaine nodded. "We had her and the Porn Star—I mean, Lance—over to dinner when we finished the first phase of the remodel. We were going to have him come back and do the basement, but we never got around to it. We couldn't afford it. Anyway, the two of them came over. I set the dinner table, the good china, very fancy. The kids ate in the kitchen. I remember the wife being a bit of a pill. She was snippy and sarcastic toward her husband the whole night. And I got the distinct impression she didn't like me at all. Maybe she thought I was interested in Lance, I don't know. She bought a bottle of wine with her, which I thought was nice. But we never got around to opening it. Then at the end of the evening, she took it back. I thought that was strange. And this part I won't forget. When she first came in, I gave her a tour, and she was pretty quiet, very distant. Then right after dinner, she disappeared. Chandler found her wandering around upstairs from bedroom to bedroom. She sure was a strange one."

Elaine finally stepped into the living room. "This was the paint color we chose," she said, assessing the area. "I'm sure it's been freshened up a few times. I like how you've decorated it. You wouldn't believe how this house looked when we first bought it. The place hadn't been occupied for seventeen years. Most of the windows were broken or cracked. The house caught fire several times during that period, mostly cosmetic damage. The police said it was because kids were breaking inside and smoking or playing with fireworks. But guess what? After we moved in, we had one fire after another. The garage caught fire. We had two kitchen fires, two more outside, and then there was the Great Labor Day Barbecue Disaster of 2012." She pointed to the pink and red scars on the side of her face. "That's how I got this. I went to start the barbecue for a little family celebration. I'd doused the coals very lightly. I've started hundreds of grills. I knew what I was doing. But when I set the lighter wand to it, the thing practically exploded. I think someone sabotaged me. I really do. Anyway, I was in the hospital for five weeks. Three plastic surgeries . . ." She waved her hand in front of her face. "This was the best they could do to fix it."

She wandered back into the hallway and then peeked into the dining room. "I picked out that chandelier," she murmured.

"It's pretty," Caitlin said. "It's one of the things I've always liked about this house."

"I found it in an antique shop in Bellingham. May I see the rest?"

"Please." Caitlin nodded, then followed her down the hallway into the study. "What did you mean when you said you thought someone had sabotaged you?"

"I always liked that fireplace," she remarked, looking at the wall behind Caitlin's desk. "Those French doors are new."

"Oh, those are windows," Caitlin said.

"Well, they didn't go down all the way to the floor before. They were just regular-sized windows."

Caitlin figured that must have been one of the changes Carrie Sewell had made with Lance. "Who do you think was sabotaging you?"

Elaine leaned against the door frame. "Well, when all those little fires started, I thought we might have had a house squatter who was upset with us for moving in. I figured someone was trying to drive us out of the house. We had windows broken on three separate occasions . . ."

Caitlin remembered what Sandra at the B and B had told her about someone throwing a rock through the windows here—and at the inn. Sandra had thought it had been Teri.

Elaine squinted at her. "Do you really want to hear this? I mean, I didn't intend to come here and unload on you. It's all in the past . . ."

"No, I want to hear it. I want to know," Caitlin told her.

"Well, I hope you don't feel bad about buying this house. It's a perfectly beautiful house—and I'd like to take some of the credit for that. You might end up being very happy here. But for me and my family— well, I think your daughter's friend may be right. We came here very happy. But it was a different story when we left. The scars I carry from my time here, they run a lot deeper than this one." She touched her face. "You know, I think I will have a glass of water, if you don't mind."

They moved into the family room and kitchen. Elaine mentioned that the appliances were all new, and she liked Gabe's and Lindsay's pumpkins. Caitlin poured her a glass of water from the Brita pitcher, and they sat down at the kitchen table.

"So—for the first six months we couldn't move in here, because the renovation was going on," Elaine explained. "There was delay after delay. One thing after another went wrong, and it got more and more costly. It was almost as if the fates—or *somebody*—didn't want us to move in. But then when the work was finally done, I was so happy, positively delirious. I thought my husband, Chandler, was happy, too. But looking back, I have a feeling during that time he might have started seeing this woman. I think she was the one sabotaging the whole project—a home wrecker, literally." She let out a defeated laugh.

"I think she started those fires and broke the windows. Do you want to know how I found out about Chandler and her?"

"How?" Caitlin asked.

"I got a wedding card in the mail, you know, one of those Hallmark jobs with the bride and groom dancing in a misty field—with the bridal veil billowing. Inside, all the preprinted sentiments were scratched out with a pen. And someone had scribbled '*Chandler has a girlfriend.*' I mean, talk about juvenile. Not '*Chandler has a mistress,*' or '*Chandler's fucking somebody behind your back.*' No, it was '*Chandler has a girlfriend*'— with a little sad face."

Caitlin just stared at her.

"What?" Elaine asked. "Does this sound familiar?"

She nodded. "Go on."

"Well, my husband denied it and got so angry with me for asking that I knew it had to be true." Elaine sipped her water. "I'm sure he was upset at his girlfriend for sending the card. She sent me another card when my son, Peter, wiped out on his bike and nearly killed himself. The front wheel of his bicycle somehow got loose—just sitting in the garage. How do you figure that? So this card, it was a get well card, no signature, just the sad face.

"She did it again when my nine-year-old, Jason, drowned. He fell off a pier and hit his head on some pilings. I got a sympathy card—again with a sad face instead of a signature. Chandler thought I was crazy, but I'm almost certain that bitch caused both accidents. I still believe that. Of course, Chandler denied he was even seeing anyone, so how could this girlfriend who didn't exist possibly do any harm to our sons? But those cards were addressed to me. And each one arrived the day after the accident—the very next day. She had to have put the cards in the mail before anyone else even knew. I wouldn't be surprised if she sent the sympathy card before Jason even fell off that pier. I wanted to go to the police, but Chandler wouldn't allow it. After Jason died, Chandler practically turned me into a junkie. He and our doctor had me taking antidepressant and sleeping pills . . ."

She dug a Kleenex out of her pocket and blew her nose. "You must think I'm crazy, too. I can't believe I'm telling you all this. I guess it's because I'm back in this house again. I was here in this kitchen when the fire department called me about Jason."

"I lost a son, too," Caitlin said quietly, "in a bicycle accident two years ago."

"You never get over it," Elaine muttered, looking down at the table.

Caitlin sighed, then she glanced up at the cabinet where she kept her wine. "I get the feeling that someone's been inside this house when I'm gone. Did you ever feel that way when you were living here?"

Elaine shook her head. "I think that bitch might have broken into the garage and screwed around with my son's bicycle. But I don't believe she got inside the house at any time. I would have known if she had."

"Do you think this other woman might have been Teri Spangler?" Caitlin asked.

Elaine chuckled. "Oh, God, no, she wasn't Chandler's type at all."

"Did you ever find out anything about her—who she was?"

She shook her head. "Nope. If I'd had the money, I would have hired a private detective to track her down—or a hit man to kill her. And I'm almost a hundred percent serious about that. But I've managed to put it all behind me—as much as possible. Except for those awful cards, I have no proof that she even existed. She covered her tracks pretty damn well."

"Your husband never admitted . . ." Caitlin started to ask, but then she trailed off.

"No, Chandler denied it right up to the end. He took that secret to his grave. After we lost the house and split up, he moved to Seattle. About a month later, he died in a car wreck while in Phoenix on a business trip. He smashed his rental car into a palm tree."

Caitlin said nothing. She was thinking of Carrie Sewell and Lance Spangler—and how the brakes had given out on Lance's Jeep.

"Did things change for you after you moved out?" she asked.

Elaine seemed to work up a smile. "Yes, after Chandler died, we settled into a nice place in Port Angeles—and things started getting better. My two kids, Peter and Jennifer, are doing fine now. It's so different from when we were living here. Like I said, I had the feeling that someone was trying to make us miserable, trying to drive us out of this house. And when we moved, all of that stopped. If my husband's *nonexistent* mistress was indeed behind it all, I guess she's satisfied now. Maybe she's moved on."

Caitlin slowly shook her head. "No, she hasn't."

* * *

She took Elaine down to the basement to show her the trapdoor to the hidden room beneath Gabe's clubhouse. Elaine had no idea the room existed. "Just one more strange thing about this house," she remarked.

She said that the ladder, workbench, and tool pegboard had all been there when they'd bought the house back in 2011. So—it was indeed Ned Healy's hammer outlined on the pegboard.

Upstairs, Elaine said the bathrooms had been remodeled but the bedrooms were the same. She and Chandler had known about Denise Healy's murder back when they'd first put an offer on the place. They'd made her bedroom into an upstairs TV room—so nobody had to sleep in there. When they'd first moved in, they'd asked a priest friend to do a house blessing.

Caitlin remembered Lindsay telling her that the Goldsmiths had done something similar.

"We had him conduct part of the ceremony right here in this room," Elaine said, standing in the doorway of Lindsay's bedroom. The walls were half-bare, and Lindsay had already moved some of her furniture into the guest room. "He prayed in here for about twenty minutes and even sprinkled around some holy water."

She turned to Caitlin and gave her a sad smile. "I guess it didn't do much good, did it?"

CHAPTER TWENTY-FOUR

Echo
Sunday, October 30—11:39 A.M.

"Ken? Ken, are you home?" Judine Albright opened his front door a little wider.

She lived down the block from Ken Meekley on Smuggler's Cove. Judine was carrying an ambrosia salad for their monthly book club brunch. Ken always gave her a ride to the host's house. Today Val and Roger were hosting. Roger and Ken were the only men in the Island Book Club. The other seven members were always trying to find someone nice for Ken. He was very nice, too, and good looking. But he was a bit of an odd duck. For two years, the Island Book Club girls had been trying, and they still hadn't found a suitable match for him.

Ken was supposed to bring his usual Toll House cookies for dessert. It was the only thing he knew how to bake—and even then, Judine suspected he made them from one of those store-bought mixes. She'd left two phone messages and also emailed over the weekend to firm up their plans to get together. But he hadn't gotten back to her. Judine had wondered if—at last—he'd found someone and was off for a wild weekend.

But if Ken was gone, she wouldn't have spotted his car when she'd peeked into the garage window just a minute ago. And he wouldn't have left his front door unlocked.

"Ken?" she called again. As usual, his place was tidy. She heard a radio on in another part of the house. It sounded like a basketball game.

In the kitchen, she saw an open bag of Triscuits on the counter. Otherwise, there were no dirty dishes and everything seemed in its place. She didn't see a plate of cookies anywhere. This was so unlike him not to be ready.

"Ken, are you home?" she called, heading down the hallway to the bedrooms. "It's Judine . . ."

She passed his office. There was a small, half-full plastic trash bag by his desk. Judine figured he must have been in the midst of cleaning or throwing stuff out. The radio was on in there. But his computer was off.

On the sports broadcast, someone had just sunk a basket and the crowd was roaring. The announcer was excitedly going on and on.

Judine noticed Ken's bedroom door was open. She poked her head in. The bed was made, but the spread was all rumpled—as if someone had been thrashing around on it. But what perplexed her even more was the wall behind his bed and his nightstand. He had at least fifty copies of a page from the *Echo Bulletin* taped up there, end-to-end—so it was almost like wallpaper. The montage covered a large section of the wall and went more than halfway up to the ceiling. It was like a crazy person had created it. The page featured an article about the new librarian, an attractive woman who was a little older than Ken. There was a photo of her with the article.

Judine remembered Ken mentioning at the last book club that he thought the new librarian was pretty. But he'd sounded rather casual about it.

This was something else entirely. It was insane.

She saw the bathroom light had been left on—and the door was open.

Judine didn't hear anything—except the game on the radio in the other room.

Still, she called out to him one more time. "Ken? Are you in there?"

She hadn't even stepped inside when she noticed a photo on the white-tiled floor. It was a picture of the librarian again, a candid shot of her in the library lot, taken from a distance. She wore a peacoat and the wind had caught her red hair. She didn't seem to know she was being photographed. It was like a surveillance photo.

Judine could hear water dripping.

A trail of photos like the first one was scattered on the floor—each shot was of the librarian. They led to the bathtub, where Ken lay with one arm slung over the side. His eyes were open in a lifeless stare—as if he was gazing at the dripping faucet.

Judine could see the wide cut on his wrist and the puddle of blood on the white tiles. Some of it was already dried—a dark, dull crimson.

The tub was full of water. It came up to Ken's chest. And it was red.

A few more photos floated on the slightly rippled surface.

One of them seemed to have affixed itself to his heart.

Echo
Sunday—4:47 P.M.

BELLTOWN MAN LEAPS 9 STORIES
TO HIS DEATH

"Too Much Partying," He Writes
in Suicide Note

The story was on page three of the front section of *The Seattle Times*. Sitting in the front seat of the car, Lindsay read the article. Her mom was driving, and Gabe sat in back. Lindsay still didn't want to believe this Neal Thomas Huggins guy was Jeremy. She didn't want to think of him as an *escort and model*, as the newspaper described. She didn't want to think of him as dead.

None of it made any sense.

Lindsay had spotted her mom standing on the dock when the ferry had come in. She'd met them at the end of the passenger walkway. She asked how they were, obviously concerned about Gabe and his stomach. He'd had a bad case of diarrhea after their lunch at Dick's. But Gabe felt better by dinnertime, and he was okay today. Lindsay had decided not to go into it with her mother. So they both said they were fine.

Instead of heading to the car, her mother asked them to sit down with her on one of the benches so they could "talk for a little bit."

That was when Lindsay knew something was wrong.

The news for Gabe wasn't so tough. He was crazy for *Dungeons & Dragons*. So finding out about a place that sounded like a secret dungeon below his new club-house was actually pretty neat. He was just disappointed he couldn't go anywhere near his little man cave until the police had a look at it. Her mom thought the hidden room might have been a crime scene of some sort.

All Lindsay could think was, *Terrific, now there's another spot in the house where someone was killed.* It was like living in a chamber of horrors.

That was the other thing: the police. Her mom said they needed to talk to the police. Then her mom told her about Jeremy, who wasn't the older brother of somebody at school. No, he was a male prostitute someone must have paid to Skype with her and set her up.

Lindsay didn't understand why anyone would go to all that trouble to humiliate her. Who would do something like that?

Her mother had gone to Jeremy to ask him the same thing. She'd been right outside his building in Belltown when he'd fallen off the balcony.

Her mother gave her the morning paper to show her the story and said she didn't think it was a suicide. She also said they needed to talk to the police about the Skype session. Maybe the police could keep it from the press, and Lindsay wouldn't have to face any further humiliation.

Lindsay had read the newspaper account twice now, and she was dazed. She really didn't know this Neal person. He'd lied to her and tricked her. Yet she wanted to cry.

At a stop sign before they turned down Birch, her mother reached over and rubbed her shoulder. "Are you going to be okay?" she whispered.

"I just want to go home," Lindsay heard herself say.

Her mother drove on. "I'm so sorry, sweetie, I know this is awful for you . . ."

"I'm just so confused," she said, her voice cracking. She was looking down at the newspaper again as they turned into the driveway.

"Oh, my God," she heard her mother say.

The car slowed down to a crawl.

Lindsay looked up to see a police car there in front of them.

Caitlin climbed out from behind the wheel. But the cop stayed inside the patrol car. Another vehicle—an unmarked black Hyundai—came up the street, pulled over and blocked her driveway for a few seconds. Caitlin wondered if they planned to box her in. Did they think she planned to peel out of there with her kids in the car? After a moment, the Hyundai moved forward and parked on Birch Place. Caitlin heard a door slam. Then she saw the Echo deputy—the one who looked like Dabney Coleman—walking up the driveway toward them. He wore jeans along with a Huskies sweatshirt, which his open Windbreaker didn't hide. It was Sunday, and he'd probably been watching a game when he'd been called away.

Caitlin figured the Seattle Police had seen the Skype session or maybe Neal Thomas Huggins's phone records. Maybe someone had noticed her in front of the building on Western Avenue yesterday. Caitlin kept thinking her poor daughter wasn't going to have much time to pull herself together before the police started in with all their questions.

A uniformed cop finally climbed out of the patrol car in their driveway. He was a baby-faced blond man with a crew cut. He carried his hat in his hand.

Lindsay and Gabe slowly emerged from the Lexus. They seemed as rattled and intimidated as she was. Gabe looked as if he was about to raise his hands above his head in surrender.

"Mrs. Stoller?" the deputy said, approaching her. He nodded and extended his hand. "Deputy Bob Dana. We met at the station the other day . . ."

She shook his hand. "Of course," she said, a bit breathless. She turned toward her children. "Lindsay . . . Gabe . . . it's all right . . ."

They still looked apprehensive.

She turned to Deputy Dana again. "I've been meaning to call you . . ."

"Well, likewise," the deputy said, reaching into the pocket of his Windbreaker. He pulled out a photograph and showed it to her.

Caitlin gazed at the picture of Ken Meekley. It looked like a driver's license photo.

"I think we found your stalker," she heard Deputy Dana say. "Recognize him?"

Caitlin nodded. "He—he's a customer at the library . . ."

"And your number one fan, so it seems," Dana said glumly. "Unfortunately, he—ah, well, it appears he's killed himself."

According to Deputy Dana, Ken had about two dozen snapshots of her, which he must have taken surreptitiously in the library parking lot.

He had practically wallpapered part of his bedroom with the *Echo Bulletin* that had her photo in it.

In Ken's office, the police had found a plastic bag full of her garbage and recycling: junk mail addressed to her; a used-up lipstick container; an old *Vanity Fair* with her subscription label on it; a name tag from a library fund-raiser a while back; a Starbucks cup with lipstick marks; used candy wrappers and the like. Deputy Dana rattled off the list—all items she'd tossed out in the last two or three weeks.

Caitlin sat on the sofa in her family room, trying to process the news about Ken Meekley's suicide. Deputy Dana sat across from her in the easy chair, sipping the Coke she'd offered to him. She'd sent Lindsay and Gabe up to their rooms to get started on their homework. Gabe had been disappointed that he couldn't check out the secret lair below his clubhouse. But Lindsay had been all too willing to withdraw upstairs. The other cop remained outside. Caitlin had last seen him leaning against the patrol car and talking on his phone.

"You mentioned that Ken's neighbor discovered

him this morning," Caitlin said. "Have they—well, have they figured out how long he's been dead?"

"Our initial diagnosis is at least forty-eight hours," Dana answered. "Could be longer. The medical examiner from Oak Harbor is looking him over as we speak."

Caitlin automatically shook her head. "Well, then Ken couldn't have been the one stalking me, not if he's been dead since Friday morning. Too much has happened since then . . ."

"Happened? What do you mean?"

Caitlin explained about Lindsay's Skype session with Jeremy—also known as Neal Thomas Huggins. Caitlin told the deputy how she'd tracked him down. Then she admitted to running away from the "suicide" scene outside his building because she was scared, upset, and confused. "But I'm convinced it wasn't a suicide," she said. "I think Huggins was murdered. Whoever is behind all this, they killed him to cover their tracks. Huggins could have told me—or the police—who had hired him to Skype with my daughter. And look at the timing of his death. It was just when I had an appointment to see him. Don't you think that's too much of a coincidence? Doesn't it seem like I was set up?"

Deputy Dana's eyes narrowed at her.

"What I'm saying is—it couldn't have been Ken, because he was already dead when someone sent out the Skype video on Friday afternoon. And yesterday at noon, that same someone murdered Neal Huggins . . ."

She leaned forward on the sofa until she was nearly standing. "Do you understand what I'm saying? Poor

Ken, I know he liked me. He was awkward, but he wasn't mean or cruel. He couldn't have killed any-one—except maybe himself. And I wouldn't even be so sure of that. Whoever has been harassing me, this person is beyond cruel. They're lethal. And they're still out there. Do the research on all the people who have lived in this house since the Healys. Look at how many have died—most of them children. What are the odds?"

Seated across from her, Dana seemed to listen to her with withering patience. He drummed his fingers on the chair arm. "Mrs. Stoller, you've been through a lot these last few days. First, you had that scare with your daughter when you thought she'd been abducted. You had Ken Meekley stalking you. Throw into the mix this revelation about your new house—with a murder taking place here back in the nineties. And there's this Skype thing with your daughter, which would be dis-tressing for any mother—"

"Yes, it was," she interrupted. "But my point is that Ken couldn't have been the one sending those notes and harassing my family—"

"Listen to me for a second," he said, cutting her off. "We have overwhelming evidence that Ken Meekley was stalking you. And you're insisting he wasn't. The Seattle PD have overwhelming evidence that this hus-tler in Belltown killed himself—including a suicide note and a history of drug use. And yet you're saying it was murder—a murder made to look like a suicide. At the same time, you're telling me this hustler was killed at a specific time for the specific purpose of setting you up." He shook his head. "I'm sorry, Mrs. Stoller, but I don't understand your logic here. If someone wanted to set you up for murder, why make it look like a suicide?"

Caitlin folded her arms and frowned at him. It did sound crazy when he put it that way. She sighed. "Could you just humor me and have the Seattle Police check Neal Huggins's laptop and his phone records?" she asked. "They'd find the Skype session and the calls to Lindsay . . ."

Deputy Dana went along with her request. He strolled into the kitchen while he telephoned the Seattle Police. She heard him talking to someone, but his voice dropped to a whisper a few times. She could just imagine him telling the person on the other end, "*I have this whack-job here spouting conspiracy theories.*"

Caitlin squirmed on the sofa while he remained on the phone for another five minutes. "Uh-huh, well, thanks," he finally said. Then he clicked off. He held up his index finger for her, and then he made another call. "Say, Jim, could you send me that file with the photos of Ken Meekley's bathroom? The one I'm looking for is among the last twenty, the shots of the sink. You got my number? Uh-huh, that's right, text them to me . . . Oh, yeah? The Huskies are ahead?" He caught her staring, and he cleared his throat. "Okay, Jim, could you get those photos to me right away? Thanks."

Clicking off, he wandered back toward the family room area.

"I'm glad the Huskies are winning," she said, deadpan. "What did the Seattle Police say?"

"They'll call you if it turns out they need a statement."

"Well, what about Neal Thomas Huggins's phone records and his laptop?"

"Huggins had his phone on his person when he took the plunge," Dana said. "It was damaged beyond repair. And the Seattle PD checked his laptop for a will. Sometimes, that's where they find them in these suicide cases. They ran across a lot of gay porn sites. But they didn't find a Skype session with any teenage girls . . ."

Caitlin just shook her head.

"Are you one hundred percent positive that Neal Thomas Huggins was the person who Skyped with your daughter? I mean, did you discuss it with him when you called and made this appointment?"

"Well, no—"

"So it's still possible that your daughter was right to think that some classmate's older brother talked her into this Skype session to—*punk* her."

"Well, I suppose it's *possible*," Caitlin admitted. "But if you compare the photos—"

"Do you still have those notes your stalker left you?" he asked.

Caitlin nodded. "They're in my desk."

Getting to her feet, she led him into the study. She switched on the light, headed to her desk, and pulled the messages out of the drawer. Figuring they might be police evidence some day, she had them in a plastic zip-lock bag. "You've seen two," she said. "There are three of them now."

She laid out the notes on her desktop:

Have a nice day, Caitlin! ☺
I'm watching you.

Isn't this sad? ☹

"Nothing very threatening here," he muttered, inspecting the messages. He looked at her. "And you really don't think Ken Meekley was your stalker?"

She shook her head. "No, I'm sure he wasn't."

He took out his phone. "Bear with me for a minute," he said, bringing up something on the little screen. "Ah, here we are. This photo was taken in Ken Meekley's bathroom this morning."

He showed her an image on his phone. It was a picture of a bathroom sink—and the medicine chest mirror above it. On the mirror was a message written in a green crayon or marker:

MAKE SOMEBODY SMILE TODAY
☺

Caitlin showed Deputy Dana the hidden room beneath Gabe's clubhouse in the basement. Even though it probably fell on deaf ears, she told him her theory that someone might have been held prisoner down there at one time. She gave him the tortoiseshell barrette—also in a ziplock bag. "Elaine Hecht was over here this morning," she explained. "Elaine and her husband bought this house from the bank after the Healys moved out. She had no idea this room was here."

To the deputy's credit, he went down into the dusty little cell and looked around for a few minutes. "Interesting," he said—several times. He climbed back up the ladder, turned off the light, and almost hit his head on the underside of the stairs above them. Dusting himself off, he stepped out of Gabe's clubhouse.

"Well, Denise Healy's murder is still an open case," he allowed. "I'll let the chief know about this. In the meantime, I'd cover up that trapdoor and stay out of there—if for no other reason than to make sure nobody trips and falls into that pit. In fact, here, let me help you lift that ladder out of there . . ."

He hoisted the ladder up and carried it into the utility room, where he leaned it against the wall. Then he fixed the trapdoor back in place. Caitlin had a feeling no one would ever follow up on this.

But at least he was nice enough to help with the ladder.

Five minutes later, Caitlin had thrown on her coat and switched on the outside lights. She walked Dana to his car. The other cop had already left in the patrol car.

In the driveway, the deputy glanced over his shoulder at the house. "Well, I think you've got the place sufficiently lit."

She rubbed her arms. "I know, it's almost like the Magic Castle at Disneyland. I'm keeping my fingers crossed I don't blow a fuse."

"Now that your secret admirer is no longer with us, I think things will start to calm down for you soon," he said. "I know you're still very worried. I'll ask them to put an extra patrol on this block for the next few days."

"Thank you," she said, working up a smile. She was frustrated and confused—and too exhausted to argue with him anymore. She was sad, too, for poor Ken.

He pressed the unlock button on his key fob and his

Hyundai's lights flashed. He stopped in front of his car and turned to her. "Can I give you some advice?"

She shrugged. "Sure—I guess."

"I noticed down in the basement, you still have some boxes you haven't unpacked yet." He glanced at the house again and shook his head. "Don't unpack them. Don't unpack anything else. Put this place on the market. So, you might take a loss. There are plenty of nice, affordable houses for sale in this town. You should look around for another place, a house where you and your kids can be happy."

"You just said you thought things would start to calm down for us," she replied, puzzled. "And now you sound like you're concerned for our safety."

"Not so much your safety as—well, your peace of mind."

He opened his car door. "Think about it. G'night, Mrs. Stoller."

"Good night," she murmured.

As his car pulled away, Caitlin felt a chill rush through her. She stood at the end of her driveway and gazed at the house. She'd fallen in love with it a couple of months ago. But now, even with the lights shining on it, the place no longer seemed warm and inviting.

She would call Sally, the real estate agent, in the morning.

Maybe the deputy was right. Maybe a For Sale sign in front of the place would bring them a little peace. And yes, she'd probably have to take a loss.

But Caitlin knew if she didn't get her kids out of there soon, she risked losing much, much more.

Seattle
Sunday—6:18 P.M.

"Listen, I've changed my mind," Russ said into his phone. He paced around his living room. "I'm putting the money in the bank tomorrow. I've thought about it. Having my kids here helped get my mind straight. The last three weeks were hell. But I'm starting to feel better about myself. Plus, Jesus, I don't want those three weeks to be for nothing, y'know?"

"I understand completely, believe me," she said on the other end. "But at the same time, I have a connection, a nice little man in your neighborhood who has some excellent product—right up your old alley. The way I figure it, we've been so good for so long. We deserve a little treat. Don't we, Russ?"

"I don't think so, Bobby," he said, stopping to stare out his window. It was a view of a parking lot and some Dumpsters.

"It'll be a while before you get to see your kids again," she pointed out. "And your wife doesn't want to see you or even hear from you until—what did she say, Thanksgiving? I mean, really, how depressing. And it doesn't have to be. I'm suggesting you and I have ourselves a little party tonight—sort of a reward, a last hurrah. We're allowed to fall off the wagon once at least. I could be over there in an hour. And we could be feeling very, very good in about ninety minutes."

Russ kept staring out the window. He didn't say anything.

"I'm coming over," she said finally.

He rubbed his forehead. "Okay, Bobby."

CHAPTER TWENTY-FIVE

Monday, October 31—9:39 A.M.

It was weird trying to give a friendly smile to the Missus when he was standing there naked.

Aaron waited until he got into the pool to try making eye contact with her. When she finally looked his way, he gave a furtive little smile and nodded. He made sure the coach didn't see. She seemed sort of schoolgirl-nervous-shy about the brief exchange. She quickly glanced away and went back to her knitting. But she had a flicker of a smile on her face just the same. She looked a little less banged up than usual. But then her scumbag husband had been away all weekend, so she'd gotten a break from being his punching bag.

The coach wasn't paying attention to either one of them. He'd been studying figures on his clipboard ever since the practice session started about twenty minutes ago. Ensconced in one of the plastic chairs, Junior was rapt by something on his smartphone. It must have been pretty special because he had earphones on.

Aaron was so relieved to be back in the pool. Forty-eight hours locked in that small windowless cell with absolutely nothing to do—he'd thought he'd go out of his mind. Both he and Monica hardly talked for the first several minutes of their warm-up period. All that pent-up energy from the confined weekend was released as soon as they dove into the water. A sixties instrumental song played on the boom box. It had a lot of guitar in it and sounded like surf music. Aaron felt reenergized. After a few minutes, he finally slowed down, caught his breath, and treaded water in the deep end.

He thought about smiling at the Missus again but didn't want to overdo it.

Monica swam up alongside him. "This is my last week here," she whispered. "I really feel it. I think he found someone new. He's going to release me . . ."

"I wouldn't be so pumped about it if I were you," he muttered.

The coach blew his whistle. "Okay, listen up!" he yelled. He turned down the volume on the boom box and strutted toward the pool's edge.

Aaron and Monica swam over to the side of the pool and grabbed on to the drain ledge.

"I was in Seattle and Vancouver, Washington, this weekend, watching a lot of extremely talented high school swimmers chalk up some damn impressive times," he announced. "I think you two could perform just as well if you put a little effort into it. Maybe you need some incentive, huh? Maybe I've been too soft on you. Let's make this a little interesting, shall we?"

"Oh, shit, no," Monica muttered.

"We're going to start off with a hundred-yard freestyle race," the coach went on. "The loser will have to swim twenty laps—with a weight belt. The winner—well, *he* might just get his TV back, or *she* might have six days knocked off her graduation day."

Monica grabbed Aaron's arm. "My God, that's all I have left," she whispered. "I could be out of here by tonight or tomorrow."

The coach obviously heard her. He nodded at her and smiled with false benevolence.

Aaron didn't say anything.

He couldn't let her win. She might hate him, but in defeating her, he'd save her life. He realized now that she must have been thinking along the same lines when she'd told the coach about his escape plan. Looking back on it, his plan had been pretty lame-ass.

"The race is at ten hundred hours," the coach said. "So get ready . . ."

He walked over to Junior, who was still focused on his smartphone. The coach kicked his son's foot to get his attention and muttered something to him.

Aaron glanced at the clock. He had less than five minutes to pump himself up for this race.

"I have to win this," Monica whispered to him. "I've got to, Aaron. I can't take another night of him pawing at me, degrading me . . ."

"Are you asking me to throw the race?" he said under his breath. "You want me to lose on purpose—so that sack of shit can take you out of here and kill you?" He shook his head. "No way." Then he pushed off the wall and swam toward the other end of the pool.

Aaron hated to think about what the coach did to her.

Still, as desperate as Monica was to get out of here,

Aaron couldn't let her win. He didn't give a damn about getting his TV back, and he didn't care about having to swim all those laps with that extra weight. What he cared about was her. If he didn't win this race, she'd be dead by tomorrow.

Junior shut off the music on the boom box and waddled over to the diving blocks with his stopwatch and the weight belt. He was almost dragging the belt. It looked like it had about twelve extra pounds of weights on it. Aaron wondered how the coach expected either one of them to swim twenty laps wearing that thing.

The coach blew the warning whistle.

He and Monica climbed out of the pool and took their positions on the blocks.

"Aaron, please," she whispered. "I know you're still mad at me for ratting out on you, but—"

"I'm not," he said. "Really . . ."

"No talking, *girls*!" the coach barked.

Aaron tried to zone out both of them, clear his head, and get into competition mode. He focused on his breathing and waited for that whistle. For a few moments, everything was so quiet.

Then the shrill sound filled the pool area.

Aaron pushed off the block and dove into the water. He moved like a shark, single-minded and determined, speeding forward under the surface. Then he broke out, caught his first breath, and started kicking. He drove with his shoulders—rapid, sweeping strokes. He knew his style was perfect, horizontal, feet up. Each breath was precisely timed. He was a machine again.

He wasn't dragging at all. Still, after the first lap, at

the push-off, he sensed she was almost catching up with him in the next lane.

Poor Monica, she was so bent on winning and getting those six days knocked off her sentence—all so she could die just that much sooner. She'd been in here so long that she'd bought into the coach's lies.

By the second lap, Aaron knew he was still ahead of her. He pushed off the wall and then drove with his whole body, hips and shoulders working, arms moving in a high-speed synch. Halfway across the pool, he shot ahead even more. He kicked harder. His strokes accelerated.

On the third push-off, on the shallow cnd wall, Aaron could tell he was on his way to a personal best. But what really mattered was Monica. He wasn't giving the coach an excuse to take her out and kill her. She wasn't going to win this race. The bastard would just have to hold on to her and let her live for a few more days. He couldn't replace her just yet.

Aaron pressed himself for one last burst of speed. *Just a few more strokes*, he told himself, relentlessly driving toward the wall. Then his hand touched it. He felt that sweet little pain as his fingertips banged against the surface. With a splash, he shot up above the surface in time to see Monica finish a few seconds behind him.

He could only be happy for a few moments because he knew she was miserable. He tried to catch his breath.

Monica let out a frail cry and covered her face. When she finally looked at him, Aaron mouthed the words *I'm sorry* to her.

Monica just smoothed back her wet hair and glared at him.

Even though he'd just saved her life, Aaron felt horrible. He glanced up at the coach, waiting for him or Junior to yell out his time. The one consolation prize to this bitter victory was knowing he'd broken his own record for the 100 freestyle. It was still an achievement. It still mattered.

"How'd I do?" he finally asked the coach.

Frowning down at him, the man shook his head. "You're disqualified. You pushed off before I blew the whistle."

Dumbstruck, Aaron gazed up at him.

The coach nodded to Monica. "You're the winner— by disqualification."

She let out a gleeful shriek.

The coach smiled. "Congratulations. You're going home in a day or two. Take a victory lap."

Aaron couldn't believe it. There hadn't been anything wrong with his dive. He hadn't left the block before the whistle. "This is bullshit!" he cried.

Eyes narrowed, the coach turned toward him.

"What are you trying to pull?" Aaron asked, unable to keep silent. "That's such a complete and utter lie! I waited for the whistle—"

"Aaron, don't," Monica whispered.

"No, this is bullshit!" he repeated defiantly. "He just wants to write this off as your win so he can get rid of you. He's tired of you. Don't you get it? He's going to take you out of here and kill you—all because he found another girl he wants to abuse—"

A loud gunshot resounded, echoing off the walls.

Stunned into silence, Aaron looked up at the coach.

The man aimed the gun at him. "Don't make me, chum," he growled. "I don't want to get blood in the pool and have to drain it. But so help me, God, I'll fucking kill you right here if you say another word."

Aaron didn't move or speak.

The coach glanced at his son. "Throw in the weight belt. Let him go down and get it from the bottom of the pool."

With a smirk, Junior dropped the belt in the deep end.

"Fetch," the coach whispered.

Aaron was trembling inside. He swam over toward where Junior had dumped the weight belt. He glanced back at the coach, who still had the gun aimed at him.

Taking a deep breath, Aaron bobbed up in the water—arms raised above his head. Then he plunged down to the bottom of the pool. He had his eyes open as he grabbed the belt. It had six two-pound weights attached to it. He knew the coach never intended for Monica to wear this heavy thing. The match was rigged from the start.

The damn belt almost dragged him down as he kicked and struggled to make it back up to the surface. He gasped for air.

"Strap it on," the coach said.

Aaron paddled back until he was at a spot where he could stand. He fastened the heavy belt around his waist. He figured he could maybe do a dozen laps. Twenty without a break would probably kill him.

Clinging to the side of the pool, Monica looked at him with pity.

"Thirty laps," the coach announced. "No breaks."

Aaron swallowed hard and didn't move.

The coach moved the gun very subtly. Now it was aimed at Monica.

She didn't see. Her back was to him. She had no idea how little she mattered to him now. But Aaron knew. The coach was finished with her, and he wanted to get rid of her. Except for having to clean the pool, he probably wouldn't have had any problem shooting her right now.

He was still staring at Aaron. "Swim," he said.

Aaron was obedient.

Echo
Monday—10:58 A.M.

It was almost lunchtime, and so far today, only three people in school had said anything to her about her boobs. And their comments had just rolled right off her.

It was old news already.

What still unnerved Lindsay was the death of Jeremy Dawson—or rather, Neal Thomas Huggins. According to her mom, the police weren't so sure they were the same guy. But Lindsay compared the photos, and she knew her "Jeremy" was indeed the Belltown hustler who had died in that nine-story plunge.

It was so bizarre and unsettling to know someone who had just been murdered. Lindsay couldn't help wondering how much of it had to do with her.

She really missed her Portland friends right now.

Lindsay sat at her table in the second row of Mr.

Noll's biology lab. She was early to class—probably because ever since the video had made the rounds Friday afternoon, she'd walked a bit faster in the hallways between periods to avoid stares and catcalls. Other students were still filing into the biology lab when her phone vibrated.

Lindsay checked. It was a text from her dad:

> I need to see u right away. Can u get out of school and come to Seattle? I can explain everything when u get here. If I don't answer the door, just let yourself in. I'll leave the building and apt. keys under the gray brick in the garden in front. It's the only gray one. Please don't tell ur mother or anyone about this. I'm counting on u. Please hurry, OK?

Lindsay's chair made a loud scraping sound as she got to her feet. She hurried toward the door, almost colliding with Mr. Noll—a tall, stocky fiftyish man who always wore a loosened tie with an open cardigan sweater. "Class is about to start," he said. "Where do you think you're going, young lady?"

He gave her a disapproving look over the rims of his glasses. Lindsay had a feeling that he, too, had seen her little video.

"I have a bad headache," she answered, ducking out to the hallway.

"You better have a note from the nurse when you come back here Wednesday!" he warned.

Lindsay rushed down the corridor and didn't look back.

Echo
Monday—1:12 P.M.

As she stepped out the library's front door, Caitlin wondered if she'd discover another note on her car windshield. She almost hoped to see one there. Then she could show it to the police and tell them how wrong they were about Ken and his supposed suicide.

Her stalker could have easily planted all that evidence in Ken's house. This notion had hit her shortly after Deputy Dana had driven off last night. She'd also realized that Lindsay's Skype session wasn't on Neal Huggins's computer because the stalker had probably given Neal another laptop to use specifically for the session.

Caitlin had called Dana this morning and told him her theories. All she'd gotten back from him had been: "Well, that's very interesting. I'll run it past the Seattle PD."

At least she'd told the police about her appointment with Huggins and that she'd been outside his building at the time of his death. And no one was reading her her Miranda rights. So at least that wasn't hanging over her head anymore.

But it didn't make her rest any easier.

Lindsay said they should go stay at a hotel. But Caitlin didn't even have a credit card to pay for it. So they were stuck in the house—for at least another night or two. In fact, she was down to her last few dollars.

She was on her lunch hour and headed for the bank.

Buttoning up her peacoat, Caitlin started across the library's parking lot. As she approached the Lexus, she didn't see any notes stuck to the windows or wind-shield. But that didn't change her mind about Ken's "suicide" one bit.

A mother with her toddler got out of a car across the street. The little girl was dressed like an old-fashioned nurse—with the cap and even a cape.

Caitlin had forgotten to dress for Halloween. But her coworkers hadn't. Della wore a very elaborate witch costume. Myra was Kathy Bates in *Misery*. She sported a flat, lifeless hairdo, a jean jumper, and a flannel shirt with a turtleneck underneath. It had been strange to see Myra become so morose about Ken Meekley's death—while wearing that funny outfit. She'd actually had tears in her eyes. "I never expected anything like this to happen," she'd admitted. "All those stupid jokes I made about him, I feel like such a jerk now. I should have been nicer to him . . ."

Everyone was in a somber mood this morning.

Caitlin climbed into the front seat, started up the car, and headed out of the lot. The bank was just a five-minute drive.

She'd kept busy this morning—even during the lulls. She'd phoned her real estate agent about putting the house back on the market and shopping for a new place. Sally had warned her that it might take a while to get any nibbles on the house once they told prospective buyers about the murder there in 1992. Caitlin was more concerned about selling the "cursed" place—and the stalker who came with it—to some sweet unsuspecting family. She couldn't live with herself if she did that.

It was obvious this stalker must have become ob-

sessed with the house back when the Healys had lived
there. Lindsay's original theory about it now seemed
spot-on. If this person wasn't Denise Healy's killer, he
or she was certainly fixated with the house because of
that murder.

Right now, Caitlin's only suspect was Teri Spangler.
Had she known Denise Healy? The ages were about
the same. She could have been friends with Denise, but
there was no way of confirming that.

Stuart Healy would be able to say whether or not his
sister knew Teri. Caitlin hadn't given up her search for
him. Last night, she'd tried to Google *Stuart Rigby*,
and wasted an hour chasing down a lot of false leads.
But this morning, she'd tried Stuart's mother's maiden
name and found an article that thanked a *Stuart Arnett*,
who had been a major donor to the Woodinville Police
and Fire departments. It was the only thing she could
find on him. There was nothing on Facebook or Linked-
In. But then she tried the online White Pages and found
a listing:

Stuart Arnett
Age: 35–39
Lives in Woodinville, WA
Used to Live In: Woodinville, WA
VIEW FULL PROFILE

The age was right. If it was him, he'd returned to
Washington State. And Denise's brother would have
had the money to donate a large sum to the local police
and firefighters. His mother and aunt had come from a
wealthy family. He'd probably received a sizable in-

heritance when his aunt and uncle were murdered in
Mexico. His rich grandfather might have even tucked
away some money in a trust for him.

Caitlin clicked on the full profile. There was no phone
number or email. And no spouse or children were listed.
But there was an address:

107 Elkhorn Court
Woodinville, WA 98077

Caitlin figured in order to talk with him she'd have
to drive to Woodinville and drop by unannounced. And
of course, he'd probably slam the door in her face the
moment she asked about his murdered sister. Then
again, maybe living in his old house would give her
some leverage.

She wondered if he knew about the hidden room.

She pulled into the Island Savings Bank lot.

Inside, she wrote a check to herself for three hundred dollars. She figured that would last until the credit
cards arrived in the mail. Approaching the teller, Caitlin pulled out her driver's license. The young woman
on the other side of the Plexiglas was dressed like Raggedy Ann.

"I love your costume," Caitlin said, handing her the
check and her ID. "Could I cash this, please? And I know
you take out three dollars, which is fine with me."

"You know the drill!" Raggedy Ann said cheerfully.
She ran the check through the little machine to clear it.
"And how's your day been so far, Caitlin?"

"Great," she lied.

The woman turned to her computer to look something up. "Ah, I can cash this, but are you aware that you have an overdraft of one thousand two hundred seventeen dollars and forty-nine cents?"

"What?" Caitlin asked, stunned. "Oh, no, that's impossible. There should be close to three thousand dollars in my checking account."

"A check went through on Saturday afternoon for four thousand dollars," Raggedy Ann explained, eyes on the computer screen. "It depleted your checking and left a deficit of one thousand two hundred seventeen dollars and forty-nine cents. We covered that by taking the money out of your savings, but there's an overdraft coverage charge of one hundred and eighty dollars . . ."

Caitlin shook her head. "There's got to be some sort of mistake. I didn't write a check for four thousand dollars. Who's this check to?"

Raggedy Ann looked at Caitlin's check—and then at the screen. "It appears the check for four thousand is out of sequence. It's made out to Russell Stoller."

"But he—" Caitlin stifled herself. Had Russ somehow gotten into the house and into her desk drawer—and then forged a check to himself? There seemed to be no other explanation. Caitlin realized she really didn't know him at all anymore. She'd been right not to trust him.

Nervously clutching the top of her purse, Caitlin took a deep breath. "Ah, you know, I—I totally forgot I gave him that check. I'm sorry. Yes, of course. Yes . . ."

She wondered if Raggedy Ann knew she was covering for her embezzling husband. She transferred funds from savings to checking, had her check cashed, and then couldn't get out of there fast enough.

As soon as she climbed back inside her car, Caitlin took out her phone and called Russ. She was shaking.

It rang and rang.

Lindsay could hear his phone ringing as she stood outside her father's apartment door.

She had tried calling him from the ferry—and then again on the bus to Seattle. Both times, she hadn't gotten an answer—not even a voice mail pickup. It had just rung and rung.

Several times, she'd come close to calling her mother and telling her where she was. But her father's text had specifically told her not to say anything.

Lindsay had buzzed him from the building's front door. Again there had been no answer.

She'd found the keys to the building and his apartment on a ring that had a tiny fake basketball attached to it. The keys were under the one gray brick amid several dark red ones encircling the trunk of a withered Japanese maple in front of his building.

Lindsay's stomach was in knots as she unlocked his apartment door. Her father had never put her through something like this before. All she could think was that he was having some kind of crisis with drugs or her mom or himself. He needed her there. The text had been so vague.

Opening the door, she winced at the smell.

The phone stopped ringing. It sounded like it was in another part of the apartment.

She glanced at his shabby little living room. Clothes and papers were strewn about. The drawers of his beat-up, secondhand desk were open. Either he'd been desperately searching for something—or he'd been robbed.

"Dad?" she called, stepping into the room. "Dad, it's me!"

She peered into the tiny kitchen. It was a similar scene: drawers and cupboards left open, the counter full of junk from those drawers.

Lindsay headed into the bedroom. The acrid smell seemed to be coming from there. She put a hand over her nose and mouth. This room—like the others—was a mess. The dresser drawers were open; one had been yanked out completely. His bed wasn't made. Clothes littered the floor. The closet door was open, and the light had been left on. Lindsay couldn't figure out what had happened. What had he been looking for? Money? A stash of drugs?

The bathroom light was on, too.

She walked around the foot of bed and then stopped. She gasped.

Suddenly everything in her body locked up. She couldn't move.

He was on the floor, lying on his side—in his undershorts. Her father used to be such a fitness nut. But now he looked so pale and depleted. A thin gray rubber strap was half tied around his arm. A line of dried blood came from his left nostril, and half his face rested in a small puddle of vomit.

The phone started ringing again. It was on the floor, just a few inches away from his hand—and the syringe.

He didn't flinch.

His eyes were still open, and he didn't blink.

Caitlin counted the ringtones: four so far.

She was still sitting in her car. She hadn't even left the bank parking lot. She was too upset to drive anywhere.

She couldn't believe Russ would stoop to stealing a check of hers and forging it to himself. Did he seriously think she wouldn't notice? She wondered how much heroin he'd bought with her four thousand dollars.

She didn't know whether to curse or cry.

She'd tried his number again. Of course he wasn't picking up.

He knew it was her. He knew he'd been busted. Seven rings now.

She heard a click—then a strange wailing.

"Mom?" It was her daughter's voice.

"Lindsay?" she asked, baffled. "Lindsay, what's going on?"

It sounded like she was choking.

"Honey, what is it? Where are you?"

"Oh, God, Mom," she cried. "I'm at Dad's. I don't know what to do. He—he's just lying here on the floor. His eyes are open. Oh, God, I think he's dead . . ."

CHAPTER TWENTY-SIX

Monday, October 31—10:16 P.M.

. . . By the 15th or 16th lap Aaron was struggling to stay afloat. It was a wonder he was able to keep moving. The weight belt dragged him down more and more. He must have swallowed about a gallon of pool water. Every once in a while, he'd start to gag and cough, and he'd stop. But the coach would yell at him to quit dawdling. I don't know how poor Aaron did it. The whole time, I just stood there in the shallow end, watching him and feeling so helpless. I really thought he might drown. I tried to tell the coach that he was wrong, that Aaron didn't start to dive before the whistle. I begged him to call off the punishment. But he told me to shut up and gave me one of those looks of his.

I didn't want to win this way. Aaron doesn't deserve this. It's so unfair.

I should be happy I'm going home tomorrow, but I feel horrible. I think of Aaron when he finally finished his last grueling lap and staggered out of the pool. He tried to take off the belt and collapsed on the floor. Junior, the little shit, got a chuckle out of it.

The coach handcuffed me to the pool ladder, and I watched him lead Aaron back toward our cells. The poor guy hobbled and stumbled the whole time. My heart ached for him. He's so sweet . . .

Monica heard footsteps, and she quickly shut her journal.

From her desk, she turned toward the door and watched the speakeasy flap slide open. She felt a wave of dread. Her stomach clenched. She realized the coach probably wouldn't let her go without raping her just one more time.

His face filled the small opening in the door. He was squinting at her.

Monica was wearing a pair of jeans, which had never quite fit, and an ugly beige sweatshirt. Yet whenever he looked in on her like this, she felt naked.

"Write a nice good-bye in that journal," he said. "I'm collecting it—and the others."

Monica stared back at him. She wouldn't have survived in this place without her journals. Six months of her life were in those books. She didn't want to give them up.

He seemed to read her hesitancy. "You didn't think I'd let you take them with, did you? You aren't leaving here with anything but the clothes that were on your back when I found you . . ."

Monica didn't say a word. But she thought "*when I found you*" was an interesting way to describe her abduction.

He stepped aside and disappeared. A moment later, the pass-through drawer opened with a whoosh.

Getting to her feet, Monica took her latest journal and then slowly collected the others from her shelf. With reluctance, she set them in the receptacle. She might as well have been shedding her clothes for him and putting them in that drawer, too. Those books were full of her private thoughts, her hopes and ideas. She knew he had read the journals, but now they were all his.

She was still standing over the little bin when it snapped back into the wall with another whoosh. Then it clanked shut.

A moment later, he was gazing at her through the small opening again. "We're having your parting ceremony tomorrow at oh-nine-hundred," he said. "Be sure to look pretty. I'll be taking your picture with your swimming medal. Enjoy your last night here."

The flap slid shut.

Monica stood in the middle of the cell with her arms crossed in front of her. She had tears in her eyes. She'd been waiting for over six months to hear him tell her that. She figured giving up her cherished journals was worth it.

She'd already given up so much more.

He set the journals on his desk in the office. Then he started clearing off a space on the bookshelf for them.

There were eleven other journals already on the shelf—from four different girls before her.

The boys, he didn't care about. He didn't give a damn what their private thoughts were.

Paula had been the last one before Monica. She'd been an excellent swimmer, and beautiful, with a strong, slender build, black hair and an olive complexion. She was also an uncooperative little bitch. He hadn't gotten around to giving her a journal. Less than three weeks after finding her, he couldn't take her bratty, smart-ass attitude any longer. He strangled her and dumped her body in some woods near Lake Sammamish. She didn't deserve to be buried with the others, who had earned their championship medals swimming for him.

This past weekend, police had discovered his secret burial ground. It had been on the news. All six bodies had been uncovered.

They'd found Julie, Cooper, and Jim—along with the two hitchhikers. Those two had never even gotten near his pool. They'd been spur-of-the-moment things.

He'd planned for the third girl, April. He'd converted one of the basement storage rooms into a cell. He wired it for surveillance and installed the pass-through drawer. He did it all himself—and did an excellent job, too.

That had been over two years ago. He'd nabbed April outside a shopping mall near Centralia. The newspapers never connected her disappearance to the other missing high school athletes, because she was the first. And she wasn't a swimmer—not when he got her. April was his test case. After four months of his skillful training, the fifteen-year-old was a regular Esther

Williams. She was all his, too. It wasn't like with the hitchhikers, fast, frenzied, and over with before he knew it. With them, it was just a few fleeting moments of power.

But with April, he shaped and molded her, punished and rewarded her. He hurt her when he wanted to and had sex with her whenever he felt like it. He was in total control, and it lasted a quarter of a year.

April filled three journals. And he took over two hundred photos of her before he got tired of her. He poisoned her food one night. Then he loaded her corpse into his car and drove to the same spot in the forest preserve where he'd buried the two hitchhikers.

Of course, by then he'd already been to several high school swim meets—in Washington and Oregon. He'd already spotted Julie in Salem. He liked the idea of taking someone with some aquatic talent and making her even better.

Then, after a couple of months, he decided to shake it up a little. He had a second room just sitting there. He could oversee competitions. That was when he brought Cooper in. The boy was a great swimmer and good-looking. Something about training this young man was even more exciting than working with the girls. It was nothing sexual. It was about calling all the shots with this cocky, handsome athlete—guiding him, breaking him, and humiliating him whenever he saw fit.

He didn't give Cooper any blank journals to fill. And the only time he took Cooper's picture was the day he gave him his swimming medal and then killed him.

But Julie stayed eight months and filled up four of the journals now on his shelf. In his desk, he had two big manila envelopes full of photos of her.

There were four more journals on the shelf. And in the drawer was another envelope full of photos, dozens of them. Unlike the other shots, these were Polaroids. And unlike the other girls, this one got away. She wasn't a swimmer. But she was his favorite.

And she was never really his.

He'd stumbled upon the photos and the journals by accident a long, long time ago. He was thirteen. Despite the poor quality of the pictures, they never ceased to fascinate and arouse him. He'd lost track of how many times he'd masturbated to her. The most recent time was two nights ago.

The journal entries were candid, funny, sexy, violent, and harrowing. Some of her fantasies were deliciously filthy. She was twisted, and he liked that about her.

The photos and the diaries were twenty-five years old.

He had no idea where she was now. But not a day went by that he didn't think of her.

The last time he ever laid eyes on her was when he'd been thirteen. He hadn't recognized her at first. He'd been at the hospital, visiting his sick mother. Some stupid doctor had just told him that she might go home in a day or two. Instead, she would remain there and die within the week.

At the time, it didn't matter much to him. He was sick of his mother being sick.

When he stepped onto the stainless-steel-walled elevator on the fourth floor, he didn't pay much attention to the old woman already on board. And he barely looked at the candy striper who stepped in right after him. She was taller than him, with glasses and mousy brown hair. He wasn't interested. It might have helped if she'd smiled, but she didn't.

The old woman stepped off on three. No one else got on.

After the doors closed and the elevator started moving again, the girl suddenly reached over and hit the Stop button.

With a jolt, the thing halted. He heard a grinding noise, and the overhead light flickered. All at once, she grabbed him and threw him against the wall. Pinning him there, she held a scalpel to his throat. She grabbed hold of his arm with her other hand and held it above his head. It was so sudden and terrifying, he felt powerless.

Then he recognized the face behind those glasses— and he knew her voice when she spoke. And that was when he wet his pants. He thought for certain he was going to die.

"Where are the pictures?" she whispered. "Where are my diaries? I want that tire iron, too. Tell me where they are or I'll cut you. I mean it, you little asshole. I can cut your fucking head off with this thing."

"I don't know what you're talking about," he whimpered. "Tire iron?"

The blade tickled his throat.

"Are they somewhere in the house? Are they hidden?"

"I don't know, I swear. What pictures? Please . . ."

She twisted his arm until he thought it might pop out of its socket. Her fingernails dug into his skin. "If I find out you're lying, I'll kill your mother. And after I finish with that bitch, I'll kill you. I'll be watching you—all the time. Remember that."

She suddenly released him and then pushed the elevator button again.

With another mechanical grinding noise, the lift started moving once more.

He was so shaken that he felt sick. His eyes were closed, and he didn't even see her get out on the second floor. He merely heard the elevator doors open and shut.

He was so relieved that she'd swallowed his lie.

The tire iron she'd asked about was long gone. He'd been with his father on a ferry when the old man had tossed it overboard into Skagit Bay. That had been a few months before his father died.

He knew about the photos and the diaries, too. He'd already seen them. He'd already gotten off on them dozens of times. He had a special hiding place for them— under a floorboard in his closet.

But if he had told her that, she probably would have killed him.

He wondered if she was still alive. What is it people said? *You never get over your first.* All the journals and photos he'd collected in the past two years didn't quite match up to those old Polaroids and her sexy, sick prose.

Monica had managed to thrill him for a while. But he was tired of her now. He was ready to break in a new one. He'd been searching for a potential replacement and had it narrowed down to a couple of girls.

He opened one of Monica's journals and smiled at the neat, feminine penmanship.

The discovery of his hidden graveyard had thrown a slight crimp into things. But he'd already picked out a new burial spot.

He would break ground there tomorrow night.

Monday—11:56 P.M.

"I'm so sorry, Aaron," she whispered.

"It's not your fault," he murmured. "He had the race rigged from the start."

Aaron still ached from swimming his "punishment laps" this afternoon. Several times, he wanted to give up and let the weight belt just drag him down to the bottom of the pool. But his hatred for the coach kept him going.

He sat at the foot of his cot, slumped against the wall with another book in front of his face. He was so exhausted that he could hardly keep his eyes open. But this was Monica's last night. He had to try to talk some sense into her.

"Listen, he's going to drug you and take you to his van," Aaron said, his words starting to slur. It was hard even holding the book up. He just wanted to lie down. "In the van, he'll sort of hogtie you—so your hands are in back of you and there's another rope connecting them to the ropes around your ankles. He'll put tape over your mouth. You'll be out of it for at least a couple of hours. When you wake up, start trying to loosen the ropes around your wrists. Maybe you could put something on your wrists to make them slippery. Do you have any lotion or anything kind of slick or greasy in your cell?"

"No, just soap," she answered.

"Well, you don't have to worry about the rope around your ankles," Aaron said. "He'll cut it so you can walk from the van to wherever he's going to kill you—"

"Please, stop saying that—"

"Monica, I'm too tired to argue with you now. Just listen to me. The best time to try escaping is after he's cut the rope around your ankles. As soon as your feet are free, kick him in the balls or just run—"

"Aaron, I can't," she said. "I don't want to make him mad just when he's ready to let me go. That would be crazy."

"It's your only chance. Can't you see? Maybe you could do a head-butt like in the movies, y'know? You'll only have a minute or two between the van and wherever he's going to kill you. Do something. It's your only chance. Stun him and run . . ."

"Stun and run," she repeated. "Okay, Aaron, whatever you say . . ."

He could tell she was just trying to get him to shut up.

That wasn't too hard to do, because he couldn't keep awake.

"Good," he muttered, his eyes closed. "Monica, I wanted to stay up on our last night so we could talk. But I—I can't. I'm fading fast. I'll miss you. Just—remember what I said . . ."

"Stun and run," she said. "Aaron, we'll see each

other again. Count on that. It's funny. I hope I'll recognize you with your clothes on." She gave a nervous laugh. "Aaron?"

He was too tired to answer.

"Aaron, you won't be here much longer," she promised. "I'll work with the police to track down this place. We'll get you out . . ."

He curled up on the cot. He could still hear her talking, but her words were all garbled.

He wanted to warn her one last time.

But he fell asleep.

CHAPTER TWENTY-SEVEN

The Olympics theme music loudly played on the boom box.

Monica had just swum a ceremonial final lap in the pool, and now she was toweling off. The coach directed her to get up on one of the diving blocks, which they'd moved a little farther away from the pool.

Junior snapped photos with his smartphone while Monica bowed deeply—so the coach could drape a cheap faux-gold medal on a blue ribbon around her neck. As she straightened up again, she nodded at the coach and the Missus, who applauded. Monica looked a little ill at ease, but her smile seemed genuine and there were tears in her eyes.

She was in the exact same place and striking the exact same pose as Jim Lessing in the bulletin board photograph.

Standing in the shallow end of the pool, Aaron was naked again. He had his wrist handcuffed to the pool ladder. Even if he wanted to, he couldn't have applauded.

And he didn't want to.

It was like watching Monica get ready for her own execution.

In another day or two, her photo would be up there on the bulletin board.

Seattle
Tuesday—2:43 P.M.

"We're not going to make the three-o'clock ferry, kids, no way," Caitlin announced.

She was driving on a traffic-clogged Interstate 5. Lindsay sat across from her in the front passenger seat and Gabe was in the back. The last twenty-four hours had been horrible and surreal for the three of them.

She hadn't realized how truly frustrating island living could be, not until yesterday afternoon when she and Gabe— the two of them in shock—had to wait sixty-five minutes for a ferry to the mainland. All the while, Caitlin had thought of poor Lindsay, scared and devastated, surrounded by cops, with no one to comfort her.

And she'd thought of Russ, lying in a morgue.

During that seemingly interminable wait, Gabe had tried to reassure her: "Well, at least Dad and Cliff are together again."

She'd been trying to keep it together for a couple of hours, but completely lost it at that moment. The two of them had sat in the car together and sobbed.

The rest of the day had been a blur. Except for a few more crying jags, Caitlin had been like a zombie. And some of it had been all too familiar as she went through so many of the painful motions she'd undergone two years ago with Cliff's death.

Both Gabe and Lindsay had held up pretty well today—considering. The three of them had swung by Russ's wreck of an apartment so she could pick out a suit he'd be cremated in. They'd agreed his ashes would be scattered where they'd scattered Cliff's—from a beautiful lookout point near Cannon Beach. The family had gone on vacation there once, back in happier times.

Caitlin also found Russ's address book. Because of his drug issues, he'd been estranged from most of his friends and extended family. But Caitlin figured they needed to be notified just the same. That would be on her *Must-Do* list tonight. There was also a contact number for his SARA sponsor, Paul—with no last name.

They didn't stay long at the apartment. Sorting through the things they wanted to save or give to charity would have to wait a few days. Caitlin just wasn't ready for that yet.

They had lunch at an IHOP on Madison, and even though she didn't eat much of her Pigs in a Blanket, her stomach was still revolting. After that, they had to go to a funeral parlor on Rainier Avenue to arrange Russ's cremation and memorial service—neither of which she could afford now that she was out four thousand dollars. However, at least a couple of her replacement credit cards had arrived by express mail yesterday.

Of course, it had already occurred to her that Russ's death certainly fit the pattern of casualties for every family who had lived in that house since 1992. But then, Russ had started his descent with drugs long before she'd moved to Echo. So she couldn't really blame the house for what he'd done to himself.

Still, Caitlin couldn't ignore the timing.

As she headed north on I-5, she knew the kids were as exhausted and frayed as she was. And now they'd have to wait an hour and a half for the 4:30 ferry back to Echo.

Caitlin saw the sign for Lake City Way, Exit 522. She knew that was the route to Woodinville.

She switched on her indicator. "Listen guys, we're not getting home before five anyway," she said. "Would you mind if we took a little side trip?"

"I don't care." Lindsay sighed. She was staring out her window.

"Where are we going?" Gabe asked.

"I'll explain on the way," Caitlin said. "Lind, honey, could you reach into my bag and get me a couple of Tums? There's also a piece of light green memo paper in there with a Woodinville address on it. Could you find it for me, please? When you do, I'll need you to GPS the address for me . . ."

"I think that black car behind us is the same one I saw in the parking lot of the IHOP," Gabe said, gazing out the rear window.

Caitlin had just driven through the center of Woodinville, and according to Lindsay's GPS, it was still another mile and a half to Stuart Arnett's house. Rush hour had already started, and they were crawling from one traffic signal to another.

"Honey, what are you talking about?" Caitlin asked, checking the rearview mirror. "Where?"

"It's the black Taurus two cars in back of us, behind the MINI Cooper," he said.

"Yeah, I'm sure it's the exact same black Taurus you saw three hours and thirty miles back," Lindsay snorted. "Like there isn't another black Taurus on the road . . ."

"This one has a weird, green-haired doll on the dashboard. It was like a gremlin."

Caitlin squinted in the rearview mirror.

"Mom, watch out!" Lindsay yelled.

Caitlin suddenly noticed the three cars ahead of her had stopped for another traffic signal. She slammed on the brakes. The Lexus's tires screeched. The car came to a halt just inches away from the SUV in front of her. "Is everyone okay?" she asked, unnerved.

Gabe and Lindsay said they were fine. Siri told her to turn left in one thousand feet. Caitlin almost didn't hear the directions. She was distracted by a ten-foot-tall inflatable Santa at Sunny's Used Car lot on the corner. Over a speaker, they had Christmas music playing, and a recording broke in: "*Ho-Ho-Ho, get a sunny deal and save at Sunny's!*"

"God, talk about obnoxious!" Lindsay said. "Think they're rushing things a little? It's not even Veterans Day."

Her heart still racing, Caitlin switched on her indicator and turned at the intersection. "Gabe, honey, let me know if the car with the troll doll is still following us, will you?"

"I can't tell," he said, staring out the back window. "There's a Winnebago in back of us now . . ."

By the time they found Elkhorn Court ten minutes later, Gabe didn't see the black Taurus anymore. Caitlin was relieved to hear it. Some of her paranoia, however justified, must have infected Gabe. At least no one was tailing them. She didn't need that now. She was already frazzled enough about dropping in unannounced on Stuart Healy—if this was indeed Stuart Healy.

"*Your destination is five hundred feet on your left*," Siri announced.

Spotting Stuart's house, Caitlin realized his "*noteworthy donation*" (as the article had put it) to the local police and fire departments must have been a mere drop in the bucket for him. He lived in a grand, isolated estate that resembled one of those old Hollywood mansions. A tall fence surrounded the grounds, but the front gates were open—probably because of the crew of gardeners working on the yard.

"Wow, Mr. Got-bucks," Lindsay remarked. "Think he wants his old house back? Maybe we can switch . . ."

Caitlin turned into the driveway. Except for the gardeners' pickup, parked off to the side, she didn't see any other cars. She wondered if anyone was home. Maybe this "side trip" would be a big bust. She parked near the walkway to the front door and asked Gabe and Lindsay to wait in the car for a few minutes.

She told herself they had their phones. They were fine.

Caitlin walked up to the front door, a big, beautiful old Spanish-style door with a wrought-iron-barred little window for a peephole and an elaborate doorknocker. She rang the bell and waited. Glancing over her shoulder, she noticed a couple of the yard workers staring at her. She figured Stuart Arnett probably didn't get too many unsolicited visitors.

She heard someone coming. She figured it might be a maid—or even a butler. Then she saw the man's eyes just reaching the bottom at the other side of the little window. He was wearing glasses.

The door swung open.

Caitlin knew she'd found Stuart Healy. He looked very much like his father—but not quite as imposing. The glasses and his red cardigan made him appear a bit nerdy. He looked older than thirty-five, more like forty. He gave her a wary look. "Yes?"

Caitlin smiled nervously. "Hi, I'm sorry to just drop by like this . . ."

"Yes. Usually the front gate is closed."

"Then I'll get right to the point. My name is Caitlin Stoller, and—well, I live at Sixty-Seven Birch Place in Echo. I think you used to live there, too."

He just stared at her for a moment.

"I was hoping you could answer a few questions about the house. Do you have a couple of minutes?"

He seemed to be blocking the doorway. "What did you want to know?"

"Well, for starters, were you aware there's a trapdoor to a hidden room under that broom closet beneath the basement stairs?"

He said nothing.

"You are Stuart Healy, aren't you?" she asked.

He nodded and then peeked past her at her Lexus in the driveway. "Are those your kids in the car?" he asked. "Do they want to come inside?"

He was very cordial but still seemed a bit guarded. He mentioned it was the maid's day off. His wife was out shopping, and his two daughters had volleyball practice. He ushered Caitlin, Lindsay, and Gabe into the well-appointed, but slightly boring living room. It reminded her of a hotel lobby—with Mission-style furniture, generic-looking artwork, and a big, ugly fireplace that might have looked better with a fire in it. He asked if she and the kids wanted anything to drink.

They all politely declined. Lindsay was perched on one end of the sofa, and Gabe slouched in an easy chair. Caitlin was on the other end of the couch from Lindsay, and Stuart Healy settled in the chair across from Gabe.

"So—you're living in my old house, good old Sixty-Seven Birch," he said with a wistful smile. Then he cleared his throat and sat back in the chair. "Though I must admit my memories of the place aren't so rosy. Forgive me earlier if I seemed standoffish. I wasn't sure you were on the level. Then you mentioned the old wine cellar, and I realized you must be telling the truth."

"Then the room was a wine cellar?" Caitlin asked.

He nodded. "For a while, we used it for that, which is ironic, because my father owned a restaurant—part of a whole recreational complex he had in town—and he didn't allow alcohol to be served. But he and my mother sure drank enough at home." He laughed—a bit uncomfortably. "Anyway, they eventually decided to clear out all the wine and the racks . . ."

Caitlin wondered if it was something Mr. Healy had

done because of the mother's drinking problem. But she didn't ask.

"After that, my sister and I used to go down there and play sometimes—until my father forbid us to. He didn't think it was safe. So they covered it up."

"I turned that broom closet into my own clubhouse," Gabe chimed in. "But I can't go in there now because we discovered that dungeon room and my mom thinks it's too dangerous. It's too bad, too, because that was a really cool clubhouse."

"I'll bet it was. That sure sounds cool," Stuart Healy said, a bit condescending. He stole a glance at his wristwatch and turned to Caitlin. "Um, what else did you want to know about the house?"

"Well, if I can be candid," she said. "You're not the only one whose memories of the place aren't so rosy. Ever since you moved out, each family who's lived there has had to endure one tragedy after another while in that house. The last owners even had a stalker, who might have been responsible for the death of one child and an accident that almost killed another. The mother ended up committing suicide."

"Oh, my," he murmured, his brow furrowed.

Caitlin suddenly felt tactless. She remembered Stuart's father had killed himself. "I'm sorry," she said. "It's just that all this seems to date back to 1992."

He glanced at Gabe and Lindsay, and then his eyes narrowed at her. "So—you're talking about my sister. Is that why you came here—to talk about Denise?"

Caitlin sighed. "I don't mean to open old wounds. But as I said, this seems to have started with the death of your sister. I was wondering if, before that, you remember anything out of the ordinary happening. Do you know if anyone was watching the house?"

"Mrs. Stoller, if something like that happened, don't you think we would have told the police about it? If you did your research—and it sounds like you have—then you know, Denise's killer was never found. I seriously doubt you're going to solve a twenty-five-year-old murder case by poking around and asking a few questions."

Caitlin shook her head. "I'm not trying to do that. It's not why I came here. We moved into your family's former home about two months ago, and a lot of strange, disturbing things have been happening to us lately. I've been getting anonymous notes, emails, and phone calls. That's just a small part of it. Actually, it's much worse . . ."

She didn't want to go into the deaths of Ken Meekley and Neal Huggins—both "suicides." But she was thinking about them.

"I'm worried about my family," Caitlin continued. "I thought since all these problems with the house started back while you were living there, you might have some insight as to why all this is happening. I thought maybe you could help."

Stuart frowned a bit and said nothing.

"I'm pretty sure my bedroom used to be your sister's," Lindsay piped up. She nervously flipped back her hair. "It's the room down at the end of the upstairs hall . . ."

Stuart's face seemed to soften, and he nodded. "Yes, that was Denise's room."

"My mom said she was a championship swimmer.

Me too. Well, maybe I'm not a champion, but I've won some races . . ."

"She's being modest," Caitlin said. "She has a whole shelf full of awards—trophies and plaques."

"So did Denise," he said. "She was so proud of those awards. She didn't have many friends, but she had her trophies. She was very shy—*people-nervous*, I guess you'd say. It didn't help that we both got pulled out of school at a certain point for homeschooling. That was hard for both of us. Everyone went to our father's stables and his pool during the summer—and his restaurant year-round. But no one was really interested in getting to know me or my sister."

"Did Denise know a girl named Teri?" Caitlin asked. "I think she was a brunette . . ."

He bit his lip, and after a moment, nodded. "Yes, she was in Denise's class before we were homeschooled. I don't think she was ever very nice to my sister. I remember seeing her at my father's pool. It was hard to miss her. She always wore skimpy suits— and filled them rather nicely."

"You don't remember anything else about her?" Caitlin pressed.

"I was about eleven years old. What I remember most were the skimpy bathing suits." From behind the glasses, he winked and grinned at Gabe, who just looked uncomfortable.

Stuart cleared his throat. "I believe she got into trouble a couple of times at the club," he continued—a bit more soberly. "I don't remember what for."

"Do you recall her last name?"

He shook his head and shrugged. "No, I don't. Funny

you should bring her up. I haven't thought about her in a long, long time. Why are you asking about her?"

"If it's the same Teri, she later married a contractor who worked on the house for two different owners. His name was Lance Spangler. Does that ring a bell?"

He shook his head again.

"Well, that's another tragedy related to the house," Caitlin said. "He died in a Jeep accident with one of the owners. I tried talking to Teri on the phone a couple of nights ago, and—well, let's just say she wasn't as gracious as you've been. She definitely has a lot of—animosity toward the house."

Stuart took off his glasses and rubbed the bridge of his nose. "I don't see how that could have started with us. As I said, she didn't know us very well."

He put his glasses back on and got to his feet. "I'm really sorry I can't be more help."

Caitlin realized he was ending the conversation—and ready to show them out. Befuddled, she stood up—and so did Lindsay. Caitlin signaled Gabe to get to his feet.

"Well, you've been very nice," she said, following him to the door. "Thank you for your time."

She'd been hoping to get something more from meeting Denise Healy's brother, she wasn't sure what. But all she had now was an unsatisfied feeling.

He opened the door for them. He smiled at Lindsay. "What's your specialty?"

For a moment, she seemed stumped. "Oh, you mean for swimming? Freestyle, backstroke, everything I guess. I just love being in the water."

"Well, keep practicing—um, *Lindsay*, right?"

She nodded. "Right."

"Lindsay Stoller," he said, patting her shoulder. "I'll look for that name in the next Olympics lineup."

She nodded again. "Thanks," she said, and then she headed out the door.

Gabe was already halfway to the car. Some of the yard crew stopped to look at them.

Caitlin shook Stuart's hand. "Thank you again."

"I'm sorry to cut things short," he said. "It's been a while since I've talked about my sister. It's still diffi-cult—and painful."

Caitlin nodded sheepishly. "I'm sorry. Well, thank you again."

With a little grimace, he reached under his glasses and wiped his eye. "Drive safely," he said. Then he stepped back inside and closed the door.

As Caitlin headed to the car, she thought it was a lit-tle strange.

He'd wiped a tear away—when there weren't any tears.

Stuart closed the door and leaned back against it. He took off the glasses, folded them, and shoved them in his shirt pocket.

He remembered that sultry night when he'd re-turned home with his parents from the Fourth of July fireworks show at Equestream. His sister had missed an awesome spectacle. In past years, locals bitched and moaned about how cheap his dad was with the fire-works, and how it wasn't even worth the buck-a-head admission he charged. Stuart and Denise would hear about it for days afterward.

But this year was different. People were actually thanking and congratulating his dad afterwards. For a change, he and his sister would be able to hold their heads high at Equestream—for at least the next few days.

His parents were still coming through the kitchen door from the garage when Stuart raced ahead of them and scurried up the stairs. He couldn't wait to tell his sister about the fireworks show—if for no other reason than to rub it in that she'd missed a really fantastic one. She'd been kind of a pill all night because of her cold. "Hey, dum-dum!" he yelled as he got to the top of the stairs. "You blew it. You should have come. This year was the best—"

He stopped dead in her bedroom doorway.

Denise was sprawled across the floor, near her bed. Blood oozed from a gash in her forehead and ran into her open eyes. A dark crimson pool had formed on the pink shag rug beneath her. She was perfectly still.

A hammer was almost indistinguishable in the puddle of blood.

Stuart stood frozen. For a moment, he couldn't breathe.

Finally, he screamed for his parents. He didn't stop screaming until he heard them rushing up the stairs.

When his mother saw his sister, she became hysterical. She ran to her, kneeled down in all that blood, and cradled Denise. His father just stood there in the doorway, shaking his head.

Stuart kept saying they should call the police.

"We can't," his father said. "We have to wait."

"But Dad—"

His father turned and slapped him hard across the face.

Stunned, he rubbed his tear-stained cheek and stared back at the old man. It took Stuart a moment to understand why his father demanded they wait.

Stuart swiveled around, raced down the front stairs and into the kitchen. He grabbed a knife out of the utensil drawer. Flinging open the basement door, he noticed the light was already on down there. He hurried down the steps, through the family room, and into the utility room. The door to the closet under the stairs was open. Most of the time, it was closed and locked. Most of the time, a linoleum cutout covered the closet floor. But the floor-piece was leaning against the wall. The trapdoor to the hidden subterranean room was open. The ladder had been lowered into the cell.

Stuart looked down into the dim cell: the cot; the old, chipped dresser; the bookcase full of books; and the travel posters on the unfinished walls.

But the secret room was unoccupied—for the first time in six months.

Clutching the knife, he bent over the trapdoor to make sure no one was down there.

Stuart remembered how his face had still throbbed from his father's slap. But the old man had been right. They'd had to wait and figure things out before calling the police.

They ended up convincing investigators that an intruder must have killed his sister that summer night nearly twenty-five years ago.

"Daddy, who was that who just left?" Stuart's wife called now from the upstairs hallway.

He sighed and closed his eyes. "Did I say it was okay for you to talk again?" he yelled. "Didn't I tell you to stay in the bedroom?"

He heard her footsteps above him as she retreated into their bedroom.

Stuart headed down the hallway and opened the door to the basement. He ambled down the stairs to a small exercise room—with an elliptical machine, some free weights, and a small TV on the wall. There were three doors off this room. The one he went through accessed a long, narrow hallway with cinder-block walls. It led to a laundry area, where in addition to the washer, the dryer and a sink, they also had a refrigerator and a microwave oven. In front of the window above the dryer, his wife kept some plants in tacky little pottery containers on the sill. She also had more plants on top of the fridge. She'd made the ceramic pieces ages ago in some stupid pottery class.

From the laundry area, Stuart walked down another hallway. He stopped at a metal door on his right and pushed open a speakeasy flap that hit him at face level. He gazed in at the girl in the cell.

Startled, Monica got up from her cot. "Is it time?" she asked.

"Not yet," he said. "We still have about four more hours before we start the preparations. I just wanted you to know, I've been looking around, and for the longest time I didn't think I could find a girl to take your place here. But I—well, I just found her."

He smiled at her, and then shut the little door.

CHAPTER TWENTY-EIGHT

The coach had the window open in the front of the van.

Even with the duct tape over her mouth, Monica relished breathing in the fresh, cold air. She hadn't been outside in over six months. It had seemed like an eternity. She hadn't seen the sun, moon, or sky in all that time. But tonight she would be free. She'd earned her release.

She had managed to poke her head out from under the sheet that covered her. She'd been stripped down to her bra and panties—and blindfolded. Aaron had been right about the way the coach tied her up. Her hands were trussed behind her, and her feet had been bound around the ankles. She'd been drugged, so she had no recollection of being taken from her cell, tied up, and loaded onto this thin mattress in the back of the van.

She'd woken up about a half hour ago. Monica wasn't sure how much time had passed or how far the coach had driven. But she knew he was at the wheel and he was alone. She heard him humming quietly.

She remembered what Aaron had told her about trying to loosen the ropes around her wrists. She'd been wiggling and twisting her hands for a while now, and she didn't think it had done much good. Besides, it didn't seem necessary, not if the coach was letting her go.

The drug gave Monica a bit of a hangover, but she didn't mind. She'd be home soon. She could hardly wait to see her dad, her sister—and her brother and his family. She wondered if her little niece, Jessica, would even recognize her.

A part of her felt horrible, leaving poor Aaron behind.

Monica intended to work with the police to find him. Of course, that meant she'd have to break the contract she'd signed for the coach, the one saying she wouldn't reveal anything about these last six months. She'd also promised to stick to the cover story he'd assigned her—the one about how she'd run away and drifted from menial job to menial job, and how she'd still had plenty of time to swim, exercise, and take care of herself.

Monica had her doubts. If she really tried to tell people that story, would anyone believe her? How could she be held prisoner for all this time and not tell people the truth? She wondered how Jim Lessing had managed it.

Obviously, the coach had figured it would be nearly impossible for anyone to keep that part of the bargain. So there was another stipulation to her release, one she'd seen coming.

"If you break our contract or breathe one word to the police about me, I'll kill Aaron," the coach had told her—through the little peephole flap in the doorway of her cell. "And I won't stop there. I'll kill your father, your big sister, and your brother's family. I know where they all live. And of course, I'll kill you, too. If you don't think you can keep the confidentiality clause of our agreement, Monica, tell me now."

"I won't say anything," she'd promised.

She'd had no choice but to agree. She would have been killed right there in her cell if she hadn't gone along with it.

"What could I tell them anyway?" Monica had said. "I don't know your name. I don't know where I've spent these last several months. What I do know is that—as tough as this has been for me, I'm leaving here a better person and a better athlete. And it's all thanks to you. I really respect you, and you have my word that I won't let you down."

It was a total lie, of course.

But the stupid son of a bitch seemed to have bought it.

Monica had figured it wouldn't hurt to keep sucking up to the coach right until the moment he freed her. She didn't want him doubting her loyalty for even a second.

She knew she'd need to be careful about telling the police. They'd have to agree to a news blackout. They couldn't allow the coach to catch on that something was up because he would certainly keep his promise about killing Aaron—and coming after her and her family.

From the smooth ride and the traffic sounds, Monica guessed they'd been on a highway for a while—at least since she'd been awake. There hadn't been any stops. But now they were slowing down.

She heard the radio of a nearby car. They were at a traffic stop, maybe at an off ramp. Someone was listening to the Eagles' "Hotel California." They must have had their window down, too. If she didn't have the damn tape on her mouth, Monica would have smiled.

It felt wonderful to be outside that little cell, hearing sounds from other people. Her dad was a huge classic rock fan with an extensive vinyl collection. That was how Monica knew who the Eagles were.

Listening to that music made her feel even closer to freedom—and home. Monica almost started crying, she was so happy.

But she was scared, too. Something could still go wrong.

She heard a hum. The coach was raising his window. She couldn't hear the music anymore. As chilly as it was, she'd kind of liked the cold, fresh air.

"Okay, now, Jefferson Street," the coach was muttering to himself. "Here we are . . ."

Monica knew where that was. It was in Olympia, not exactly walking distance to her house, but still, it meant the coach had kept his word.

She was on her way home.

It was just what he'd promised—to leave her alone in a remote spot within a mile of her house. He would cut the rope around her wrists. Then she would count to five hundred before she removed her blindfold. After that she could find her way home.

The van started moving again, more slowly now.

Squirming under the sheet, Monica figured this whole ordeal might be over within less than thirty minutes. It was really happening. She'd had her doubts before, especially after listening to Aaron go on and on about how the coach was just going to take her someplace and kill her. But now she was in Olympia. The coach wouldn't have taken her all this way and so close to home if he wasn't living up to his end of the deal. He wouldn't have taken these precautions and given her so many warnings if he was going to murder her.

Another thing, he wouldn't have spent the last six months training her to become a better swimmer, getting her technique and timing to the level she'd reached—all just so he could kill her. He'd have to be crazy.

But of course, he was.

Damn it to hell, he was.

Stuart knew she was awake.

The drug he'd given her had probably worn off about twenty minutes ago. He'd been driving for only an hour now. But she had no way of knowing that.

He'd just mentioned a street he knew in Olympia, pretending to be looking for it.

Actually, he was on Highway 2 in the little town of Gold Bar—at least two hours away from the state capital. He was on his way to some woods outside of Skykomish to start a new burial ground.

He would be there within the half hour. And when he led Monica to her final resting place in those woods, she'd believe she was somewhere in Olympia, walking distance from her home—just as he promised. He found from past experience that they were always docile and cooperative right to the end if they thought they were close to home and about to be freed.

He had a shovel in the back, a tank full of gas, and his passenger was appeased.

There was just one little glitch.

Stuart thought someone might be following him.

He'd noticed a black Taurus some distance behind him shortly after he'd left the house. It had been there again when he'd gotten onto Route 522 in Woodinville. This time of the evening, traffic was pretty light.

He was extra watchful tonight. Now that the cops had found those bodies, he was wary of them tracing his DNA or figuring out where those swimming medals had come from. Of course, he'd paid for the ribbon and medals in cash over two years ago at two different shops in Portland. So they weren't very traceable. Still, he had to be cautious. And this black car in his rearview mirror was bothering him.

Of course, it might not have been the same car, but he saw one just like it—three cars behind him at a stoplight on Highway 2 in Monroe. He'd turned and drove around some Monroe side streets for a bit—just to lose them. He was back on the highway again, going through a couple of small towns. There was an SUV two cars behind him, and it blocked his view of the vehicles in back of it. But he was pretty sure he'd lost the black Taurus.

He'd know in just a few minutes, when he took the turnoff at Skykomish. The narrow old roads and trails into the woods wouldn't have much traffic at all. Anyone tailing him would be easy to spot.

He'd spent most of the afternoon looking up Lindsay Stoller's times from several of her school team's competitions—all the way back to when she'd been living in Portland. He was impressed. She showed promise. With a little training and discipline from him, she'd be outstanding.

He thought of her, sitting on his living room sofa this afternoon, flicking back her long brown hair. It was like she'd just dropped into his lap.

His wife would clean the cell and have it ready for a new occupant tomorrow. Hell, he might even do it himself—he was that excited about this new girl. He could hardly wait to get rid of this one in the back of the van.

Stuart knew he would start to miss her in a few weeks. But then he'd have her journals and the photos. A part of her would always be with him.

So it was on to the next. And he didn't even have to do that much research to track her down.

After all, he knew just where she lived.

Now Monica couldn't hear any traffic at all.

They took one turn and then another. Monica wondered how close they were to that *remote spot* near her home in Olympia.

They slowed down to a crawl and turned onto what seemed like a driveway or a trail. She could hear gravel ricocheting against the underside of the van. She felt the van going over bumps and potholes.

"We're almost there," the coach said. "Tap your foot on the floor if you're awake."

Monica hesitated. Then she kicked her foot against the floor.

"I figured you were up," he said. "You remember our deal now, don't you, Monica?"

She tapped once.

"I don't mind saying, I'm going to miss you. Of all the kids I've coached, you've been the best. I'm very proud of you . . ."

The car stopped.

The coach shut off the engine. It was deathly quiet. "Think it would be okay if I called you sometime— just to check in? I'll be using one of those disposable phones, of course. Think it would be okay?"

Monica tapped once.

"Good," the coach grunted.

She couldn't believe he actually wanted to keep in touch with her. Maybe that was to make sure she kept her end of the bargain. Did he do this with Jim Lessing, too?

Monica heard him climb out of the van and shut the door. Then there were footsteps and humming again. The back of the van opened, and she felt the cold air on her. She heard a clatter as the coach moved around something in back. It sounded like tools of some kind.

He grabbed her by the feet and pulled her closer to the back door. The mattress moved with her. Monica felt the rope around her ankles become tauter, pinching against her skin until she heard a faint snap. She realized the coach had just cut the rope. Her feet were free now.

She remembered what Aaron had told her: "*The best time to try escaping is after he's cut the rope around your ankles. As soon as your feet are free . . .*"

But she couldn't go anywhere with her hands tied and a blindfold on. Besides, it would be stupid to run away now—when she was this close to being let go.

Taking hold of her arm, the coach guided her out of the van. "C'mon, upsy-daisy, watch your head. You might feel a little dizzy . . ."

The guy was so gentle with her that Monica could almost forget what a brutal, sadistic bastard he could be.

The fresh night air on her skin made her shiver, but it was wonderful, too. Even the rough ground—the rocks and grass—felt good under her bare feet. She couldn't stop trembling. She was so nervous and happy and scared.

The coach carefully peeled the duct tape off her mouth. It hurt, but Monica didn't care. She could breathe through her mouth again—and she was *outside*. A tear stained the blindfold.

"Follow my lead here," the coach said, holding her arm again. "We need to walk a bit. I don't want you to see my vehicle. You'd have to go to the police if you got a look at the make and model. I mean, it would be too tempting. How could you keep your promise if you had info like that to tell them?"

"I'll keep my promise," Monica said, trying not to stumble as the coach led her across an uneven terrain. She figured they must be in some woods. She could smell the trees.

"So—no grudges?" the coach asked.

"No grudges," Monica lied.

"Now, we're only about a mile from your house. You should be able to find your way from here."

"I'll find my way," she said, nodding.

They stopped.

Monica felt him pulling and tugging the back of the blindfold.

Then it came off. Monica saw an indigo sky full of bright stars over the shadowy treetops. She could hardly breathe. "Beautiful," she whispered.

She heard the coach behind her. Something moved over her face again, and Monica flinched. She thought he might be putting the blindfold back on. But then she saw that it was her gold medal on the cobalt blue ribbon. The coach placed it over her head and hung it around her neck.

"You didn't think I was going to let you go without this, did you?" he said.

Monica just nodded. She waited for him to cut the rope around her wrists.

"You aren't having your period, are you?" he asked.

It was a bizarre question. "Ah, no," she replied. "Why?"

"They say bears can be attracted to menstrual blood. I don't know if that's completely true or not. When I released Jim in some woods like these, it didn't attract any bears . . ."

"But Jim's a boy . . ." she started to say. They wouldn't have had to worry about anyone menstruating when he'd released Jim.

But there had been blood.

He'd killed Jim in those woods—just as he was about to kill her now.

She should have put it together. The coach was doing things out of order. He wasn't supposed to take her blindfold off yet. He was supposed to cut the rope around her wrist first. She was supposed to count to five hundred, and then she would take off the blindfold herself—after the coach was gone.

Monica could see the van—with its back door open. The interior light was on.

A shovel stuck out of the back.

He needed it to bury her body.

Aaron was right. What did he tell her? *Stun and run*.

"Promise you'll go easy on Aaron, okay?" she said.

"I promise," she heard him say. He was still standing behind her. "Just look up at those stars . . ."

"I need to tell you something about Aaron, what he's planning," she said, nervously stalling for time. "Please, don't punish him for it. I'm just worried if I don't tell you, he might take you by surprise . . ."

"What is it?" he asked. "What does that little bastard have in mind now?"

She turned around. She could see the coach had a knife in his hand. And she knew that he wasn't about to cut the rope around her wrists with it.

"I just don't want to see anyone get hurt when he does this," she said, stepping back. She faked a fall, but slammed her elbow as she hit the ground. The pain was excruciating.

"Well, what the hell is he planning?" the coach asked impatiently. He reached down to help her up.

Stun and run, she thought.

All at once, Monica leaped up and slammed the top of her head into his face.

He let out a yowl, reeled back, and toppled onto the dirt.

Monica caught a glimpse of him, writhing there, momentarily helpless. Blood covered the bottom half of his face. It looked like she'd broken his nose.

He'd dropped the knife. She started to go for it but realized it would take too long and too much contorting to grab the blade with her hands tied behind her.

As she stood there indecisive, the coach tried to grab her ankle.

Monica screamed and bolted away. Through the trees ahead, in the distance, she thought she saw a car's headlights. So she headed in that direction. Twigs and stones cut into her cold, bare feet, but that didn't slow her down.

Her head throbbed. It was because of the drug, but also from slamming into his face like that. She felt dizzy and sick.

She could hear him cursing back there, where she'd left him in the clearing.

It was hard to run with her hands restricted behind her. It threw off her balance. She kept scratching up her arms and legs as she brushed against shrubs and low branches. The cold night air nipped away at her bare skin, but she tried not to think about that right now.

She'd spotted those headlights earlier and figured there must be a road or maybe even a house somewhere in that vicinity. It was her only salvation.

"Where are you going, Monica?" he yelled. "Listen, it's—it's okay—what you did. I forgive you. I know you're scared. For God's sake, come back here! Your house is in the other direction!"

She paused and glanced back at him. He was being very clever, but she didn't believe a word.

The coach was hunting for her with a flashlight—probably from his phone. The beam haphazardly swept across the trees.

"There you are!" he called. "I see you! Come here, honey . . ."

Monica turned around and ran.

Dizzy, scared, and cold as she was, she just kept running.

CHAPTER TWENTY-NINE

Tuesday, November 1—11:55 P.M.

The pass-through drawer whooshed open.

Aaron hadn't heard any footsteps, and the sudden noise made him flinch. He was already wired. He nervously paced around his cell, bathed in a dim blue hue from the night-light. He was thinking of Monica. If this were any other night, they would have been whispering through the vent to each other.

He'd already broken down and cried a couple of times. He was almost certain she was dead by now.

Moving over to the drawer, he found a Milky Way bar in there.

Aaron heard the Missus's footsteps as she started to walk away. "Thank you!" he called. "This is really nice of you. And thank you for dinner tonight. The chicken pasta was really good!"

It was Lean Cuisine, nothing special. But he figured he needed her on his side.

"You're welcome!" she murmured in her nervous, little-girl voice.

"My name is Aaron," he said.

There was a long pause. "I know."

"You seem too nice for this—too nice for him," Aaron dared to say. "You know, the other night, he came down here and attacked Monica. He—forced himself on her. I could hear it . . ." He almost said, *through the vent*, but caught himself just in time. "He took her out of here tonight. He said he was going to release her. But I know he's going to kill her—if he hasn't already. You know it, too . . ."

She didn't say anything. But he didn't hear her walk away, either.

"He beats you up, doesn't he?" Aaron asked. "You don't deserve that, nobody does. And look what he's got you doing. I'm sorry, but you're so much better than this. Listen, please, between you and me, I think we might still be able to help Monica . . ."

"No, we can't," she whispered. "It's too late."

The words hit him like a punch in the gut. Aaron doubled over and started to sob.

He heard the Missus retreating.

"My name is Aaron!" he cried out. He wanted to tell her again, to remind her that he was *somebody*—not just a thing that was fed, trained, and killed. "I miss my mom! And I'm scared! You must know that. He's going to kill me, too—maybe not right away, but eventually. And he's going to kill you, too—eventually. I—I think we're both alike. We're both prisoners here. If you help me escape, I'll help you escape . . ."

On the other side of the wall, it sounded as if she'd come back.

"I'll help you," Aaron repeated. "You won't have to be scared of him anymore. You deserve better. You can take your son away from him—before he turns into someone like his father. He's still young. He could change if you gave him a chance. We can help each other . . ."

Aaron wiped the tears from his eyes. "Are you there?"

There was no response.

"Guess I've been talking to myself," he muttered. *And for the camera, too*, he thought. If he was being recorded and the coach reviewed tonight's footage, he was a dead man.

Aaron peeled off the candy wrapper and took a bite out of his chocolate bar. He had a hard time swallowing because he'd been crying. So he fixed the wrapper back around his Milky Way and set it on his desk.

He glanced down at the vent, and he thought of Monica again.

The drawer suddenly whooshed and snapped into the wall. A moment later, the receptacle popped back into the cell again.

"Are you there?" Aaron called. "Did you—did you hear me earlier?"

There was no answer.

He glanced down into the drawer and saw a small, very sharp-looking knife.

She'd heard him.

Crouched down behind some shrubs, Monica couldn't see him anymore. But she saw the flashlight as he weaved through the dark woods in search of her. He was getting closer. He kept calling out her name, very calmly—like she was his lost cat.

Her feet bled. Her shoulders and arms ached from having her hands tied behind her for so long. She was covered with scratches, dirt, and sweat. Because of the night chill, she couldn't keep her teeth from chattering.

Soon he'd be close enough to see her pale skin—and her breath in the chilly night air.

She'd found an old, narrow road that snaked through the forest. She was almost certain this was where she'd spotted the car's headlights earlier. But she didn't see a car or a house anywhere around. There wasn't a single sign or streetlight—just that flashlight flickering amid the trees.

Monica figured if she stayed hidden behind the bushes and trees, then followed the road, it would eventually lead to something—some semblance of civilization, maybe a campsite or a cabin, or a stranger who might be able to help her.

She kept glancing over her shoulder. She couldn't see the flashlight anymore. She wondered if the coach had turned it off to save the batteries—or if he had wandered off in the other direction. Was it too much to hope that she'd lost him?

Emerging from the thicket, she took a chance and staggered closer to the roadside where the ground wasn't so hard on her sore feet. Her cold, sweaty skin felt prickly, and she couldn't even rub her arms to get warm.

Monica noticed a light again—farther up the road. A panic swept through her. She thought it might be his flashlight—and here she was, running toward it.

But then she saw there were two lights. It was a car, and it was getting closer as it zigzagged through the woods. Every once in a while, as it passed behind a cluster of trees, the light would disappear for a moment or two. And then, she'd be so grateful to see it again—stronger, brighter, and closer.

It wasn't a van. It was a black car. It looked like a Taurus.

Breathless, Monica hobbled into the car's path, hoping it would stop. She just wished she could use her hands to wave it down.

The headlights blinded her. Monica heard the tires screech.

She couldn't get a breath to scream for help.

The car had stopped. Whoever was inside the Taurus didn't do anything for several moments.

Monica squinted in the headlights' glare. She couldn't see the driver. Why weren't they doing anything?

"Help me, please!" she cried, taking a chance the coach would hear. If he was anywhere in the area, he must have seen her in the headlights' beams.

She staggered closer to the vehicle. She could see now, there was just one person in the car—in the driver's seat. It wasn't the Missus, Monica could tell that much. But the driver was a woman. Her face was in the shadows.

She just sat with her hands on the wheel and didn't move at all.

For a moment, Monica couldn't move, either. She stood there frozen—uncertain whether this stranger was going to help her or kill her.

* * *

"Stuart, you bad boy, look at what you've done," she murmured, staring at the dirt-covered, near-naked girl standing in the middle of the road. Her skin looked so ghostly pale in the headlights she may as well have been an apparition. Her hands were tied behind her.

The woman in the driver's seat smiled.

So—it turned out Stuart was a regular chip off the old block. Like father, like son.

She'd always figured Denise's kid brother was still alive. But she'd let him fall off her radar. He never really mattered. She'd been pretty certain he'd moved on and had nothing to do with his father's secret pastime. But obviously she'd been mistaken.

She had Caitlin to thank for her finding Stuart again and discovering the hobby he'd shared with his late father. Or was it something he'd inherited?

She wondered if—like the old man—he was a holyroller hypocrite, too.

She'd followed Caitlin and her brats onto the Echo ferry this morning. There were always plenty of places for her to hide on the commuter boat. But this black Taurus she'd recently stolen was hardly inconspicuous, thanks to the medium-sized green-haired troll doll glued to the dashboard. Yet if Caitlin suspected someone was following her, then that was fine, too. It was part of the plan. She wanted Caitlin to feel someone was always watching.

She tailed them from the ferry to Russ's apartment building to the IHOP. She parked and waited for them outside the funeral home on Rainier Avenue. But then, on the interstate, instead of taking the Mukilteo Ferry exit, Caitlin pulled a fast one and got onto 522. She followed the Lexus to Woodinville—all the way to Elkhorn Court and that mansion. She drove to the side of the house in search of a recycling bin outside the tall hedge-bordered wrought-iron fence. She hoped to find an old letter, catalog, or magazine with the name of the person who lived here. But she didn't see any bins, and she didn't want to attract the gardeners' attention. So she turned around and pulled over about a quarter of a block away, where she could still follow Caitlin when she left the place.

On her smartphone, she looked up real estate agents in Woodinville, then called the one at the top of the list. Giving a phony name, she asked about the mansion on Elkhorn Court and was told the house wasn't on the market. "I'm still interested in buying the property," she told the woman. "And money's no object. You'll get your commission, of course. Do you have the name of the owner?"

The woman called her back five minutes later with the name: *Stuart Arnett*. It didn't take much figuring. It was the same first name, and his poor drunken mother's maiden name. The real estate woman also had a phone number but wasn't positive if it was still current.

She waited in the car outside Stuart Healy's estate on Elkhorn Court. She wondered what kind of lies Stuart was telling Caitlin and the kiddies. She decided to remain there—even after she saw Caitlin and company drive away. She'd become more interested in the comings and goings of Stuart. While waiting in the car, she went online but didn't find much about Stuart *Arnett*.

Several times, she thought about driving up to the front door—or phoning him. But she sat it out. At eleven o'clock, she was just about to leave when those front gates opened and an old silver van slowly pulled out of the driveway. The dumpy vehicle just didn't go with the rich real estate, but it had come out of his garage.

In the light traffic, it was pretty easy for her to stay on his tail and stay inconspicuous. But then he turned off at Skykomish and started onto these old rural roads and trails that wove through the woods. She couldn't follow very close and often had to switch off her headlights to keep from being seen. For several stretches, she drove by the moonlight—her knuckles turning white as she gripped the steering wheel. She wondered if Stuart had a cabin around here somewhere.

At one point, she lost him. She stopped the car, stepped outside, and listened.

He must have stopped and gotten out of his vehicle, too, because she heard him talking to a girl. The words weren't clear, but from the gruff baritone voice, he sounded like his father. Through the trees, she spotted his van, parked in a clearing with the back door open and the interior light on.

She still couldn't see Stuart—or the girl with him. But she heard someone cry out.

Moving around to the Taurus's trunk, she dug out the tire iron. She had a gun in her purse, which was certainly a better weapon. But the first time she'd ever killed someone it had been with a tire iron. It had also been in the woods. And she was feeling sentimental tonight.

Back inside the car, she switched on the headlights and drove around in search of a trail that might lead to where Stuart's van was parked. She rolled down her window. She heard Stuart calling to the girl. Her name was Monica, and it sounded like she'd somehow managed to break free of him. Obviously, she'd been in his van all this time—and in his house before that. Did he have a secret, special room down in the basement— just like his daddy?

All at once, this helpless pretty young thing stumbled into the middle of the road. The girl squinted in the headlights' beams.

The woman in the driver's seat slammed on the brakes and caught her breath.

She couldn't help thinking that this girl might have seen her face—or the license plate of her car.

She glanced over at the tire iron on the passenger side. It would have been so easy to get out of the car and kill her.

But really, why help Stuart?

Besides, the car was stolen and couldn't be traced to her. She planned on ditching it the next morning. If the girl could somehow see her face, it didn't matter. To follow Caitlin around, the woman had donned a wig—along with a pair of glasses she used for driving at night. There was no way the girl could identify her later.

Finally, the strongest argument for allowing this girl to live was that the two of them were so much alike.

On a beautiful snowy night twenty-five years ago, she was in practically the same predicament as this girl. She almost felt sorry for her.

"Help me, please!" the girl screamed. She hobbled toward the car.

Shifting into Reverse, the woman backed up and then shifted again to Drive. She stepped on the accelerator and turned the wheel to avoid hitting the sad, hapless girl. One side of the Taurus drove into the dirt on the roadside.

Gravel and clouds of dirt sprayed from the tires as she sped down the trail.

She pitied that girl. But that didn't mean she had to do anything.

After all, twenty-five years ago, no one had helped her.

"Where are you going?" Monica whispered. Her teeth were chattering. "What's wrong with you?"

She wanted to scream it at the top of her lungs, but she didn't dare. She knew the coach was still somewhere around there, searching for her.

The woman—that soulless jerk woman—must have been coming from *someplace*. So Monica kept moving in that direction, hoping to find a busy road where she might have better luck flagging down someone else.

She had no idea where she was.

One thing she'd figured out. She probably wasn't anywhere near her home—or Olympia for that matter.

She veered away from the roadside, back into the cover of the dark, dense woods. If the coach was still looking for her, she didn't want to make it any easier for him. Her skin felt as if it were on fire she was so cold. The only way to keep warm—and alive—was to keep running. The twigs and rocks on the forest floor chewed away at her cold, bloody, bare feet. She was in agony. Every step hurt, and tears streamed down her face.

But Monica pressed on. She kept telling herself she was better off than she'd been yesterday. She was better off, because now she was free.

The girl in her rearview mirror had disappeared.

Tightening her grip on the steering wheel, the woman pressed harder on the accelerator. She glanced at the tire iron on the passenger seat once again.

She remembered that snowy night in December 1991 when she and her friend, Lilly-Anne Wilde, had been stranded in those woods. She was already furious at Lilly-Anne for acting like such a slut with Mitch Towner at the movies earlier in the evening. Then her friend had to drive like a maniac in the snow. Instead of taking her home, Lilly-Anne took her for a joyride in some woods, where they'd gotten a goddamn flat. Neither one of them had the first clue how to change a tire.

Then this mysterious minivan showed up and parked about two hundred feet away. She couldn't figure out what was wrong with the driver. She and Lilly-Anne were obviously in trouble. Lilly-Anne had even switched on the Accord's hazard lights. But the minivan didn't move. No one got out to help them.

She remembered how scared she was. She had picked up the tire iron in the snow.

"Asshole!" Lilly-Anne screamed as the vehicle

turned around and drove away, abandoning them. Her voice seemed to echo in the wintry woods.

"You're the asshole," Jill said to her friend, "for getting us stuck here."

Lilly-Anne turned toward the Accord's open trunk. "Shut up and help me get out the spare," she sneered. "You're lucky to be here with me. You're lucky I'm even friends with you . . ."

"What's that supposed to mean?"

"It means you're a total drag," she replied, unscrewing the spare from its mount inside the trunk. "Everybody thinks so. You're so pathetic to think Mitch Towner likes you. If you weren't my friend, he'd barely know you exist. And by the way, your new hairstyle? You look like a lesbian."

Lilly-Anne started to hoist the spare tire out of the trunk, but set it down again. "Are you going to help me with this or what? Could you possibly be more useless?"

Jill shook her head. "You got us stranded here, and now you're giving me this shit? You know, I've been putting up with you all night, and I'm sick of this. I'm sick of you. God, you're such a skank! Listen, if you don't want to be friends, then that's fine with me."

"Good," Lilly-Anne snapped, "because, seriously, I've been getting pretty tired of you. I'm glad we're finally having this conversation. You're clingy—and boring. And I'm sick of driving you everywhere. God, you're just like your mother—tacky, white trash." She bent down, scooped up some snow, and threw it in her face.

There was gravel in the snow, and it stung Jill's

cheek. She shrieked in anger. "That hurt! You fucking brat!"

"Talk about a drama queen!" Lilly-Anne sneered, hurling another handful of snow and gravel at her. Then she gave her a shove. "It's just a little snow. Get over it. Would you help me with this fucking tire?"

Unhinged, Jill wiped the snow and soot off her face. She stared at Lilly-Anne, bent over the open trunk again. She was so furious, she couldn't stop shaking. For a few moments, she'd forgotten she was holding on to the tire iron. Now she gripped it even tighter.

She just wanted her to shut up.

"Drag, drag, drag," Lilly-Anne grumbled. "I really hope you mean it about not wanting to be friends, because I honestly can't stand you anymore. I'd have dumped you ages ago, but shit, you're so needy, I was afraid you'd have a meltdown and kill yourself or something. It's suffocating. I hit a point last week when you became so annoying and I was so embarrassed for you . . ."

Before she knew what she was doing, Jill swung the tire iron.

She heard it crack against the side of Lilly-Anne's head.

Her friend let out a stunned cry. Then she spun around and glared at her. Blood started to leak from the gash, mingling with her blond hair. Lilly-Anne's hand went up to the wound, and then she gazed at the blood on her fingers. She let out another cry—almost as if she couldn't form any words. She looked like a crazy woman. She lunged at her.

Jill swung the tire iron and hit her again and again and again.

Blood sprayed her with each blow. She lost track of how many times she smashed her friend in the skull. Then Lilly-Anne finally crumpled onto the snowy ground.

All at once, everything was so quiet.

The snow continued to fall gently. Lilly-Anne was sprawled out in front of her. The white-covered ground around her body had splotches and specks of red. She wasn't breathing. But steam rose from the gashes in her head.

Jill looked at the bloody tire iron in her own hand. *Fingerprints*, she thought.

She dropped it on the ground and then frantically rubbed snow on it.

That was when she heard a car door slam in the distance.

Still trying to get her breath, Jill took a few steps away from the car to look farther down the trail. There it was—in the distance. The minivan had never really left.

Jill glanced back over her shoulder at her dead friend.

She already had tears in her eyes. It wouldn't take much acting to pretend she was crying and hysterical. She let out a scream and started running toward the minivan.

"Help!" she cried. "Oh, God, help me! Somebody killed my friend!"

She saw the man in a lumber jacket standing by the minivan's front door. He was in his mid-forties and somewhat handsome with salt-and-pepper hair. He folded his arms.

Jill staggered up toward him. "Help me," she gasped. "Someone killed my friend . . ."

He smiled. "I know. I saw everything, girlie."

Jill stared at him.

He took a step toward her and then suddenly punched her in the face. It knocked her unconscious.

That was how she'd met Ned Healy.

The woman in the black Taurus slowed down. She didn't see Stuart's van. She didn't see any sign of him. Ned's son was somewhere in these dark woods, hunting down some defenseless, near-naked girl.

Twenty-five years later, she thought, *it was too perfect*.

She wondered what Stuart was going to do with that girl once he caught her.

He had to give up his search.

His whole face was throbbing. Stuart had blood splattered down the front of him, and had to breathe through his mouth. He wouldn't have been surprised if that bitch had broken his nose. He could feel it swelling up. He figured he might not even be able to see in an hour. The thing to do was get an ice pack on his face as quickly as possible.

Stuart kept checking his rearview mirror. He'd noticed those headlights in the distance earlier. They seemed to be on one of the other trails nearby. He wondered if the driver had seen him or the van. Maybe they'd rescued the girl.

He hoped not. But the possibility of that happening was even more incentive for him to give up and go home. He couldn't stay in the area any longer—not if someone had already called the police.

Turning the car around, he headed for Highway 2.

With a little luck, he'd be home in an hour.

As for the Monica problem, with a little more luck, if the cold didn't kill her maybe the bears would.

She was lost. There were no signs for the highway along any of these winding trails. And the trees were creating havoc with her phone reception, so she couldn't use her GPS.

The woman in the black Taurus felt like she was driving in circles.

She wondered if she might run into that girl again. Even if she wanted to help her, she couldn't. She couldn't get involved. There would be police and the press. And since age sixteen, she'd been a fugitive.

That was something Ned had held over her. She'd committed a crime.

Ned was a deeply devout man, bent on redeeming her. At least, that was his excuse for tying her up, throwing her in the back of his minivan, and taking her to his house. He locked her in that cellar dungeon and made her write down all her secret thoughts—her sexual fantasies, fears, and the things she was most ashamed of. It went on for months. He said it was how she could achieve salvation.

Ned liked to remind her that he'd collected the tire iron from that night. He said he'd saved it as evidence and even had it in a big plastic bag. "I know you tried to rub off your fingerprints with snow, but I'm sure you missed some spots." He had the tire iron well hidden someplace. "If you're not cooperative, I may just have to send it to the police and give them your name."

She always had that hanging over her head, but that didn't mean she always cooperated. As punishment, he slapped her around a lot or starved her. And she took the abuse. The thing he did that always destroyed her was shut off the power to her little room. She could wrap herself in a blanket to fight the cold, but she couldn't take the insidious darkness. With the lights out down in that cell, there was nothing—just solid black. It paralyzed her. She couldn't handle being blind like that. Just an hour of it seemed like an eternity. She'd scream and scream—until he finally opened that little trapdoor overhead. Then at last, she'd see some light—and his silhouette hovered over the opening. And she'd apologize.

Ned's doormat of a wife and his homeschooled children knew she was there. Hell, they were probably relieved someone else was now the object of Ned's beatings and sexual abuse. They had no friends, so there was hardly any risk of them incurring their father's wrath and telling someone about the girl in their cellar.

As part of her rehabilitation, Ned raped her—repeatedly. He'd open the trapdoor and toss her a pair of handcuffs. It was standard operating procedure for all his visits. She had to handcuff herself to a pipe in the corner of the room. She was supposed to tug at the cuff and let it clang against the pipe—to show it was really secure. Then Ned would lower the ladder.

To this day, whenever she heard that same clanging sound, it would still make her sick.

Ned used to take Polaroid photos of her naked—in various poses. He'd make her write in a journal about these experiences. He would take the journal away from time to time so he could read it. She knew he was getting off on some of the candid sexual talk. In fact, it gave her a tiny feeling of power over him. Over the months, each time she started a blank journal, he'd confiscate the one she'd just finished.

It turned into a sick, perverted relationship—with Ned often accusing her of "corrupting" him. His wife rarely communicated with her—except to lower meals down to her on a special pulley. She was a shitty cook. Of course, everything was cut up ahead of time because Jill couldn't have a knife. The forks were plastic. Jill felt like a family pet that Mrs. Healy ignored—except for those twice-daily feedings.

Sometimes bratty little Stuart would open up the trapdoor and squirt water at her, hurl things at her or tease her. For Stuart, she was the family pet he could torture. Once he gave her a rubber ball and a set of little steel jacks—throwing them, one at a time, down at her. She still had a tiny scar on her forehead from one of them. But Jill also remembered that once he had tossed down a Nestlé Crunch bar to her. It must have been around Christmastime.

Denise was a bit of a simpleton. But at least she was kind. The reason that cellar dungeon became remotely livable was because Denise gave her some hand-me-downs. She threw down tape and posters—mostly foreign travel posters: Paris, Rome, London, and New York. On the meal pulley, she lowered a transistor radio, a blanket, old clothes, cheap lotions, and hair-care products. Sometimes there was a soda and a bag of junk food. When her parents were gone or asleep, Denise would sit in that little broom closet and talk down to her like they were best friends or sisters.

Jill often begged Denise to help her escape. But Ned's dear daughter would always shrug and say it was impossible. "Besides, it would spoil everything," she once explained. "You'd stop being my friend . . ."

But then on the Fourth of July—while Ned, Phyllis, and Stuart were out watching the fireworks—Jill convinced Denise that she really wanted to see her bedroom with all her swimming and equestrian trophies. As long as nobody else was home, they'd never know.

"If I let you come up, you have to swear you won't try anything funny," Denise said.

She remembered Denise lowering the ladder. Jill climbed up to the basement level and stepped into the utility room. For the first time in six months, she breathed air that wasn't musty and dirty. She also noticed Ned's workbench and the wall of tools. She told Denise she needed socks for her dirty feet. And while the poor fool dug a pair of her white ankle socks from the dryer, Jill stole the hammer.

The weird thing about it was that during that bizarre year, Jill ended up killing the only two girls who had become her friends.

Once Denise was dead, all Jill could think about was washing off the blood, stealing something to live on for a while, and getting out of there. For a while, she got as far away as she could.

It wasn't until afterward that she became obsessed with that tire iron, the journals, and the photographs Ned Healy had taken.

The last time she saw little Stuart Healy, his father had already blown his brains out and his mother was in the hospital. Jill surprised him in the elevator. Stuart swore he didn't know anything about the journals, the pictures, or the tire iron.

Jill believed him and let him live.

After all, Stuart couldn't go to the police.

She couldn't go to the police, either, of course, because they were still looking for her—or her remains. They believed she'd been abducted and killed by whoever murdered Lilly-Anne.

That was in one of her journals, too—all about how she'd slain her best friend.

Lilly-Anne used to say she got obsessive about things. It was how Jill felt about those elusive journals. It wasn't just that they were incriminating and full of her deepest secrets. They were also *hers*, and she wanted them back.

Knowing they were somewhere in that house drove her crazy. It was what made her keep returning to Echo. While the house was unoccupied after Mrs. Healy's death, Jill broke in several times and searched every room. She even tested the floorboards in the closets for any slats that might be loose, concealing a hiding spot.

She went so far as to revisit the hidden cellar room where she'd been held hostage all that time, thinking the journals might be hidden down there.

When she didn't find them in her former prison, Jill closed the trapdoor and covered up the closet floor with the linoleum cutout they'd used. Then she gathered up anything she could get her hands on that had been lying around the old, deserted house: wood scrap, bricks, old blinds, pipes, and trash. She dumped it all in that little room beneath the stairs. She didn't want anyone to ever find the secret room. She felt so much shame about it. And that was the closest she could get to making her onetime prison cell disappear.

Several times, Jill tried to set fire to the house. She figured if she couldn't find the evidence Ned had collected, then she'd destroy it. But the blazes she set never did much damage, and the fire department's response times were frustratingly quick.

The worst was having a family move into the house. Jill did as much as she could to sabotage the remodel, but the project persevered, and eventually the Hecht family took occupancy.

Not only was she constantly worried about someone finding her journals, those Polaroids, and the tire iron, Jill also resented their very presence in that house. How dare some happy family move into the place of her nightmares and make it their home? She had total contempt for them. So it became her goal to make each family who moved into that Birch Place house utterly miserable—until they were driven out.

The once oppressed became the oppressor.

It was her mission. In fact, she'd become so bent on

making the place unlivable and torturing its occupants that she'd practically forgotten about the evidence of her time there: a murder weapon, those old Polaroids, and a few diaries.

Seeing Stuart Healy tonight helped her remember.

She'd been driving around these wooded back roads and trails for over an hour now. And she'd been lost at least half that time. But at last she'd spotted a sign at an intersection of trails indicating the route to Highway 2—in three miles. She turned in that direction.

Until she'd let Stuart sidetrack her, she'd had grand plans for Caitlin tonight. She was ready for the first casualty. The ex-husband didn't count. It had to be one of the kids. She had a feeling it would take only one dead child to make Caitlin pack up and move. She couldn't figure out why little Gabe was still up and around and looking healthy. Maybe he wasn't drinking his chocolate milk—or maybe she hadn't put enough solution in it.

She wanted to take care of that tonight. In fact, she was determined to make it Caitlin's final night in the house.

The last ferry to Echo had already crossed, but there was always Deception Pass Bridge, which she knew very well. It would give her a little bit more time to drive and think.

She wondered if Stuart had lied to her in that elevator over twenty years ago. Maybe he knew about her journals, the photos, and the tire iron. Maybe he even had them, hidden away somewhere in that big, beautiful mansion of his.

It could be she'd been searching through the wrong house all those years.

Well, she knew where he lived.

She thought about that as she finally found the high-way. She could always return to Stuart's place and get what she was after. That would come later.

Tonight, she'd clean her own house.

CHAPTER THIRTY

Echo
Wednesday, November 2—2:48 A.M.

Caitlin couldn't sleep. She couldn't read, either. She had a stack of books at her bedside that she was eager to get to—some of them advance copies of books not yet published. But she just couldn't concentrate on anything right now.

The outside lights cast bright beams that peeked past the edges of her bedroom shades. It almost felt like daytime. She kept listening to all the sounds the house seemed to make only in the wee hours—the same sounds Denise Healy had heard, the same sounds Sara Goldsmith had heard as she'd slowly gone crazy. Caitlin could have used a pair of earplugs and one of those sleeping masks, but she couldn't imagine making herself so vulnerable. The truth was she needed all of her senses right now.

She kept thinking about her conversation with Stuart Healy this afternoon. It had been strange how he'd suddenly ushered them out of the house. He seemed to be holding something back, something important.

She thought about another conversation she'd had later in the afternoon—when she'd called Russ's SARA sponsor, Paul, to let him know that Russ had died.

The man had seemed genuinely upset. And he'd seemed genuine when he talked about what a great guy Russ was. Caitlin needed to hear it from someone. Paul said he would let his fellow SARA members know about Russ's memorial service next week. Then he mentioned that he'd have to track down Bobby. Apparently, she was a new member to the SARA family, and she and Russ had gotten close. "It was nothing romantic, I assure you," Paul told her. "If you don't mind me getting a little personal, Russ was still very much in love with you. He talked all the time about you—to me and the group. He and Bobby were getting to be good rehab friends, really helping each other out. She didn't show up at the meeting last night. I don't have a contact number for her. I wonder if she knows about Russ . . ."

Caitlin had a feeling she knew.

She thought about Chandler Hecht and Dr. Goldsmith, whose marriages were ruined by a mystery woman. She couldn't help wondering if this new SARA member, Bobby, was that same woman.

Then again, drugs had ruined her marriage to Russ, not some mystery woman. Could she really blame someone connected to the house for what had happened to Russ?

Still, it was strange, now that Russ was dead, this woman hadn't shown up for any SARA meetings.

Caitlin climbed out of bed and went into the bathroom. She was wearing a Peter Gabriel T-shirt that used to be Russ's. It had always been too big on him, but it was a perfect nightshirt for her.

She switched on the light and opened the medicine chest. She had a bottle of melatonin in there. Maybe that would help knock her out.

All at once, the lights went off.

Caitlin was suddenly swallowed up in blackness. Panicked, she turned toward the bedroom. The flood-lights weren't coming through the shade edges any-more. She couldn't see a thing. "Shit," she murmured.

Waving her hands in front of her, she found the doorway to the bedroom. Blindly making her way to the nightstand, she knocked over her stack of books. She felt around for her phone. Her eyes were adjusting to the darkness, and there was enough moonlight for her to see the outlines of the bedroom windows now. But for all she knew, someone could have been in the bedroom with her. She finally found her phone and switched it on. She clicked on the flashlight and held it up.

No one else was in there.

But then she thought about the kids' rooms.

Heading out to the hallway, she opened the guest room door. Lindsay was asleep. The digital clock on her nightstand was blank. The power outage was in this room, too. Next door, Gabe was asleep and safe.

Caitlin made her way down the hall. She shined the light into the bathroom. No one was there. The beam seemed to shake along with her trembling hand as she aimed the light down the hallway to the unoccupied bedroom—Denise Healy's old room. She made her way there, then reached past the door and tried the light switch. Nothing happened. She swept the flash-light beam over the deserted dark room.

She almost expected to find someone standing in a corner, grinning at her in the light's glare.

But the bedroom was empty. She turned and hurried downstairs, using the iPhone light to navigate each step. She knew if she didn't keep moving, she'd never have the guts to go down there. She kept telling herself it was just a regular power failure. Those damn outside lights had probably put a strain on the circuit.

The front hallway switch didn't work. She shined the light on the front door lock. The chain was still on; the dead bolt was set. Caitlin peeked out the window by the door. Across the street, in the distance, she could see the neighbors' front porch light was on. So it wasn't a neighborhood outage. It was just this house, this damn house.

She aimed the flashlight into the living room—and then the dining room. She started to move toward the kitchen but stopped dead. She heard a rumbling sound. It couldn't have been the refrigerator or the furnace, not with the electricity out. She waited and listened for it again, but didn't hear anything.

Caitlin made her way into the kitchen. The door to the outside was locked and dead-bolted, and the base-ment door was locked. She took that as a good sign—for a few moments. Then she wondered if someone had switched off the power just to lure her down there.

She wanted to call the police. But they'd already tagged her as a paranoid nutcase. What would they think if she called 9-1-1 to report a power outage—that her six high-wattage floodlights had probably caused?

She decided to double-check the refrigerator to see if it was off, too. As she swung open the door, something fell off the shelf. It hit the floor with a thud. Caitlin almost dropped the phone and fumbled to recover it. She felt a cold puddle forming around her bare feet.

Shining the light on the floor, she saw a near-full carton of chocolate milk was the casualty. She grabbed a dishtowel, wiped off her feet, and then threw it on top of the puddle. Padding over to the counter, she took a steak knife out of the rack.

She unlocked the basement door and headed down the stairs. She had to walk slowly to navigate her way in the blackness—plus she had the knife in her hand.

Nothing looked disturbed in the never-used second family room. She moved into the utility room and shined the light on the outside door. It was locked, and the chain was in place. Of course, someone could have done that after they broke in.

She made her way around all the junk she'd moved out of Gabe's clubhouse and headed to the little closet with the circuit box. Tucking the knife under her arm, she opened the gray metal box. All the switches were in the On position—except the main switch. Biting her lip, Caitlin flicked the switch.

She heard a click and a humming noise. Then she realized it was just the furnace starting again.

Light from the outside flood lamps poured though the basement windows. Caitlin let out a sigh. She headed back toward the door and switched on the overhead. There was no one else down here with her. She even checked Gabe's clubhouse just to make sure. The linoleum cutout was still covering the trapdoor.

Switching off the utility room light, she started through the family room. But then she heard a noise upstairs. It was the same rumbling sound as before—only louder. She stopped and listened. It was quiet again. She wondered if one of the kids was up. Or was it someone else?

Caitlin hurried up the stairs.

In the kitchen, the refrigerator door was still open—as she'd absentmindedly left it. The dim light cast an eerie glow that spilled into the family room area. But it was bright directly in front of the refrigerator, where a tabby cat was licking up some of the spilled chocolate milk.

As soon as Caitlin aimed the flashlight at it, the cat looked up and scurried away. That was the rumbling she'd heard earlier. It was the cat running. She wondered how in God's name the feline had gotten in. She couldn't help thinking the stray must have snuck in along with whoever had tampered with the circuit box downstairs.

She quickly switched on the kitchen light and headed up the stairs to check on Lindsay and Gabe again. They were still asleep. She peeked into her own room and saw the bathroom light was on—just as she'd left it. If someone had snuck in, they didn't seem to be up here.

Back downstairs, she found the cat in the kitchen again, lapping up more chocolate milk. She was pretty sure chocolate—and milk—weren't good for adult cats. As she approached it, the tabby scampered past her again—in the same direction as before. It darted into the study.

Still holding on to the knife and her phone, Caitlin

followed the cat. She switched on the study light and saw the stray beside the tall French window to the left of the fireplace. The cat scratched at the glass—as if it wanted to go outside. *Why there?* Caitlin wondered. She'd thought the cat would have returned to the door it had used to slip inside the house. It should have been scratching at the kitchen door or the front door.

She glanced over her shoulder to make sure no one else was there. It didn't seem possible that the cat had snuck in when she and the kids had gotten home earlier today. Someone would have noticed.

The cat stopped scratching at the glass, arched its back, and let out a choking sound—like it had a hairball or something. It blinked and shook its little head. Then the tabby put its paw back on the window again.

Caitlin remembered something Elaine Hecht had said when she'd been in this room on Sunday: "*Those French doors are new.*" Caitlin had told her they were windows. Elaine had said that the windows hadn't extended all the way to the floor before. Caitlin figured it must have been one of the changes Carrie Sewell had made with Lance.

But maybe Elaine Hecht's original observation had been correct.

And maybe the cat had indeed returned to the spot where it had first slipped into the house.

The tabby backed away as Caitlin pushed aside the light drape on the window's edge. There were no door hinges on the side. She pushed at the window frame, and it rattled a bit.

She tried the window on the other side of the fireplace. Again, no hinges. But when she pushed at the frame, nothing happened. The windows were different. Was one actually a door?

Caitlin got a pair of boots and her coat from the front closet. The cat followed her out the front door. It let out another strange raspy sound. She thought it might scuttle off into the woods, but the tabby remained at her side as she walked around to the side of the house. The floodlights were almost blinding. But the study windows and the chimney were in the shadows behind some shrubs.

She stepped around the bushes and inspected the tall "window" the cat had been scratching. There were several tiny hinges down one side of it. Caitlin hadn't seen them at all from just a few feet away. On the other side, where a doorknob might have been, was a small plastic tab. Caitlin pushed it aside and saw a keyhole.

"So that's how they've been getting in," she murmured.

Behind her, the cat started gagging again.

Backing up, Caitlin nearly stumbled over it.

The tabby arched its back and kept rapidly shaking its head. Caitlin crouched down beside the stray and stroked it. The cat's whole body shook. Horrible, raspy sounds came out of its mouth. Caitlin wondered if this was all a reaction to lapping up a little chocolate milk.

The poor thing seemed to be dying.

CHAPTER THIRTY-ONE

Wednesday, November 2—8:25 A.M.

Aaron sat at the desk with his breakfast in front of him: orange juice, a banana, and a not-bad microwave breakfast burrito. But he was too nervous to eat.

He told himself he had to get out of here this morning.

He was dressed in a T-shirt, jeans, and white socks. He had the small knife concealed in his right tube sock. The cuff of his jeans covered the bulge. He'd nicked his ankle twice already—just pacing around his cell with the damn thing hidden in there. Fortunately, it hadn't bled too badly. The small red dots on the sock were barely noticeable.

His socks were usually the last thing he took off when they made him strip for practice. So that would give him a little extra time to figure out the logistics of a surprise attack. He figured he'd bypass Junior and lunge directly at the coach. He'd go for the coach's neck. That would put the son of a bitch out of action quickly enough.

Aaron realized he had no choice. Now that he had the knife, he had to use it—today. He couldn't exactly leave it in his cell while he was in the pool. Junior might find it, or maybe the Missus would change her mind and decide to take it back.

She'd been very quiet dropping off breakfast this morning. Aaron had called out a thank-you, and then he'd heard the retreating footsteps. She hadn't responded at all, nothing.

He couldn't help thinking something was wrong, something besides Monica's execution last night.

Around one in the morning, he'd thought he heard a door slam upstairs. He knew it must have been the coach, back from killing her. He assumed the son of a bitch must not have buried Monica, because he hadn't been gone that long. He couldn't have driven too far, either.

Aaron had wanted to weep, but by that time, he'd been all cried out.

So he'd curled up on his cot and prayed for Monica—and himself.

Now, as he nibbled on his burrito, he wondered if the coach knew about the concealed knife. Maybe the Missus had confessed to him that she'd had a "weak moment." Then again, all the coach had to have done was review the cell-surveillance video from last night—and he'd know. If that was true, Aaron knew he was every bit as dead as Monica.

Suddenly, the little speakeasy door slid open.

Aaron almost dropped his bottle of orange juice. He gaped at the slot opening. He thought he'd have a few more minutes to think about his escape. But the coach was a little early today.

The man glared back at him. His eyes were puffy and bruised, and his nose looked broken.

"Did Monica do that to you?" Aaron dared to ask.

The coach didn't say anything. He slid the door shut again.

Aaron sat there for a moment. He didn't know what to think—except *That a girl, Monica*. His eyes welled with tears. Was it too much to hope that she might have gotten away? Maybe that was why the coach had come back as soon as he had last night. There had been no body to bury.

Something was screwy, because it was almost time for practice. Yet he could hear the coach's footsteps getting fainter.

Aaron stood up, crept to the door, and pressed his ear to it. He didn't hear anything.

But with just that little movement, the sharp blade nicked his ankle again.

Watching the small TV in his office by the pool, Stuart was filled with dread. The little bitch who had escaped last night was on the local morning news.

"Just days after the discovery of a mass grave outside Darrington that held—among others—three of the missing high school swimmers, there's some good news this morning," announced the fortysomething Asian American anchorwoman with the wedge hairdo. *"Seventeen-year-old Monica Leary of Olympia, who*

disappeared in May, is safe this morning, having escaped from her captor in a wooded area north of Skykomish late last night . . ."

They showed footage of a visibly exhausted Monica, wrapped in a gray blanket and sitting on the back fender of an emergency vehicle. Police lights were swirling, and camera flashes went off in the background. Whoever rescued her must have called the police—and every news station around.

"Seattle residents Jeff and Tammy Palmer were driving along Beckler Road to their Skykomish River cabin when they noticed someone staggering along the roadside . . ."

The picture switched to a friendly-looking, fiftyish man with a mustache. He was wearing a ski jacket. A handheld mic was thrust in front of his face. *"We saw this poor girl wandering out in the cold night with hardly anything on and her hands tied behind her,"* he said. *"She looked pretty beat up, too. Well, we stopped for her, and we managed to untie her wrists. I gave her my jacket. We had some water in the car, and my wife gave her a drink. That's when she told us some guy had just tried to kill her . . ."*

The screen switched back to the anchorwoman. *"Police sources have informed us that Monica Leary suffered some minor cuts and injuries during her escape, but is otherwise in good health. She was told about the mass grave in Darrington, which held three of the missing swimmers. She was extremely upset to hear that James Lessing of Bellingham was among the dead. Police are confident Monica Leary will be able to provide them with details about her abductor and her six-month ordeal, details that will help their investigation. We weren't able to confirm whether another swimmer, Aaron Brenner, missing since October twenty-third, is still alive. KOMO News will bring you updates as they develop . . ."*

They showed another clip of Monica swaddled in the blanket. She nodded and seemed to work up a weary smile for the news cameras. Then she looked away.

The image on TV switched to the co-anchor, a handsome gray-haired man. *"A brave young woman,"* he commented solemnly. *"Next on KOMO-News, a five-car traffic pileup on the Aurora Bridge last night caused delays—"*

With the remote, Stuart muted the TV. "A goddamn bitch is more like it," he muttered.

He imagined her, right now, giving the police a very accurate description of him, his wife, and his son. She could also tell them all about the indoor pool—and she'd seen his van, too.

Stuart reminded himself that his friendless son had a private tutor. His wife never left the premises. All their food and shopping items were delivered. But then, what about the boy's tutor and the various delivery people? What if they figured out that this little wench on TV was talking about him and his family?

All the police had to do was look at a map. Darrington and Skykomish were two hours apart. But each was about an hour and a half away from Woodinville. They were probably trying to pinpoint his exact location right now.

He was glad he hadn't stopped by Evergreen Health

Urgent Care last night to have them look at his nose. Monica had probably already told the police that she'd broken it. There would have been records of his visit if he'd had it looked at. Besides, they couldn't have done much that he didn't do for himself at home—a bag of ice, aspirin, and bourbon.

Stuart caught his own reflection in a dark patch on the window looking out at the pool. His eyes were bruised, and his nose was still swollen. It hurt like hell just to touch it, and he did all his breathing through his mouth.

He wondered if he should go to the bank, take out his money, and then disappear. Of course, his wife and son would weigh him down—and make it easier for people to identify them. Maybe he could just leave the two of them here.

They were upstairs right now, eating breakfast. They had no idea what was happening. Stuart had a device built into all the TVs in the house—as well as his son's smartphone. The news stations were scrambled—except for his little TV here in the office.

It sometimes occurred to him that he was just like his father. Now he understood why the old man used to knock him and his mother around. He understood the frustration when certain family members were a disappointment. Ned had favored Denise, who had been a bit slow and stupid, but very athletic. Stuart had never been very good at sports. He'd always admired his sister but resented her, too. Now, nothing gave him a bigger thrill than coaching these swimmers, showing them how to be better, and completely dominating them. He felt so powerful having them under his thumb.

He looked at his collection of journals on the shelf. And he thought about the envelopes full of photos in his drawer. He couldn't leave them behind. He could never part with them.

He thought about going to Europe, staying on the move, and following the local news reports from here on the Internet. If the police weren't looking for him, he'd come back—back to his wife and son, who disappointed him. But he'd also be coming back to his beautiful home. And after a while, he could start coaching swimmers again.

It seemed like the best plan.

The girl was probably telling the police that Aaron Brenner was still alive. She knew about the mass graves now. She knew Jim and Chris were dead. There was no reason for her to hold back anything, no reason for her to honor her contract.

Aaron Brenner—that was something Stuart couldn't exactly leave behind, either.

He needed to get rid of him—tonight.

The phone rang, startling him.

Stuart immediately thought it could be the police.

His wife and son knew better than to answer the phone. Stuart checked the caller ID: UNKNOWN CALLER. He let it go to voice mail. The caller hung up without leaving a message. Stuart couldn't help thinking it was the police, trying to be clever.

He picked up the remote again and clicked it. The TV showed a split screen of the six locations where he had cameras: the two cells, the front gate, the front door, a side entrance, and the back door. He had a grainy godlike view-from-above of Aaron lying on his cot. But right now, Stuart was more concerned about the front gate. He wanted to make sure the police weren't out there. He didn't see anything, no cars at all.

The phone rang again. "Goddamn it," he muttered. It was UNKNOWN CALLER again.

His home intercom buzzed. He reached over and pressed the switch to the speaker on his desk. "What?" he barked. He could hear feedback echoing throughout the house. They had to fix the stupid thing.

"Should I pick this up?" his wife asked timidly.

"No, goddamn it," he growled.

The call went to voice mail again. And once more, the caller hung up.

To Stuart's utter annoyance, the phone rang yet again.

He couldn't take any more. He snatched up the receiver. "What do you want?" he hissed.

"Well, now, Stu, that's no way to talk to an old friend," the woman purred.

"Who is this?"

"You mean, you don't recognize my voice? I was your father's houseguest for over six months. I was practically part of the family. I'd think you'd remember my voice."

Stuart said nothing. He was stunned. He thought of those journals on his shelf—and the girl in the Polaroids in his desk drawer.

"I remember you," he said—at last.

"I'd like to see you tonight," she said.

"That—that's impossible, I'm sorry," he muttered, unnerved.

"Make it possible. I just saw on the news—the *other*

girl that got away. I had no idea, Stu. You've certainly got old Ned beat—a whole stable of captives, girls *and* boys . . ."

"I don't touch the boys," he said automatically.

"But the girls are another story, right?" She chuckled. "Do you take their pictures, too—like old Ned did with me?"

He said nothing for a moment. He wondered if she was taping their conversation. "What do you want?"

"I want those old photos back—along with my journals," she explained. "You still have them, don't you? Naughty boy, you lied to me in that elevator all those years ago, didn't you?"

"I don't know what you're talking about," he lied—once again.

"Yes, you do. And I don't expect these things for free, Stu. You'll be buying my silence. Plus I'll sweeten the deal for you . . ."

"I still don't know what you're talking about."

"I'm talking about a pretty young thing who visited you yesterday—along with her mommy and her kid brother. Did Lindsay tell you? She's an excellent swimmer, Stu. She has a whole shelf full of swimming trophies in her bedroom—just where Denise used to keep hers. I'll bring her to you tonight—in exchange for those pictures and my journals. We'll swap. What do you say, Stu?" She paused. "Are you ready to do business?"

Stuart said nothing for several moments. Then he licked his lips.

"What time tonight?" he asked.

Echo
Wednesday—4:37 P.M.

Caitlin had thought as soon as her head hit the pillow, she'd be asleep. But she couldn't switch off everything going on in her mind. She couldn't stop thinking about the last twelve hours.

Hustling her sleepy children into the Lexus, she'd driven like a maniac to take the sick stray tabby to a twenty-four-hour veterinary hospital fifty miles away in Oak Harbor. The entire way, the cat had shivered, convulsed, and farted. They rolled the windows down and nearly froze to death. Lindsay tried to comfort the poor thing, but the cat only seemed to get worse and worse.

The cat died just minutes after they got it to the clinic.

Lindsay broke down and sobbed uncontrollably. Caitlin knew it had more to do with Russ than some stray.

She asked the vet how the cat could react so violently to just a little bit of chocolate milk. The middle-aged blond veterinarian frowned and shook her head. "No, a small quantity of chocolate milk might make a cat very sick, and in a few cases, it could be lethal. But it wouldn't do this—not if he seemed healthy less than ninety minutes ago like you say. No, this cat was poisoned."

Caitlin called the police when they got home. The Jennifer Lawrence lookalike showed up with her stocky, fiftysomething partner. Then they had to wait around for an hour for Deputy Dana and another detective to show up and take samples of the chocolate milk. Caitlin offered to make coffee for anyone who was willing to risk it—considering that the milk in her refrigerator was probably tainted. She didn't have any takers.

Caitlin figured someone had been poisoning Gabe's milk for a while, perhaps with not as lethal a dosage. It explained why Gabe threw up on Friday night. Then he got better the next few days because he hadn't been home. He hadn't drunk any chocolate milk on Monday because she'd tossed it out.

Whoever broke in to tamper with the circuit box in the basement must have poisoned the newly opened milk as well. Caitlin imagined what would have happened had she not knocked that milk carton off the refrigerator shelf. If Gabe had drunk his chocolate milk this morning, she would have been rushing him to a hospital—and not some cat. Then Gabe would have been the latest in a long line of children to perish while living in this house.

Deputy Dana examined the secret door, and at last, he seemed to take Caitlin's fears seriously. He asked to see the notes from her stalker again, and this time, he wanted to keep them. He also asked if she had any suspects in mind.

The only person she could think of was Teri Spangler.

"I called her on Saturday and left a message asking if she might possibly still have her husband's plans or blueprints for this house," Caitlin told him. "She called back later and just lit into me. She said she didn't want anything to do with this house and that I should leave her—pardon me—*the fuck* alone. I think she didn't want me to see the house plans because I would have noticed the specifications for this secret door. She must have known about it. The only other people who probably knew were her husband and Carrie Sewell—and both of them are conveniently dead."

Exactly why Carrie Sewell wanted a door like that for her new B and B was a mystery. Then again maybe it was something Lance had done on his own—or at the behest of his wife.

Caitlin remembered Elaine Hecht saying she didn't think her tormentor had gotten inside the house while they'd been living there. But all that had changed by the time the Goldsmiths had moved in. The secret door had been installed. So no one could detect a break-in when a news clipping was shoved under a bedroom door in the middle of the night—or later, when a figurine was smashed, when wine magically disappeared, or when the power was switched off.

Elaine had dismissed the idea of Teri as the other woman who had seduced her husband. But otherwise, Lance Spangler's widow was the perfect suspect. Her association with the house dated all the way back to when Denise Healy was alive and Scary Teri was getting into trouble at the Healys' recreation center all the time.

Deputy Dana promised to have a talk with Teri Spangler.

By the time he left, Watchmen Home Security arrived for their on-site assessment and consult. They were a little late in the game, but Caitlin let them check the place over. Once the home security assessor finally wrapped up shortly after one, Lindsay announced that she and Gabe were starving. Caitlin wouldn't let them eat or drink anything in the house that had been opened, which limited them to Coke, orange juice, a box of Ritz crackers—and a bunch of things neither one of them would touch with a ten-foot pole.

They went out for a late breakfast at Happy Baker's Table near the recreation center—or The Sappy Baker, as Gabe called it. From there, Caitlin phoned the Bayside B&B. She still had the brochure in her purse. She told Sandra what had happened—right down to the discovery of the secret door this morning. "Do you have any idea why Carrie would want that kind of door there?" Caitlin asked.

There was a pause on the other end of the line. "You mean in that room with the fireplace?" Sandra asked. "Not a clue—unless Carrie wanted it for carrying logs in from outside. But she never said a thing to me about it. I don't understand why she kept it a secret . . ."

"Well, maybe Teri Spangler knows," Caitlin said. "The police are supposed to be talking with her right now."

"Good," Sandra said. "I hope they're able to nip this thing in the bud. Meanwhile, I'll shift a few things around on this end. I should have a couple of adjoining rooms ready for you and your kids by three o'clock . . ."

The rooms were charming and connected to each other with a Jack and Jill bathroom. They both had their own outside entrances, too. The kids were content because they had Wi-Fi and cable television. Caitlin was happy because they wouldn't have to stay in the Birch Place house tonight. She was imagining an evening when she could go to bed without checking every room and every closet of that place for the umpteenth time.

She desperately wanted a nap, but couldn't fall asleep.

At the same time, it felt good just to lie there on the extra-soft bed in a darkened room. She was just starting to drift off when her phone rang.

She snatched it off the nightstand and checked the caller ID. She sat up. "Hello, Deputy Dana," she said into the phone.

"At this point, you can call me Bob," he said. "So—I just had a nice visit with Teri Spangler. I'm not completely ready to write her off yet, but at the same time, I don't think she's behind all this."

"Really?" Caitlin asked. "Why?"

"Well, she has alibis for some of the times you say certain things happened. For example, at noon on Saturday, when Neal Thomas Huggins took that half gainer off his balcony, Teri was at a writers' workshop in Port Townsend. She's writing her memoirs and looking to publish. I'm sure they'll be lining up around the block at Barnes and Noble for that."

"Did she say where she was at three o'clock this morning?" Caitlin pressed.

"Believe it or not, she claims to have been home, asleep in bed."

Caitlin sighed. "You don't sound like you're taking this very seriously."

"I am," he said. "I'm sorry. It's just that between you and me, talking to that woman was kind of exhausting. And I went in there pretty exhausted already. Anyway, Mrs. Stoller, rest assured we're on top of this. We've let the Seattle PD know about the Huggins connection here, and Ken Meekley's death is still an open investigation . . ."

"Did you ask Teri about the blueprints of the house?" Caitlin cut in.

"Yes, she said she doesn't have any of her husband's work documents. She said she threw everything away—'*including his tool belt*.' I'm quoting her here. Again, I'm not writing her off as a suspect just yet. But I thought you'd want an update on our conversation. By the way, we have the chocolate milk samples at a lab in Everett, and we should have the results for you by tomorrow morning. Meanwhile, try to get some rest this evening. We'll put extra patrols on your block . . ."

"The kids and I are staying at the Bayside B and B tonight," she said.

"I'm glad to hear that," Dana said. "We'll still be watching the house for you. Talk to you soon . . ."

After she clicked off, Caitlin lay back on the bed again. She could hear the TV in Lindsay and Gabe's room—and them murmuring to each other.

A minute later, there was a knock on the bathroom door.

"Come in," she called, sitting up in time to see the door open.

Gabe stood in the doorway, looking like he'd had a successful nap. His eyes had that just-woke-up look. His shirt was wrinkled, and his unruly red hair was flat on one side from his head pressing against the pillow. "Do you need to use the bathroom?" he asked. "I thought I'd take a shower."

"Knock yourself out, honey," she said.

"Okay, I might be a while," he said.

"You might be a while?" Lindsay called from the other room. "Like we don't know what you're doing in there. You're not fooling anybody."

"Shut up!" he yelled. Then he closed the bathroom door.

After a moment, Caitlin heard him close the other bathroom door.

The phone rang again. Caitlin checked the caller ID: UNKNOWN CALLER. Biting her lip, she stared at it for a moment and then clicked it on. "Hello?" she answered.

"You sent the police to my house, you bitch!"

Caitlin tensed up. "That's because I didn't know anyone else who might know about a secret door your late husband installed on the first floor of my house."

"You told them I poisoned a cat!" Teri Spangler hissed. "I love animals. I'd never do anything so horrible. Shows how much you don't really know me . . ."

"No, I didn't tell the police you poisoned a cat," Caitlin said, trying to keep calm. She tried to keep her voice down, too, because Gabe hadn't started his shower yet. "But you're right, Teri, I don't know you at all. The only thing I know about you is that you have an unlisted cell phone. And this is the second time you've called me on it—the second time I know about, and once again, you've been rude, shrill, and abrasive to me."

Caitlin's heart was racing. She was waiting for Scary Teri to rip into her again—or maybe just hang up.

"If you knew how much that goddamn house has cost me, you'd understand," Teri finally replied. "I want nothing to do with that place or anyone who's living in it. I hate that house. My husband nearly got killed there several times during the first remodel. He had one setback after another—so many freak accidents. And after all his efforts with that place, Lance had to go back and do even more work on it for the B and B conversion. I didn't want him to. He didn't want to. But the money was too good to pass up. And then he started in with that slut from the B and B. It's because of that house he's dead. If it were up to me, I'd burn the place to the ground."

"Well, I understand from Elaine Hecht someone tried that very thing several times," Caitlin pointed out. "Their windows got broken, too."

"I don't know anything about that," Teri muttered.

"And you know nothing about a trick door in the study, the one you've been using to sneak into my house?" Caitlin asked. She planned to phone Deputy Dana as soon as she hung up. She would have to remember this conversation word for word.

She heard Gabe start the shower in the bathroom.

"This particular door looks like a window," Caitlin continued. "All the hardware is hidden. It was obviously installed by your late husband when he was working on the B and B remodel. Are you pretending you don't know about it?"

"Why the hell should I?" Teri snapped. "I just told you! I've never wanted anything to do with that goddamn house. If you want to know about the work Lance did for that whore, why don't you ask her?"

Caitlin let out a stunned laugh. "You want me to ask Carrie Sewell? You want me to ask a dead woman?"

"I'm not talking about Carrie," she growled. "Lance

wasn't ever serious about her. Okay, yes, he had sex with her a few times. That was Lance, always out for a good time. He liked Carrie, but she was almost twenty years older than him. No, I'm talking about the other one—the one who had him wrapped around her little finger. I'm talking about that scheming bitch, Sandra."

"What?" Caitlin murmured.

"You don't really know her any better than you know me, do you?"

Caitlin said nothing. She didn't believe her.

"Sandra came to town around the time Carrie bought the Birch Place property," Teri explained. "And boy, what a schemer! She started to work on Carrie— and got hired to help manage the B and B. She had Carrie bamboozled. She was over there at the house half the time, giving Lance orders. I wouldn't be surprised if she was the one who spread it all over town about Carrie and Lance. Well, they stopped their harmless little fling. Then Sandra took over and started fucking my husband—in every sense of the word. Near the end, she was calling all the shots. You want to know about a secret door? You ask Sandra . . ."

Gabe had left the TV on the Syfy channel, but Lindsay wasn't paying attention to it. She was waiting for the news to come on.

Half sitting up on top of the bed, she wore a beat-up, old black V-neck sweater, jeans, and thick pink socks. She had her earbuds in and her iPhone in front of her. After all her Internet news source browsing, she was pretty certain she'd seen the latest updates on that girl's escape from the creep who was killing all those swimmers. But she figured the TV news was still worth checking out. It would be on in five minutes.

The police had interviewed the girl, Monica Leary. She said the missing swimmer, Aaron Brenner, was still alive as of yesterday. Lindsay was glad because she thought he was pretty cute, and was sort of rooting for him. Apparently, this psycho they called *the coach* kept them locked up—except when they trained and competed against each other in his indoor pool. The whole thing sounded really twisted.

With the aliens on TV, the newscasts on her iPhone, and the shower going full blast in the bathroom, Lindsay couldn't hear anything else. If someone had knocked on the outside door, she didn't hear it.

But she saw the door slowly opening.

It had been locked.

The skinny blond woman who ran the B and B, Sandra Something, obviously had a passkey. She wore jeans and a bulky bronze-colored sweater with pockets. She slipped the key into her sweater pocket. In her other hand, she held a gun.

Staring at her, Lindsay sat up. She took out her earbuds.

The woman put her finger to her lips. "Toss the phone on the floor," she whispered.

Swallowing hard, Lindsay obeyed her.

"And keep your mouth shut unless I tell you to talk—"

The bathroom door swung open, and Gabe stepped out in his T-shirt and jeans. His feet were bare. The shower was still roaring, and steam escaped into the bedroom. He saw the woman and gasped.

"Close the bathroom door, Gabe," the woman whispered.

Gaping at her, he stood there frozen for a moment.

"Do it," she said, "quietly."

His skinny body started to shake as he closed the door.

"Now go to the dresser and open the bottom drawer," she said, nodding toward it. She still had the gun aimed at him. "You'll see a couple of rolls of duct tape I put in there earlier—just for you kids. You're going to tape up your sister's wrists for me. You'll do it efficiently, too—because you don't want your sister to get hurt, and neither do I. I need her for something tonight. You, little man, I don't need. So—you better make yourself as useful to me as you can. Do you understand?"

With a timid little nod, he hurried to the dresser and opened the bottom drawer. He had tears in his eyes as he took out the rolls of tape.

Lindsay sat very still on the bed. She did her damnedest not to tremble or cry. She didn't want this woman to know how scared she was.

"Now, just do what I say," Sandra whispered. "And we'll be out of here in a couple of minutes. The three of us are going on a little trip . . ."

As soon as Caitlin clicked off with Teri Spangler, she got the B and B brochure out of her purse again and dialed the number. She didn't want to believe

Teri's rants about Sandra. After all, the woman was obviously unstable. Deputy Dana had said she hadn't been written off as a suspect yet. And as far as Caitlin was concerned, Scary Teri still seemed the most likely culprit in all this.

Most of what she knew about the B and B, Lance Spangler, and Carrie Sewell she'd learned from Sandra. Everything else that she'd picked up since then seemed to confirm what Sandra had told her—including the irrefutable fact that Teri seemed unbalanced. Caitlin just needed to hear Sandra explain how bogus Teri's claims were.

But Sandra wasn't picking up the phone. It went to voice mail.

Caitlin clicked off without leaving a message.

The only thing Teri had going in her favor was an unshakable alibi for her whereabouts at noon on Saturday, when Neal Thomas Huggins was killed. Someone else had to have killed him. Caitlin knew Sandra couldn't have had anything to do with it. She'd left Sandra at the B and B to catch the ferry for her noon appointment in Seattle. She would have noticed if Sandra had been following her.

Then again, she hadn't really been looking—and she didn't know Sandra's car.

Caitlin tried to convince herself that it wasn't possible. But she remembered telling Sandra before she'd left the B and B that she had a noon appointment.

Caitlin reached over and grabbed the brochure again, the same brochure that had been sticking out of her purse the whole time she'd been with Sandra on Saturday morning. There, scribbled across the top of it, was the Western Avenue address for "Dack," right down to the apartment number.

Sandra had known exactly where she was going. She could have been on the same ferry. And while Caitlin had been roaming around Sculpture Park, Neal Huggins could have been buzzing Sandra into his building.

Everything Scary Teri had told her about Sandra suddenly made sense.

Caitlin sprang to her feet.

All she could think about was getting the kids out of there. Then she'd phone Deputy Dana.

She could hear the shower was still running.

Caitlin pounded on the bathroom door. "Gabe!" she called. "Gabe, honey!"

She turned the knob. Locked.

"Shit," she muttered, heading for the outside door.

Her phone rang, and she stopped to look at the caller ID: UNKNOWN CALLER. Was it Teri again?

Caitlin clicked on. "Hello?" she said, out of breath.

"Don't call the police, Caitlin," the gravelly voice croaked over the line. "They're never any help."

"Sandra, I know that's you," she said, her heart racing.

"Yes, well, after you found that door, it was only a matter of time before you figured it out," she said—in her own voice. "But the important thing is that you haven't told the police yet. And the reason it's important, Caitlin, is because if you tell the police about me—if you call the police at all—I'll kill Lindsay and Gabe."

With the phone to her ear, Caitlin ran outside and tried the door to the kids' quarters. It was unlocked.

Swinging it open, she stood in the doorway and gazed at the empty room. The TV was still on, and the bathroom door was closed.

"Where are they?" she asked. She still couldn't get a breath.

"They're with me, of course," Sandra said. "Now, once again, you're not to call the police. You understand that, don't you?"

"I won't call the police," she said, a tremor in her voice. "You have my word. Now, what do you want?"

"I want you to follow my instructions. Stay there in Gabe and Lindsay's room. Don't call anyone. I'll know if you do. You believe that, don't you?"

"Yes. Listen—"

"I'll phone you back in just five minutes."

"Wait—" Caitlin said. But she heard a click on the other end.

She figured they couldn't be far. She'd just seen Gabe in the bathroom less than ten minutes ago. She wondered if they could still be in the B and B—or maybe even right here.

Caitlin listened to the shower running.

She tried the bathroom door. It was unlocked. She flung it open.

Steam had filled the room. No one was there. But Sandra had been expecting her. She'd left a message in the steam on the bathroom mirror—already dripping and half-obscured, but still legible:

POOR CAITLIN
☹

CHAPTER THIRTY-TWO

Wednesday, November 2—5:20 P.M.

S he sat in her car waiting for the ferry.

Sandra knew it was a tremendous risk taking the commuter boat with the special live cargo in her trunk, but sometimes she liked to push the envelope. The two siblings fit rather snugly in the trunk of her Chevy Impala.

Getting them tied up and locked in there had been easier than she'd anticipated. One thing she could say for Caitlin, her children were very obedient. She'd made Lindsay lie facedown on the bedroom floor while her little brother taped up her wrists. Then she'd had the boy lie down beside his sister. Tucking the gun in the waist of her jeans, she'd knelt on his back and taped up his wrists. Working with tape was so much faster than ropes. And it was amazing how cooperative the kids were—once she assured them that she wouldn't hesitate to blow the backs of their heads off.

There was only one other guest staying at the B and B—with a room on the other side of the house. So no one had seen her walking the two of them to her car.

Once she'd gotten them into the trunk, she'd taped up their ankles—and put tape over their mouths. Then she gave each one a shot to put them to sleep for a couple of hours. She was very good with a hypodermic. If their father were still alive, he would have attested to that.

Getting rid of Caitlin's ex had been a lot more complicated than she'd anticipated. She'd figured once Russ Stoller got his hands on Caitlin's money, he'd buy a weekend supply from the closest dealer and have himself a little party. Then slipping him a hot dose wouldn't have been a problem. But Russ pulled a fast one and suddenly turned into a Boy Scout. He'd insisted he didn't want to let down his wife and kids. So she'd had to buy the drugs herself, get him good and drunk (a SARA no-no), and then inject him with the stuff while he was nearly passed out. But she had a delicate touch with the needle.

He'd hardly even flinched when she'd given him that lethal dose.

She didn't think his children felt the needle sting, either.

She'd put a blanket over them—to keep them warm in the trunk. She didn't want Stuart Healy's new plaything to get sick on him.

Sandra glanced at her wristwatch. If she didn't run into bad rush hour traffic, she'd be pulling up to Stuart's house in Woodinville around six thirty.

She was racing against the clock. That was another reason to risk this ferry crossing—instead of going via the Deception Pass Bridge. The bridge was safer but added at least another hour onto her travel schedule.

It was only a matter of time before the Echo Police finally woke up. After discovering the secret door at Birch Place and talking to Teri Spangler, they'd certainly want to ask her some questions, too—and maybe even do some background checking. The fake birth certificate for a Sandra Watts of Vallejo, California, worked well to establish credit, take up residency in Echo, and inherit that fool Carrie's B and B, but it wouldn't hold up under close scrutiny.

Caitlin had already figured out that she wasn't quite who she appeared to be. The police wouldn't be far behind.

So—in addition to the two brats in her trunk, Sandra also had four packed suitcases on the backseat. She'd ditched the stolen Taurus early this morning in Coupeville and had taken the bus back to Echo. She would have to sell her Impala and buy or steal something else tomorrow—just to throw the police off her trail.

She wondered how long it would take them to connect her to Jill Ostrander, who had been missing and presumed dead since December 1991. Then again, maybe they'd never put it together.

Either way, Sandra Watts would soon join the ranks of the missing as well.

She'd have to disappear and reinvent herself. It wouldn't be the first time. She planned on squeezing some getaway money from Caitlin. And maybe she could get some fast cash from Stuart, too. She'd certainly squeezed enough money out of men in the past.

So—Stuart would have a new girl swimmer, and she would have some traveling money and maybe some pieces of his wife's jewelry she could hock. Most important, she'd have her old journals back—after all these years. She'd have those photos, too. She might sell a few to Stuart if he was stingy about giving up any cash. The journals were what really mattered to her.

As for the house, she now knew it no longer had anything that she wanted.

And no one would ever be interested in living there again—not after every member of the last family to occupy the place was killed. Lindsay Stoller would end up as a victim of a serial killer now called *The Coach*— at least, that was what they were calling him on TV today. Depending on how long Stuart could elude the police, Lindsay could remain missing for months or she could be dead by tomorrow.

Lindsay's mother and brother would end up shot in the woods north of Highway 2. That would definitely happen tonight.

She'd considered tampering with Caitlin's car. That had worked well for her in the past—in Phoenix with Chandler Hecht, and later with Lance and Carrie. On both occasions, she'd had to do a lot of planning and research online to make sure she didn't screw it up. And there just hadn't been enough time to do that today.

It would be fine, better than fine. Sandra certainly knew those woods pretty well now. She would collect some money from Caitlin, kill the two of them, and continue east.

She planned to keep Caitlin close and cooperative

most of the night, stringing her along and using her children as pawns until that final rendezvous in the forest.

"Welcome aboard Washington State Ferries . . ." the announcement boomed. Sandra could hear it—even inside her car with the window rolled up. She waited until the announcement was over, and then she dialed Caitlin's number.

Caitlin picked up after half a ring: "Sandra, is that you?"

"Go to Island Savings Bank and take out the eleven thousand two hundred dollars that's left in your savings account. I want it in cash, of course—mostly twenties, if they can. Don't pretend you haven't got the money. I've been in your house. I've seen your most recent statements. You keep them in the bottom left drawer of that desk in the study—"

"Where are my kids?" Caitlin asked. "So help me God, if you—"

"I'll have someone watching you at the bank," she said, cutting her off. "So don't even think about contacting the police. This person will be watching you all night, Caitlin."

"What do you mean, '*all night*'?" Caitlin asked. "How long will this go on? When am I going to see my children again?"

"Soon enough," she said. "Just get me that money. The bank closes in half an hour. That's when I'll call you again with some new instructions. And don't forget, Caitlin. Somebody's watching your every move. I mean, you seriously didn't think I was alone in this, did you?"

She clicked off. Then Sandra smiled.

* * *

"That's eleven thousand two hundred," said the same teller who had been Raggedy Ann on Halloween. Stacks of bundled twenties and hundreds were piled up on the other side of the Plexiglas window from where Caitlin stood. The young woman had gone to the bank's safe for some of the money. And of course, she'd had to let the manager know.

The chubby blond man now stared through his office window at Caitlin.

She did her best to ignore him. Nervously drumming her fingers on the counter, she glanced out at the parking area. Earlier, when she'd pulled into the lot, she'd spotted a man in a red Jetta, talking on his phone. She hadn't gotten a good look at his face and couldn't quite see him now. But he was still out there and still on his phone. She wondered if he was Sandra's partner.

The only other customer in the bank was a middle-aged woman using the lobby cash machine.

Caitlin checked the clock above the bank's door: about two minutes to six. Sandra would be calling again soon.

"Would you like a small tote bag for that?" the teller asked.

Caitlin turned to her and nodded a few more times than necessary. "Yes, thank you very much," she said.

The woman slipped a purple Island Savings Bank cloth tote into the slot under the window. Then she started to slide through the bundled bills. "What kind of car are you getting?"

"Pardon?" Caitlin said.

"You said you needed the money to buy a used car."

As she filled up the tote bag, Caitlin nodded again. "Yes, a—a practically new Volkswagen . . ."

"Well, nice," the woman said. "Good luck."

Caitlin thanked her and hurried outside with the tote bag and her purse.

The man in the Jetta backed out of his space and headed to the lot exit.

Caitlin got into her car. She set her purse and the tote bag on the floor of the passenger side. She took out her phone and waited.

She watched the Jetta turn onto Main Street. She wondered if she'd see the car again at her next destination—wherever that was.

The lobby lights turned off inside the bank.

Caitlin started up the car so she could roll down the window. She felt sick and couldn't quite get a breath. She couldn't let herself imagine what poor Lindsay and Gabe were going through right now, because she would fall apart.

She kept looking at her phone, waiting for it to ring. She thought about the last time she was here in this bank lot—and on the phone. She'd listened to Lindsay on the other end of the line, crying over her dead father.

Caitlin wondered if she was doing the right thing—not calling the police. If the man in the red Jetta was Sandra's partner, he was long gone.

Her phone rang.

She clicked it on. "Yes?"

There was no response on the other end. But Caitlin could hear faint traffic noise in the background. It sounded like a truck passing.

"I have the money," she heard herself say.

"I know," Sandra said. "Be on the six twenty ferry. I'll call you again when you get to Mukilteo."

"Are Lindsay and Gabe okay?" she asked.

But Caitlin realized the line had gone dead, and she was talking to no one.

"Your attention please. We are now arriving at our destination. Please take a few moments to make sure you have all your personal belongings before disembarking the vessel . . ."

Caitlin sat in her car on the parking deck and listened to the announcement over the ferry's loudspeaker. She was near the front of her lane, but still had only a limited view of the Mukilteo terminal as the ferry eased toward the dock ahead. People were starting to return to their cars.

If Sandra was true to her word, she'd be calling again soon with more instructions.

But the word of that murderess was hardly trustworthy. Caitlin had been on the lookout while in the Echo ferry terminal—and again here, on the parking deck. She hadn't spotted the red Jetta again. Unless the guy had switched cars, no one seemed to have been following her. And hell, even if he were just two cars over on the deck, he still wouldn't be able to see if she was talking to the police or texting them, not if she was careful about it.

Gabe had noticed a car following them yesterday— from the IHOP near Russ's place in Seattle to Woodinville. Caitlin had figured he might have been imagining things. But now she tried to remember the make and model of the car. It was a black car: a Toyota . . . no, a *Taurus* with a green-haired troll doll on the dash.

She quickly looked around for a car like that one in the general vicinity. In the passenger rearview mirror, she spotted a black Taurus behind her on the right. She turned to see if someone was inside the car—and if a troll doll was on the dash. Just then, a woman and her young daughter climbed into the car.

Caitlin sighed and looked at her phone again.

She wondered if Sandra had been driving the black Taurus yesterday—and again today. Clearly, she'd been in traffic when she'd called forty-five minutes ago.

Caitlin listened to passengers chattering and the car doors opening and slamming. She told herself she'd wait until she spoke to Sandra again. She'd demand to talk with Lindsay or Gabe. If Sandra refused, then it would be time to call the police.

She felt the ferry come to a stop.

Her phone rang. Once again, the caller ID showed UNKNOWN CALLER.

The timing was almost too spot-on. Maybe Sandra herself was watching.

Caitlin answered it. "I want to talk to my kids before we go any further," she said—in lieu of a greeting.

"Impossible. They're both fast asleep, but quite safe . . ."

Caitlin could hear traffic noise in the background—and then Christmas music.

"Why the hell should I believe you?"

"Because you don't have any choice," Sandra replied. "You're to proceed north toward Everett and turn off at Highway Two. Go to Monroe. Stay on Two, and you'll see a Safeway on the left. Pull into the parking lot and wait for my next call."

Caitlin heard someone talking in the background. The voice was muffled, but she could still make out the words: *"Ho-Ho-Ho, get a sunny deal . . ."*

There was a click on the other end. Sandra had hung up.

"*'Get a sunny deal and save at Sunny's,'*" Caitlin whispered to herself. "She's in Woodinville . . ."

Sandra was in a car, only a few blocks from Stuart Healy's house.

CHAPTER THIRTY-THREE

Woodinville
Wednesday, November 2—7:03 P.M.

Hunched over the desk in his office, Stuart had the remote control in his hand. He switched from the evening news to what his surveillance cameras were monitoring. The spot he was most interested in was the front gate. She'd said she would be here between six-forty-five and seven. She was late.

He was actually nervous—as if he were on a date with the girl of his dreams. Of course, in a way, he was. For twenty-five years he'd been studying her nude photos and getting off on them. He'd been reading all her secret thoughts and her erotic fantasies until he felt they were his own. None of the other girls quite compared to her. She'd murdered his sister, but somehow that didn't matter. He still desperately wanted to possess her.

Stuart knew it was silly, but he'd showered, put on cologne, and changed his clothes twice—all for her. He finally decided on a sports shirt, blazer, and khakis.

He even used some of his wife's makeup to cover the bruises under his eyes from his broken nose.

He'd just watched the latest updates on the evening news, and they showed a police composite sketch of him from Monica's description. It didn't look that much like him, especially with his nose in its new altered state. That had been on the news, too—the fact that she'd broken his nose. So—he wouldn't be able to step outside or answer the door for at least a week or two. Jill's visit was an exception, of course.

At six thirty-five, he'd sent his wife and son up to the second floor—and forbidden them to come down again until he gave the okay.

Monica had given the police descriptions of them, too, no doubt. But there weren't any artist's renderings of them on the news. His former captive had told the police how none of them had names—except for him. The police knew all about the setup here—thanks to that little bitch. Stuart had already made up his mind to pay her back for her disloyalty. Once things calmed down, he would visit her and her father. He'd kill the father first—so she could see it before she died.

The newspeople were calling him *The Coach*, which he kind of liked. Apparently, the authorities were checking the sex offender registry for swimming instructors and coaches. They were reviewing records at high schools and colleges throughout the Pacific Northwest for any coaches who had been fired—or received complaints.

Now that he'd seen how far along—and far off—the authorities were with their investigation, Stuart wasn't so worried anymore. If he kept the van in his garage for the next few weeks, he'd be okay. He wasn't concerned about tire tracks he'd left in the woods. He'd bought the current set of tires on his van two years ago, shortly after he'd killed and buried the first hitchhiker. He'd figured he'd eventually—and quite literally— have to cover his tracks. The tires were purchased with cash at an auto garage in Longview that was closing. Stuart paid one of the yardmen to mount them on the van for him. There was no way the tire tracks could be traced to him.

So—for now, he didn't see any need to pack up, cut his losses, and disappear. Aaron had no idea how close he came to having his throat slit tonight.

Stuart figured he'd just have to lay low for a while— no more scouting talent at swim meets, no cruising around in his van. With that in mind, how perfect was Jill's timing? She was bringing him a new girl—very pretty and a good swimmer. He wouldn't even have to risk leaving the house for this one. She was being delivered to him.

Still, he didn't quite know what to expect from Jill. The last time he'd seen her was in that hospital elevator when he'd been thirteen. She'd scared him so much he'd wet his pants. If nothing else, she was unpredictable. Was she really just after her journals and those Polaroids? There had to be something else she wanted from him.

He knew what he wanted from her.

He had the bottle of chloroform, a rag, and rubber gloves in the same little leather shaving kit case his father had used back in 1991. Stuart had used it on all his pupils. It was on the table by the front door right now. Stuart was also carrying a gun inside his blazer.

She wasn't leaving here.

Stuart still wasn't sure about the arrangements. He'd probably give Jill her own cell—and have the girl and Aaron share quarters. It might be interesting to let nature take its course there, and watch the two teenagers on camera, cohabitating and copulating. He'd have his own private reality show.

Then again, perhaps he'd just want Jill for one night. After all, it had been twenty-five years. She was no longer a nubile teen. Maybe the years hadn't been kind to her. Maybe he wouldn't be the slightest bit interested in keeping her here.

He'd know when he saw her.

The image on his TV went back to the split screen of all six surveillance spots. There still wasn't anyone driving up to the front gate. But he noticed Aaron hobbling around his cell.

Stuart wondered why he was limping—and if it would affect his swimming. He clicked on the image so that it filled the screen.

Aaron sat down on his cot and rubbed his right ankle.

Stuart hit a couple of keys on his computer keyboard to control camera number six. He zoomed in for a better look at the boy's feet. The right white sock had blood on it.

Aaron lowered the sock slightly and then adjusted something inside it.

It looked like a knife.

*   *   *

The slat in the little speakeasy window slid open and the coach peered in at him.

From the edge of his cot, Aaron gaped back at him. Just seconds ago, he'd been adjusting the knife so it would stop nicking his ankle every time he walked across the cell. He quickly pushed the cuff of his jeans over the bulge in his sock.

"Strip down," the coach growled.

"Now?" Aaron said, slowly getting to his feet.

He was worried the knife might fall onto the floor. Something was wrong. They couldn't be getting ready to practice. It was after seven. He'd eaten dinner an hour ago, and once again, not a peep out of the Missus—even though he'd thanked her and asked how she was doing today. Maybe this surprise visit had something to do with her silence. Had she confessed to her husband about the knife? Or maybe the coach had been watching him on camera just a minute ago.

"C'mon, get undressed, damn it," he grumbled. "I don't have all day."

Trembling, Aaron took off his T-shirt, jeans, and undershorts. He was naked—except for his white socks. Out of habit, he covered his crotch with his hands. He tried to turn to one side to conceal the telltale lump in his right, bloodstained sock.

"Everything off," the coach said. Then he moved away from the peephole window.

Suddenly, the pass-through drawer popped into the cell.

The coach came back to the little speakeasy door. "Put the goddamn knife in the drawer."

Aaron did what he was told.

After a few seconds, the drawer retracted with the usual *whoosh-clank*.

Then he heard another clank, and the cell door swung open. Before Aaron knew what was happening, the coach charged into the room with his gun raised high.

All at once, the coach slammed the butt end down on his forehead.

Aaron collapsed onto the hard concrete floor.

He was dazed, but still conscious. He almost wished he weren't. Then maybe he wouldn't have felt the full force of the coach's kick to his side—just under his right ribs. The pain was horrible. Aaron couldn't breathe.

Naked and in agony, he coiled up on the floor.

"Sneaky little bastard," he heard the coach mutter.

Then the cell door slammed shut and the lock clanked.

Stuart stashed the knife in the top drawer of his desk.

He didn't have to guess how the kid had gotten ahold of one of their steak knives. His dingbat wife must have given it to him. But why? To cut his food? Stuart wondered if maybe he'd belted her one too many times and had rattled her brains loose.

On the monitor, he saw Aaron, still naked and lying on the floor of his cell.

Then he noticed activity in one of the other surveillance spots: the driveway entrance.

He saw a Chevy Impala pulling up to his front gate.

Hunched over his keyboard, he switched to full screen for the front gate monitor. The car wasn't quite close enough to the gate yet for him to see her face. Stuart's heart started racing.

His phone rang. She hadn't used the gate intercom.

He snatched up the receiver. "Yes?"

"I have a special delivery for Stuart Healy," she announced in a tone dripping with irony. "It's an aquatic creature, sixteen years old and pretty, a nice little body, and I believe she's a virgin."

"I'll open the gate," he said, pressing the code on the phone.

He watched the gate open and the car pull into the driveway. He caught a glimpse of a blonde on the phone in the driver's seat. He couldn't really see her face. But she seemed to be alone in the car.

"Where's the girl?" he asked.

"With my partner," she said. "He's at another location, very close by. He doesn't know about you. For your sake, I'm keeping it that way. He has your name and address in a sealed envelope, and if he doesn't see or hear from me in a half hour, he'll open that envelope. He'll find details about you—along with my instructions for him to make an anonymous call to the police. So—if you had any notions of keeping me any longer than I intend to stay, you can forget them, Stuart."

"I didn't have any notions like that at all," he lied.

"Once I see you have the journals and the photos, we'll make an exchange. I guarantee it'll take less than five minutes. The girl won't give you any trouble.

She's been sedated. And you won't have any contact with my friend. It'll all be very easy."

"That sounds fine by me," Stuart said. "I—I'm hanging up now. I'll see you at the door."

He clicked off and then hurried out of his office and up the stairs. He was disappointed he wouldn't have more time with Jill. And it bothered him that she was out there somewhere, a loose end. But then, she'd eluded the cops for the last twenty-five years. It wasn't as if she could blow any whistles on him without incriminating herself.

Still, he didn't like this idea of a partner. He couldn't help wondering if all this was some kind of trap. For now, he would hold on to his gun.

He grabbed his little kit off the table in the front hallway. "Someone come down here and take this!" he yelled, slightly out of breath. Through the window by the door, he saw the Impala pulling up in front of the house. "C'mon, somebody get down here!"

His son raced down the stairs. His wife came to the top of the steps.

Stuart handed him the kit. "Hold on to that for me," he grunted. Then he looked up at her. "How the hell did that boy downstairs get ahold of one of our steak knives?"

Wide eyed, she stared back at him and put a hand over her heart. "Why—I—I don't know . . ."

"I'll deal with you later," he said. "For now, I don't want to see either one of you until I say it's okay to come down here."

The boy scurried back up the stairs, and his mother

took the kit from him. She gave Stuart an apprehensive look, and he glowered back at her. She led the boy away.

The doorbell rang.

Stuart quickly checked his reflection in the mirror, felt for the gun in his blazer, and then opened the door.

With the threshold between them, Stuart and his onetime fantasy girl stood and stared at each other. Stuart could tell the awe and wariness was mutual.

She finally cracked a smile. "Well, Stu, you sure look like your dad," she said. Then she squinted at him. "But, boy, that girl did a number on your nose. That must smart. I'd say you look good, but actually you look pretty tired—and old, a hell of a lot older than thirty-five or thirty-six. Then again, you had a rough night last night, didn't you?"

Gazing at her, Stuart couldn't help feeling disappointed. For over two decades, she'd been his dream girl, forever sixteen. He was still aroused by her photos from twenty-five years ago. But in all that time, he never imagined her as a mature woman. Despite her hard-edged features, she was still attractive. But she wasn't a girl anymore. It just wasn't the same. Seeing her now—this fortysomething woman standing at his door, spouting these catty remarks—it sort of spoiled everything.

"I guess we've both gotten older," he said, clearing his throat.

She pulled a gun from the pocket of her bulky sweater. It was strange how she was so casual about it. "So are you going to ask me in or what?" she said, pointing the revolver at him. "Don't let the gun rile you. It's just for self-protection. Believe me, Stu. You'll be pleased with how this visit goes . . ."

Taking a deep breath, he opened the door wider and stepped aside. "My wife and son are upstairs. I'd just as soon leave them out of this—if that's all right with you."

She stepped inside. "That's fine with me. I'm not worried about them. I mean, it's not like they'd call the police, right?" She glanced around the front hall, obviously taking in the view of the living room and dining room. "Well, you're certainly doing pretty well for yourself. Congratulations, Stu."

Frowning, he nodded. "Stuart."

"Would you relax? You look so tense. I already told you about the gun. And I'm not going to make you do anything you might not want to do—except this . . ." She looked him up and down. "The jacket and pants need to come off. I can see you're carrying something in the jacket. So why don't you just toss that over there . . ." She nodded at a chair in the living room.

He hesitated.

"C'mon, Stuart, I only have a half hour here."

Stepping into the living room, he carefully took off his blazer and draped it over the back of a chair. The gun slipped out of the pocket and landed on the seat cushion.

"Just leave it there," she said. "And now, take off the pants and pass them over to me."

He unfastened his belt and undid the front of his trousers. His change and house keys jingled as he let his pants drop to the hallway floor. Then he kicked them over toward her. He stood there in his sports shirt, black briefs, shoes, and socks. His face was turning red.

Still eyeing him, she bent down and felt the pockets of his pants. "Turn around," she said, straightening again. "Let's see you . . ."

He raised his arms and turned around for her.

Backing away, she nodded at his pants in a rumpled pile on the floor. "Thank you, Stuart. As much as I like looking at your white legs, you can put your khakis on again."

He stepped back into his trousers.

"So—you were lying to me that time in the elevator," she said. "You've known all along where the journals and those racy Polaroids were. And you still have them, don't you?"

"You wouldn't be here if I didn't," Stuart said, zipping up his pants.

"What about the tire iron?" she asked.

"It's at the bottom of Skagit Bay," Stuart explained. "My father tossed it off a ferry during a crossing a while after you escaped. I was with him."

"But you have my diaries and the photos—and they're here?" she pressed. She still seemed doubtful.

"Yes, I have them," he said—with a tiny smile.

Stuart realized it didn't really matter that she had a gun. As long as he had those journals and the pictures, he was the one with all the power.

Hunched close to the wheel, Caitlin ran a yellow light on Route 522.

She kept checking her rearview mirror. She'd been

driving for about twenty minutes now and hadn't noticed anyone on her tail. If Sandra truly had a partner,
he was damn slippery—invisible, in fact. It seemed
like the partner story was a lie to throw her off, to keep
her obedient and scared. Most of all, it kept her from
calling the police. But if someone was really following
her, they would have contacted Sandra by now and let
her know that the woman carrying the money wasn't
headed to Monroe at all—but in the opposite direction.

She wondered why Sandra had instructed her to go
there.

Caitlin had made up her mind. She wasn't driving to
Monroe only to sit in a Safeway parking lot and wait
for someone who might never show. She was going
where she thought her kids were.

She had to slow down for traffic—and a red light
ahead. "God, please," she whispered, tapping the
brake. "C'mon, c'mon . . ."

Caitlin checked her rearview mirror again—and then
the clock: 7:24. She did the math in her head. From the
Mukilteo ferry terminal, Woodinville was closer than
Monroe. She would get to Elkhorn Court before Sandra called her again.

What Sandra had to do with Stuart Healy was still a
mystery. But Caitlin was pretty certain Sandra must
have followed them to Stuart's house yesterday—probably in that black Taurus Gabe had noticed.

The light changed, but people weren't budging.
Texters probably, Caitlin thought, her hands tightening
on the wheel. At last, traffic started moving to a slow
crawl to the next traffic signal.

Up ahead, she could see it: the big inflatable Santa

at the edge of the used car lot on the corner. Sandra had called her from that corner about forty minutes ago. Was she still at Stuart Healy's house? Had she even gone there?

Caitlin would be at Elkhorn Court soon. If she saw a black Taurus in front of Stuart's house, she would know her hunch was correct.

Then she would call the police.

Aiming the gun at his back, Sandra followed Stuart down the basement stairs to a small exercise room with some cardio equipment and a TV. A door was open to a short hallway that led to his indoor pool. In the alcove was another door—this one to a little office. Sandra had attended enough high school swim meets before her disappearance to recognize how Stuart had set this up. It was just like a swimming coach's office—with a window looking out to the pool.

She imagined bratty little Stuart, all grown up and rolling in money, making demands on contractors about his custom-built pool. Meanwhile, she'd been living under the radar and hustling for a little bit of change in her pocket every day.

"My swimmers spend about eight hours in the water—every day," he boasted—with a nod toward the big pool. "It's not like what my father did with you, throwing you down in a dark, cold room. My kids get a lot of exercise. I see they eat right, too—as long as they cooperate."

"Are my journals somewhere around here?" she asked impatiently.

"Right here," Stuart said, leading her back into the alcove—and then into his office. He pointed to the cabinet by his desk.

Sandra recognized her old diaries on the bottom shelf with several other untitled bound books. For a few seconds, she couldn't breathe. After all these years, the endless hours of hunting through the Birch Place house, all the lives she'd snuffed out—she'd finally found her diaries.

Squatting down by the cabinet, Stuart pulled the books off the shelf and set them on his desk.

Sandra couldn't help noticing all the other journals on the shelf. She wondered how many girls had filled those books, girls who were now dead.

He opened one of her journals on the desk. To Sandra, it felt as if he was violating something. She knew that for years he'd been reading these journals. Maybe he'd even gotten off on them. But they were hers again. Seeing him casually open one of her private journals and glance at it almost sent her over the edge.

"Stop that," she whispered. "Don't touch those."

He smiled a bit as he stepped back from the desk.

Sandra stared down at the open diary. She recognized her own girlish penmanship, and it broke her heart.

Reaching into his desk drawer, Stuart took out an old, crinkled manila envelope. He gave it a little shake, and about a dozen Polaroids spilled out onto his desk blotter. It looked like at least another dozen photos were still in the envelope.

Sandra had to remind herself to keep the gun on Stuart—and keep her guard up. At the same time, she couldn't help herself. She gazed at the dark, slightly blurry old photos. She felt sorry for that sixteen-year-old girl who—in a moment of anger at her friend—had destroyed her own life.

Stuart pulled a second envelope out of the drawer and set it on the desk. "This is the whole collection," he said. "Some of them didn't turn out so good, and some of them didn't really interest me, so I burned them."

"Did you . . ." Sandra paused. She was getting choked up and had to clear her throat. "You sure you aren't keeping any for yourself?"

"This is it," he said—with a nod at the two envelopes on the desk.

Earlier, she'd toyed with the idea of selling some of the photos back to Stuart for some getaway money. But she didn't want to anymore. Something inside her needed to protect that teenage girl from twenty-five years ago.

Maybe that was what she'd been trying to do all along.

She looked at Stuart and cleared her throat again. "Do you have a box or bag—something I can put this in?"

As she turned down Elkhorn Court, Caitlin switched off her headlights. She stopped across from Stuart Healy's front gates, which were closed. She saw a car in the driveway—in the same spot where she'd parked yesterday afternoon. It wasn't a black Taurus. It was a silver car.

"Shit," she whispered.

Of course, that didn't necessarily mean the car wasn't Sandra's. It could just mean that Sandra wasn't driving the black Taurus today. Caitlin couldn't be sure yet. It was all still a hunch—and not enough to call the police.

She hated to think she might have been mistaken about the Sunny's Santa announcement. Was Sandra right now waiting for her in a parking lot in Monroe?

No, she had to follow her gut. Lindsay and Gabe were here. And once she confirmed that, she would call the police.

Caitlin didn't want to linger too long in front of the house. She slowly cruised farther up the street and then around the block. She needed to get onto the grounds for a better look at that car. At the same time, maybe she could see what was going on inside the house. Coming up along Stuart's side yard, Caitlin studied the wrought-iron fence, bordered by a tall, perfectly trimmed hedge. The place was like a fortress.

She spotted a tree on the parkway—with lower branches that were almost reachable from the ground. One of them extended over the fence and the hedges into Stuart's side yard.

Caitlin pulled up onto the curb and onto the parkway lawn—until her Lexus was directly under the tree branches. She shifted into Park and switched off the car.

On the ferry, she'd gone through her purse for anything she might use as a weapon against Sandra. She'd found a small, old canister of pepper spray that no longer worked and a nail file.

Now she popped the trunk, climbed out of the car,

and checked the trunk space. A tire iron was the best she could do for now. It beat trying to defend herself with a nail file.

Tucking the tire iron into the waist of her jeans, Caitlin quietly closed the trunk and headed around to the front of the car. She climbed up on the hood so she could reach the tree branch. She hoisted herself up onto the limb. Leaves and twigs fell onto the car as she climbed across the branch to the tree's crown. Then she scrambled onto the limb that extended over the fence. She tossed the tire iron onto the grass, about eight feet below. It landed with a thud.

She almost expected dogs to start howling or an alarm to go off. But it was quiet.

The rough tree bark tore at her hands as she lowered herself from the branch. Dangling from the limb, she let go and dropped to the ground, feet first. But her legs gave out and she fell on her side. It knocked the wind out of her for a moment, but she sprang to her feet and snatched up the tire iron.

Then she crept toward Stuart's house.

At the sink, Aaron splashed some cold water on his forehead—and his ankle. Both were sore and bleeding. He could feel a bump forming on his head where the coach had struck him with the gun. Aaron's side ached, too. For all he knew he could be bleeding internally.

He'd managed to put his clothes back on, but left his socks on the floor.

He figured whatever he'd just gotten, it was nothing compared to what the coach would do to his poor wife.

Aaron felt horrible for her. And without her sympathy and help, he felt doomed.

As he shut off the water, Aaron heard snippets of conversation.

He moved over to the door and put his ear to the speakeasy window. It sounded like the coach was talking to someone in the pool area. It was a woman, but not the Missus. He knew her little-girl voice by now. From the woman's tone, she didn't sound scared. So she wasn't some new "recruit." Aaron couldn't quite make out what they were saying. But he heard her call the coach *Stuart*. Or was it *Stewart*—for the man's last name? Either way, at least Aaron now knew the son of a bitch's name.

He wondered if this woman was a friend of Stuart's— and if she had any idea what went on down here.

He took a chance—and then a deep breath.

"Help!" he screamed. "Help me! I'm locked up in a cell here in back of the pool! Help me! My name is Aaron Brenner! He kidnapped me! I can hear you. I know somebody's there! Please help me . . ."

She realized the doors to the pool area must have been open. Even up in her bedroom on the second floor, Stuart's wife could hear Aaron screaming from his basement cell.

Her son heard him, too. Stuart Junior stood near the top of the stairs.

She watched him from her doorway. "You should be in your room," she whispered. "You know what he'll do if he finds you out of your bedroom . . ."

He glanced over his shoulder at her. "I'm not afraid," he sneered. "You're the one who's in trouble. I can't believe you actually gave that kid a knife. You're really going to get it . . ."

With a sigh, Stuart's wife stepped back into the master bedroom. The boy followed her in there.

Aaron's cries for help were just slightly muted background noise. It happened sometimes, when Stuart left one of the doors open down there. She'd hear one of the teenagers crying or screaming out—especially the new ones when they just woke up and didn't know where they were.

She was almost used to the screaming now.

But Stuart's wife wasn't used to having one of his prisoners actually say nice things to her. Aaron seemed to understand her. And for the last day or so, she'd been forced to understand him, too.

Stuart's wife wandered over to the bedroom window. She kept her back to her son. Some of the things Aaron had said last night about Stuart Junior had really sunk in as well.

"So why did you do it?" her son asked. "Why'd you give that loser a knife anyway?"

"I realized it has to stop," she admitted.

"He's right about you," her son said. "You're stupid."

She winced. But she didn't turn around. She didn't want him to see that his words hurt her.

Below, Stuart's wife spotted a woman moving across the side yard toward the house. She gasped.

"What is it?" her son asked. "Let me see . . ." The

boy practically shoved her out of the way. He stared out the window.

Stuart's wife bumped into the dresser, almost knocking the old leather shaving kit case to the floor. Stuart had left the pouch unzipped.

"What did you see down there?" her son asked, still looking out the window. His breath was fogging the glass. "Wait a minute. Shit, who is that?"

He obviously couldn't see his mother's reflection in the darkened window. He couldn't see what she was doing. Otherwise, he would have turned around quicker.

"Hey, Dad!" he started to yell. "There's somebody—"

But he didn't get another word out.

His mother slapped the chloroform-soaked cloth over his open mouth. She'd seen it done several times before.

Her boy struggled for only a moment, before he started to sink into her arms.

This time, as Stuart Junior slipped into unconsciousness, he wasn't faking.

He was heavy, but his mother dragged him to the bed and gently lowered him onto the mattress. She hovered over him for a moment.

"It has to stop," she whispered.

Darting from tree to tree in the front yard, Caitlin made her way to the silver Impala. She peeked in the driver's window. A smartphone was in the cup holder. It was the same brand as Lindsay's, but that was no proof the phone actually belonged to her daughter.

Still, who would go into a house and leave behind a phone?

Caitlin tried to open the car door, but it was locked. She didn't want to force it and risk setting off the car alarm, so she backed away. She glanced at the trunk. It looked like it might be roomy, maybe even big enough for two young people.

"Lindsay?" she whispered, leaning over the trunk. She tapped on it. "Gabe? Honey, are you in there?"

No response.

A shadow swept over her.

Caitlin looked up and saw a woman standing in a window on the first floor. It wasn't Sandra. The woman seemed to be looking directly at her.

Caitlin ducked behind the Impala. She heard a window slide open.

She peered over the roof of the car in time to see the woman moving away from the open window. Perhaps it was Mrs. Healy—or *Arnett*—or whatever Stuart's wife called herself.

Caitlin couldn't help wondering if it was a trap. It didn't seem possible that the woman had failed to notice her. And yet she was opening the window. From where Caitlin stood, it didn't look like there was a screen on the window. The woman might as well have laid out a welcome mat.

Caitlin made a beeline for the window and looked inside the house. It was a plush, formal dining room. No one was in there.

As she hoisted herself up over the windowsill, the tire iron slipped out from the waist of her jeans. It fell onto the hardwood floor with a loud clank.

Caitlin froze just inside the dining room window. Had she given herself away?

She didn't hear footsteps.

But in a distant part of the house, she heard someone screaming for help.

It wasn't Lindsay or Gabe. It was a young man yelling.

"*My name is Aaron Brenner!*" she heard him cry.

With a shaky hand, Caitlin pulled out her phone and dialed 9-1-1.

"Shut up, goddamn it!" Stuart yelled.

Sandra listened to the young man's cries. She remembered screaming like that on several occasions when she'd been Ned Healy's prisoner. "Aaron Brenner," she echoed. "That's the boy who went missing about a week ago . . ."

"A week ago Sunday," Stuart corrected her. "Would you like to meet him?"

Stuart's prisoner was still screaming for help.

Sandra followed Stuart as far as the pool area and then stopped abruptly. She didn't want to go near the young man's prison cell. It might be too tempting for Stuart. He might just want to throw her in there with the kid. Maybe Stuart didn't really believe she had a partner nearby.

"Scream all you want!" Stuart bellowed. "She's not going to help you, stupid! No one's going to help you!"

The boy stopped his yelling.

Stuart turned and frowned at Sandra. "What's wrong?" he asked. "Don't you want to meet him? I figured you might be curious to see what the cells look like. It's a lot more civilized than the conditions you were living in."

"I believe you," she said. "But instead of bringing me to the boy, why don't you bring the boy to me?"

Stuart smiled. "All right, I can do that, but only if you bring me the girl first."

She thought about it for a moment and then nodded. "I need to get something out of my car."

"You mean, the girl?" he asked. "Let me guess. She's in the trunk, isn't she?"

Sandra managed to smile back at him. "Maybe." She stepped toward his office to pick up her journals and the photos. He'd found a Nordstrom bag for them earlier. The bag was on his desk.

"That stuff stays down here with me until I get the girl," Stuart said, blocking the door. "Your purse can stay here, too, so I can be sure you're coming back."

She let out a stunned little laugh. "What makes you think you can call the shots all of a sudden? You seem to forget, I have the gun, Stu."

"Well, fair is fair," he said. "I'm just looking out for myself. You can take your car keys, of course—and your phone. You might want to call your friend. Our half hour is almost up. We don't want him calling the police when he shouldn't."

Sandra nodded. "I'll just be a minute."

"I'll have the boy here when you get back," he called. "Maybe I'll have them both race for us. Don't worry about a swimsuit for her. He doesn't have one . . ."

Sandra headed into the exercise room and then up the stairs.

Stuart was getting awfully cocky. Had he known all along that Lindsay was in the trunk of her car? Maybe it was just a guess. Still, she'd caught the irony in his tone when he'd suggested she call her partner.

He was even more disgusting than his father. The sleazy son of a bitch had naked teenage swimmers competing for his amusement and titillation.

She was almost tempted to shoot the bastard, and let Lindsay, Gabe, and this Aaron Brenner kid go free.

Almost.

Caitlin picked up the tire iron and then tiptoed through the front hallway. She glanced into the living room, where she and the kids had talked with Stuart yesterday.

The screaming had stopped. Now, all she heard was a faint murmuring. She couldn't quite tell where it was coming from.

She'd given the 9-1-1 operator Stuart's address and said she'd heard screams coming from inside the house, a boy claiming to be the missing swimmer, Aaron Brenner. "I know it sounds crazy," Caitlin had whispered into the phone. "But I heard him, and he keeps yelling for help. I don't think this is a joke."

"Where are you calling from, ma'am?" the 9-1-1 operator had asked.

Caitlin had hesitated and then switched off her phone.

Now, she started down the hallway—closer to the sound of those voices in murmured conversation. One of them was obviously Stuart Healy. He'd just yelled out for the boy to shut up, that no one was going to help him.

Caitlin hoped the police would prove him wrong. She hoped they were on their way.

The other person sounded like Sandra.

Caitlin peeked down a stairway to the lower level—just as someone started up the steps. She quickly ducked around the corner.

Tightening her grip on the tire iron, Caitlin watched as Sandra came through the front hallway. Sandra shoved her phone inside her sweater pocket. In her other hand she held a gun.

Sandra started for the front door but seemed to hesitate. Then she stepped into the living room and picked up a gun lying on a seat cushion. The chair had a blazer draped over the back of it. Caitlin hadn't noticed the revolver until now.

With a smile on her face, Sandra tucked the second gun into her sweater pocket. Then she headed outside, leaving the front door open.

Caitlin padded over to the door and ducked behind it. Through the space between the door and its frame, she peeked outside.

Sandra tapped on the trunk and called out in a singsong voice: "C'mon, sleepyhead, wake up! C'mon, Lindsay . . ." She pressed the button on her key fob to pop the trunk. Then she reached down and started poking someone with the gun. There was muffled moaning.

On her tiptoes, Caitlin tried to get a look at who was in the trunk. Was it Lindsay and Gabe—or just Lindsay?

Sandra went around to the front of the car, opened the door, and dug out something from under the driver's seat. Shutting the door, she returned to the trunk. She had a box cutter in her hand.

It was all Caitlin could do to keep from running outside to stop her. But a tire iron wasn't much good against a gun. She could end up getting her kids and herself killed.

Sandra leaned over the trunk and started to cut away at something. "Hold still, you little bitch," she hissed. "Don't make me nick you . . ."

Caitlin finally caught a glimpse of Lindsay's feet. She recognized her daughter's fuzzy pink socks. Sandra was cutting at some duct tape that bound Lindsay's ankles together.

Caitlin wondered what was taking the police so long. They should have been here by now.

Tossing the box cutter on the pavement, Sandra sat Lindsay up in the trunk. Lindsay looked half-asleep. She had a piece of duct tape over her mouth. Her wrists were tied behind her.

"All right, c'mon now, get out of there," Sandra grunted, grabbing her by the arm. She held a gun to Lindsay's head. "Careful, I don't want to blow your pretty little head off . . ."

But Lindsay was groggy and unresponsive.

Letting go of her arm for a moment, Sandra slapped Lindsay hard across the face.

Caitlin winced. Helpless, she watched Sandra slap her daughter again.

Moaning past the tape that covered her mouth, Lindsay seemed disoriented.

Pressing the gun to Lindsay's head again, Sandra helped her out of the trunk. She stopped to gaze back down. "Sit tight, Gabe. Your turn's coming." Then she shut the trunk.

She pushed Lindsay along the path toward the front door. But in the doorway, Sandra stopped dead.

This close, Caitlin could see the tears streaming down her daughter's face—and the red marks on her cheek.

For a moment, she thought Sandra had spotted her behind the door. But Sandra was looking directly ahead, not at all in the direction of the doorway hinge.

"Goddamn it, Caitlin," she whispered. "Why aren't you in Monroe?"

She glanced over her shoulder and saw Sandra's reflection in a mirror on the wall. Sandra stared back at her in the mirror. She pressed the barrel of the gun against Lindsay's cheek. "Get out from behind the door, Caitlin," she said.

Caitlin tucked the tire iron behind her leg and backed toward the living room. Sandra hadn't told her to drop the tire iron. Caitlin prayed she hadn't seen it.

Neither of them said a word. Lindsay had stopped moaning.

From the basement, the theme to *Rocky* suddenly started up.

Sandra chuckled. Something about the music seemed to amuse her. She led Lindsay inside the house and kicked the door shut with her foot.

"You don't have to do this," Caitlin said.

"But I do," Sandra replied. "Now, where the hell is the money?"

* * *

Stuart listened to the music from his boom box.

His father's former prisoner and plaything could probably hear it upstairs. She'd thought she was being so clever. But she was all bluff. Stuart knew she was lying about that partner of hers. She was alone.

He'd let her make this deal. He would come out ahead. Hell, he'd even let her go. He wouldn't miss the journals and those Polaroids. He didn't want them anymore. Seeing her now—as an adult—had tarnished them. In the months ahead, Lindsay Stoller would fill several journals for him, pages and pages full of her private thoughts and sexual fantasies. He would take hundreds of photos of her—erotic pictures that would put the blurry old Polaroids to shame.

He pulled a second revolver from the center drawer of his desk. Did that stupid bitch really think he owned only one gun?

He took his coach's whistle out and put it around his neck.

He was the one calling the shots now.

Aaron heard the music start up.

He was usually undressed, showered, and in the pool before the old boom box was turned on. If they were having an evening practice session, the coach was changing the order of things around tonight.

There was a clank and the door opened to his cell.

The coach—Stuart or Stewart—hadn't even looked in at him first. Aaron was completely caught off guard.

He'd been sitting on his cot with a cold, wet washcloth on his head.

"Let's go," the coach said. He had a gun in his hand.

Aaron dropped the washcloth and got to his feet. "Where are we going?" he asked.

This was usually when Aaron had to strip down to nothing. And Junior wasn't here, helping his dad. Everything was out of whack.

Aaron had a feeling he was going to die—not just tonight, but very soon—within minutes. A part of him was afraid the moment he stepped outside the cell, the man would put a bullet in his head.

"Move," the coach grunted, nodding toward the open door. "We're going to the pool."

Warily, Aaron followed the coach's orders. They moved through the corridor—past the showers and toward the pool area. Aaron figured if he was ever going to escape, this was his last chance.

"We're doing everything out of order tonight," he said. "What's going on?"

The coach didn't answer.

It was strange to be in the pool area with his clothes on—with just his captor. Aaron started to walk toward the shallow end of the pool, where the old boom box was propped on the chair.

"Other way," the coach barked, poking the gun in his back. "I want you to start out at the deep end. You'll get undressed for this woman, then dive in and start your laps. You just might be joined by a pretty young swimmer . . ."

But Aaron kept walking toward the boom box. He pretended he didn't hear. His pace didn't quicken. He tried to act like nothing was wrong. But his heart was racing. He saw the boom box and the long extension cord plugged into the wall—a potential trip hazard.

"Didn't you hear me?" the coach yelled over the music. He grabbed Aaron's arm. With the gun, he jabbed him in the back again. "Goddamn it, have you forgotten that I *own* you? Do you think—"

Aaron swiveled around. "Son of a bitch!" he roared, pushing him with all his might.

The coach flew through the air, and the gun fell onto the deck. With a stunned cry, he toppled into the pool and hit the water hard. He came up flailing helplessly in the shallow end. But then he seemed to notice the gun and sloshed his way through the water to reach for it.

In one motion, Aaron swiped the boom box off the chair and hurled it into the water.

A loud pop echoed off the tiled walls. Sparks shot out from the wall outlet and the plug. The lights flickered.

Frozen, Aaron stared down at the pool.

His mouth open in a silent scream, the coach thrashed in the water as the volts surged through his body.

Finally, he stopped moving.

The lights flickered again, and everything went black.

Caitlin jumped as a loud pop resounded from the basement.

The lights flickered.

In a split second, everything froze. Her back against the hallway wall, Caitlin still had the tire iron concealed behind her leg. But as long as Sandra had the gun barrel pressed against Lindsay's cheek, Caitlin was powerless. A tire iron was no match for that.

Trembling, Lindsay whimpered past the tape that covered her mouth. Tears welled in her eyes.

Then the lights flickered again.

All at once, Lindsay swiveled around. She slammed into Sandra and broke free.

Suddenly, the hallway was black.

Caitlin heard Lindsay moaning in one corner of the hallway. Directly in front of her, she heard Sandra hiss: "You're not going far, you little brat—"

Caitlin could just barely see her silhouette.

A shot rang out. Caitlin saw the spark.

She hauled back and swung the tire iron. She heard a crack as the weapon connected with Sandra's skull.

Sandra let out a feeble cry. There was a loud thud as she collapsed on the hallway floor.

Caitlin heard something else hit the floor. It was Sandra's gun. But she couldn't see where it landed. She couldn't see Sandra, either, but she was groaning. She almost sounded like a madwoman. Her hand thumped on the floor as she blindly groped for her gun.

Just before everything went black, Aaron saw the coach in the pool. He was already dead. His face had turned crimson, and his eyes were open wide in wonder—as if he couldn't comprehend how this had just happened to him.

His body had started to sink beneath the surface. But his whistle on the string had somehow come off his neck.

It floated on the water.

Aaron couldn't see anything now—not even his hand in front of his face. He was shaking uncontrollably.

He heard voices upstairs. In the darkness, he tried to make his way toward the sounds of the other people. There was a thud. Something—or somebody—had fallen on the floor upstairs.

Aaron tried to get his bearings and find the window to the coach's office. He knew the exit was right beside that. He knocked over a plastic chair as he tried to make his way to the wall. It seemed to take forever, but at last, his hand brushed against the slick tiles.

He almost tripped over something else, probably the bucket of rubber balls the coach liked to hurl at him. Aaron finally felt an indentation in the wall—and the window to the office. From there, he found the door to the hallway.

A gunshot made him jump. For a few seconds he couldn't move.

From above, there was a boom—like something heavy had hit the floor. Then he heard scuffling and someone moaning.

The light from upstairs was very faint. He could just barely see a stairway in front of him. Aaron crawled up the steps, unsure what to expect upstairs. For all he knew, he could be getting himself into an even worse situation—if that was possible. He realized he should have searched for the coach's gun on the pool deck. But he hadn't been thinking. He'd just wanted to get out of there.

As he reached the top step, he heard someone gasping and groaning.

He could also hear a police siren in the distance.

About fifty feet in front of him, Aaron saw the outlines of some windows. He could sense someone thrashing around, but it was too dark to make out what was happening.

Terrified, he started toward the windows but tripped over a body on the floor. He heard a muffled groan.

A flashlight went on—from above.

Aaron saw that he was in a foyer—obviously the front hall of the house. He looked at the stairway on his right: someone stood near the top step with the light. As the flashlight's beam swept across the area, he could see two women in front of him. One of them, a fortyish blonde, was on the floor. For a second, Aaron thought she was dead. She lay faceup with her eyes closed. Blood matted her blond hair and formed a small puddle on the tiled floor.

"Lindsay, honey," he heard another woman pleading. "Where are you?"

The light swept over her. She had a gun in her hand. He recoiled.

She gaped at him. "Are you Aaron?" she whispered. The police siren almost drowned her out.

Dumbfounded, he just nodded.

"Thank God," she said.

The dark room was now bathed in red flashing light from the approaching police cars' strobes. He could see everything now.

He'd stumbled over a teenage girl. Her hands were

tied behind her, and a piece of duct tape covered her mouth. But she was alive. Aaron wondered if this was the "pretty young swimmer," the coach had been talking about.

The woman dropped the gun and almost knocked him over to get to her. "Lindsay," she cried. "I'm here, sweetie . . ."

The sirens stopped wailing.

Aaron saw who was on the stairs. It was the coach's wife with the flashlight in her shaky hand. Staring back at him, she sat down on a middle step. "Where is he?" she murmured in her little-girl voice. "Where's my husband?"

Aaron slowly shook his head. "He's dead."

"Then it's finished," she whispered.

From outside, flashlight beams swept through the windows. Aaron heard chatter over a police radio, footsteps and policemen talking.

Hovering over the teenager, the woman peeled the tape off the girl's mouth. They both started crying.

Aaron realized they were mother and daughter.

"Can you help us?" the mother asked him, trying to pull the girl to her feet.

Aaron lifted her up and then tried to help tear the tape from around the girl's wrists. "I'm okay, Mom," the girl said. "Go get Gabe. He's in the trunk of her car . . ."

The woman rubbed her daughter's shoulder. Then she hurried to the front door and opened it. She raised her hands over her head. "Do you have my son out there?" she called to the police. "Gabe?"

"Are you Caitlin?" one of the cops asked.

"Yes, I can't see anything," she called back. "Those lights are in my eyes. Is my son out there?"

Aaron kept peeling away at the tape around the girl's wrists—until he was down to the last couple of layers.

She glanced over her shoulder at him. "Thank you," she said, catching her breath. "Who—who are you anyway?"

"My name's Aaron," he said. "I'm a swimmer—like you."

The ambulance was parked with its back doors open. Huddled in a beige blanket, Caitlin leaned against the bumper and held on to Gabe. He rested his head on her shoulder. Despite all the police lights and excitement around him, he barely stirred. The drug Sandra had given him was still in his system. A medic had looked him over a little while ago and said he would be fine.

The medics had loaded Sandra into another ambulance, which had already peeled away, its siren blaring. She was still alive, but unconscious. "Severe head trauma," Caitlin had overheard one of the medics say amid all the chaos.

She hoped Sandra would live—and then maybe they could find out what all this was about.

The police were inside the house talking with Stuart Healy's wife. Somewhere along the line, they'd gotten the power back on.

Caitlin realized that Healy had lied to her about having a couple of daughters. He had a son, who was heavily sedated in an upstairs bedroom.

As for Stuart Healy, apparently a couple of police officers had used a garden hoe from the garage to fish his corpse out of his indoor swimming pool. The body was still inside the house.

A little farther up the Healys' driveway, two more cops were interviewing Aaron Brenner. Lindsay was at his side.

Caitlin noticed her reaching over and rubbing his shoulder.

Just then, she felt someone gently touch her own shoulder.

"Ms. Stoller?" a stout black policewoman asked over all the background chatter and humming car motors.

"Yes?"

She handed her a mobile phone. "Deputy Bob Dana from Echo," she said. "He's been trying to get ahold of you for the last half hour. I guess your phone's switched off."

"Thanks," she said. She put the phone to her ear, trying not to move too suddenly and stir Gabe, who was still asleep on his feet.

"Deputy Dana?" she whispered into the phone.

"Well, I heard you've had quite a night," he said. "I'm not sure if you're ready for this . . ."

"Ready for what?" she asked.

"I've got some bad news. Teri Spangler decided to pay your house a visit about forty-five minutes ago. She's in police custody right now."

"What for?" Caitlin asked. "What did she do?"

"Well, she said she knew nobody was home. So she took that opportunity to torch the place. I'm—I'm terribly sorry, Caitlin. There's practically nothing left."

Dazed, Caitlin let out a surprised little laugh.

She stared at her daughter, leaning against a nice, cute boy—another swimmer.

Caitlin felt Gabe stir, but then he rested his head on her shoulder again.

They didn't have a house anymore.

"It doesn't matter," she heard herself say. "I'm here with my kids, and they're okay. Nothing else matters."

EPILOGUE

The gravelly-voiced nurse had just taken away her lunch tray. Sandra had actually managed to feed herself a few bites. But most of the meal still ended up down the front of the bib she wore. The nurse had offered to feed her, but Sandra had refused.

A part of her didn't want to get used to being blind. The doctors said there was a very good chance she would get her vision back. In head trauma cases such as hers, it sometimes took a few weeks to heal.

But for certain people, in certain cases, cortical blindness was permanent—like prison.

Sandra knew if she got her sight back, she would survive. Hell, she was famous. Her lawyers were fielding book offers, for God's sake. Everyone wanted to read about her life—and all the nasty things she'd done. She'd keep busy in jail writing her memoirs.

Ned Healy would have gotten a kick out of that. He was the first person to lock her up with a pen and paper. She'd learned back then how writing about herself could make the time fly by.

But she didn't know what she'd do if she stayed this way—with nothing to see but this bleak, dark gray. She remembered how Ned had punished her by shutting off the lights, and how it always left her paralyzed with fear. She could never get used to it.

Even as she lay in this hospital bed—with a police guard outside her door—she felt as if she were back in that black, black subterranean dungeon once again. And she was waiting for that little bit of light from above as the trapdoor opened.

She was still waiting.

Bellingham, Washington
Saturday—3:17 P.M.

In his warm-up jacket and Speedo, Aaron started his customary walk around the pool. They were up against Bellingham High School—on the Red Raiders' home turf. The bleachers were packed, and someone on the other team led cheers. It was a noisy, restless crowd.

His friend Nestor, who had already peeled down to his swimsuit, gave him a subtle thumbs-up signal. As Aaron smiled and nodded back, he remembered a couple weeks ago, thinking he'd never see his friend again.

This was his second meet since returning home, and Aaron still sometimes felt like he'd come back from the dead.

He stayed in touch with Monica, who said she felt

the same way. She said she was wary of strangers and constantly looking over her shoulder, too.

It was strange. Back when he'd been in his cell, whispering to her through the vent, he'd figured if the two of them survived their ordeal, they'd be inseparable. He'd even imagined Monica becoming his girlfriend. Maybe it was because she lived nearly two hours away in Olympia, but he'd seen her only once since their release from captivity. It had been at a press conference—with a mob of reporters and the two of them seated at a table together. The array of microphones on the table had been intimidating. At one point early on, Monica had nudged him and whispered, "I almost didn't recognize you with clothes on."

He'd just gotten a text from her yesterday. She said that Wayne State and Colorado Mesa had offered her swimming scholarships.

Aaron was fielding offers, too. As he strolled around the pool with his hands in the pockets of his warm-up jacket, he knew several scouts were there in the bleachers to watch him. Being in the news had called attention to his swimming record, but Aaron knew it was also great public relations for any university to offer a scholarship to this famous kid who happened to be financially strapped. There was a story in that—and lots of free publicity for the school.

Still, that didn't stop Aaron from being nervous about the meet.

He knew his mother wasn't there in the crowd. He'd taken the team bus here. She had an appointment with a potential buyer at a gallery in Seattle. His abduction had gotten her a lot of attention, too. She'd sold thirteen paintings in the last month.

Aaron was looking for someone else in the crowd. And as he finished walking around the pool, he finally spotted her—the pretty, longhaired brunette in the third row.

Lindsay whistled at him.

Aaron smiled and gave her a subtle little wave.

Lindsay lived less than an hour away. Aaron was getting to know the ferry schedule by heart. She had a meet the next day in Lynnwood. And he would be there in the crowd to cheer her on.

Tossing his warm-up jacket on the bench, he swung his arms to limber up some more. Coach Gunderson whispered some advice in his ear about his main competition in the 100-yard freestyle. Aaron nodded, but he'd barely heard what the coach had said. He was already starting to get into his own zone.

The ref called the swimmers to their blocks with a few short blasts of his whistle. Aaron put on his goggles and took his position.

His times from the last meet were his best ever. He hated the idea that Stuart Healy had actually helped him become a better swimmer. So instead, he gave the credit to Monica for being such a skilled competitor. He'd done so well last time because he'd imagined Monica in the lane beside him. He'd imagined the two of them, swimming for their lives.

He would be thinking the same thing as he hit the water in just a few seconds.

Aaron heard the starting horn.

Then he pushed off.

Cannon Beach, Oregon
Saturday, November 26—11:33 A.M.

The lookout spot was on a bluff off the Oregon Coast Highway. It was just secluded enough so that Caitlin, Lindsay, and Gabe were the only ones there. Of course, the weather helped. It was chilly and overcast. But somehow that made the rugged coastline, the beach and the ocean seem even more heartbreakingly beautiful.

It was a perfect time to scatter Russ's ashes—and the perfect place, too.

Caitlin remembered scattering Cliff's ashes from this same spot on a summer morning two and a half years ago.

The ritual wasn't much different from last time. They all said a simple good-bye as Caitlin emptied out the urn over the low rock wall between them and the precipice. Lindsay sobbed—just as she had two and a half years ago, while Caitlin and Gabe remained solemnly dry-eyed—as they had last time.

They had driven down yesterday and planned on leaving this afternoon to beat the Thanksgiving-weekend Sunday traffic. Lindsay didn't have a swim meet this weekend. Neither did Aaron. So he'd come along with them. He was at the hotel right now. They would be meeting him for lunch in a little while. He and Gabe shared a room. She and Lindsay doubled up next door.

Lindsay was crazy about Aaron. As a result, she'd finally stopped talking about how much she missed Portland. Whenever he wasn't in school or swimming or working at the supermarket, Aaron was over at their house. He'd managed to become like a big brother to Gabe.

For Caitlin, he was like a godsend—polite, thoughtful and sweet. She'd met his mother, who was a bit of a flake. But Aaron was nothing like her. He seemed very solid. Caitlin felt he was perfect for Lindsay, but of course, she wasn't about to spoil things by letting her daughter know that.

Their new home in Echo was walking distance from the ferry. It was mission-style, totally new construction. It lacked any old world charm. But it also lacked any history—and that was a good thing.

In a strange way, Scary Teri Spangler had done them a huge favor burning down that cursed old place. Caitlin hadn't wanted to remain there—and she would have felt horrible selling it to another family.

She'd bought the new house with the insurance money.

Still, it was hard losing so much in the fire—the photo albums especially. But when she'd cleaned out Russ's place, Caitlin found dozens of photos that he'd copied or kept. He'd also held on to a few knickknacks from their happier times, too. So it wasn't a total loss.

She'd found something else at Russ's place—inside the mailbox in that grimy little lobby. It was a letter he'd sent to her. He'd gotten the address wrong, and the post office had returned the letter to his mailbox days later. He'd written it on the night he'd died.

Caitlin had already figured out Russ hadn't stolen that check from her. Lindsay had told her about how Russ had driven to a check-cashing place shortly after getting a letter from her. Sandra's confession simply verified what Caitlin had suspected—and filled in a few blanks. Russ hadn't overdosed. He'd been murdered.

Caitlin had brought the letter with her here to Cannon Beach.

She handed the empty urn to Gabe. "Honey—kids—could you guys give me a minute alone here?"

Wiping her eyes with a Kleenex, Lindsay nodded. "No sweat," she murmured. Then she steered Gabe toward the car.

Caitlin sat down on the rock wall. She took the letter out of her purse and read it again. The page fluttered slightly in the wind.

Hey, You,

I know you said you don't want me contacting you. But tough. You can't send me all that money and expect me to accept it silently. You can't expect me to accept it—period. The first thing I did as soon as I got the check was cash it. The first thing I thought of buying with the money was drugs. But then I realized I just couldn't.

One of my recovery pals is on her way over right now. She thinks we're going to get high together. She's going to hate me when I tell her I sent the money back to you. I'm writing this from one of those crummy check-cashing/money order/bail bonds stores. They take out a big chunk for every transaction. So this check isn't as much as the one you mailed to me. But I'll

*send you the difference later. Maybe I can give it
to you when I see you at Thanksgiving. I hope
so.*

*Well, I should mail this and head back to the
apartment. Notice I didn't say home. It can't be
home to me if you're not there.*

*I miss you. I know I've let you down in the
past. But I'm trying hard to make sure that never
happens again. Kiss the kids for me.*

*Love,
Me*

The money order was for $3,796.

Russ was right. He hadn't let her down.

Caitlin carefully folded up his note. She held it to her heart for a moment, and then she slipped the letter back into her purse.

Getting to her feet, she took a deep breath and started toward the car. Gabe and Lindsay were waiting there for her. They had to go pick up Aaron and their bags. Caitlin hoped to get checked out and on the road within the hour. They could grab lunch at a diner along the way. It didn't matter where.

Right now, Caitlin just wanted to get home.